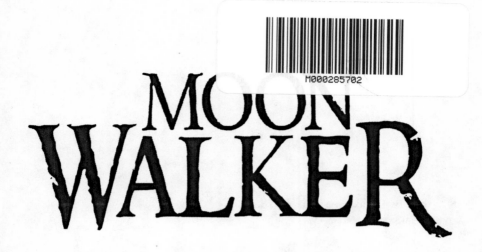

M000285702

# MOON WALKER

By

## RICK HAUTALA

*Cover design by Jeremy Robinson*

**BREAKNECK BOOKS**
PUBLISHING COMPANY

Published by Breakneck Books (USA)
www.breakneckbooks.com

First published by Zebra in 1989
Reprinted by Breakneck Books in 2007

Printed in the United States of America.

ISBN: 0-9796929-1-1
ISBN-13: 978-0-9796929-1-8

Visit Rick Hautala on the World Wide Web at:
www.rickhautala.com

ATTENTION: SCHOOLS AND BUSINESSES
Breakneck Books' titles are available at bulk order discount rates for educa-
tional, business or sales promotional use. They are also available for fund-
raiser programs. Please e-mail: info@breakneckbooks.com or write us at:
Breakneck Books - PO Box 122 - Barrington, NH 03867 for details

# Books by Rick Hautala

Untcigahunk
Four Octobers
Occasional Demons
The Mountain King
Poltergeist: The Legacy: The Hidden Saint
Bedbugs
Impulse
Beyond the Shroud
Shades of Night
The Mountain King
Twilight Time
Ghost Light
Dark Silence
Cold Whisper
Dead Voices
Winter Wake
Moonwalker
Little Brothers
Night Stone
Moonbog
Moon Death

## Written under the pseudonym A. J. Matthews

Waiting
Unbroken
Follow
Looking Glass
The White Room

## The Body of Evidence Series
## written with Christopher Golden

Last Breath
Throat Culture
Brain Trust
Burning Bones
Skin Deep

## Screenplays

Lovecraft's Pillow
Dead @ 17

# Note to Breakneck Edition of *Moonwalker*

I've written enough novels now, under my own name and the pseudonym A. J. Matthews, so the generation and execution of my books have begun to blur. Maybe that's my age showing. In any event, *Moonwalker* (not my original title, by the way, but that's another story for another time) was about in the middle of the novels I did for Zebra Books back in the late 80s and early 90s. I have a fond memory of this novel simply because I remember writing it (or did it write itself?) so quickly and easily.

Usually that's not the case. Writing a novel is never really "easy." Anyone who tells you differently is either a liar or a fool and, ultimately, a lousy novelist.

Novels take time. You can't work in a frenzy. The journey takes too long. You have to plan carefully and you have to build and develop and revise as you go. Most novelists I know are never satisfied with the end results. A novel is so vast you can always go back and make it better ... or worse with too much meddling. In some cases, usually with—I won't say "bad" books ... I'll say "unsatisfying" books, the writers didn't really conclude their books; they simply stopped writing. Once, years ago, F. Paul Wilson commented on a writers' panel that: "Revision is like sex. You know when you're done." To which Chet Williamson added: "Or you can't do it anymore."

Maybe ... I know that's often been my experience.

But *Moonwalker* was a fun book for me to write because the story simply poured out of me. Looking back on it now, I am amazed—and jealous—of the energy I had to plot and write such a large story. Sure. The prose may not be the most glistening example in the world, but the energy of the story swept me and—I hope—you, the reader, along.

I was tempted to revise the book for this new edition, but I finally decided against it. I'll admit there are many grammatical and stylistic "twitches" I wouldn't do today and would have liked to change. But all in all, I think the writing and the story hold up quite well, considering it's the product of a much younger "me."

So all I ask is that you take the story as it is, warts and all.

I had a blast writing it more years ago than I want to remember, and if nothing else, I hope it sends a nice little frisson though you a time or two.

Enjoy!

—Rick Hautala
Westbrook, Maine
August 16, 2007

# PART ONE

"And then I dived, In my lone wanderings, to the caves of Death, Searching its cause in its effect; and drew From withered bones, and skulls, and heaped up dust Conclusions most forbidden." —Lord Byron

"Run to escape, for they hurl their ghostly tracking against you, serpent-fisted and blackened of flesh, offering the fruit of terrible pain." —Euripides

# CHAPTER ONE
## "HEADING NORTH"

### I

—*Who's dead now?*—

That was Dale Harmon's first thought when the harsh ringing of the telephone sliced into his sleep. Through sleep-blurred eyes, he saw the glowing red digits of his alarm clock —

*2:37 AM.*

"Damn!"

The numbers were swimming in his vision as his hand fumbled for the receiver. He knocked the empty water glass from his bedstand, but luckily it didn't break before it skittered off somewhere into the darkness. Finally, after one more nerve-jangling ring, he found the phone and, grunting, rolled into a sitting position on the edge of the bed. Chills darted up the back of his legs when his feet hit the cold floor.

—*Who's dead?* his mind screamed.

Angie was safe in bed—he knew *that* much even through the haze—so how bad could it be?

A dash of fear as cold and numbing as ice jabbed at him from the surrounding darkness and slammed into his stomach. Suddenly, in his confusion, it was eight and a half years ago . . .

*That* telephone call had come at 11:30 P.M., more or less.

It was back in the days when he didn't have a digital wristwatch, and he rounded off time to the nearest quarter hour. Even back then, though, any call after ten o'clock usually meant some kind of trouble, unless it was his brother, calling from Omaha and not keeping the time difference in mind.

*That* telephone call hadn't caught him asleep because he had been sitting up watching Dave Letterman . . . watching ... and waiting! Angie had been just shy of four years old then, and she had been blissfully asleep for hours, but not Dale . . . not as long as Natalie still wasn't home.

Her class at the University of Maine in Augusta should have been cancelled as soon as the storm started, even though the forecasters said it wasn't going to amount to much, Especially with 20/20 hindsight, Dale knew he should have pushed harder to make her stay home. How serious could it be to miss one class? She had the highest grade going into the final week of the fall semester, and he had seen no sense taking any chances on the hour-long drive from Thomaston to Augusta and back, especially if the roads near the coast iced up.

And then *that* telephone call had come . . .

—"We're sorry to have to tell you this, Mr. Harmon, but there's been an accident."

—"What happened?" he remembered saying, although even before the state trooper told him, he knew Natalie was dead. He had felt it coming like a hammer-fisted blast of Arctic wind.

—". . . lost control on Route 17 . . . skidded ... crashed ... just outside of Coopers Mills."

—"Is she ... all right?" Dale had asked, his throat raw. His mind was blank. He wasn't even listening to what the trooper was saying. The details—the exact time and place—could wait. What he wanted . . . what he *had* to know was is she . . .

-". . . *killed instantly, I'm afraid. . .*"

The words drove into his brain like an overheating drill. Dale remembered looking at the television and seeing people's mouths move but not hearing anything they said because of the rushing sounds in his ears. His vision had blurred so badly Letterman's face looked like water-colors left out in the rain.

—". . . trucker never even saw her ... The snow must've masked her headlights."

The state trooper had spoken some more, had offered to come and pick him up, but Dale couldn't think of anyone he could call to have come and sit with Angie while he went down to the police station. Probably the person closest to him, someone who wouldn't mind getting a call to help out at this late hour, would have been Larry Cole, his co-worker. He didn't live very far away.

. . . That was eight years ago . . .

"Hello, Dale?" the voice on the phone said.

"Umm ... yeah," Dale replied sleepily, his gaze still fastened on the glowing red digits of the clock. He recognized the voice on the other end; it was Bob Nichols, his boss at the Department of Transportation.

The receiver was slick in his hand as he groped for the light switch with his other hand, found it, and snapped it on. Yellow light filled the room, hurting his eyes.

"Sorry to call you so late," Nichols said gruffly.

Still staring at the clock—*2:38* AM—Dale said, "S not late. It's early."

His hand muffled his voice as he rubbed his face, struggling to haul his awareness up to the surface.

"There's been an accident up north," Nichols said, and for the first time Dale registered how strange his boss' voice sounded. It was wound up so tight Dale feared it would crack. He tried to imagine gruff old Nichols so upset his voice almost cracked.

"What?"

Dale was confused. As far as he knew, there wasn't any major construction up north. All they had going now was the preliminary survey work on the road between Haynesville and Houlton, and that was being handled by. . . .

"Oh, no," Dale said as a chilling thought filled his mind. "Not *Larry!*"

"Fraid so," Nichols said. "He lost control on one of the back roads and went straight into a tree."

"Is he——?"

"He's dead, Dale," Nichols said, and now it happened—his voice *did* crack. Dale clearly heard his boss sob.

"Christ on a crutch!"

"I'm sorry to have to tell you this," Nichols said, fighting to control his voice. "I know how close you two were."

"Yeah."

Dale was numb all over as the realization that he'd lost not just a co-worker, but a close friend as well, worked deeper and deeper into his mind.

—*First Natalie! ... Now Larry! ... Christ!*

"I haven't got all the details yet," Nichols went on, "but I assume, since he was from up that way, he'll be buried in his hometown. Where was he from?"

"He, uh, he grew up in Dyer," Dale said. Coming through the receiver, his own voice sounded oddly distorted, as if someone else was using his mouth to talk.

"Course, I figure you'll want to go up for the funeral. You've still got two weeks vacation coming, right?"

"Huh?"

"You have some time off coming," Nichols repeated. "I assume you'll drive up for the funeral."

"Yeah ... Of course."

Now, even though Dale's eyes were fully adjusted to the bright light, he noticed that the red digits on the clock shimmered and shifted. He jumped when the minute number changed. He assumed it turned to *2:39*, but he couldn't be sure. Warm tears made it all but impossible for him to see.

Nichols was respectfully silent for a moment, then he cleared his throat and said, "I wish I could make it, too, but we've got that budget meeting on Tuesday morning. You'll have to represent the department. 'Course, we'll send flowers and condolences to the family."

"There's just his mom left," Dale said, surprised he could talk through the jumble of memories flooding his mind. And at the bottom of it all was the icy thought that it was all over—

*Larry was dead and would be buried in a few days!*

No more chances to store up any more memories, not even the slightest ones.

*It's horrible how life can turn so suddenly,* he thought. Already he could feel the anger churning inside him … just like when Natalie died … anger mixed with that hollow, empty feeling of grief and loss.

"Thanks—ah, thanks for letting me know," he said.

Nichols started to say something, then stopped himself and simply grunted. For some reason, that made Dale like him all the more. His boss knew there was nothing he or anyone could say to take away the razor-edged pain.

"Thanks for the time off, too," Dale said. "I'll just take a week."

"You've got two coming," Nichols said, almost brightly, as if the offer could help.

"Thanks … one's plenty." Then Dale hung up. He had to restrain himself from slamming down the phone. After a while, he turned out the light and lay back down in bed, his hands cradling his head as he stared wide-eyed at his bedroom ceiling until morning stained the sky a burnished gray.

# II

"This is really friggin' stupid! I don't see why we don't just get on the turnpike and hitchhike," Tasha Steward said. She didn't care if her irritation showed. They had been walking since sometime around three o'clock in the morning, and she was much too uncomfortable to care what her companion thought.

She stared angrily at the back of the man she had been traveling with since they joined up near Fredericksburg, Virginia, and she wished for the millionth time she had left him behind long ago. He, like her—although for very different reasons—was heading to northern Maine, and any company was better than none.

At least that's what she had supposed.

His name was Roy Moulton, but because of his habit of frequently clearing his throat and spitting, especially when he was nervous or upset, she had taken to calling him "Hocker." And it hadn't taken her long to realize something was definitely weird about him … a lot of somethings …

For one thing, and she knew she should have ditched him as soon as he told her this, he had readily admitted that he had "walked out of" (escaped, she figured) a mental hospital in Athens, Georgia. During their journey north, she's had plenty of time to wonder why he had been hospitalized. She wasn't entirely convinced by the reason he gave—that his aunt and uncle had wanted to "get rid of him" after his mother died. His father, he told her, "Big Russ," had gone to the store for cigarettes and never come back when Hocker was six years old.

For another thing, Tasha had to consider how he traveled. It had taken her a while to see the pattern, but there *was* a definite pattern. They would hitchhike just as bold as could be along major turnpikes, even getting stopped and questioned by the cops now and then, but then, for no apparent reason, Hocker would suddenly demand that they leave the highways and take back-roads for a while, and they would spend several days passing through one small, nameless town after another. Then, acting as if some danger of which only he was aware was over, he would just as suddenly say it was all right for them to get back onto the highway, which they would travel a few days until they were off again onto some twisting two-lane back roads.

That had slowed their progress down considerably. Tasha was beginning to wonder if, at the rate they were going, they'd even make it to northern Maine before snow fell. But most of all she just wondered why Hocker used such a strange leapfrog method of travel.

It made no sense at all.

It wasn't to buy food or other supplies because they could get everything they needed in any of the sprawling shopping malls close to the turnpike. It was almost as if Hocker was on a mission ... or that he felt suddenly threatened or pursued.

By *what,* Tasha didn't know, and she wasn't so sure she wanted to find out.

Whatever the reason, Tasha had learned not to question or defy him. The first and only time she had done that, he had threatened to "make her *real* sorry" if she didn't come with him. And there had been something in his eyes that made her comply without question.

Lying awake late at night and on early morning walks like now, Tasha wondered if maybe Hocker had been hospitalized for something a bit more serious than "family problems," as he said She wondered if he might not have it within him to kill her and leave her corpse buried in some nameless, shallow grave along the highway. Maybe he was one of those serial killers who cuts a notch into his belt for each woman he murders. But, of course, Tasha was pretty sure she could handle herself. Anyway, she figured if Hocker was going to off her, he would have done so long before now.

No, there were a lot of things wrong with him, but he wasn't a murderer ...

As they walked along, Tasha kept staring at the wispy gray traces of morning mist that still hovered in low spots along the side of the road. She imagined tattered, shrouded ghosts—*maybe all the ghosts of mass-murderer Hocker's victims*—drifting noiselessly along the road with him, following them north. Droplets of dew clung to grass and bushes like ripe berries, ready to fall or fade as the sun angled its light through the leaves overhead. They were on the outskirts of a small town named Holden, Maine, Hocker told her. Tasha could just about care. All she was interested in was grabbing breakfast at a roadside diner because she was so damned sick of beans and soup heated in their cans over a smokeless campfire.

Hocker made a deep rumbling in his chest, worked a wad of spit back and forth in his mouth, and then sent it sailing into the air. It arched gracefully, two globs joined by a silver filament that twisted end over end before landing—*splat!*—on a dew-slick stop sign.

"Hot damn!" Hocker said, pausing to watch with child-like intensity as his saliva slid down to the edge of red metal, hung suspended for a moment, and then dropped to the pavement. The sound it made when it hit reminded Tasha of her mother's parrot, when his turds hit the newspaper that lined his cage.

"This is bullshit, and you know it," Tasha said as they resumed walking. "I'm cold and wet, and my friggin' legs are so tired I can barely feel them."

"It's refreshing to take the scenic roads now and then," Hocker said. "Gives us a chance to really *see* where we're goin'."

"You've gotta remember, I was born in New Jersey," Tasha said. "The turnpike *is* the scenic road as far as *I'm* concerned."

Hocker shook his head vigorously. "Turnpike isn't really for traveling—it's just for *getting* there," he said. He glanced back at her over his shoulder and frowned deeply. Whenever he did that, it made Tasha want to laugh out loud because he looked so damned dim-witted, but beneath the surface smoldered a crazed intensity, like the fire hidden inside an ash-gray coal. It was what kept her on her guard around him.

"You're still dressed like a damned teeny-bop hooker from Miami, that's why you're so damned cold," Hocker said. He twanged his words with an exaggerated Southern drawl. "So you can quit your complainin', all right? I mean — " Again he rumbled in his chest and spat. "What do you expect, a chauffeur-driven Cadillac or some-thin'?"

Tasha smiled wanly. "That'd be nice," she said, as much to herself as to him.

The mere mention of a Cadillac made her think of her parents, back in Port Charlotte, Florida. If she was still back with them, or at least with her father on every other weekend, she would have had the Cadillac, if not quite the chauffeur. But that and a whole pile of other reasons was why she had left Port Charlotte five weeks ago. She was tired of feeling like a wishbone in her divorced parents' emotional tug-of-war, and her goal in leaving home was to make it to the tip of northern Maine—to be as far away from her parents as she possibly could get without actually leaving the country.

With Hocker leading the way, they walked down the road toward town, taking only a passing notice of their surroundings. Lights glowed in a couple of houses as three or four cars whispered by in the early morning stillness. The cars were heading in the opposite direction from the way they were walking, so they couldn't stick out their thumbs. Tasha couldn't help but wonder what kind of impression they made.

As they rounded a corner into town, they saw up ahead a rusted pickup truck pulled over on the side of the road. A grizzled old man—old enough to be her grandfather, Tasha thought—was leaning over the rear wheel well on the passenger's side. He had a star wrench in his hand and was busily spinning the lug nuts off the back tire.

Hocker jolted to a stop, holding his arm out to stop Tasha. Before she could complain, he held his fingers to his lips, silencing her.

"Not exactly a Cadillac," he said. He spoke so softly Tasha wasn't exactly sure what he had said.

In silence, they watched as the old man worked the last lug nut loose and dropped it into upturned hubcap. The clanging sound it made was as loud as a gunshot in the early morning stillness. The old man put down the star wrench and picked up a car jack, as rusted and dented as his truck, and inspected it to see if it was still functional. Leaning over to concentrate on his work, he didn't hear Hocker and Tasha when, on Hocker's silent signal, they started to creep slowly and quietly toward him from behind.

The jack made a loud ratcheting sound as the old man worked it up and down. He was just standing up to place the jack under the rear fender when Hocker spoke up.

"'Morning," he said. "Got a flat?"

With a loud grunt of surprise, the old man spun around. At the same instant, he let go of the jack. It fell to the road with a loud clang. The top end hit the lip of the hubcap, and before he could react, the lug nuts catapulted into the air. If the shot had been planned, it probably never would have worked, but with the perversity of fate, the lug nuts bounced off the curb, and then all four of them disappeared through the iron grating of a storm drain. There was a loud splash as they hit the black, subterranean water and sank to the bottom.

"Jumped-up, bald-headed *Christ!*" the old man shouted, shaking his gnarled fist inches beneath Hocker's chin. "Why'd you go 'n spook me like that? Damn yah eyes!" He looked past Hocker at Tasha, who was standing several steps behind him.

Hocker, unblinking, took one step back, spit to one side, and said softly, "Sorry . . . didn't know you were so jumpy."

The old man's scowl deepened. The lines in his face looked like cracks in old granite. "Well, Christ! I can't 'xactly say I was expectin' anyone to be sneakin' up on me from behind. Not at this hour."

Hocker squinted one eye, regarding the old man as though measuring him. "I said I was sorry," he said, but there was a sarcastic edge in his voice that Tasha didn't like.

"Well, now, what in the name of Christ am I gonna do?" he said. He slapped his hands on his thighs, raising little puffs of dust, then shoved his gnarled hands into the front of his bib coveralls. "I ain't gonna be able to change the tire without lug nuts, now, am I?" He eyed the iron grate of the storm drain as if he expected to see his missing lug nuts suddenly, miraculously return.

"Here," Hocker said, bending to pick up the tire iron from where it had fallen. It was slick with dew, so he wiped it on his pants leg before going over to the truck and kneeling down. Working quickly, he removed one lug nut from each of the three good tires and, with a smirk curling one side of his mouth, handed the three lug nuts to the old man.

"What the—?" the old man said. He couldn't refrain from smiling at the obvious brilliance of Hocker's idea.

"Now each tire will be missing only one," Hocker said. "It'll get you by until you can pick up some new ones. I can give you the money for 'em, if you'd like." As he started reaching for the wallet in his hip pocket, he was still smiling that wide, friendly smile of his, but to Tasha, at least, it held a vicious undercurrent.

"I'll be a son-of-a-bitch," the old man said. "Never would'a thought of that." He rattled the three lug nuts like dice in his hand.

"Name's Roy," Hocker said, extending his hand and giving the old man a firm shake.

"Pleased to meet yah," the old man said. "M'name's Buddy—Buddy Conners."

"Look, I've caused you enough aggravation for one day," Hocker said. "Let me finish getting that spare on for yah. Maybe you can give us a lift out of town."

The old man handed the lug nuts back to Hocker and stepped back to the curb to give him plenty of room to work. "I would 'predate the help," he said, casting a questioning glance at Tasha. "My rheumatiz been actin' up something fierce. The old bones don't feel quite right 'till sometime 'round noon."

"No problem," Hocker said.

He dropped the three lug nuts into the upturned hubcap and started to whistle as he fit the jack under the bumper and began cranking away. The ratcheting sound echoed in the early morning stillness, and the truck's rusting springs groaned as the chassis slowly rose higher and higher. Each crank got harder as the jack took more and more of the weight of the truck.

"The emergency brake's on, I hope," he said.

"A-yuh."

Hocker kept a cautious eye on the base of the jack. Under the weight and swaying of the truck, it had shifted forward and was working one edge into the asphalt of the road. He considered lowering it to start over but decided to go ahead anyway. What the hell? It wasn't his truck, so what did he care if it fell and broke an axle? It'd just be another problem for the old fart to deal with today.

"Kinda risky, removing all the lug nuts before you jack it up, don't you think?" Hocker asked the old man. "If the jack shifts before it's clear of the ground . . ."

As if in proof of what he was saying, the jack suddenly heaved to one side. There was a sharp, metallic *twang* followed by a slow, grumbling crunching sound as the old asphalt powdered away. Hocker kept one hand loosely on the tire iron, but he backed away, ready to dart aside if the jack suddenly sprang out.

"Hold on a second," Conners said. He walked to the side of the truck and gave the side rail a firm push. The crunching sound got louder as the truck shifted away from him, but the jack base leveled out, looking firmer than before.

Hocker glanced at the old man and shot him a wide smile. "Risky trick," he said as he gave the jack neck a few quick tugs to make sure it was secure and then started jacking again.

After a few pumps, the flattened tire cleared the ground, and Hocker slid it off. He coughed up a wad of mucous and spit before picking up the spare tire and wiggling the rim onto the wheelbase. Once the tire was in place, he quickly spun the three lug nuts into place, tightened them by hand, and then started lowering the truck.

When the truck was back down solidly on the road, Hocker pulled the jack out. The base fell to the ground with a loud clatter as he swung the jack and tire iron into the flatbed of the truck. Then he bent down and picked up the flat tire and threw that into the back. Brushing his hands on his pants, he looked at Conners.

"That wasn't so bad now, was it?" he said. Again he smiled, and again Tasha saw more meanness than friendliness in his smile. The old man didn't seem to notice a thing.

"I 'preciate the help," Conners said, "but I'm late for work as it is. I ain't goin' to downtown, but I'll be glad to give you a ride in. You look like you could do with a cup of coffee. There's a nice little place called Feeney's just this side of the corner of Main and Railroad."

Tasha nodded agreement as she rubbed her bare arms, trying to drive away the chill that didn't seem to want to leave.

Hocker's smile wavered for just a fraction of a second. "You should've said something before I did all that work," he said softly. "Now I'm all sweated up, and we still ain't gonna get any further than downtown? Shee-it!" He glanced at Tasha. "Oh, well. What the hell? Hey!" He pointed at the jack base on the roadside. "Don't forget that."

"Right," the old man said. He turned and bent down to get it, and as he did, Hocker snatched the tire iron from the back of the truck. Just as Conners was standing up, Hocker brought the tire iron around and hit the old man hard on the base of the neck. Tasha let out a high-pitched scream as the old man spun in place and then slowly crumpled to the ground. His shoulder hit hard on the curb, but it broke his fall so his head didn't hit hard.

"What the hell are you—? Are you crazy?"

Tasha looked frantically up and down the road, but there were no cars or people in sight. Not yet, anyway.

"Bastard should have told us he couldn't give us a ride *before* I did his fuckin' job for him," Hocker said. He worked up a big wad of spit and let it fly at the crumpled form of the old man. It left a slug-white glob on the back of his bib coveralls.

"The keys still in the ignition?" Hocker asked.

Tasha stood, immobile. All she could think about was that now, in a split second, everything had changed. *Everything!* It wasn't just the two of them, hitching across the Eastern states anymore. Now Hocker had committed a real crime, and she was an accomplice. The old man might even be ...

"Is he dead?" she managed to ask. Her mouth went dry as dust; her lips felt cracked.

"I dunno." Hocker bent over the fallen man and touched his neck behind the left ear. "Nope. I can still feel a pulse," he said. Actually, he couldn't feel anything close to a pulse. He wasn't even sure he was feeling in the right place. "Check the truck for the keys while I drag him out of sight."

Tasha still couldn't move. It was as if her feet had suddenly grown rope-thick roots that held her there, terror-stricken.

Hocker glanced up and down the street. Still no traffic. Their luck was holding. He slid his hands under Conners' shoulders and lifted him off the ground just enough so his hips cleared the curb. He dragged him up a gentle slope and into a thin stand of trees. It wasn't much, but it was enough so they could get a few miles out of town, anyway.

"Will you go check for them goddamned *keys!*" he shouted from the top of the knoll. "We ain't getting very far if we don't have 'em!"

Tasha still didn't move. She was debating whether or not she should do now what she had been thinking about doing before—just walking away; leaving Hocker to get himself into and out of his own damned messes. If that old man was dead ... then she was—what did they call it on T.V. cop shows?

*An accessory to murder!*

She was in almost as much trouble as Hocker was if they got caught.

"Car comin'! Duck!" Hocker suddenly yelled. He flattened himself on the ground, his eyes visible over the grassy knoll.

Thinking only to keep herself out of trouble, Tasha darted around behind the truck, scooched down by the cab, and waited. Seconds seemed to draw out into minutes as she waited ... waited to hear the approaching car. At last, she heard the whisper of tires on the road as a car crested the hill, heading toward town.

*What if the driver recognizes the old man's truck?* she wondered. Pressure built in her bladder, and she nearly wet her pants in fear. *What if it's someone the old man knows or works with, and they stop to see what's the matter?*

The car moved slowly down the road, its engine hushed by the early morning stillness. The tires made a soft tearing sound on the moist asphalt.

Tasha held her breath and glanced fearfully up to where Hocker was hiding. She couldn't see him at all now, and she wondered if he had taken off, leaving her to take the rap.

Wouldn't *that* be a laugh riot?

He leaves her with a broken down truck and an unconscious man.

— *Who's maybe dead!* her mind screamed.

She' be arrested for assault or maybe *murder,* and he'll be back on I-95, heading up to Fort Kent or Canada or maybe the edge of the known world.

*Would that be just Jim-dandy-roo?*

The car seemed to take forever to drive by, but Tasha didn't dare peek out to see how close it was. By the sound of it, it must be the size of three stretch limos moving at a whopping four miles per hour.

*When the driver sees the old man's truck,* she thought, panic-stricken, *he'll stop and a whole SWAT team will burst out and spray the truck with automatic weapons.*

"Stay down!" a voice called out, oddly hushed. It took Tasha a moment to recognize Hocker's voice. At least for now, he was still up there in the woods. Still, if they had to bolt and run, he'd have the advantage.

At last, there was no doubt in Tasha's mind that the car was right next to the truck. She clung to the rusted door like a tick on a mongrel and bit down on her tongue to keep from crying out, as she waited … waited for the car to move past. The pressure in her bladder made her eyes water.

The car slowed down. At least it *sounded* like it was slowing down.

*What if it was the police, and they were looking for the old man!*

They'll find him, all right—right up there in the woods with his brains leaking out of his crushed skull!

But then with a gentle rush of wind, the car sped past. Tasha let out her breath in a slow, shrill whistle. Once she was positive it was safe, she peeked out around the edge of the truck and watched the tail lights disappear around a gentle curve.

"Now for *Christ's* sake! Will you check the truck for the *keys?*" Hocker shouted.

Tasha's back felt like a rusty spring as she slowly straightened up. Glancing toward the woods, she saw Hocker stand up and brush leaves and dirt from his knees. Then she turned and glanced into the truck cab. The keys were dangling from a faded orange rabbit's foot in the ignition.

"Yeah," she said, barely loud enough for Hocker to hear. "They're in there."

"Thank you, ma'am," Hocker said as he walked as bold as could be down the slope to the truck.

"You can't just leave him up there," Tasha said. The fear of being implicated in a murder was still working into her mind like a worm into an apple.

"Aww, don't get your panties in a bunch 'bout him." Hocker waved one hand over his head. "He'll wake up with a bit of a headache that a bottle of whiskey will cure. Come on. Hop in. We can at least drive this sucker 'till it runs out of gas."

"Hold on a minute," Tasha said. She dashed up the slopes and into the woods, keeping as far away from where Hocker had ditched the old man as she could before she lowered her pants and released the pressure in her bladder. While she peed, she considered that she still had her backpack strapped on. She could finish her business and run off deeper into the woods. Maybe she could get a half mile between her and Hocker before he even realized she'd taken off.

From below the slope, she heard the truck labor as Hocker turned the key in the ignition. It churned, sputtered, and stalled out a few times until— finally—it roared to life. A blue haze of exhaust kicked out from the tailpipe and rose into the air. Suddenly, the horn sounded a long, blaring blast.

" Come on! Get a move on!" Hocker shouted, his voice muffled by the distance.

Tasha stood up and buckled her pants. Her eyes flashed back and forth from the woods to the road and then back to the woods.

She could do it now!

She could boogie before he could stop her. Then again, why *would* he stop her. He didn't seem to care one way or the other if she was with him or not.

"I ain't waitin' all goddamned day!" he shouted.

"Just a sec," Tasha answered. She looked over to where the old man lay, and curiosity suddenly overruled her fear.

*I should check him myself,* she thought. *Then, if I stay with Hocker, I'll at least know if I'm wanted for assault or murder.*

Hitching up her pants, Tasha moved slowly toward the dense brush. She could see the matted trail, a wide streak through the dew-soaked grass, where Hocker had dragged the body, so she had no difficulty finding him.

*What did he say his name was? Buddy ... Buddy Conners?*

In spite of her fear, she almost laughed out loud when she saw how Hocker had left him. He was lying flat on his back beneath the bushes, his heels together, and his hands clasped on his chest like he was laid out in his coffin. A spring of dried flowers was stuck in the top pocket of his bib coveralls. He looked for all the world like a parody of a low-budget funeral.

*But was he really dead?* she wondered.

*It won't be so funny if he's dead.*

Again, the truck horn blared.

"I'm leavin' in ten seconds," Hocker shouted.

Tasha was going to call back to him, but instead she remained silent as she approached the motionless man. Bending low, she licked her fingers and brought them close to his nose. She braced herself, ready and waiting to see his eyes suddenly snap open. He would grab her by the arms or throat and pull her to him, crushing her in the steely grip of his thin arms.

But there wasn't the slightest breath chilling the moisture on her hand. Fear flooded her.

*He's dead!*

Hocker had *killed* a man, and for what?! All because the old man had told him he couldn't give them a ride out of town!

"Oh, shit … Oh, *Jesus,*" she muttered as she knelt down beside the old man and stared at his pale, drawn face. But then she saw something that made hope stir within her. She might not have felt his breath, shallow as it was, but the artery in his neck was pulsing. She could see it throb beneath his skin.

"Last chance!" Hocker shouted.

Tasha stood up slowly, silently regarding the unconscious old man.

*Yes!* she thought. *Unconscious … Not dead!*

For another second or two, she considered running off into the woods and letting Hocker go his own way. But then, she thought, it may not be a chauffeured Cadillac, but it's wheels, and it sure, as hell beats walking all goddamned day. The more distance she got between herself and this old duffer the better. She turned and sprinted down the slope to the waiting truck, swung open the door, and jumped inside.

"Come on," she said breathlessly. "Get this mother-fucker *moving.*"

Hocker stomped down on the accelerator, and the truck lurched forward, leaving a good three inches of warm, black rubber on the road.

"We'll avoid town in case anyone recognizes the truck," Hocker said. He turned left just before they reached the first business buildings on Main Street.

The fuel needle bobbed between three-quarters and full, so Hocker was satisfied that they wouldn't have to put any money into the truck before they got out of Holden. Draping his left arm out the window, he settled back comfortably in the seat as they drove across the bridge, heading to Bangor.

Tasha still felt uncomfortable with the thought that they had just added grand theft auto to their list of crimes, but all in all, things weren't turning out so badly. At least, for a while, they had wheels!

"You know," she said as they darted up the entrance ramp onto I-95, heading north, "that was quite a stunt you pulled back there."

"What, blindsiding the old man?"

"No, with the lug nuts," Tasha said. "I wouldn't have thought to use one from each tire."

Hocker glanced at her and smiled that lopsided grin that bothered her so much. "Fuckin-A. I may be crazy, but I ain't *stupid.*"

# III

Finally, once the sky was completely light, Dale gave up on trying to sleep. He got out of bed and shambled into the kitchen to make breakfast. Angie was a sound sleeper, and he figured she would stay in bed at least until eight. School didn't start for another few weeks. Then, she'd be up at six o'clock every weekday morning. No sense waking her up early just to tell her Larry was dead.

"Uncle Larry," Dale said, shaking his head as he dropped two slices of wheat bread into the toaster slots. He folded his arms across his chest and leaned back against the refrigerator.

Ever since Angie could talk, she had called him "Uncle Larry," and in many ways, that's exactly what he had been to her. He never forgot her birthday, and he always gave her a present that Dale ... and Natalie, when she was alive ... thought was a bit *too* much. But he always made Angie feel special. Unlike some adults who condescend to kids and either patronize them or act as if they don't deserve attention, Larry had always made a special effort to include Angie in the conversation whenever she was around. He was warm and friendly toward her, always saying how, since he didn't have wife or any children of his own, she would do as his niece, and Angie was more than happy to oblige him.

*Not any more,* Dale thought. Again, his eyes started stinging as they filled with tears. *No more presents ... No more talks ... No more nothing!*

Dale jumped and let out a startled gasp when his toast popped up. Moving mechanically, he put both pieces on a plate and went to sit down at the table. The knife made a harsh, grating noise as he spread a thin coat of grape jelly over each piece. He got up, poured a cup of coffee, and then sat down to eat.

Instead of eating, though, he ended up staring blankly at the two pieces of toast as his mind sifted through memories of Larry ... especially of Larry and Angie. There were so many memories of their deep-rooted friendship, of caring and helping. Dale recalled his kindness during the years it took him and Angie to get over Natalie's death. So many memories, now spiked with pain and loss.

As Dale stared at his meager breakfast, his eyesight began to blur. At first everything on the table top went out of focus, but then, starting in the middle of his vision, a swirling black hole began to form. Dale was barely conscious of his attention as it funneled into the spinning void spinning before his eyes, but his body reacted. His shoulders and arms began to tremble as if embraced by an icy wind; his neck and throat pulsed in time with his heartbeat, and each pulse grew louder and louder until hard-hitting hammer blows thumped his inner ears; his throat was squeezed shut as though bony fingers—

*hands reaching from the grave!*

—were slowly choking him.

"Why are you up so early?" a voice said from behind him.

Dale choked back a scream as he spun up and stood up, knocking his chair over backwards. His left knee hit the underside of the table, and his coffee slopped onto the plate, soaking his uneaten toast. A jolting pain darted up his leg, but he barely noticed it in his flood of panic as he stared at his daughter.

"Gosh. I didn't mean to scare you," Angie said.

The expression on her face shifted back and forth between surprise and laughter. To break the awkwardness, she bent down and righted her father's chair.

Dale tried to soak up the spilled coffee with a napkin, but when he saw that the toast was doing a good enough job of it, he went to the sink and scooped the whole mess into the garbage disposal. He flicked the switch, and the disposal whirred loudly, gobbling up his meal. More than anything, he wanted just to stand there with his back to Angie and lose himself in the whining sound of the disposal.

*Anything* if he wouldn't have to turn to face her.

As soon as she saw his face, he was convinced she'd know something was terribly wrong.

When the throat of the disposal was clear, Dale slowly turned around. Already he could see it there on her face ... the thin lines of concern and questioning that, in mere seconds, would come crashing down like a poorly built brick wall.

"I thought I'd better practice getting up early for school," she said, "so I set my alarm for early." There was a forced brightness in her voice that cut Dale to the quick.

Sunlight poured in through the kitchen window, backlighting her and giving her dark hair a wispy nimbus. Her blue eyes sparkled, and her skin was a deep nut brown from spending most of the summer at the shore with her friends.

*She's the perfect picture of a healthy, happy, twelve-year-old,* Dale thought, *and when I tell her what I have to tell her, it'll put lines in her face that will* never *go away!*

"You all right?" Angie asked when Dale didn't speak to her right away.

"No, I ... I'm not. I'm afraid I've got some ... some terrible news."

She could read from his face that he meant it.

This was a *bad* one.

With a trembling hand, she drew her chair away from the table and lowered herself into it. Not once did she break eye contact with him as he came over and sat down beside her, pulling up close.

In as few words as possible, and struggling not to break down, he told her about Larry—everything Nichols had told him in his pre-dawn call, and he sat there and let her pitch forward, burying her face into his chest as her tears spilled, hot and wet, soaking into his shirt.

She cried for more than fifteen minutes. Sobs shook her entire frame, making it difficult for her to take anything more than shallow, halting breaths. Before long, her throat was raw, and her crying took on a ragged wheeze that worried Dale; but he let her cry it all out: to cry for Larry, to cry for her mother, to cry for anyone and everyone whoever suffered the loss of a close friend. She cried and moaned until her body was as wrung out as a tattered washcloth.

When it was over, although Dale knew it would never really be *over,* but when her crying had subsided, he went to the counter, got a box of Kleenex tissues, and handed it to her. Taking several, she rubbed her eyes vigorously and blew her nose. Her shoulders still shook with deeply repressed sobs, but she made a bold effort to pull herself together.

"It's just not . . . not fair!" she said, her breath catching like a fish hook in her throat. "It's . . . not. Larry was . . . was so . . ."

"I know, babe, I know," Dale said, still leaning close and stroking the back of her head.

When she was four and her mother had died, Angie was too young, really, to register the true depth of her loss. It had seemed like one day her mother just stopped being around, and after a long while she got used to it; Mommy had "gone away from us—gone back to God," her father had told her. Figuring she was too young, Dale hadn't let her go to the funeral or anything, so she had never really experienced a deep, personal loss before.

"Why doesn't stuff like this happen to ... to other people?" she sobbed. "Larry never hurt anyone."

Dale's eyes were stinging, but he knew he had to be strong for Angie now, like he had been when Natalie died.

"No one ever says life is fair, babe," he whispered. "And I think that's one thing, maybe the *only* thing, that separates kids from adults. You begin to realize that life never has been and never will be fair."

Angie looked at him with grief twisting like smoky clouds over her face and said, "We maybe realize it, but do we have to *accept* it?"

Dale shook his head as he got up and went to the refrigerator. He took out the juice jug and poured each of them a tall glass of orange juice. He got a couple of ice cubes from the freezer and dropped them into Angie's glass, the way she always liked it.

He sat back down, and they drank silently together, each reassured by the nearness of the other. The only sound in the kitchen was Angie sniffing back her tears.

"Well," Dale said at last, once their juice was gone and neither of them had moved from the table.

"Well, what?"

"Nichols said the funeral would be Monday afternoon, up in Dyer," Dale said. "I've got the week off so I can go up. I was thinking you could probably stay at Mary's for a couple of days."

"I want to go, too," Angie said.

There was willfulness in her voice that Dale had never heard before. He looked at her and saw the resolve in her eyes. She was biting down hard on her lower lip, turning it a bloodless pink. She looked so small and scared, Dale wanted to smother her in hugs.

"I don't think that's such a good idea," he said solemnly. "I mean, funerals aren't exactly the finest things going, you know."

The resolve in her eyes got steelier, but then she let her gaze drift past her father and out the kitchen window to the arc of clear blue sky.

"You know," she said, almost dreamily, "I always thought funerals were such a waste of time. Like—you know—like they were just so the people still alive could get rid of guilt and stuff they were still feeling."

Dale smiled gently. "Well, I don't expect the person who has died really cares one way or another."

"I never did, either," Angie said. "But you know, with . . ." For an instant she paused, almost unable to say his name, but she braced herself and went on. "With Larry, though, I have this feeling that it's . . . it's different somehow. Like it's important for me to go to his funeral so I can help keep his memory fresh in my mind."

Standing up quickly, Dale walked over to the sink and, leaning on the counter, looked out over the backyard. His mind was a confusion of half-thoughts and scattered memories, but the over-riding thought was that the void, the black, bottomless void had opened up and swallowed another person he loved, just as someday it would slide open and pull him and Angie and everyone down. He knew he had to deal with it his way, and he also recognized that Angie was old enough to decide for herself how she would deal with it.

"You know, it'll be like—like a part of him is still alive as long as I remember him."

Dale turned, unable to distinguish his daughter's face through his swirl of tears.

"What you said before, though," Angie said, "about how the person who's dead doesn't care one way or the other. Do you think that's really true?"

"What do you mean?" Dale asked, controlling his voice only by an immense effort.

"I mean, do you think that once you're dead, that's it? Or do you think the person—like goes on, somehow, like to Heaven or something."

Dale shook his head and ran the cuff of his shirtsleeve over each eye. *She's not four years old anymore,* he told himself. *She's growing up. She's starting on that rocky road to adulthood, and it would be dishonest not to tell her the truth as I see it.*

"No," he said, still shaking his head. "I think when you're dead, that's it. It's final. You go back to where ever the hell you were before you were born, and all that's left of you is what they bury in the ground."

"So then it is important," Angie said, a sudden intensity in her voice. "Cause, like, if I don't go to Larry's funeral, if *I* don't *remember* him, then it'll' be like he never ever lived."

Dale nodded and, sighing deeply, ran his hand over his forehead.

"Okay," he said. "You better get packing if you're coming with me. I've got a few things to take care of, but I want to be on the road before lunch."

# IV

Donna LaPierre had thought, foolishly, perhaps, once upon a time, that she would never have to see the town of Dyer again, but it came into view as she created the hill just as she remembered it. After too damned many miles of twisting, narrow roads through Mattawamkeag and Haynesville, the pine forest thinned out, giving way to a scattering of houses and stores that marked the center of town, such as it was. North of town, toward Houlton, the woods had been pushed back, leaving low-knolled hills and wide, flat fields, covered now with the green vines of potatoes nearing harvest time.

Donna looked at the photograph taped to her dashboard just above the AM/FM radio. On the drive north, she had done something incredibly immature; it hadn't made her feel good then, and it didn't make her feel good now . . . put *still,* she thought, *he deserved it!*

With the tip of her cigarette, she had burned two small holes through the eyes of Bradley Phillips, the man in the photo ... the man standing on a white-sand beach in Jamaica dressed in cut-off shorts and a T-shirt with the logo *NO PROBLEM* ... the man with his left arm draped lovingly over Donna's shoulder . . . the man whose bright gold wedding ring sparkled in the Caribbean sunlight . . . the man who had told Joan, his wife, he was in Jamaica "strictly on business" . . . the man who had finally told Donna . . .

"You self-centered, chicken-shit little *prick!"* Donna said, feeling her upper lip curl into a nasty snarl. She stuck up her middle finger and waved it savagely in front of the photograph, but the ash-rimmed eyes didn't look back at her ... or if they did, they were as sightless as if he were dead.

In spite of her embarrassment about what she had done, though, Donna didn't just take the photo, shred it, and cast its tatters to the wind. She liked keeping it there—for just a while longer—as a memento of a love affair gone bad.

The two hundred and fifty dollar fine for littering wouldn't be worth the pleasure, she thought, replacing her hand on the steering wheel as she slowed to a stop at the blinking red light in the center of town.

"Bradley, my man, you've littered up my life enough already!" she said, automatically snapping on the turn signal for the left turn onto Burnt Mill Road.

Taking the turn, she glanced over at the Mill Store, and sure enough, Sparky Wilson was sitting there, slouched in the shade of the gas pumps with his hat pulled down over his eyes to shield them from the afternoon sun. Donna couldn't remember a time when Sparky *hadn't* been propped out there by the pumps, and she seriously wondered if maybe, in the time she was away, Sparky had died and the town had put a life-sized statue out there to commemorate him. But no. As she completed her turn, she gave her horn a quick beep, and Sparky shook awake, glanced at her, and waved even though she could tell by his squint that he didn't know who in hell she was.

Some things around here never change, she thought. And that was exactly why, as soon as she graduated from high school, she had left town for college with the intention of never coming back. That had been eleven years ago, and she had pretty much done just that. Only twice within the last five years had she come back to Dyer. And both times it had been for funerals, first her mother's in 1984 and then her father's, in 1986.

As she drove slowly through town, Donna noticed plenty of other things that hadn't changed. It was spooky how much it felt like she had never left and in some ways, that was exactly true. Small towns like Dyer do seem to create their own little sinkholes in time. While the rest of the world spins along, changing and growing, towns like Dyer stay the same. The population remains almost constant, the birth rate balancing the death rate. A few new houses go up on the outskirts of town, but lumbering and potato-growing have already seen their boom days, and nothing, not even the new varieties of potatoes, could revive them to their former glory days. There's no influx of new jobs to lure new families. Sons and daughters assume their parents' jobs and social positions, and only a few, usually the brightest students, get away to college and never come back.

Maybe that wasn't Sparky back there at the pumps, Donna thought. Maybe Sparky got married, and that was Sparky Jr. out there, manning the pumps for the old man. It was possible . . . But she liked the Sparky memorial statue idea better.

"And here *I* am," Donna said under her breath. "The one that almost got away."

When she saw the yellow siding of her sister's house up ahead on the right, she fished a cigarette out of her purse and lit it with the car lighter. She slowed for the turn into the driveway and a weary sense of sameness came over her. The driveway was still unpaved; it still had its Mowhawk center strip of grass and weeds where the wheels from Barbara's car and Al's truck hadn't worn it away.

How many years had it been since Barbara had said she wanted to get it paved? Donna wondered. Maybe she should just give them the money to get the damned thing done while she was here visiting. Then, when she left again, she would be secure in the knowledge that at least *something* had changed in Dyer recently!

The screen door in the shade of the boxed-in porch opened up, and Donna saw a wide smile spread across her sister's face as she came quickly down the steps into the sunlight. Donna pulled in behind the family car, an old, sun-bleached blue Volvo station wagon, knowing she was taking Al's parking space, and killed the engine. By the time she pulled the keys from the ignition and dropped them into her purse, Barbara had run down the steps and was reaching in through the open driver's window to squeeze Donna's shoulder.

"Oh, you're early," she said, her voice nearly squealing. "I wasn't expecting you until 'round suppertime."

Donna popped open the door and stepped out to be engulfed in a warm hug. She held her cigarette away from them at a safe distance and gave her sister a quick kiss on the cheek.

"Radar detector," Donna said, nodding toward her car. "A great invention if you want to make good time on the road."

Barbara shook her head as she stood back, holding Donna at arm's length and studying her.

"You've lost quite a bit of weight since I saw you last," Barbara said.

Donna took a puff of her cigarette, and snorted out a thin burst of smoke with her laughter. "Yeah, I have, about a hundred and eighty pounds of dead weight."

Again, Barbara shook her head as though in disapproval of her sister, or at least of her life style. "I'm sorry to hear about you and Brad," she said, "but you didn't really expect him to give up his wife and family, did you?"

Donna expelled smoke and dropped the cigarette to the driveway, grinding it out in the dirt with her heel. Drawing her hair back with her fingers, she sighed deeply and said, "Come on, now. Don't start in with your big sister routine with me already, okay? I've had a bitch of a week."

"Okay, okay," Barbara said, and again she clasped her sister in her arms and squeezed her. "I've got the guest room all ready for you, and like I told you on the phone, you're welcome to stay with us for just as long as you like."

Donna smiled wanly as they broke their embrace. Reaching in through the open car window, she popped the trunk release. Hoping her sister hadn't yet seen the photo on the dashboard, she reached over and flicked it to the floor. It landed face-up, and now it *did* look as though Brad was staring up at her with a blank, zombie stare. She repressed a shiver as she walked around to the back of the car to get her luggage.

"Do you want me to try and find Junior to help with this stuff?" Barbara asked as Donna unloaded three large suitcases and several tied-shut boxes.

"If you can take this, I can get the rest," Donna said. "Gosh, I'll bet he's grown up some since I saw him last."

Barbara smiled with parental pride. "You should see him. He's already up to here on me." She tapped her arm almost at the shoulder, then held her hands out for the package Donna was holding out to her.

"Be careful with that," Donna said. "It's breakable. A little surprise for you."

"What is it?" Barbara asked, giving the box a gentle shake.

Donna's smile widened slightly, and she glanced to one side. "Remember that table lamp from the house? The one I took after Dad died?"

Barbara nodded, and a small scowl appeared on her face. "I sure do," she said softly. "I remember us arguing like cats over who was going to get it."

Donna nodded. "Yeah, well, I figured now that I don't have any place to live, and you're so settled here . . ."

Barbara snorted. "Hell, I don't think blasting powder will get us out of this town."

"I decided to let you have it," Donna said. Then, swallowing with difficulty, she added, "And I wanted to apologize for being such an asshole about it."

"Oh, you don't have to apologize," Barbara said warmly. "I know how much that lamp meant to both of us, and I think we both just kinda used it to focus everything we were feeling about Mom and Dad being gone. Tell you what. You can use it in your room for as long as you like."

Donna shook her head. "You have to use it in the living room where everyone can see it. Otherwise, I'll take it back. Another thing I'm going to do, too. I'll give you the money so you can finally get this driveway blacktopped."

"You don't have to do that."

"I know I don't," Donna said. "But I've been hearing you say you're going to get that done for years now, and I figure, since you insist you won't take any rent from me, that it'll be one thing I can do to help you guys out."

Barbara shrugged and cast a furtive glance at the gravel-strewn driveway. "Well, it *is* something I've wanted done for a long time."

"It's settled, then," Donna said. "Call someone this afternoon and have them start tomorrow morning." Bending down, she gripped a suitcase handle in each hand and, grunting, hefted them and started up the walkway toward the house. Barbara followed behind her with the box with the lamp in it.

After three more trips, the car was unloaded. Donna felt a measure of relief that that was all. After Brad had left her, she had quit her job at John Hancock in Boston, sublet her apartment until her lease expired, and sold most of her clothes and furniture to a second-hand store in Chelsea. Nestled into one corner of the small guest room in her sister's house in Dyer, Maine, were her entire possessions. She was just about a vagabond, and, at least for now, that was all she wanted.

As the sun started its westward slide toward the horizon, the two sisters sat side by side on the front porch with their feet up on the railing and tall glasses of iced tea in hand. Their conversation wound in lazy loops and curves, like an old stream, as Barbara filled her sister in on the latest doings around town: who was married or divorced or cheating or whatever.

All of Barbara's children were off for the afternoon: Heather, who had just turned fourteen, was off to Houlton with some friends to see a movie, or she said. If Donna and Barbara guessed right, she was using that as an excuse to meet up with some boys somewhere. Kelly, the next in line, was taking piano lessons from Mrs. Plaisted, who played organ for the local Baptist church. And

Al Junior, whose sixth birthday was only weeks away, had gone swimming with his friend's family at Beaver Brook Pond.

Mention of Beaver Brook Pond sent a rippling chill up Donna's back. The swimming hole was out on Mayall Road, the same road as the old homestead. When she and her sister were growing up, it was the site of hundreds of days of fun, the place for swimming in the summer and skating in the winter. But with those memories came memories of the house, once a thriving, warm, love-filled home. Now, Donna didn't even want to think about it. Three years ago, when she came home for her father's funeral, the place looked worn-out, tired and small. She tried not to imagine how it looked now, after three more years of desertion.

"Did you drive by the graves on your way in?" Barbara asked. She looked directly at Donna, but she didn't seem to notice the cross-fire of emotions Donna was sure were playing across her face.

"No, I came straight here. I've been driving since five o'clock this morning."

"And here I am, talking your ear off," Barbara said, shifting forward and standing up. "You should go inside and take a nap before everyone gets home. *Then* the house will sound like there's an army in town."

"No, no," Donna said, waving her sister back down. "I'm comfortable right where I am." She took a sip of iced tea and, as if in proof, smacked her lips with satisfaction.

"You're sure?"

"I'm positive," Donna said. "I wasn't hinting or anything. If I was that tired, I'd tell you."

"Well, I certainly hope so," Barbara said. "After everything you've been through, I think you deserve to spoil yourself a little."

Donna smiled and nodded, thinking to herself, you don't know the half of it, sister dear. Lucky you! She hoped her voice didn't betray her when she said, "I was thinking of driving out to the cemetery and maybe by the old house this afternoon, but I think I'll wait 'til tomorrow."

"I told you I was renting the fields to Higgins for growing potatoes, didn't I? He doesn't pay much, but every bit helps."

Donna took another sip of tea. She tried to settle back deeper into the lounge chair, but one of the straps was digging into her back. "Old Sam Higgins," she said. "Christ, he must own or rent pretty much every farm in the area by now."

Barbara nodded agreement. "He's got quite a business going. He was hounding me about selling the farm to him, but I couldn't quite bring myself to do it. I still kinda have hopes you'll move back to town for good."

Donna looked down at the porch floor. "I don't know. I don't have any idea what I'm going to do. After what I've just been through, and what with Mom and Dad gone now ... I don't know."

"I put flowers out whenever I can," Barbara said, "but lately I've been so damned busy."

While she was talking, a pickup truck drove slowly past the house, raising a fantail of dust as it went. Barbara followed the truck lazily, but then she suddenly cut herself off mid-sentence and bolted forward in her chair.

"What the dickens?" she muttered. One had gripped the porch edge so tightly her knuckles went white.

Donna looked quickly from her sister to the truck.

"I swear to God, that's the strangest thing," Barbara said softly, as if talking to herself. She eased back into her seat, but a deep, worried frown wrinkled her brow, and her eyes looked cold and hard, like ice caps, as she tracked the truck until it disappeared over the crest of a hill.

"I forgot to tell you something else. You remember Larry Cole, don't you?"

Donna nodded. "Sure do. We went steady in junior high school, for a total of three days, as I recall. Remember? What, was that him?"

Still frowning, Barbara shook her head tightly from side to side. "No, no. I forgot to tell you. He died last night in a car accident out on the Haynesville Road."

Now it was Donna's turn to frown, "I thought he was working down in Augusta. Was he home visiting or something?"

Barbara shook her head again. "No, he was working for the State Transportation Department. I don't know the whole story, but he was up here doing some survey work for a project to widen and straighten some of those roads."

Donna didn't really feel much emotion because of Larry's death. True, they had known each other right up to graduation, but after their brief romance in junior high, they had drifted apart into their own circles of friends. She remembered that he had shown up at both her mother's and father's funerals, but that was to be expected, in such a small town as Dyer. Staring out to where the truck had disappeared, Donna thought she would probably attend *his* funeral.

"Was he married? Have a family or anything?" Donna asked once the sound of the passing truck had faded.

"No, I hadn't heard that he was. Al will probably know more about it when he gets home from work. That's the strangest thing, though," Barbara said, still shaking her head. "I could *swear* that was him driving that truck."

"It's a nice trick if you can pull it off," Donna said. She snorted a quick laugh, but after all this talk of deaths and funerals and the old home, she decided she would take a quick nap before Barbara's family got home.

# CHAPTER TWO
## "THE SECRET PLACE"

### I

Jeff Winfield, one of Dyer's two full-time policemen, hated the first day of the morning shift after a week of third shift, especially after the fatal car accident on Route 2A, known locally as the Haynesville Woods Road, last night. What it all boiled down to was one long, sixteen-hour shift starting at midnight; and not even three cups of coffee at Kellerman's at five A.M. could get him going. And after that last visit to his doctor, he decided not to chance a fourth cup because of the havoc it might wreak on his bladder. He was only forty-two years old, but nineteen years on the Dyer police force made him feel much older!

The morning was clear and cool, with a hint of on-coming autumn in the air as he steered into the parking lot beside the police station. He cut the engine and sat for a moment, gazing vacantly at the back lot behind the station. Beyond the ten-foot high hurricane fence, a meaningless precaution in such a small town as Dyer, Winfield always thought, a thin screen of maple trees were already turning yellow and red, and it was only August! Beyond the maples, he could see a long expanse of potato fields, their dark green vines dying, waiting for the tractors to come and churn up their harvest. The sky was a dull, cloudless blue, overhanging everything with a hazy oppression.

The pressure in Winfield's bladder demanded that he head into the station soon to relieve himself, but he took a minute to appreciate the scenery, thankful that for the past nineteen years he hadn't had to work in the potato fields during harvest. That was backbreaking work, and he'd had enough dirt under his fingernails when he worked the fields through high school. Becoming a cop saved him from ending up like his father and older brother, working sixteen or more hours a day every day of the week with nothing to look forward to but decreasing yields, lower prices, increasing costs, and no hope for improvement.

It struck him as strange, though, that looking out over the potato fields made him feel so down. The harvest would start soon, and most everyone in town would pitch in to bring in the crop. Even school, which started in mid-August, would close for the few weeks of harvest so sons and daughters, and even teachers could help. Whatever jobs weren't filled by local people would be taken by the migrant workers who followed harvests around the state from blueberry barrens to apple orchards to potato fields. As long as there wasn't any trouble with the migrants, and there *usually* wasn't, except for those unexplained disappearances last year up in Caribou. Things should be all right.

Of course, Winfield wouldn't be expected to help with the harvest. As a police officer, he was expected to stay on duty and sometimes even put in a little overtime; with the influx of migrant workers and everyone working so damned hard during the day, nights and weekends downtown saw more action than usual, especially at Kellerman's, the only local bar. Of course, Dyer at its most active would still strike someone from down south—say, Bangor or Portland—as a sleepy little town. And that's just how Winfield liked it, sleepy and quiet. So quiet, in fact, that now more than ever he couldn't see any need to double up shifts, especially for someone who had been with the force for as long as he had. Maybe today he would mention it to Chief Bates, again.

He swung open the cruiser door and stepped out, pocketed the keys as he stood up straight and then, yawning, stretched his arms over his head. A sudden twinge of pain shot through the small of his back, and he massaged it as he went up the walkway to the front door.

"Mornin'," said Pam Lessard, barely looking up as the heavy front door slammed shut behind him.

Pam was the daytime desk officer and radio dispatcher who had been with the department almost as long as Winfield had. Still, in all those years, he felt as though he barely knew her. She was married and lived out on Ridge Road, past the town dump. She had two boys, both in high school now, and her husband had a job at one of the banks in Houlton, he knew that much. But Pam kept pretty much to herself; she did her job and went home at the stroke of four, and that was it. She never even made it to the few social events the department had.

Winfield knew one thing, though, especially on days like this: he knew he envied the regularity of her work hours: seven to four, Monday through Friday, and a Saturday morning every now and then, like today, to help catch up. That's police work the way it *should* be.

He nodded a greeting as he walked past her glass-fronted desk, heading toward the bathroom. He tried to walk without revealing the urgency he felt.

"Oh, Jeff," she said. Her voice was flat and nasal, and when she looked at him, her eyes seemed lifeless and dull. "This just came in over the wire. You might want to have a look at it." She held a sheet of paper out through the slot in her window and gave it an impatient shake.

"Uh, yeah," Winfield said, biting down on his lower lip. "Just a sec."

He made it to the bathroom, just in time as far as he was concerned. He vowed he would limit himself to *two* cups in the morning from now on.

Back at the front desk, he looked for the Teletype Pam had tried to give him. She had it on the edge of her desk and was sitting with her back to him, busily typing.

"So," he said, feeling much relieved. "What've you got?"

"Nothing much," Pam said. She stopped typing and, turning, handed him the paper. "A File-13 from Detective Maloney in Westbrook. Seems they've had a few suspicious fires down their way and they all sort of fit together. State fire marshal indicates they were all set the same way. No real serious damage, just a couple of abandoned warehouses and one old barn. But according to this, whoever's setting them seems to be moving north."

Winfield frowned as he quickly scanned the sheet of paper. A File-13 went out on the Teletype to all police stations in New England as a general, informational bulletin. In these days of manpower shortages and budgetary restraints, not every crime could be pursued with full vigor. A File-13 was pretty much a catch-as-catch-can notice. If something happened to catch your eye, you could give the station of origin a call and offer what information you had. Usually, they just piled up and, after a week or so, made their way to the *real* File-13, the waste basket.

This particular bulletin concerned straight arson, and because no people so far had been hurt or killed, the FBI hadn't been called in. In time, either the arsonist would stop and disappear, or he would do some serious damage, or someone would get hurt or killed. Then more effort would be exerted to bring him in.

What caught Winfield's eye, though, was the warning to watch locally for a "cluster of suspicious fires."

Westbrook's had a few fires recently, he thought. So what? It could be coincidence just as easily as it could be someone setting those fires.

"I don't get it," Winfield said when he was finished reading. "Why does this detective think the arsonist is heading our way?"

Pam quickly returned to her typing, but she heard his question over the loud clattering sound she was making, and without slowing down, tilted her head toward the telephone on her desk. "I know as much as you do. Give him a call if you're so interested."

Winfield groaned as he massaged the small of his back with his fist. He glanced again at the File-13, his eyes getting caught once more by the phrase "cluster of suspicious fires." Moving stiffly, he walked down the hallway to his office, unlocked the door, entered, kicked the door shut behind him, and sat down at his desk.

His eyes felt like they were dusted with powdered glass. From his top drawer, he took a bottle of Visine and squirted three drops into each eye, blinking rapidly as the fluid ran from his eyes and down his cheeks. It felt better, but not much. A solid eight hours of sleep was what he needed, and the last thing he wanted was for anything to happen today.

In spite of that, though, he picked up the phone and dialed the Westbrook police station. After eleven double rings, Detective Maloney picked up his receiver.

"Detective Maloney here," said a sharp, clipped voice.

"Hello, this is Sergeant Winfield up in Dyer."

"How may I help you, sir," Maloney said, sounding as though he had come to the police force straight out of the Army.

"Well," Winfield said, settling back in his chair, closing his eyes, and leaning his head back, "I just got your telex on the suspected arsons, and I had a couple of questions for you."

"Shoot," Maloney said, so quickly it almost sounded as though he had sneezed.

"Well, you say here to watch for a 'cluster' of fire, but I was wondering why you think this guy's heading up this way."

There was a short pause on the other end of the line, and Winfield could hear sheets of paper being turned. He leaned forward in his chair, bracing the phone with his shoulder.

"Since that went out, we heard from two more stations in Connecticut and another one in Massachusetts. All three of them reported several suspicious fires and putting them together with the others we've had, it appears as though they're all the work of a person or persons heading north, up I-95."

"What time frame are we dealing with here?" Winfield asked. It surprised him that, after listening to Maloney for only a few seconds, he adopted his military-sounding speech pattern.

"Each local incident has been a day or two apart for the space of approximately a week or so. The time between local incidents seems to vary between two and three weeks. My gut feeling is that whoever is doing this is traveling on foot or hitchhiking. Anyone traveling in a car would be too noticeable. They'd be in the local area too long."

"But you've had no reports of any arson north of Portland recently, correct? Nothing around Augusta or Bangor?"

"Affirmative."

Winfield nodded and, glancing up at the ceiling, blinked his eyes rapidly. The Visine was starting to work now, and the small dots on the overhead acoustic tiles no longer blurred together. The caffeine from Keller-man's was finally starting to kick in, too, so he was actually beginning to think he might make it through the day without falling asleep over lunch.

"Look Sergeant Winfield, I have a call on the other line. I appreciate your call and any help you can give me."

"Sure," Winfield said, but before he could say good-bye, Maloney's line went dead.

Winfield hung up the phone and, looking down at his desk, realized for the first time that he had been doodling on the telex the whole time he had been talking to Maloney. A faint smile curled his upper lip as he looked down at the face he had drawn at the bottom of the page, but he also felt slightly unsettled as he studied his drawing. On top of a smooth, rounded, rather sexless-looking face, a shock of thick, long hair streamed out in all directions. It took him a moment to realize that the hair looked, really, more like a raging fire than hair. The mouth he had drawn was open in a large oval that might have been a scream, but what unnerved him most of all were the eyes he had drawn, round, blank circles, opened wide with what?

*Surprise? . . . Pain? . . . Fear?*

In the middle of the message from Maloney in Westbrook, he had also underlined the phrase "clusters of suspicious fires" with heavy, dark lines. So heavy, in fact, his pen point had worn right through the paper and marked his ink blotter.

"Burn, baby, burn," he whispered as he pushed his chair back with the backs of his legs and stood up. He clicked his pen shut, not even remembering when he took it from his pocket to begin doodling, and replaced it in his shirt pocket. Shaking his head as though waking up from a nap, he went down the corridor to the front desk.

"Any calls today?" he asked Pam, whose fingers still flew over the typewriter keyboard as though they had a mind of their own.

Pam shook her head and continued with her work.

"I guess I'll take a swing through town," Winfield said. "Maybe drive out by Higgins' farm and see if he's started harvesting yet. He's usually the first."

Pam nodded and kept typing.

"I won't be far from the radio," he said. He was just turning to go when the Teletype beside Pam's desk suddenly chattered into life. Between that sound and Pam's typing, Winfield began to understand, maybe, why Pam was so antisocial. Fifteen years of that much noise was as bad as working with a drop hammer in an iron forge.

The Teletype finished its brief flurry of activity and then fell silent. When Pam made no move to tear off the bulletin and give it to him, Winfield came around the side of the desk and got it for himself. He read it quickly and then left it on the desk for Pam to file later. It was nothing important, just a File-13 on an assault and motor vehicle left in Holden early that morning:

BE ON THE LOOKOUT FOR A RUST RED 1967 FORD PICK-UP. AS-SAILANT OR ASSAILANTS UNKNOWN BUT CONSIDERED DAN-

GEROUS ANY DEPT. HAVING INFO. PLS CONTACT: SGT. MCCOR-
MICK HOLDEN 29 AUG 08:27

Winfield went out into the parking lot and got into his cruiser thinking, as usual, that it was the towns in the southern part of the state that got all the action, and that was just the way he liked it!

"Good luck finding your rust-red Ford pick-up, Mc-Cormick," he said as he started up the cruiser, backed around, and pulled out into the street.

# II

It'd be a great day for a drive, Dale thought, if they weren't driving north for the funeral of their best friend.

After packing, they took off just before noon, driving up Route One, stopping for a quick lunch at Burger King in Bangor, and then continuing up I-95 to Houlton. North of Bangor, though, the highway got pretty monotonous, just pine trees and open fields punctuated here and there by maybe a swamp or lake thrown in for variety. Between the boredom of the drive and the sadness they both felt, any pleasure they might have felt at having some time together quickly evaporated.

Larry's death left Dale with an icy feeling in the pit of his stomach. It was a physical emptiness that made him think of the dull concussion of a gun going off too close to his ear. What was worse was seeing his loss reflected in Angie's face. She looked pale and aged beyond her years, and he found himself worrying how much of her youthful vigor would be lost forever. Through much of the ride, she sat silently, her head leaning against the window, her eyes staring blankly at the road unscrolling in front of them.

Several times along the way he had tried to talk to her about it, but after a few empty-sounding platitudes, variations of "Larry wouldn't want you to be this way," he fell silent, deciding that first of all, she had to absorb this loss at her own pace; and second, they would have plenty of time during this week and the months ahead to share their memories and feelings. He tried to resist the thought that he was simply avoiding dealing with it; but after losing Natalie, he knew emotional shock when he felt it.

They got off the Interstate at Exit 62, crossed the Meduxnekeag River, and after a quick "pit-stop" for gas and rest rooms at LeDoux's Mobile station, started south toward Dyer on Route 2A.

The road wound through thick, green-shaded pine forest. Dale had the impression that they were driving through a twenty mile-long tunnel from Houlton to Dyer, but at last they hit the north end of town. It had taken them longer to get there than Dale had expected and it was almost six o'clock when they pulled into an empty parking spot right in front of Kellerman's restaurant.

"Looks like the local pizza-and-beer joint," Dale said as he leaned over the steering wheel, regarding the restaurant.

Angie smiled weakly and nodded. "Looks like they serve breakfast here, too."

Dale nodded. "Well, I guess it's too much to expect to find a McDonald's around here. Do you want to get something to eat now, or should we find a place to stay for the night and then come back?"

Angie let out a long, whistling sigh as she looked at the dirt-streaked front window of Kellerman's. Sun-faded posters in the window announced the local fair and a variety of church suppers and social events.

"Let's look for some place to stay, first. Maybe we'll see a better restaurant," she said tiredly.

Dale backed out into the street and started back up Main Street. He figured they called it Main Street around here because it didn't look like there were too many other streets in town. They passed a church on the right and a combination town hall and police station on their left and came to an intersection with a blinking yellow light. Across the intersection, Dale saw the Mill Store with its stand of gas pumps. An overweight man in faded bib coveralls was slouched by the gas pumps when Dale pulled in.

"Excuse me," Dale said, easing up to the pumps but positioning his car so it would be obvious he didn't want gas.

The snoozing man snorted and, shaking his head, looked up with a furrowed squint. He pushed his hat back on his head, exposing thin, brown hair that looked like it needed a good wash.

"Ayuh," he said, heaving himself up in his chair but not bothering to stand.

"I was wondering if you could tell me where I might find a room for the night."

The man leaned back and scratched the underside of his unshaven jowls. His eyes remained half-closed as though in deep thought or half-sleep. For a moment, Dale thought he was trying to ignore him.

"Well," he said, drawing out the word as if it was the required way to respond to an out-of-towner. "If yah come up 2-A, you must'a passed the Twin Oaks Motel right outside 'a Haynesville."

Dale shook his head. "We drove down from Houlton. I was hoping, to find someplace right here in town, though."

The man shifted forward again, and Dale thought for an instant that he was actually going to bother to stand up, but he merely leaned forward and hitched his thumb in the direction of the road leading back to Houlton. He looked down the road, as if to assure himself it hadn't disappeared while he was napping.

"Just 'crost the street up there, on your right, didn't you see the sign for Appleby's?"

Dale glanced quickly at Angie, and they exchanged shrugs.

"Lil Appleby rents out a couple of rooms, 'specially now with harvest comin' up. I dunno. Maybe she ain't got any right now. You might wanna check there first."

"Okay, thanks," Dale said, shifting the car into gear and starting to pull away slowly.

Now that the man was fully awake, though, he didn't seem to want to let him go. With a loud grunt, he hoisted himself to his feet and waddled over to the car. He leaned down close to the window and glanced over at Angie, who shifted uncomfortably.

"If Mrs. A. don't have any rooms left, I'd say your best bet was to head back to Houlton. If you don't mind me askin', what you want to stay in a town like this for?"

Dale felt a tingling tension in his stomach, and as the words formed in his mind, his eyes began to sting.

"Well, uh, a friend of mine died and we've come up for the funeral."

"Umm, yeah. Larry Cole, right?" the man said, nodding his head slowly up and down. His eyes squinted tighter, making him look all the more pig-like. "Pity somethin' like that could happen, and to a nice fella like Larry. Shit!"

"Yeah, well—thanks," Dale said. Without another word, he pulled out into the street. Less than half a mile down the road, they saw a sign in front of a large, white house: APPLEBY'S BED AND BREAKFAST. ROOMS BY THE DAY AND WEEK. Although there was a wide driveway leading up behind the house, Dale pulled up to the curb in front of the house and parked in the shade of a tall blue spruce.

The house sat on a slight rise well back from the road. It was a towering, three-story Victorian painted white with black shutters and trim. All along in front of the house and lining the walkway up to the front door were carefully tended garden plots, still bursting with color even this late in the summer. Obviously, someone knew how to plan and care for the flowers. Sidelight windows surrounded the heavy door. On the left side of the house was a large bay window, and as Dale and Angie looked up at the house, they saw the silhouette of someone standing there, looking out at them.

"They don't have a 'no vacancy' sign out," Dale said. "Maybe we're in luck." He was glancing at Angie, trying to gauge her reaction, but her face remained passive. She's not even listening to me, he thought. She's still thinking about Larry.

As they got out of the car and started up toward the front door, the silhouette in the front window drew away and disappeared. Dale pressed the doorbell button, and from deep within the house, they heard a faint "ding-dong."

"Avon calling," Angie said, chuckling under her breath. They were both snickering when they heard footsteps approach the door and saw motion behind the curtained sidelight. They straightened up when the door latch jiggled, and the heavy door swung inward.

"Good afternoon," Dale said, smiling at the stocky, white-haired woman who stood in the doorway. She looked to be in her late sixties and like the man at the gas station, had heavy, fleshy jowls. Dale found himself wondering if everyone in town had jowls like that. Maybe it was from eating potatoes all the time! She didn't have the gas station attendant's squinty, pig-like eyes, though. Hers were bright, sparkling blue, like ice on a sunny winter day.

The woman smiled and, stepping to one side, invited them in with a sweeping wave of her hand. Dale opened the screen door and stepped back to let Angie enter first. He eased the door shut behind him to make sure it didn't slam,

"My name is Dale Harmon, and this is my daughter, Angela. You must be Mrs. Appleby. The man at the gas station said you might have a room we could rent for a few days. I didn't notice a no vacancy sign."

"Good old Sparky," the woman said. "Call me Lil." She extended her hand to Dale and shook it firmly. "And, sure, I have a room. Just one left, but it's one of the nicest." She looked smaller now than she did standing in the doorway, and she reeked of an overpowering flowery perfume.

The house, or what Dale could see from the entryway, seemed an extension of the old woman: cozy, warm, and hospitable. A dark red runner rug covered the stairs leading up from the hallway. On one wall beside a small desk with a registration book, a delicately carved grandfather clock measured the time with a slow, steady tick-tock.

Off to the left was a sitting room whose built-in shelves, Dale could see, were lined with old books. There were leather-bound volumes and "recent" bestsellers with faded and worn dust jackets. Two pine-green leather chairs, glossy with age, faced a fireplace. Between the two chairs was a dark wood, oval table with several copies of *National Geographic* fanned out.

To the right was a small parlor with warm, dark paneling and two fringed couches facing another fire-place. In one corner, almost as an after-thought, was a small television set with a rabbit-ear antenna. Dale wondered what stations you could pick up way out here, maybe something from Canada. Throughout the entryway and two rooms, the polished hardwood floor was covered by several hand-made scatter rugs.

"I charge thirty-five dollars a night," Lil said. "That includes breakfast, if you'd like. So if you'll just fill out this registration card, we'll be all set." She led Dale over to the desk and stood aside while he leaned over the desk and signed in.

Angie, meanwhile, was still lost in looking around the house. She felt as though she had literally stepped back into another century. The TV was the only thing that broke the illusion. The house seemed to shut out the rest of the world and embrace her with a warmth she had never experienced before. She could imagine herself living in a house like this and being happy for the rest of her life, even so far away from everything.

"You must be, oh, I'd say twelve, going on thirteen," Mrs. Appleby said, propping her chin on her forefinger as she stared at Angie, smiling.

One side of Angie's face twisted into a smile as she nodded. "Exactly," she said. "Are you a mind-reader?"

Mrs. Appleby smiled and shook her head. "Oh, no. It's just that I have a granddaughter who looks about your age. Her name's Lisa. She's off some-where now, but I'll just bet the two of you will hit it off just fine."

"I can't wait to meet her," Angie said, still glancing around, trying to absorb the peaceful quiet of the house. The prospect of having someone her age in the house brightened her spirits even more.

From somewhere inside the house, there came a loud bang followed by the sound of running feet.

"Ah," said Mrs. Appleby, I'll bet that's her now."

In a flurry of activity that seemed to contradict the ancient quiet of the house, a young girl with long, dark braids bouncing on her shoulders burst into the hallway. She was dressed in jeans and a light yellow T-shirt with a brightly colored parrot design. Her face was flushed from running.

"Hi, grammy," she gasped. Breathing heavily, she leaned over to catch her breath but took the opportunity to glance slyly at Angie.

"Lisa, this is Mr. Harmon and his daughter, Angie. They'll be staying with us for a day or two. Maybe you can show Angie around town a little."

Dale had finished with the registration card and, as he handed it back to Mrs. Appleby, he glanced at Lisa and gave her a warm smile. There was no doubt that she was related to the older woman, he thought. Her eyes had the same blue intensity of her grandmother's.

"You know," Mrs. Appleby said, looking at Dale. "I shouldn't be prying into your business, but you never mentioned why you folks are up this way. Are you taking a family vacation?"

Dale stiffened as chilled fingers gripped his stomach. For a moment, he had forgotten why they were in town. Carefully placing the pen back on the desk so he could avoid eye contact with her, he said softly, "No. We've come up from Thomaston for . . ." His throat caught, and he almost couldn't continue. "For Larry Cole's funeral. He worked with me down in Augusta."

"Oh, my," Mrs. Appleby said, clicking her tongue and shaking her head. "Wasn't that a shame? I've known Larry's mother and father since they were children. As a matter of fact, I had both his parents and him in class when I taught. Of course, I've been retired for twelve years, now. I started taking a few boarders to keep myself busy. But wasn't that accident a shame? Now with his father gone, that just leaves poor Mildred. It's a terrible tragedy when you lose a child. Terrible!"

Dale couldn't shake the feeling that Lillian Appleby was speaking from per-sonal experience. It seemed obvious that Lisa lived here with her, and there had been no mention of her parents.

"Actually," Dale said, clearing his throat, "I was hoping someone could tell me where his mother lives. I wanted to stop by the house and visit her before the funeral."

"You're parked right out front," Mrs. Appleby said. "Why don't you bring the car up into the driveway and get your luggage up to your room? Lisa, why don't you take Angie downtown for an ice cream before it gets dark?"

"Well, we haven't had supper yet," Dale said. "I was thinking we'd unpack and then go find someplace to eat."

"Oh, pshaw," Mrs. Appleby said, waving her hand in front of Dale's face. "The sign says 'bed and breakfast,' but that's just because I didn't know what else to call it. You can have supper here with us if you don't mind waiting until after seven."

Dale looked at Angie, who gave him a what-the-heck shrug. "Fine," he said. "That would be just fine. A home-cooked meal will beat anything we could find in town, I'm sure."

"You two run along now," Mrs. Appleby said, shooing her hands at Angie and Lisa. "Just don't go off so far you don't hear when I call you for supper, all right?"

With quick nods of their heads, Angie followed Lisa back out of the house the way she had come in. Again, there was a loud slam as they went out into the back yard by way of the kitchen door.

Dale turned to go down to the street and get his car, but before he went, he turned to Mrs. Appleby and said softly, "I want to thank you."

She smiled widely. "For what, renting you a room? Don't worry. I'll give you a bill for that."

"No," Dale said. "I mean for everything else. Just for *being* here and even for having Lisa here. Coming for Larry's funeral hasn't been easy for me or for Angie. Larry was more than just someone I worked with. He was almost a part of our family. But I was expecting we'd be staying in some flea-ridden motel for the next two nights, and . . . and . . ."

He wanted to say more, but his voice suddenly twisted and broke. Mrs. Appleby reached out and gripped him gently by the elbow.

"Now, now," she said, almost cooing. "You just take it easy. I know what it's like when you lose someone you love, and I could tell, as soon as you mentioned Larry, that it pained you. You just get your car up, and I'll show you your room. Then I can tell you how to get to Mildred's house."

Dale smiled and nodded as he went out the door and down the walkway to his car. All the while he was thinking that it was people like Lillian Appleby, people who reach out and help people in the simplest ways by being kind and caring who can, with time, help blunt the hollow pain of loss.

# III

Angie was surprised how fast she and Lisa hit it off. It felt like they had known each other before. Even before they were out the kitchen door and walking across the back yard, they were chattering away to each other like long-lost friends. Again, Angie found herself thinking that she wouldn't mind living in a place like Dyer if she could have a house like Mrs. Appleby's and a friend like Lisa.

As they crossed the back yard, heading toward the line of trees at the margin of the well-trimmed grass, Angie paused and looked back at the house. Slanting sunlight lit up the side of the house, making it gleam so brightly it hurt her eyes. The windows reflected back the cloudless sky with a dark marble sheen.

"I thought we were going to take a walk downtown," Angie said, frowning. She heard a car pull into the driveway and saw her father back into the turn-around. When he parked and got out to get their luggage from the trunk, he glanced up and saw them standing at the far corner of the backyard. He smiled and waved.

"I want to show you something else, first," Lisa said. Her voice was hushed with repressed excitement, and Angie had a moment of doubt, wondering if she could trust her. Maybe, living in such an isolated town, she was weird or something.

"I was thinking maybe I should help my dad unpack," Angie said. She hoped her momentary doubt wasn't betrayed by her voice.

Lisa looked over and watched as Dale, a suitcase in each hand, walked up the back steps. "It looks as though he's got it. Come on. I want to show you my ... my secret place." She spoke in a low, conspiratorial whisper and, lowering her head, glanced to either side as though the surrounding trees had ears.

"Exactly what is this place?" Angie asked.

"Follow me," Lisa said, and she started off into the woods, following a well-worn path that twisted between trees and through ever-thickening brush.

Angie hesitated before following, uncertain exactly what Lisa had in mind. Growing up in Thomaston, she had never spent much time playing in the woods, although she didn't exactly define herself as a "city girl," either. But something about the forest—especially deep forest like these, stretching all the way to Canada—that unnerved Angie. A gnawing of fear filled her stomach as she watched Lisa's yellow shirt plunge deeper into the foliage.

"Uh, remember what your grandmother said about not going too far from the house?" Angie said as she started along the path. "We don't want to miss supper."

Lisa glanced back at her over her shoulder and waved her arm to hurry her along. "We won't miss supper," she said with a slight agitation. "Come on. If you hurry, we'll be back in less than half an hour."

Taking a deep breath, Angie quickened her pace until she was only three or four steps behind Lisa. The woods grew thicker as she followed her, but the path continued, unwinding like a beige ribbon up a gradual rise. Angie cast several nervous glances behind her as she went, and the gnawing in her gut got worse when she lost sight of the large house.

"Your dad said something about you guys being here for Larry Cole's funeral, huh?" Lisa said.

The woods were dark and cool, and the ground was thick with musty, matted leaves. Each step she took gave with spongy softness, and the air was full of a fresh, woodsy smell. Afraid she might trip over a hidden root, Angie didn't hazard to look up when she responded.

"A-huh, he was a really good friend of ours," Angie said, her voice low and throaty. "Did you know him?"

"I know some people named Cole," Lisa said, "but not a Larry."

Angie didn't want to say any more about it, and was thankful that Lisa let it drop. They continued along the winding path, down in a dried stream bed and then up another crest, this one quite steep. At the top of the crest, winded, Angie stopped and hung onto a tree branch to catch her breath. There was no way she was used to tramping around like this through the woods.

"If it's much further, I'm not gonna make it," she gasped. "I think I'm gonna puke."

"It's just up there," Lisa said. She pointed off to the left where the trees seemed most dense. At first, Angie couldn't see anything. The gloom of the woods closed in on everything. But then she noticed what looked like a peaked roof sticking up through the autumn-stained foliage. The little she could see of the building was weathered gray, the exact color of a hornet's nest.

"What is it?" Angie asked, still fighting the burning in her lungs.

"I told you—my secret place," Lisa said. "Come on."

They started toward the building, and Lisa explained:

"When I first moved here, after my parents got divorced, I . . ."

"You don't live with your parents?" Angie asked. Even though she couldn't really remember her own mother, the idea that Lisa lived without either parent struck her as terrible.

"No," Lisa said. "We lived in Connecticut, but my dad was never home much. Finally, he met someone else and ran off. My grammy's never told me the whole story, but I've heard from other people that he ran off with one of his students- He used to teach philosophy at the University of Connecticut. My mom, I guess, never thought she was much of a mother, so she asked her mom to take me for a while until she could get her life together. That was four years ago."

"Gee," was the extent of Angie's response as she considered what a tough situation that must have been and maybe still was for Lisa. She felt a little guilty, feeling so sorry for herself when there were other people like Lisa who had to deal with things just as bad, or worse.

"Anyway," Lisa said, forcing a smile, "that was a long time ago, and I've pretty much gotten used to it."

"Do you ever see your folks?"

Lisa set her mouth in a tight line and shook her head. "My mom comes to visit once or twice a year and she calls me every couple of weeks. It's been less and less over the years, though. I haven't seen my dad since . . ." Her voice caught for an instant. "Since he left us."

"Boy, that must've been wicked tough on you," Angie said.

"Hey, I didn't bring you out here to give you my sob story," Lisa said. They had been making their way slowly down the slope the whole time they were talking, and now they broke through the screen of brush that had been hiding Lisa's "secret place."

Angie gasped and couldn't help but wonder what such a big barn as this was doing out here in the woods in the middle of nowhere. Years ago, maybe a century or so, the land around it might have been cleared, but now big, thick-trunked trees towered over the ancient barn, almost completely hiding it. She could see where some trees had grown up inside the barn, and one was big enough to have pushed its way up through the roof.

"Pretty neat, huh?" Lisa said, her voice tinged with the pride of ownership.

Angie nodded agreement.

Most of the weathered-gray boards still clung to the sides of the barn, although many were loose at one end or the other, giving the whole exterior a random, lopsided look. Shingles had peeled off one side of the roof, exposing the skeletal structure of the rafters beneath, and the loft doors hung open at awkward angles on either side. Tumble-down fences and rusted farm equipment littered the overgrown dooryard. The big front doors were closed, but the side door was torn off its hinges and lay like a platform entrance. Dappled shadows thrown by the setting sun cast the whole structure in a deep gloom. When the breeze stirred the leaves, the whole barn seemed to vibrate with a weird sort of energy.

"I found it one day when I was taking a walk in the woods," Lisa said solemnly. "I used to do that a lot when I first moved here."

"You must have been pretty lonely," Angie said. She locked eyes with her newfound friend, surprised she could feel so close to her after so short a time together.

Lisa shrugged. "I have no idea who owns the place," she said. "But I come out here a lot when I want to be alone so I can—you know, think and stuff. You're the first person I've ever shown it to."

Angie smiled, acknowledging the honor she had been given.

"Somebody else knows about it, though," Lisa said. "'cause sometimes I find stuff moved around, and the ground inside the barn sometimes looks like a lot

of people have been inside. Lots of times, 'specially in the late summer, I find
burned out campfires. But I've never seen anyone else here."

"Maybe you're not the only kid in town who comes out here," Angie said.
"I'll bet maybe some of the local teenage boys come out here drinking or something."

"Or to make out with their girlfriends," Lisa said with a giggle. "But I don't
usually find empty beer cans lying around."

"We have the returnable bottle bill to thank for that," Angie said. She stood
for several seconds, silently admiring the barn and absorbing what it must have
meant to Lisa, to have a place to come to when she needed to be alone. Since
her father told her about Larry's death, she understood even more how important a place like this could be.

"Well, don't you think we ought to be getting back?" Angie said after a
while. She glanced at her watch. "Your gram said supper would be at seven and
we've already been gone more than half an hour."

"Before we go, though, I want to show you the hay loft," Lisa said. "Come
on." She tugged at Angie's arm until she followed her into the barn.

As soon as she stepped inside the barn, Angie felt a shiver run up her spine
to the back of her neck. It wasn't just being out of the sun that chilled her, either. There was an eerie . . . *deadness* inside. It was a dead-ness that went beyond
the broken stalls and rusted tools that littered the scuffed dirt floor. Sunlight
lanced through the cracks in the wall, and slanting bars of golden-lit dust sliced
downward at hard angles, giving what should have been a large, open space a
tight, claustrophobic feeling.

Angie tried to take a deep breath, to get rid of the choking sensation she felt
in her throat, but the dusty air only made it worse. She wanted to tell Lisa that
she didn't like it, not here inside the barn, but Lisa was heading toward the
back wall where a ladder of rough-cut two-by-fours led up into the hay loft.

"Up here," she said, and in a flutter of arms and legs, she scampered up
through the hole in the ceiling. "Come on," she called, her voice muffled by the
ceiling between them.

As Lisa walked slowly across the loft floor above, small bits of dust and hay
chaff sprinkled down like thin snow through the cracks in the floor. Angie
sneezed and, wiping her nose with the back of her hand, cast a wary glance
back at the door. Through the opening, the shimmering green woods outside
looked somehow unreal, as though the barn was all there was, and the woods
outside merely a tiny glimpse of a better, purer reality.

"We don't have all day," Lisa called out. From the direction of her voice,
Angie could tell she was near the front of the barn.

Finally Angie took a deep breath and made her way over to the ladder,
grabbed the first rung, and slowly started up. The rusty nails holding the boards
in place creaked softly, but Angie figured they had held for nearly a century;
they weren't about to pull out now.

She poked her head up through the opening and was surprised to see that the loft was full of hay. Most of the wires holding the hay into bales had broken long ago, and rotten straw had fanned out all over the floor, leaving a thin, yellow carpet.

Lisa was standing in the open loft doorway, looking out at the brightly lit woods. She was leaning with one arm on the door frame, her other hand cocked on her hip.

"I don't think the world could look any prettier than it does from up here," she said, not bothering to turn around as Angie hoisted herself up through the trap door opening and came slowly toward her.

Again, Angie was struck by how the woods seen from inside the barn looked strangely unreal, shimmering, like a fantasy world. "It is nice," she said, leaning on the other side of the open loft doorway. She inhaled slowly through her nostrils to clear out the dust and musty smell from down below.

"I used to spend hours and hours, just sitting here, looking out," Lisa said, her voice hushed with remembered awe. "I got so I thought I knew every tree and stone and bush like they were friends."

"Didn't you have any friends to play with?" Angie asked.

Lisa shrugged. "I'd hang around with some of the kids from school, but you know, this town is weird. I mean, not spooky weird, like those stupid towns in scary movies where everyone has a deep, dark secret. But to most of the kids, I was a stranger, and it was a really long time before they accepted me."

"I'll bet," Angie said, only half paying attention. Her own thoughts were turning again to how much she was going to miss Larry; and this lonely, old barn seemed too *sad*.

"Uh-oh!" Lisa said, suddenly standing up straight and stiffening. She looked at Angie, then dropped to a crouch inside the doorway. "Get down!"

"What?" Angie said, following Lisa's example and flattening herself against the barn wall.

"Shhh! There's someone coming," Lisa hissed. "I can hear 'em over there." She indicated the direction with a quick nod of the head. Cautiously, Angie leaned forward and looked out, careful to keep in the shadow inside the doorway. Sure enough, she could see some kind of motion through the thick brush, and when she concentrated, she could hear the heavy tread of feet.

"Can you see 'em?" Lisa asked, unable to look for herself without revealing herself fully.

"I think it's some men," Angie said. She held one finger up to her lips, and waited, watching. The muscles in her thighs tightened, getting ready to run; her left leg started to tremble. The only real problem she saw was that the ground was far below her.

The footsteps got louder, and the two girls clearly could hear the snapping of branches as several people made their way toward the barn.

"Why do you think they're here?" Angie whispered.

Lisa shrugged, clinging to the barn wall.

"What are we gonna do?" Angie asked, her voice tight and dry. She was afraid she was going to throw up.

Lisa shook her head. "I dunno. Maybe they're just passing by. Let's just stay here and hope they don't see us."

"Oh God, Lisa! I'm scared!" Angie whined.

"Just be quiet. We'll be all right."

The footsteps grew louder and louder, and then suddenly several people— Angie counted eight before she ducked deeper into the shadows —stepped out of the forest, heading straight toward the old barn. Now she *knew* for sure she was going to throw up!

None of the people spoke as they crossed the clearing and entered the barn. Listening from above, Angie and Lisa could hear labored, watery breathing and deep-chest grunts, but neither one of them could imagine what these men were doing here. Angie merely glimpsed them as they approached, and her overriding impression was that they looked old and poorly clothed, like TV hoboes.

Moving as quietly as she could, Angie made her way over to Lisa. She cupped her hand to Lisa's ear and whispered, "We've got to get out of here. Your grand-mother and my dad are gonna be worried if we don't show up at the house soon."

"It sounds like they're planning on staying down there for a while," Lisa whispered back. "But why aren't they talking?"

Angie shrugged. Now that Lisa mentioned it, it did seem strange that with eight or more men all together down there, that there was no conversation, but only their heavy breathing and what sounded like them shifting around, maybe sitting or lying down on the barn floor.

"You know what?" Lisa whispered, her breath hot in Angie's ear. "I think they're gonna be staying here for the night. It sounds like they're settling down."

"How are we gonna get out of here?" Angie said. She could feel her eyes stinging as tears welled up in her eyes, and she wanted nothing more than to be back at the house with her father.

"We'll think of something," Lisa said.

"You stay here," Angie said. "I'll tiptoe over to the trap door to see if I can figure out what they're doing down there."

Before Lisa could respond, Angie had started moving stealthily back across the loft floor, putting down her feet with the utmost care. Every now and then, a floorboard would creak under her weight and she would freeze in place, waiting for long-drawn out seconds to see if the men below responded. She kept glancing back at Lisa by the loft door, and they could read the growing terror in each other's eyes.

Angie was a little more than half-way to the trap door when one floor board creaked particularly loudly. She stopped instantly, with one foot still in the air, but almost instantly she knew they were in trouble. From down below, the men shifted and grunted; the watery rattle of their breathing grew louder, sounding more agitated.

"Shit! *Angie!*" Lisa hissed.

Angie remembered the dust that had sifted down through the cracks in the ceiling when Lisa was up in the loft alone. She wondered if that's what had alerted the men. Right now, though, it didn't matter!

For several heartbeats, Angie stayed as she was, with one foot frozen in mid-air. A jolt of pain shot through her thigh muscle. Then she heard louder sounds of motion from below, and she knew it was time to act. This was *big* trouble! Quickly, she dashed over to loft door and, leaning into the opening, peered down. What she saw froze her blood.

In the dimness of the barn, there appeared to be more than eight men in the barn. It looked like there might be twenty or more. Her first impression was right, though; the men were wearing tattered, dirty clothes. Some wore pants with gaping holes in the knees or shirts with sleeves that hung from the shoulders by mere threads. She only had a second to register their faces, but what she saw sent waves of panic through her. Beneath the dirt, their skin looked pasty pale, almost transparent. As they looked up through the opening at her, their eyes glowed with a peculiar, dull gleam.

Thinking fast, Angie grabbed the trap door and, ripping it from the hook that held it open, slammed it down just as the man closest to the ladder gripped one of the rungs and started up. One small part of her mind registered that still none of the men had spoken. As if in mutual, unspoken agreement, they started together to come toward the loft ladder.

"*Lisa! What do I do?*" Angie wailed. She couldn't shake the memory of those blank, dirty faces, staring up at her as she knelt on the trap door, hoping to keep it shut.

Lisa scrambled over to where Angie crouched and looked frantically around for anything they could use to keep the trap door closed. The best she could do was to grab one of the unbroken hay bales and start dragging it toward the trap door.

Angie let out a loud scream when a heavy blow hit the trap door with enough force to lift her into the air. Pain jolted her jaw, and she tried to ignore the splinter of wood that jabbed into the heel of her hand as she willed herself to be heavy enough to keep the door shut until . . .

—until *when?*

— *what could they do?*

Two girls couldn't very well expect to hold off that many men all night, and sooner or later, one of them was sure to think of climbing up through the open loft doors!

"Hurry! *Hurry!*" Angie wailed, watching Lisa struggle to move the bale. The hay was old and rotten, and with each push, dust and chaff swirled like smoke into the air, choking Lisa and making her cough.

A heavy fist hammered in rapid succession on the trap door from below. Every hit jolted Angie, sending waves of pain up through her body. She shifted to one side to allow Lisa to push the hay bale on top of the door, but they both knew it wouldn't be enough weight. Lisa quickly went back to get another.

It sounded now like two or more men were pounding on the door from below. Their efforts bounced Angie as if she were a rider on a bronco. Her frantic cries were nothing more than strangled whimpers, caught like fish bones in her throat.

Lisa grabbed another bale by the wires, but as she leaned back to pull, the wire snapped. She fell back in a shower of flying hay and pinwheeling arms, landing hard on her butt. Pain like a white heat shot up her tailbone.

"Come—*on* — Lisa!" Angie shouted. Her jaw was clenched tightly, distorting her words.

Lisa tried to move another bale, this time pushing it from behind. But once she moved it near the door, she realized that Angie would have to get off to make room for it. There was no way she could lift the new bale to put it on top of the other one.

Suddenly, one of the boards in the trap door exploded upward and a clenched fist shot up through the smashed wood in a choking swirl of dust. The long fingers extended and, before Angie could jump away, they grabbed her wrist. The hand clamped her like a shackle. Angie looked down, horrified, as dirt-crusted fingernails pressed into her skin.

"*Lisa!* . . . *Help!* . . . *Help me!*" she wailed as the hand pulled her down. Through the splintered door she saw a man's face glaring up at her. His eyes flashed with a cold, dull anger.

To Angie, the man looked hopelessly insane. His eyes glowered with a wild intensity and a wide grin split his face, exposing a row of stained and broken teeth. Black gunk rimmed his mouth and teeth, as though he had just eaten a mouthful of dirt. His tongue darted out at her, wiggling like a colorless slug, and a deep, rumbling laughter erupted from his chest.

The pressure on her wrist, pulling her down, was impossible to fight. Angie watched, horrified, as the man's fingernails bit deeper into her flesh.

Now, she thought, almost laughing aloud, *would be a great time to throw up! All over him!*

"Lean back!" Lisa suddenly shouted. Angie didn't notice during her struggle that Lisa had left the bale and was searching in a far corner of the loft. She came running back to the trap door now with a pitchfork. The tines were rusted and dull-looking, but still useful.

"Oh, shit! Be careful!" Angie said with a groan. She pulled back as far as she could and tensed, while the hand kept pulling her down.

Lisa knelt down and with a sudden grunt, drove the pitchfork home.

The man bellowed as one of the pitchfork tines skewered his wrist and stuck out the other side. For an instant, his grip relaxed, and Angie took that instant to break free.

"Come on!" Lisa shouted.

Angie got off the trap door, and as soon as she did, it started to lift up. Lisa ran over to the open loft door, but before she followed her, Angie sat back and kicked the bale of hay through the opening door. She heard another bellow of anger but didn't waste time to see what happened. She ran to where Lisa waited at the loft door.

"We've gotta jump!" Lisa shouted. "It's our only chance!"

Angie didn't pause to consider. She flexed her legs and shot out into the air, her arms and legs flailing for balance. The ground came up fast, and she hit it hard. She knocked the breath out of herself, and was only dimly aware of Lisa landing in a sprawl on the ground beside her.

They both looked frantically at the barn door, but none of the men had come out yet. Most likely, they were, even now, scrambling up the loft ladder, frantically looking for them.

"Let's get moving!" Lisa shouted.

Fists clenched and hearts pounding, the girls ran as fast as they could into the woods. As they crested the hill and before the barn disappeared from sight, they slowed for a moment to see if they were being pursued.

Nothing. There was no sign of the men. The loft door hung open, a black empty rectangle, but no leering faces leaned out, watching them. The barn looked entirely deserted, and what had just happened seemed little more than a dream.

"Let's boogie before they come," Lisa said, tugging Angie's sleeve.

Turning quickly, the girls found the path and ran as fast as they could until the roof peak of Lisa's grand-mother's house came into view. Then they stopped and, panting heavily, sides aching, tried to catch their breath.

"I don't . . . want to go in . . . yet," Angie gasped, bent at the waist. Then she noticed the gray splinter sticking in the base of her thumb. Her fingers were sticky with blood starting to dry to a dark, brick red. Wincing, she took hold of the splinter end and, with one quick flick, pulled it out. Fresh blood started to flow, falling to the ground with a faint *plop-plop*.

"Hey, Lisa," she said, her voice still cut by gasps. "Thanks for ... showing me that . . . place." She squeezed the wound to make it bleed more to clean it out.

Lisa forced a smile, but it was twisted and tight. Her hair was full of hay seed, and her face was streaked with sweat lines that cut through the grime. Angie was thinking, if she looked even half as bad as Lisa, then they were a sorry pair.

"We'll have to go there again sometime," Angie said, forcing firmness into her voice. "Maybe camp out overnight and party with those guys. Sound like fun?"

"I'm really sorry about that," Lisa said. "I wouldn't have taken you out there if I knew they were gonna be there." She found it difficult to make eye contact with Angie, but when she looked down, her eyes locked on the dime-sized splotches of blood on the ground.

"It's all right," Angie said, fighting the trembling in her voice. "Do you have any idea who they were?"

Lisa shrugged. "I dunno. Probably some of those migrant workers who come to work during the potato harvest. All sorts of strange people show up for those few weeks."

"But did you notice how *weird* they were?"

"What do you mean?"

"Those men," Angie said. Her memory filled with the vision of that one man's face, staring up at her through the shattered door, his eyes aflame with cold fury. "The whole time that was happening, they never said anything. Not a single word! Just all that grunting and groaning."

Lisa glanced warily down the trail, but all was silent and calm. No one had followed them.

"Do you think we should call the police about this?" Angie said, following her friend's gaze back along the trail. The sun was just on the horizon, and it edged the trees with soft, golden light. They were surrounded by the soft sound of crickets.

Lisa shook her head. "I don't think we have to," she said thoughtfully. "Besides, if they're just here for the harvest, they'll be gone in a couple of weeks. I just won't go out there for a while." She shook her head, resolved in her decision even though it obviously bothered her.

"Well," Angie said huskily. "I think we ought to get cleaned up before your gram calls us in for supper."

"We can use the outside faucet," Lisa said, starting across the lawn the cellar bulkhead. "Less explaining to do that way."

"Good idea," Angie said.

"One other thing," Lisa said, but she cut herself off and kept her gaze fixed firmly ahead.

"What?" Angie said, and she snagged Lisa's arm, making her stop and turn to face her. "What *other* thing?"

Lisa's face did a slow, agonized twist, and Angie thought she was going to cry. Maybe the stress had finally gotten to her, and she was set to fall apart now that it was all over.

"Did you notice? When I stuck that pitchfork into that man's wrist, he . . ." She stopped herself and looked down at the ground, her jaw clenching and unclenching.

"Yeah?" Angie said, pressing.

"Did you notice that when the pitchfork went right through his wrist, his wrist . . . didn't *bleed?*"

# IV

The closest Dale could come to describing supper at Mrs. Appleby's was that it reminded him of Thanksgiving dinner at his grandmother's house when he was a boy. He couldn't remember how long it had been since he had had a real home-cooked meal that included home-made wheat rolls, roast beef, mashed potatoes with gravy, peas, carrots, and tossed salad with three kinds of lettuce. Dessert was something else, too: a choice between homemade blueberry pie or fresh-made strawberry shortcake. Dale and Angie both tried some of each.

"I'm glad we're only going to be here for a few days," Angie said, "'cause if we were here very long, I'd go home a blimp." She laughed, but when she saw the sadness that flashed across Lisa's face, she let her laugh die. It didn't take her long to feel close to Lisa, and the sudden realization that she would soon lose her newfound friend hit her like a splash of icy water.

Dale tried to smile, too, but as soon as he remembered that they were here for Larry's funeral on Monday, the quiet pleasure of supper instantly evaporated. He sat silently sipping his coffee while Lisa and Angie scram-bled around, clearing the table and getting the dishes ready to wash. Mrs. Appleby was sitting back, enjoying an after dinner cigarette. It surprised Dale that she smoked, and he commented on it.

"I know I should quit, but I only smoke Carletons, now," she explained, chuckling. "They're not much more than colored air."

Dale nodded agreement, having fought his own battles with nicotine. "I think it's nice the way Lisa and Angie have hit it off so quickly," he said. "I mean, here we are, not even in town for three hours, and she in fact both of us, feel like we're home visiting for the holidays."

"Well, like I said," Mrs. Appleby replied, blowing out a pale plume of smoke, "I started renting out rooms so I wouldn't be lonely once I retired. 'Course, once Lisa moved in with me, I had all the company I needed, but by then I was used to having a few other folks around."

"I can't imagine all of your boarders get a meal like this, though," Dale said, leaning back and patting his stomach.

Mrs. Appleby flicked the tip of her cigarette into the ashtray and then took another shallow drag. "You know, I must admit I had a bit of an ulterior motive," she said. Her eyes flicked quickly at the kitchen doorway before she continued. "You see, Lisa's been living with me for almost four years, now, but she still ... I don't know, she just doesn't seem to have much of a knack for making friends around town. She's pretty much a loner, and frankly, I liked the looks of both you and your daughter right from the start."

"I think it works out fine because it gives Angie something to do besides mope around in a motel room," Dale said. "And I think Lisa's a very nice girl. You must be proud of her."

"Very," Mrs. Appleby said, smiling warmly at Dale. "You know, I kind of sensed right off that they'd like each other, and I don't know. I guess I was being a little selfish hoping Lisa would have someone around for a few days, someone her own age. I mean, here she is, stuck in this house with her old granny, and I, well, never mind. Listen to me. I could blab on all evening. You wanted to go over to Mildred Cole's tonight?"

Dale stroked the side of his face and heaved a deep sigh. "Yeah. I suppose I should. I just want to, you know, speak with her before the funeral and tell her how sorry I am about what happened."

"It's terrible, isn't it?" Mrs. Appleby said, snubbing out her cigarette in the ashtray. "The longer you live, the more you see of death, but I'll never understand why the young have to die like that." She looked at Dale, and her blue eyes glistened brightly. "It's about the only thing that sometimes shakes my faith in the Lord."

Dale nodded his tacit agreement, not wanting to say anything about his own faith or more truthfully, his lack thereof.

"Well," he said, sliding his chair back and standing up slowly. "If the girls are going to do the dishes, I'll guess I'll go."

"You know where to go now, right?" Mrs. Appleby said.

Dale nodded. "Yup. Down through the center of town, the first left after the police station."

"Ridge Road."

"Right. Second house after the school on the left."

"You'll know you've gone too far if you see a sign on your right for the town dump."

As it turned out, Dale did miss the house on his first pass and ended up turning around at the entrance to the dump. As he pulled up in front of the house, he saw two cars in the Cole's driveway. He knew Larry's father was dead, so that must mean someone was staying with Mildred.

Actually, now that he thought about it, Dale guessed that Larry would probably be buried right next to his father. On their way into town today, he had noticed a small cemetery named Brooklawn and had assumed that's where Larry would be buried. The funeral, Mrs. Appleby told him, would be at Rodgers' Funeral Home, and he reminded himself to look for it before returning to the boarding house.

Dale idled the car for a minute before killing the engine. Then, taking a deep breath, he got out and walked up to the front door. There was only one light on in the house, and from behind a drawn curtain, he could see the flicker and hear the low buzz of a television set.

The night air was chilly, and a faint puff of steam came out of his mouth as he blew out his withheld breath and rapped gently on the door.

At first, there was no response, but after a second knock, he heard someone approach the door. There was a loud "chunk" as the deadbolt lock turned, and the front door opened a crack. One eye peered out at him through the crack. Dale saw the safety lack chain stretched to its limit.

"Yes?" a woman's voice said, muffled by the door between them.

"Mrs. Cole?" Dale said. "I'm . . ."

"Mildred's asleep right now," the person said, her voice a sharp whisper. "Can 1 help you?"

"Well, I'm Dale Harmon. Larry and I worked together in Augusta."

"Oh, yes," the woman inside the house said. "Just a minute." The door closed, and Dale could hear it as the woman slid open the chain lock and opened the door wide.

"Good evening," she said, extending her hand out to Dale. "I'm Roberta, Mildred's sister."

"Pleased to meet you," Dale said, shaking the thin, dry hand. "I only wish it was under better circumstances."

Roberta rolled her eyes heaven-ward and took a deep, sighing breath. "I know, I know, It's been very difficult on Mildred. Other than me, she's left alone in the world."

Dale smiled grimly, waiting to be invited in, but so far, it appeared he would spend his time visiting on the Cole's front steps.

"Mildred said Larry mentioned you quite often, and yes, I think I recall some flowers arriving from your department."

Dale nodded, grateful that Nichols had gotten right on it. "Perhaps I'd better come back another time," he said, feeling awkward. "I just wanted to speak with Larry's mother for a minute."

"I told you," Roberta said, "Mildred's asleep right now. The doctor prescribed a tranquilizer for her, and the damned things knocked her right off her feet. 'S probably just as well, I suppose."

Dale shrugged and took one step backward, about to leave.

"You know, Mr. —Harmon, was it?"

"Yes."

"Well, Mr. Harmon, you being from Augusta and working for the state and all, maybe you could help us out."

Dale frowned, genuinely confused. He wondered if maybe Larry's death had seriously affected his aunt. She was staring at him with rounded eyes and a deep furrowed brow, looking for all the world like she just took a short trip around the bend. Maybe, he thought, she should try one of her sister's "tranks."

"Ahh, how do you mean?"

"Maybe you could use some of your pull in Augusta to help us to get to see Larry."

Dale shook his head and reached into his pocket for his car keys for a bit of reassurance. "I don't understand," he said, holding one hand up helplessly.

"They won't let us *see* him," Roberta said. Her voice was low and thin, and she leaned forward as though afraid even now she might wake her sister.

"Franklin Rodgers, the funeral director, won't let us look at the body. He says the accident was so horrible, he's insisting on a closed casket service, and he doesn't even want my sister to see him, not the way he is now."

The first thought Dale had was that he hoped Mildred had someone, a minister or close friend to talk to. anyone but her sister. If Larry's death affected her this much, then Mildred was going to need some serious counseling to get her over it all.

. "I'm sure there's a good reason for that," he said. 'I | mean, if he was really, you know, bad off, it might be too much of a shock for her to see him like that. I'm sure this Mr. Rodgers wants you and your sister to re-member Larry the way he was when he was alive."

Roberta shook her head viciously from side to side "No! No!" she hissed. "Just the opposite. I think my sister *has* to see him, dead like that, so she can start to accept it and live with it."

Dale took another step backwards, wishing he had just waited until the funeral to speak with Larry's mother. He hadn't counted on a crazy aunt.

"I'll see what I can do about it," he said, jingling his car keys in his hand. "Tell Mildred I was by when she wakes up, okay?" He wasn't entirely sure how much of his visit would be relayed to Mildred, and he started to think that the less said, the better.

"I will, don't you worry," Roberta said as she started to ease the door shut. "You just do what you can so my sister can see her boy one last time, all right?"

Dale nodded and, turning, started down the walkway to his car. He resisted his impulse to run the distance, and he felt a slight measure of relief when he heard the Cole's front door slam shut and the rattle of the chain lock as Roberta ran it back into place.

# V

Angie pretended to be sleeping when her father came up to the room sometime after midnight. She heard him stumbling around in the dark, tripping over unfamiliar furniture and fumbling through his suitcase. Her body tensed as she forced herself to breathe evenly and deeply.

After supper, her dad went out to visit with Larry's mother, but he had returned quickly, saying it wasn't the right time. So after a mug of hot chocolate, she had said goodnight to him, Lisa, and Mrs. Appleby, and zone upstairs to bed. For more than two hours, though, she laid in bed, listening to the buzz of conversation downstairs in the living room.

What stuck in her memory, replaying with frightening intensity, was that face, a grinning, leering face with insane, glowing eyes, looking up at her through the shattered wood of the loft door. Her wrist still burned where the man had held her; and when she had washed up for bed, she had carefully studied the bright red half-moons where his grimy fingernails had dug into her skin. The cut from the splinter still hurt, too, but she and Lisa had secretly washed and bandaged it up without anyone finding out.

Most frightening of all, though, was when Angie thought about that steely grip. It didn't feel like it was around her *wrist;* she couldn't get rid of the sensation that those bony fingers were closing around her *throat,* cutting off her air and making her pulse hammer in her ears.

*Hammering! . . . like those fists, slamming on the door as she tried, frantically, to hold it down!*

*Hammering! . . . like that hand that had shot up through the door and grabbed her!*

*Hammering! . . . that kept sleep at more than arm's distance away!*

*Hammering . . . until she thought her eardrums would explode!*

She stirred, rolled over onto her side facing the wall, and groaned when her father sat down on the edge of his bed, making the bedsprings creak. He took off one shoe and let it drop to the floor.

*Like soft hammering!* Angie thought, and a surge of panic almost made her cry out.

He took off the other shoe and let it drop; then he got up and went into the guest bathroom down the hallway.

The whole time he was gone, Angie lay, staring wide- ! eyed at the blank wall no more than a foot from her face. Her father left the door open a crack, and the light from the hallway cast her rounded shadow on the wall. Then the door opened, and she saw another shadow loom up over her own. Again, she almost cried out in fear. The shadow looked too large, too slouch-shouldered, too misshapen to be her father! It got bigger and bigger as it came toward her bed.

A sheen of sweat broke out on her forehead as she gripped the sheets into tight-fisted balls. The shadow grew larger as the slow, steady thumping of its tread got closer and *closer!*

Angie tried to keep the thought out of her mind, but all she could think of was that, with a sudden, inhuman grunt, the shadow would suddenly materialize and come crushing down on her. Its bony fingers would reach for and find her neck, and then slowly . . . painfully crush her throat to pulp.

"Dad?" she whispered, her voice a gravelly gasp.

"Sorry, Ange," her father said softly. "I didn't mean to wake you." The bedroom door eased shut again, and the room darkened.

Angie frantically wished she could get enough air into her lungs and enough courage so she could tell her father about what had happened out at the barn. She knew she should tell him about it, but then again, she and Lisa hadn't been hurt and maybe Lisa was right. They should keep quiet about it and make sure they never went to the old barn again!

She stirred and rolled onto her back, smacking her lips and muttering a string of senseless words, pretending to talk in her sleep.

Her father came over to her bed and placed his hand lightly on her shoulder. "Are you awake?" he said, so softly she could barely hear him even at this close range.

She snuggled down into her pillow and again smacked her lips, wondering if she was laying it on too thick. As much as she wanted to say something, as much as she wished she could just fall apart and cry on his shoulder, she forced herself to keep her eyes shut and to feign sleep.

Lisa was right, she decided after all. Just forget all about what happened out there at the barn. Keep the secret of Lisa's "secret place"!

But that didn't stop the nightmares that came later, once she fell asleep.

# CHAPTER THREE
## "SOME UNANSWERED QUESTIONS"

## I

At six-thirty on Sunday morning, Kellerman's Cafe had all the smells and warmth that only a small town, working-class greasy spoon can have. Over the snap and sizzle of frying eggs and bacon, and the shouting of orders to Herbie, the cook, and requests for coffee refills, the steady drone of conversation was reassuring to Dale that even in the face of death, life *did* go on. He found that, ever since Natalie's death, he took to noticing such reassurances.

Between the much too-soft mattress, the sounds of Angie's disturbed sleep, and thinking about his awkward conversation with Larry's Aunt Roberta, Dale hadn't slept very well. He figured Mrs. Appleby saw through his lie when he told her he had "slept like a baby." He hoped she wasn't offended when he refused her offer of breakfast but said, instead, that he wanted to take a few hours to look around town. Angie was sleeping soundly, finally, when he tiptoed downstairs.

Even on a Sunday, when most families were either sleeping late or getting ready for church, Kellerman's was busy. Farmers, truckers on a long haul, and a couple of mechanics sat around at the worn mint green linoleum counter or in the padded booths by the window. Two waitresses in light pink uniforms, one white-haired and elderly, the other well on her way to looking old before her time, dashed back and forth between counter and booths and the ordering window. Dale learned there was a bar downstairs, making Kellerman's practically the only local entertainment short of a drive into Houlton. He imagined seeing these same faces in the bar on a Saturday night.

For the money, though, Herbie slung some mean hash-browns and sunny-side-up eggs. Dale knew the cook's name because every other sentence he heard was a sharply barked, "Herbie, I need *this!* Herbie, where's my order?", from one or the other waitress. He wondered if Herbie was Kellerman, but from the way the waitresses yelled at him, he doubted it.

Dale finished scooping up the last bit of yolk with his crust of toast when he looked up and saw a policeman walk in from the back door. The cop was middle-aged, maybe mid-forties, Dale guessed, and beneath his well-pressed uniform, he looked a bit worn out. Although sturdily built, his gut looked flabby and hung out over the edge of his belt. His service revolver looked heavy and mean riding on his right hip.

" Mornin', Cloe! Hi 'yah, Ruth," he said, nodding at each woman as he hoisted himself up at the counter near the cash register.

Herbie glanced up. When he saw the policeman, he touched the rim of his grease-stained chef's hat in a weak salute and immediately reached for two eggs and broke them open onto the griddle.

Before the policeman said anything else, Cloe, the older waitress, slid a cup of coffee down the counter to him. "How goes the battle?" he asked, looking down as he stirred two packets of sugar and a squirt of milk into his coffee.

Cloe snorted as she turned away. "Nothing a year's vacation in the Bahamas wouldn't fix," she said.

It was times like this that Dale yearned for a cigarette, but he pushed aside the dented green ashtray—color coordinated with the countertop—and contented himself with his refill of coffee. Sitting back in the booth, he took a moment to size up the policeman.

One of the first things that crossed his mind was to ask this policeman if he knew anything about Larry's death. Dale figured he must, in a small town like Dyer. If there was anything to Roberta's claim that Larry's mother hadn't even been allowed to see her son's body the policeman would know. He also realized, in a town like this, that such questions, would be considered prying by an outsider. Maybe, though, if he explained that he was Larry's boss at the D.O.T., it would be seen as nothing more than concern for Larry's survivors.

*Good questions,* Dale decided as he swallowed the last bit of coffee and put his cup down.

"Get 'cha anything else?" Cloe asked, coming up on Dale from behind.

Startled, Dale looked up at her and shook his head. "Ahh, I guess not," he said. "The bill, I suppose, if you have to."

It was a stale joke, and Cloe surely had heard it a thousand times before because her face remained passive as she took the order pad from her stained apron pocket and hurriedly totaled it up.

"You can pay at the register," she said, tearing off the sheet and handing it to Dale. "Have a nice day," she added, sounding so automatic, Dale was sure she couldn't repeat it if he asked her what she just had said.

With one last wipe across his face with his napkin, Dale stood up and fished in his pocket for some loose change. Not finding enough, he unlimbered his wallet and slipped out a dollar bill. He left it under his plate and strode over to the register.

He didn't miss the side-long glance the policeman gave him, so he nodded a friendly, wordless greeting. He could practically hear the cop's mind, questioning him: *New fella . . . Ain't seen you 'round here before . . . What 'cha doin' in town?* Dale chastised himself for slipping into small-town, redneck cop cliché.

Cloe, still unsmiling after snatching up the monstrous tip Dale left her, walked to the register and rang up the sale. Dale handed her a twenty-dollar bill and waited patiently for her to count his change.

The whole time, Dale could feel the policeman's gaze burning into his back. His neck felt flushed as he put the bills into his wallet, folded it closed, and slipped it into his back pocket. He was about to stride on out of Kellerman's, but impulsively he turned to the cop and met his gaze.

"Good morning," Dale said, letting his smile widen as he held his hand out to the policeman. "My name's Dale Harmon. I was wondering if I could ask you a couple of questions."

The cop shook his hand firmly and then, letting his hand drop, said "M'name's Jeff Winfield." Gesturing at the empty stool beside him, he added, "I see you already had breakfast, but have a seat and tell me what I can do for you."

Dale pulled nervously at his ear lobe as he sat down. Suddenly, he felt very foolish, but now that he had started, he felt compelled to continue.

"Well, you see," Dale said, shifting on the stool, trying to get comfortable, "I worked down in Augusta with Larry Cole. My daughter and I came up for the funeral tomorrow, and I was wondering if you could answer a few questions for me to clear a few things up."

Winfield squinted as he regarded Dale. "I knew Larry since he was a boy," he said softly. "'S a shame what happened. He was a good kid growing up, 's far as I was concerned. Never got into any trouble with me, anyway." He glanced up when Cloe slid his breakfast plate in front of him. "You don't mind if I eat while we talk, do you?"

Dale shook his head. "Go right ahead. I just wanted to get a bit more about what happened last Friday," he said. "You see Larry was pretty close to me and my daughter, and I just won't feel right unless I know how it happened."

Winfield stripped back the foil from a small container of grape jelly and, squeezing it tightly between thumb and forefinger, squirted it onto a piece of toast. He spread it evenly with his knife, then took a huge bite. Jelly squirted out from between his front teeth.

"Not all that much to tell, really," he said between grinding chews. "He was driving south on Route 2-A, in a section the locals call the Haynesville Woods. What was he doing up here, anyway? Was he just home for a visit?"

Dale damned well knew that the cop already knew what Larry had been doing up in the area and was just feeling him out. "There's some highway money appropriated for some work on that stretch of road. I guess some folks consider it too dangerous and want it straightened out."

Winfield nodded his head. "Folks have an expression for that stretch of road. They say there's 'a tombstone every mile,' because of all the accidents out that way."

"So what happened to Larry?" Dale asked with a sudden intensity that caught Winfield by surprise.

"Like I said, not much to tell. The road's pretty curvy most of the way to Haynesville, and it gets pretty monotonous pretty fast. Lots of times, it's something as simple as a deer suddenly darting out onto the road or a logging truck pulling out from one of the tote roads. A driver gets startled and *blam!*" He slapped his fist into his open hand. "He doesn't make the turn and he meets a tree or a rock head-on. That's all she wrote."

"Larry went off the road sometime around midnight," Dale said. "You can't tell me there was a logging truck out there that late."

Winfield shrugged and put a forkful of eggs into his mouth. "I'm not saying I know what made Larry go off the road," he said, chewing noisily. "I'm just saying he went off the road as he was going into a curve. He went straight into a rock embankment. There wasn't a whole hell of a lot of his car or him left."

"You don't have any idea why he was driving out there, so late at night, do you?" Dale asked.

"You sure do seem to have quite a few questions," Winfield said, leaning away from Dale and scanning him up and down. "You sure you aren't from the press or maybe the insurance company?"

Trying to keep the intensity he felt out of his voice, Dale shook his head. "Like I said, Larry was like family to me and my daughter, and I really feel like I have to know what happened."

"Look here, Mr. Harmon. From Haynesville, you have two choices. You can either drive south to Bangor or you can go north straight off the edge of the world." He paused, took a deep breath, and added, "I guess we know which way Larry went."

Dale nodded and looked away, feeling a sudden iciness in his stomach. He tried hard not to imagine the squealing sounds of tires and brakes, the smashing of glass and groaning of twisted metal, and the soft, thudding impact of human flesh that had taken his friend's life.

"As it was," Winfield continued, "I was on patrol that night, and I was the first one on the scene after we got the call." He shuddered and swallowed. "T'weren't very pretty."

"I can imagine," Dale said softly. "But what you're saying is, you haven't really determined the cause of the accident, is that right?"

"No, but we sure as hell know the cause of death," Winfield said. He scooped up some more eggs and shoveled them into his mouth. "Is that all you wanted to know?"

"Well," Dale said. Cold fingers still gripped his stomach. "There was something else I was wondering about. Have you heard anything about the funeral?"

"Oh, yeah. That's tomorrow afternoon."

Dale nodded. "At two. Have you heard anything about the funeral being closed-casket?"

Winfield took a swallow of coffee and wiped his chin with his napkin. Shaking his head, he said, "I hadn't, but it wouldn't surprise me any. Like I said, I was there on the scene and, frankly, if I hadn't found his registration and his wallet, I never would have recognized him. The car burst into flames on impact, and he was . . . Look, you just finished eating. I don't want to be responsible for any indigestion, all right?"

Dale shifted to his feet, about to leave, but still, he didn't want to let it drop, not quite yet. "I went out to Mildred Cole's last night," he said.

Winfield shook his head solemnly. "I had the dubious honor of going out there myself to tell her what had happened. I understand she's taking it pretty hard."

"Actually, I never got to speak with her," Dale said, "but I spoke with her sister."

"Roberta," Winfield said, unsuccessfully disguising a small laugh.

"Uh-huh. Roberta told me Mildred wasn't allowed to see the body, that the funeral director, what's his name?"

"Franklin Rodgers," Winfield said.

"Right. He's insisting that Mildred can't see the body."

Winfield shrugged. "After seeing what I saw, I can understand why," he said, taking another sip of coffee.

"And you don't consider that unusual?" Dale asked. It struck him as strange how, in talking about this to Winfield, the whole thing grew in intensity for him. He suddenly felt very committed to finding out exactly what the hell had happened out there on the Haynesville Woods Road last Friday night.

Winfield shook his head slowly. "Look here, Mr. Harmon," he said. "No one tells me how to do my job except for Captain Bates. Frank Rodgers is the local undertaker, 'n in my estimation, no one, including some state worker from Augusta, is going to tell him how to do it. Can I be any clearer on that?"

Dale shook his head and paused to scratch the back of his neck. "I'm not telling anyone how to do their job, Officer. Look, you knew Larry Cole, didn't you?"

Winfield shrugged. "Course I did. Not very well, but like I said before he always stayed in line. Never any trouble 's far as I was concerned."

"And you knew his mother and his father before he died."

Winfield grunted agreement.

"Well, then, think about how his mother must feel! She gets a call sometime after midnight . . ."

"Actually," Winfield said softly, shivering from the recollection, "I went over to her house to tell her."

"Okay, fine, and you tell her that her only son, her last surviving family member is *dead*. Gone, just like that!" He snapped his fingers in the space between them. "Think about it! She has to absorb all that grief, and then, how do you think she feels when she's told that she can't even *see* him one last time? How do you think she feels?"

Winfield looked down at his lap, where he had shredded his napkin. He glanced nervously around the restaurant to see if anyone overheard their talk. Cloe was checking customers for coffee refills; Ruth was nowhere to be seen; Herbie was leaning out the back door of the kitchen, smoking and gazing off into the distance.

"I know how she feels," Winfield said softly.

"Do you?" Dale said, pressing. "Did you ever lose someone that close? Did you ever have a child of yours, or your wife die in an accident like that?" He earnestly hoped Winfield hadn't; his purpose wasn't to scratch open old wounds. It was obvious Winfield was still shaken up from what he had seen that night.

Winfield shook his head. "No, I haven't. I meant I know how she feels 'cause I saw her fall apart when I told her the news. 'N I happen to know from talk around town that her doctor prescribed some pretty hefty tranquilizers."

"So I'm not telling you or Mr. Rodgers or anyone in this town how to do their respective jobs," Dale said. "All I want you to do is one favor not for me but for Mildred Cole. I want you to ask Rodgers if he'll let me see Larry's body."

Winfield's head snapped up, and he nailed Dale with a harsh look. "Why you?" he asked. He laughed softly as he shook his head. "After all this bullshit, I was pretty much expecting you to ask if Mildred Cole could see him."

Dale stroked the side of his face. "You know, if he really is as bad as you say he was, maybe it wouldn't be a good idea for her to see him. Rodgers is probably right. Let her keep the memories she has. But if I saw him, I could reassure her and comfort her. It would be the voice of someone who had been close to her son, telling her that her son was at peace."

Winfield picked up his coffee and contemplated it for several seconds before drinking. He wrinkled his nose and, putting the cup back on the saucer, hailed Cloe. "Yoh! I could use a warm-up."

Cloe immediately started toward him.

"So?" Dale said, leaning both elbows on the counter.

Winfield smiled and nodded as Cloe filled his cup. He took his time adding cream and sugar, and stirred thoughtfully. The spoon clattered loudly when he placed it on the countertop, where it left a little brown ring.

"I *just* want to know why *in* hell you're so all fired-up about all this," he said. He leaned back slightly, puffing out his chest as he hitched his gun belt. "You want to see his body, and I want to know why you think I should help you do something like that."

Dale came up close to him, meeting his eyes on the level. "Larry Cole was a damned close friend of mine," he said, his voice a harsh whisper, "and since you scraped him up off the road, no one, not even his mother, has seen him. I think that's pretty damned peculiar! That's why!"

Winfield thought for several seconds, seconds that seemed to drag out into minutes for Dale. At last, he took a huge gulp of his coffee, wiped his face with his shredded napkin, and hefted himself off the stool.

"Okay, Mr. Harmon," he said, as he fished a five dollar bill from his wallet and left it on the counter beside his plate. "I'll give Rodgers a call later on today and just sorta broach the subject with him. You give me a call this afternoon, 'n I'll tell you what I find out. Will that satisfy you?"

Dale knew he had pressed the man far enough, so he smiled and held out his hand. They shook, and Dale smiled, "Thank you very much," he said.

Winfield started for the door, but before swinging it open and leaving, he looked back at Dale. "Just give me a call 'round one o'clock. We'll see what's what. I ain't promisin' anything."

# II

The day was turning into shit, as far as Hocker was concerned, but last night had been pure glory!

After "borrowing" the old man's truck, he and Tasha by-passed Bangor and I-95, taking Route 2 north through Old Town and Lincoln. They didn't dare stop until they had some healthy distance between them and the town of Holden. By the time they stopped for "breakfast" in Mattawamkeag, it was well past noon.

The "old man," they had discovered, was in the bad habit of keeping his wallet on the seat beside him as he drove. Perhaps, Hocker thought, the truck seat drove the bulging wallet into his skinny, little ass, making driving uncomfortable. In any event, Hocker was surprised to find a fat wad of bills in the wallet, along with assorted credit cards, a driver's license, and ragged-edged family pictures.

"Righteous bucks," Hocker said, whistling between his teeth as he held the steering wheel with one hand and hastily counted the bills with the other. "We got close to a hundred bucks here."

"Whoopee," Tasha said. She was unimpressed by the money or at least that was the impression she tried to give him. Throughout the drive to Mattawamkeag, she was silent, either staring out at the road ahead or else, eyes closed, leaning her head against the side window. Every bump in the road made her head bounce against the glass, but at least she didn't have to look at or talk to Hocker!

What she really felt was a cold, stark fear that Hocker really had killed that man back there! It was fear that, even now, an All Points Bulletin was out for their arrest! It was fear that she might have made the biggest mistake of her life when she ran away from home and hooked up with this asshole Hocker!

Somewhere along Route 2, after Mattawamkeag, Hocker spotted a deep-rutted logging road and, without even slowing, jerked the wheel hard to the left. The truck's chassis groaned and snapped as it rattled over the wash-board road bed. A yellow wall of dust fantailed behind them.

"Christ! Slow down before I lose all my fillings, will you?" Tasha yelled. Her voice was almost lost beneath the rattling sound coming from underneath the truck.

Hocker leaned his head back and laughed aloud, but a sudden, hard bounce threw him right out of his seat so that he hit his head on the truck roof. That suddenly sobered him up, and he eased up a bit on the gas pedal.

"What the hell are you doing, anyway?" she asked. She looked back longingly at the asphalt road through the rear window. It may not be much, but at least it connected towns. This road was going nowhere!

Hocker's jaw was set grimly as he negotiated the bumpy dirt road around several turns, but before long he drew to a stop and killed the engine. "I guess this'll about do," he said. "Come on, everybody out. We'll set up camp for the night here."

Tasha scowled as she stepped out of the truck and looked around. Dust swirled in the air and settled slowly. Other than the curving dirt logging road behind them, there was no sign of human life anywhere. Towering pine trees speared up into the sky, swaying with a soft hiss in the gentle wind. Birds called from surrounding woods, and looking up, she could see what appeared to be a hawk wheeling overhead, riding the thermals. The brightness of the sky made her eyes begin to water, so she turned away.

"Look," she said, her anger continuing to bubble, "it's one thing to hitch-hike and camp somewhere along the road. But I never said I was Pioneer An-nie! I don't want to sleep out here in the goddamned wilderness!

"Sssh!" Hocker said, holding his finger to his lips and glancing around. "You hear that?"

Tasha shook her head angrily. "All I hear is the frig-gin' wind!"

"No! Listen!" Hocker said. He suddenly bolted forward, running into the brush, leaping over moss-covered deadfalls and waving for her to follow him. "Come on!" he shouted, his voice echoing and growing fainter.

Tasha stood for a moment beside the truck, watching him go. Soon, all she could see was his head, bouncing up and down further into the brush. Every-where, the woods vibrated with intense shadows and light. After another moment, she swore softly under her breath and started after him. It was better than standing there alone.

Hocker was out of sight by then, so she called out to him as she ran in the same direction he had taken. She was filled with a sudden fear that a bear or moose or something worse would charge out of the woods at her, but on she went, hoping to find Hocker before the wild animals found her, for all the good Hocker would be!

As she went, though, what she had thought was the sound of the wind in the trees grew steadily louder until she broke through the brush and jerked to a stop, astounded. She stood in a clearing on a cliff, maybe twenty or thirty feet high, looking straight down into a rolling foam-twisted river.

Hocker was some distance upstream, staring out over the twisting ribbon of water as it wound its way south. Rocks glistened in the bright sunlight and white-capped water splashed into the air as it rushed downstream. Fallen trees, stripped of their bark, littered the riverbed, looking like giant toothpicks scattered everywhere.

"A river. Big deal!" Tasha said. She shouted over the roar of the water. "You never saw a river before?"

Hocker glanced at her and shook his head as though he heard some very sad news.

"We've been driving north along a river. What did you call it? Penob . . . whatever! Who the hell cares?" She waved her hand at him in disgust. "Come on. Let's get out of here. Look," she said, brightening. "The road comes through there. At least we won't have to bushwhack our way back to the truck."

Not entirely confident of her sense of direction, she turned and started along the dirt road, hoping it would lead her back to the truck. If she was lucky, she thought, Hocker left the keys in the ignition. She could take the truck and drive the hell out of here alone. If she got stopped by the cops before she got to wherever the hell she wanted to get, she'd tell the truth about how she had hooked up with Hocker and how she had had nothing to do with hurting that old man! She could make up some story about how she had to steal the truck to get away from Hocker.

As it turned out, Hocker had taken the truck keys with him, so she ended up waiting nearly an hour before he came back, walking along the dirt road, whistling a merry little tune to himself even though his face was bathed in sweat. Pioneer Annie or not, they ended up camping in a small clearing next to the logging road. After another supper from a can, it took Tasha several hours to fall asleep, and even then, the sleep was thin and practically useless. She lay there with her sleeping rag pulled up to her chin, expecting at any moment to hear a loud roar as a snarling, clawing bear, or worse, tore through the tent and ripped her to shreds!

But the roaring sound that did wake her up, some time after two o'clock in the morning was the sound of the Ford pickup starting up.

Tasha jerked up out of her sleep, thinking crazily, Oh, Christ! The bears found the truck keys! A "Far Side" cartoon popped into her mind and almost made her laugh. . . . Almost.

In a flurry of arms and legs, she kicked free of her sleeping bag, ran up the tent zipper, and stared out at the logging road. Overhead, the stars were so thick the sky looked like one huge luminous gray wash. That only accented the heavy, black shadows of the forest. She thought she could discern the silhouette of the truck against the sky, but she wasn't sure.

"Hocker?" she called out. She reached out in the darkness to pat his sleeping bag, but she felt only slight relief when she found it empty.

Good, she thought. That's him out there. Not someone else!

But what in the name of God was he doing? she wondered. She wanted to call out louder, but then she thought he had decided to leave her. That didn't make sense because if he wanted to dump her, he seemed like the kind of guy who simply would "off her.

So, if he's not leaving without me, she thought, what the hell is he doing?

The truck's ignition ground over and over, came close to starting but then died several times. In the silences between his attempts, she heard the long string of curses Hocker laid on the old Ford.

Tasha eased out of the tent into the chilly night air, watching the misty plumes of her breath as she breathed shallowly. Her legs and back ached as she stretched upright and started to move cautiously forward.

As she got closer, the grinding ignition and the cursing got louder. Hidden behind a thick-boled tree, she heard the truck catch and turnover, chugging unevenly.

"All-fuckin'-right!" Hocker shouted.

Tasha could see him clearly, sitting at the wheel, an inky silhouette against the gray night sky. He snapped on the headlights, flooding the forest with light so bright it hurt Tasha's eyes. She was convinced she saw other eyes, shining from the bushes around her. But she ignored that fear as she waited, wondering what Hocker would do next.

The truck ground into gear and haltingly moved forward, the suspension groaning over the rutted road, and the tires spinning out particularly deep ruts. Once she was sure Hocker couldn't see her, Tasha left her hiding place and, picking her way carefully, followed along behind.

At least he's not heading out to the road, she thought. He's not leaving me behind. There was small comfort in that thought. It was as bad as being alone in the woods at night.

Hocker drove along the road until he came to the point where the road came closest to the river's edge. Tasha crouched behind some bushes and watched Hocker get out of the truck.

Leaving the engine running, he went to the truck bed and fished around. The old man who owned the truck may have been foolish about where he left his wallet, but he was no dummy when it came to preparing for emergencies. Hocker shook the ten gallon gas can, apparently satisfied by the feel; it was practically full.

Despite the chilly night air, Hocker stripped off his T-shirt and twisted it into a thick knot. Then he unscrewed the gas can and stuck one end of the shirt into the top. He shook the can several times to saturate the shirt with gas, then he took off the truck's gas tank cap and stuffed the shirt half-way in.

Tasha shivered as she watched, not sure what was going on. She knew, finally, what was happening when she saw Hocker open the truck door and splash gas from the can all over the front seat of the truck. When the can was empty, he tossed it into the seat and then suddenly turned around to face Tasha.

She was sure he had seen or sensed her hiding there, but when he started moving toward her, he suddenly kneeled and felt around on the ground. At last, with a grunt of satisfaction, he found what he was looking for and went back to the truck.

She heard a soft scratching sound, but before she could guess what it was, she saw a cigarette lighter flare up in Hocker's hand. The flame looked like a solitary orange teardrop. Hocker went to the rear of the truck and, poised like a track runner in starting blocks, held the flame to the rag stuck into the gas tank. When a thin tongue of fire licked up one side of the cloth, he ran to the front of the cab. The engine roared to life, and Tasha guessed that he had dropped a heavy rock onto the gas pedal. There was a soft click as he shifted the truck into gear, and then he dove away from the truck. He hit the ground with a thud as the truck leaped forward.

The ground was uneven and cluttered with thick brush, but with its wheels spinning and squealing, shooting dirt and rocks up behind it, the Ford sped toward the edge of the cliff. Hocker got up quickly and, leaping into the air with a joyous *whoop,* ran after the truck, tripping and stumbling in its wake. The trailing flame from the gas tank got brighter, and Hocker followed it as though it were a fleeing will-o-the-wisp.

At the cliff edge, the truck almost stalled trying to run up over an edge of rock, but dinosaur-like it plowed up and over, and then shot out into the darkness of the ravine.

It wasn't dark for long! As Tasha watched, horrified, the night flashed bright with an oily yellow explosion. Hocker stood at the edge of the cliff, looking like a demon poised at the brink of Hell. Flames and thick, curling smoke roared skyward, blotting out the dusting of stars. Tasha cringed when she heard Hocker shout his joy, his animal-like howls echoing from the stark rock walls across the river.

But it wasn't over yet. As the sky filled with light, there was a sudden, thunderous boom as the truck's gas tank exploded. The flames intensified, underlighting the roiling black smoke with a wicked yellow glow.

Tasha huddled in the cold, dark forest, fighting the impulse to scream. Another, smaller explosion ripped the silence of the night, and then the flames slowly ebbed, leaving the silhouette of Hocker on the cliff edge, more afterimage than reality.

She listened to him at last turn away from the scene of destruction. She quickly got up from her hiding place and started back toward the tent, stumbling in the dark. She was sure he would see or hear her, so half-way back, she turned and started running toward him along the road. They collided in the dark.

"Jesus Christ!" she shouted, letting her panic out in a high-pitched wail. "What the hell's happening?"

Hocker pulled back a step and held her by both shoulders. She felt like a quivering mess in his grip.

"Hey! Hey! Take it easy, Tash," he said. He was trying to calm her down, but she could hear the guy wire tension in his voice.

Tension? she wondered, or excitement?

"What the hell was that noise?" she wailed, thinking it would be just fine to let him think the explosion had woken her, and that she had run blindly out of the tent. "What in the name of Christ happened?"

"Now, now," Hocker said. "Don't get all freaked out. I did what I had to do."

His voice was soothing, but the grip on her arms closed tighter. She tried to pull away but couldn't break his grip. Behind him, the distant rock wall still glowed with a fading, flickering orange. She could see, despite the chill, that his face and bare chest were slick with sweat. He looked like someone who had just finished a long bout of love-making.

"Was that the truck?" she shouted. "Did the truck blow up?" Again, she tried to pull away, but his grip held.

"Well, now, we can't very well go riding around the countryside in a stolen truck, now, can we?" Hocker said. "That wouldn't be too smart. 'Specially after what we did to that old man back there."

"What *you* did," Tasha screamed. "Not me!"

Hocker snorted with laughter and spit to one side. "I did what I had to do," he repeated. "Maybe I should have gotten you up so you could've seen it." He glanced back over his shoulder at the fading light. Darkness closed like a blanket over the river gorge. "God!" he said, almost sighing. "You should have seen it. It was fucking *incredible!*"

Well, Hocker thought the next morning, last night might have been incredible, but today is turning to shit!

They were awake and packed, ready to move when the eastern sky began turning from black to the color of soot. Pre-dawn bird calls sounded a raucous chorus all around them as they started down the dew-covered road. Three hours later, once the sun rose and drove away the chill of night, they were still walking down the road and hadn't yet seen a single car.

"You know, this really sucks," Tasha said over her shoulder to Hocker, who always walked a few paces behind her. Her backpack bounced painfully in the small of her back. Every bone in her body seemed to ache from sleeping on the ground for so many nights. And last night, after the truck-burning, she hadn't really slept at all! She had still expected a bear or something, angered by the fire and explosion down by the river, to attack them.

The seams of her jeans rode up uncomfortably into the crack of her ass, and she wiggled now and then, trying to loosen up. She wondered if, while they walked, Hocker ever looked at her ass. She was amazed that Hocker never made any sexual advances toward her. He was alone with her, night after night, and could have easily overpowered her. Who knows? Maybe he's a faggot. But it suited her just fine that he left her alone.

"It'd suck even more if the cops put the make on us 'cause of that truck," he replied.

The road twined back and forth like a lazy snake. It seemed whoever had planned it couldn't make up their minds where they wanted it to go. Eventually, the thick forest yielded to wide, cleared hills, most of which overflowed with potato plants. In the distance, weathered barns stood like sentinels on the horizon.

"Do you even know where we are?" Tasha asked. She, like Hocker, was damned sick and tired of all this walking.

Hocker snorted and spit into the woods alongside the road. Yeah, he thought, somewhere between Bangor and nowhere!

"You wanted to go to Canada, right?" he said, his voice laced with sarcasm. "Well, Houlton can't be too many miles up ahead and that's right on the Canadian border."

"You might have just spit into Canada, for all you know," Tasha said under her breath.

They continued walking, and they didn't see a single car until after they had stopped for a short lunch, but it was traveling in the wrong direction.

Tasha sat on the side of the road, watching the car disappear over the rise in the road. For a long time after, she could hear the tearing sound of its wheels on the asphalt. She wished she had flagged the driver down and headed south as far as he was going.

Anything to get away from Hocker.

She vowed to herself that, as soon as they hit a town large enough to get lost in, she would dump the creep. He served his purpose; now that he had committed a crime, maybe even murder, she wanted to be rid of him.

"We'll go just a little more," Hocker said. His frustration at having to walk for so long was written all over his face. "We'll try to find a place where we can set up camp for the night. We're gonna need some supplies, too."

"You're sure there are towns around here?" Tasha asked.

Without consulting his map, Hocker nodded, then spit. "You betcha. Hey look! See? What'd I tell you?"

He pointed down the road, toward a small rectangular sign bolted to a wooden post. The paint was peeled but they could read what it said: WEL-COME TO DYER POP. 1247

"Dyer, Maine, huh?" Tasha said, shaking her head, as they got closer to the sign. "I never heard of Dyer." Hocker laughed aloud as he shifted his back pack.

"They probably never heard of you, either," he said.

Then, snorting loudly, he spit. The glob of spit arced in the air and landed with a "splat" right on top of the town's name.

"Bull's eye," Hocker said, laughing out loud.

# III

After a late breakfast, Donna got into her car and backed out of her sister's driveway. She didn't tell Barbara where she was going; she didn't feel the need to, and she certainly didn't want to explain herself, not any more.

Driving slowly down Burnt Mill Road, past the Mill Store, she waited at the blinking red light to turn left onto Main Street. There was Sparky in his customary slump beside the gas pumps. She wondered if he might spend his nights there as well. Tooting her horn a few times, she stuck her hand out the window and waved to him. As she turned onto Main Street, it amused her to think Sparky would be wondering all day who the hell that woman was in the blue Toyota.

Donna made her way down Main Street, taking her time to check out what few changes had occurred since her last time in town. A few of the houses sported fresh coats of paint, but generally, the downtown store fronts, if any different at all, looked smaller and seedier than ever.

When she saw two girls running and skipping along the sidewalk, she thought back to when she and her best friend, Lorrie Parker, used to do the same thing. Some things about Dyer never changed, she thought, for better or for worse.

On the edge of town, Brook Lawn Cemetery was as neat and well-trimmed as ever. The old maple at the front gate had already changed color, and every passing breeze sent brilliant red leaves spiraling to the ground. The spiked wrought-iron fence had a fresh coat of paint that glistened like polished ebony.

A shiver ran through her as she saw the grounds-keepers digging a new grave. Bright ochre earth was heaped up in a rounded hill, and their shovels flashed in the sun. She could faintly hear their conversation as they worked. One of the men, the overseer, sat on a small John Deere tractor, smoking a cigarette. His wide girth made the tractor look like a toy.

"Ann, shit. Poor Larry," Donna whispered once she realized who that grave was for. She stepped on the gas to get by the cemetery quickly.

The town gave way to wide open hills, crisscrossed by rows of potatoes fields. A quarter mile down the road, Donna slowed and, out of habit, snapped on her turn signal for the left turn onto Mayall Road. Insects whirred in the dying grass alongside the road.

She passed the Larsen's farm on the left. It looked like she remembered it, not much worse, anyway; maybe one or two additional rusty cars around back, but it looked as though the Larsen's were still hanging on. After Larsen's, there was a small grove of trees marking the stream where she used to play. Then, on the left, was the driveway up to her old house.

The car wheels crunched over the gravel, setting her teeth on edge as she turned into the driveway. All around her, a summer's growth of grass swayed in the wind, its ripe, yellow heads bowed heavy with seed. The insect noises got louder, filling the air.

Donna eased up the driveway, leaning over the steering wheel as she stared up at the house. From the dormers down to the cellar windows, it was obvious the hose needed a good scraping and at least two coats of paint. If she was going to do it, she would make damned sure not to use the same dull yellow her mother favored.

Several balustrades were broken out of the porch railing and gave it an odd, broken-tooth look. By the living room window, one shutter hung down at an awkward angle. Rotting branches and last season's dead weeds littered what had once been a well-kempt front lawn, and the shrubs out front had grown rampantly.

But Donna knew it would take more than paint and a little cleaning up to lay to rest the ghosts that hovered inside the house. She wondered if the house could ever be resurrected to its former beauty. Probably not, but she was sure of one thing. She wouldn't be the one to do it! When she got back to Donna's, she would press her sister harder about selling the place, before it was so dilapidated they couldn't get a decent price for it.

She stopped the car at the foot of the walkway and sat for several minutes staring up at the front door. The screen on the storm door had been ripped down from the top, leaving a large, hanging triangular flap. It looked like someone had tried to break into the house and, failing, had torn the screen out of spite. She cut the engine, dropped her car keys in her purse, and stepped out.

The walkway, like the driveway, was chocked with weeds and grass that grew through the cement. At the bottom of the stairs, Donna's heel caught on a tuft, and if she hadn't grabbed the newel post, she would have fallen to the ground. Straightening up quickly, she looked around in embarrassment, even though no one was nearby to see.

Her heart was pounding in her chest as she searched her pocketbook for the front door key. Holding the screen door open with one hand, she slipped the key into the lock and gave it a turn. The rusted tumblers gave with a little effort, and the door clicked and slowly swung open.

The stale, stuffy smell of a house long closed as-sailed her when she stuck her head into the entryway. She closed her eyes for a moment to let the aroma carry her memories back, but beneath the familiar smell was the deeper, pungent smell of decay. She figured, most likely, a rat or mouse or something had gotten caught behind the walls and died there. With that in mind, she left the front door open as she walked from the entryway into the dining room. She walked from room to room, soaking up the atmosphere as she circled the house from the dining room to the kitchen to the mudroom to the living room and back to the entryway.

Although the house had been empty for three years, there were still several pieces of furniture in each of the rooms. She and Barbara had agreed that each of them could take whatever they wanted, but there were some pieces neither of them wanted; but neither had had the heart to throw them away yet, either. The only problem had arisen when each of them had insisted on taking their mother's favorite table lamp.

Donna couldn't shake the confusion of memories that flooded her mind as she made the circuit again, pausing in each room to look around. Dingy trim work in need of paint and yellowed wallpaper peeling from the walls added to her sense of loss. In the living room, she screwed up her courage enough to look into the closet under the stairway, the place where she used to huddle while her sister told her ghost stories. As for the cellar, well . . . she never played down there much as a child, so she didn't bother looking down there.

At last, she climbed the stairs to the second floor, pausing momentarily to glance into both her parents' and sister's bedrooms before going down the hallway to her own bedroom. The doorknob felt cold in her hand as she stood there rigidly, neither daring to open it nor wanting to leave without looking inside.

"One last time," she whispered. Sucking in a shallow breath, she turned the doorknob and pushed the door in.

She expected to see the room as it had been years ago: walls festooned with posters of rock stars, her dresser cluttered with jewelry and make-up, her big double bed covered with white ruffle bedspread and piled high with stuffed animals. She also expected to see one of the ghosts she knew was still there in the house: the ghost of the little girl she once was.

She found it difficult to realize, that she had once been the little girl who had played and slept in this room. In her imagination, she thought that little girl had grown up, gotten married, had two or three beautiful children, and now lived in a beautiful house in Portland or outside of Boston, living a life with no problems or complications. She thought, sometimes, she wasn't the person that little girl grew up to become; she couldn't be because her life had too damned many complications! What she wouldn't give to be that little girl, all grown up!

Moving slowly, so as not to disturb the dust that covered the floor like a glaze of ice, she went over to the window and pressed her face close to the glass to look out over the back yard. To the right, she could see just a small corner of the barn, its boards weathered the color of storm clouds. She wondered how some houses, in a few years could deteriorate so fast while some barns stayed the same for decades. No matter how weathered or rotten, barns stood up to the unmerciful Maine winters. She found herself wondering if her own life was more like a house or a barn.

Next to the barn, in the seed-choked back yard, the old chicken coop roof had finally caved in. The two peaks at each end pointed upward, like useless wings, and the whole structure looked like an airplane crash. Next to the chicken coop, dangling from a limb of the old apple tree, was the rope that had once been part of her swing. Its frayed end swayed gently in the wind, and Donna shivered when it reminded her of a hangman's noose.

Beyond the barn, over the gently rising hills, stretched acre after acre of potato fields right up to the horizon. A lone tractor creeped along in the distance, the sound of its passing no more than a dull buzz. Toward the south she could see the thin screen of trees that separated their land from the Larsen's. Through those woods, less than a mile away, was Beaver Brook Pond, where she had spent girlhood summers, swimming and sunning herself.

Donna withdrew from the window and looked at the two ovals of mist that had formed where she had breathed onto the glass. She pulled her shirt cuff to the heel of her hand to wipe the spots away. When she was young, she always got into trouble for messing the windows, but she loved looking out her bedroom over the fields, even on the bleakest winter day. Back then, of course, her life had no complications.

But the little girl who once lived in this room had grown up to a life full of complications. As Donna looked around, breathing deeply, she wept quietly as she wondered if she could ever return to where she once had been. She ran quickly down the stairs and out the door to her car.

Driving into town, tears blurring her vision, her mind a jumble of confusion, she was sure of one thing: if she was ever going to get her life back the way it should be, it sure as hell wasn't going to be in that house or in this God-forsaken town!

# IV

Winfield didn't get back to Dale until after three o'clock. He was alone in the station for the afternoon and had used the time to catch up on his paper work. Hunched over the typewriter at his desk, he was pecking his way through one of the dozens of forms he needed to fill out about Larry's fatal accident. His concentration broke, though, when the Teletype in the front office unexpectedly chattered to life.

"Goddamn!" he hissed, glancing up at his open of: door, wishing Pam was there to take care of the report. He swirled the last gulp of cold coffee in his cup, and grimaced as he poured it down his throat. What the hell! he thought as he pushed himself away from the typewriter. It's a good chance to get a fresh cup.

He moved out by the front desk, refilled his cup, then checked the telex. The printer stopped as suddenly as it had started, and the page rolled up with a grinding of gears. He tore along the perforation and glanced at the sheet. He froze in place when his mind registered what he read.

Then he walked as fast as he could back to his office, being careful not to spill hot coffee on his hand. After scanning the report a second time, he started digging through his files until he found what he was looking for. Quickly, he dialed the police station in Holden.

"Hello. Holden Police," a woman's voice, all business, said.

"Hello, this is Officer Winfield, up in Dyer. I was wondering if Sergeant McCormick was in today."

"I'm sorry," the woman said, actually sounding as if she could barely care. "You can either leave a message or speak with the duty officer."

Winfield considered for a moment. Granted, it wouldn't take a Sherlock Holmes to figure out that the report he had just received from Haynesville, concerning a red Ford pickup truck that had been torched and dumped into the Mattawamkeag River some time during the night, was in all likelihood the same red Ford that had been boosted in Holden on Saturday morning. It probably wouldn't even be necessary to check the plates. If Sergeant McCormick didn't know this already, he'd sure as hell put it together when he came to the station on Monday.

Actually, Winfield was thinking his first phone call should have been to Detective Maloney in Westbrook. McCormick would easily recognize his stolen truck, but Maloney might not even hear about it. Winfield was sure that the torched truck was the work of the pyromaniac who, apparently, was heading north. Winfield had learned through years of police work, not to put too much faith in "hunches": a hunch and a quarter would always get him a cup of coffee at Kellerman's, but that was about all.

Still, it all seemed so right.

"No, I'll give him a call tomorrow," Winfield said. He still held the bulletin, but now he put it down on his desk and smoothed it with the flat of his hand.

"Just leave a message for him to get a make on the truck they found in Haynes-ville this morning, all right?"

"Yes, fine. Thank you for your help," the woman said, and before Winfield could say good-bye, the phone clicked in his ear and went dead.

Winfield propped his feet on his desk as he sipped his coffee and thought. The best he could do for now, he figured, was be on the alert for this pyroma-niac. Of course, it all depended on why the person, or persons, was heading north, burning buildings as he went. If it was just a lark or a spree, he could just as easily pass by or through Dyer without being noticed, especially at this time of year with so many migrant workers coming into the area to work the potato fields. The person he was looking for could be anyone.

Hell, Winfield thought, it could even be this guy Dale Harmon.'

He chuckled out loud at the idea, but one thing about police work he knew for certain: never ignore anything! Ever! Any kind of mindset or tracked think-ing could blind you from seeing what's really happening.

Thinking of Dale reminded Winfield that he hadn't yet called Franklin Rod-gers. He looked the number up in the phone book and dialed the funeral home. After a quick word or two with Maggie Sprague, Rodgers' receptionist, Franklin himself came on the line.

What Rodgers told him, after this Harmon fella had got him started think-ing, didn't satisfy him at all. Winfield asked, as politely and friendly as he could if Dale and he could view the body. He didn't want Rodgers to think this was in any way "official." Without a second's pause to consider the request, Rod-gers refused. He told Winfield that the family had insisted the funeral service be "closed-casket." In as few words as possible, Rodgers stated that his skills as a mortician were limited and, in Larry's case, completely insufficient.

Winfield thanked Rodgers, trying to make light of his polite refusal. But something didn't "feel" right to him. Dear God, help me! Not another hunch! Winfield thought. Maybe it was that Dale had been so damned intense about wanting to see the body, or maybe it was because he, quite frankly, was still shaken up by what he had found at the crash site. Whatever it was, it left a bad taste in his mouth. As soon as he hung up with Rodgers, he dialed Dale at Mrs. Appleby's and said he'd pick him up in half an hour. Then they'd both go to the funeral home in person.

Winfield finished his coffee and the report he was working on before leav-ing the station. He drove down Main Street, toward Appleby's, when he saw a young girl walk out of the Mill Store with a bag of groceries under her arm. Now usually it wouldn't have been too unusual, even the fact that Winfield didn't recognize the girl. He had never noticed her around town before, but there was something about this particular girl that drew his attention. It might have been her pale face, framed by long, dark hair, or maybe it was the back pack she had slung over her shoulders, even though she didn't look at all like your typical hiker. Or maybe it was because she wore a jacket entirely too thin for this time of year. Whatever the reason, Winfield slowed and pulled up to the curb in front of the store.

Sitting over the pumps, Sparky looked up and touched the bill of his baseball cap in greeting. Winfield waved without taking his eyes off the girl for an instant. What he didn't expect was that, as soon as she looked up and saw him, she bolted and ran across the street.

# V

Even after she had selected the food and paid for it, Tasha was still fuming that Hocker had made her go into town for supplies. Again she thought about taking off without him, leaving him in the dust, but although she hated to admit it to herself—she had actually come to depend on Hocker. At least it was nice that he never tried to screw her. It was almost refreshing compared to the guys she knew in Port Charlotte! And traveling alone, this far north, leaving Hocker was simply out of the question!

Her anger flashed into panic though, when she saw a cop pull up to the curb in front of the store just as she as leaving. All she could think was that somehow, they had found her! The cops had gotten a description of both Hocker and her, and now it was all over!

With no time to think, she reacted instinctively. She turned and ran down the sidewalk away from the cop's cruiser. If he had to screw around turning, if might give her enough of an edge to get away.

She ran in a blind panic, occasionally daring to glance over her shoulder to see how close the police car was to her. But before long she heard the long wail of the siren and, looking back, saw the flashing blue lights.

This wasn't her town. She had no idea which way to run. Her only clear thought was to lead the chase away from where Hocker was waiting. If she was bagged, she'd wait and see how bad it was going to be first. She wouldn't hesitate to turn Hocker in if she thought it would help, but it didn't make sense to tip her cards by leading the cops right to him.

Her feet went "slap-slap" on the sidewalk as she dashed past a rundown shoe store. Up ahead she saw a narrow road leading behind a church, and beyond that, thick woods. If she could just get to those woods, she'd be free, she thought.

The air in Tasha's lungs felt like flames and her arm clasping the bag of groceries started to ache furiously, but she ran for all she was worth toward the alleyway beside the church. If the wailing siren wasn't enough, a glance over her shoulder told her that the cop was close behind . . . and closing.

As she ran full speed down the alleyway, Tasha saw that the alley suddenly dead-ended!

"Oh, shit! *Shit!*" she shouted as she turned and stared as the cruiser, lights flashing like summer lightning, slowed and closed the distance between them.

Tasha's shoulders sagged, and she looked down at the ground, letting her breath out in one long, heavy sigh. The only thought in her mind was, This is it! I'm heading to jail!

The cruiser's engine rumbled like a caged beast as it came closer until Tasha was practically pinned against the hurricane fence that separated her from the woods. Hell, she thought, that might be Canada right there!

The cruiser stopped, and the siren gave one last, warbling wail before falling silent. The blue lights kept flashing as the policeman opened the car door and stepped out. His hand rested lightly on his service revolver, and there was a trace of a smile on his face as he approached her.

"Well, now, little girl," the cop said. "Where might you be going in such a hurry?"

Tasha read his shield number and vowed that, every night, she would pray for this man's gonads to dry up and blow away. The man's eyes were bright blue and made her feel as though he could look right through her.

"None of your goddamned business," Tasha said. She straightened up and met his gaze squarely.

The cop smiled and nodded. "When I see someone in town I don't recognize, someone who looks for all the world like a runaway, and as soon as she sees me she runs. Well, I sort of think that makes it my business."

"Fuck you!" Tasha shouted. She held the bag of groceries defensively to her chest, but with her free hand she flashed her middle finger at him. He looked tough, but she didn't think he was going to slug her.

Winfield laughed as he approached the girl. Either he was just getting old, or kids these days were really turning into wiseguy smart-asses. Either way, he had heard and seen it all before. It seemed as though young girls, especially, thought their foul language would shock him and then, for whatever reason, let them off.

"If you'd please step over to the cruiser, I'd like to see some identification," he said, standing in front of her, his arms folded across his chest. Between him and his cruiser, the alleyway was pretty well covered. He could snag her easily if she decided to run.

Tasha scowled, chewing on the inside of her cheek as she shifted her weight from one foot to the other. This is going badly, she thought. Her mind raced through her options and came up blank.

"It's in my back pack," she said. She bent down and placed her bag of groceries on the ground. She started to stand up, turning as she did. Then she struck out.

Winfield realized later that thinking he had seen it all before was his first mistake, but it was mistake enough. Tasha came up out of her crouch, twisting her body to one side. Before he could react, her left foot flashed out at him. The heel of her sneaker caught him squarely in the balls.

Pain shot up his spine, all the way to the base of his skull. Pinpoints of yellow light spun like fireworks through his field of vision, and the air left his lungs in a single, painful *whoosh!* Clutching his groin the source of all his pain, he fell to his knees. The sound was like a bull moose in rut when he sucked enough air into his lungs to groan.

When he looked up, he understood the rattling sounds he heard. Tasha had snatched her bag of groceries and tossed it over the fence. Now she was scrambling up over the ten foot high fence, her arms and legs a blur of motion.

At the top of the fence, she paused, one leg on either side, and looked down at the kneeling man. He coughed and sputtered while he held his groin, but she knew she had it made. It would take him a few minutes to crawl to his radio and call for help. If he doesn't draw his gun and shoot, she thought, there will be time enough to get to the woods and back to Hocker.

"Eat shit and die, pig!" she said, loud enough for the cop to hear her. Again, she extended her middle finger and jabbed it skyward.

The cop opened his mouth and tried to say something, but all that came out was a high-pitched grunt. He didn't reach for his gun and, in his blinding pain, hadn't even thought of it.

Tasha swung her other foot over onto the side of freedom and then, kicking back, dropped to the ground. Her legs hurt when she landed, but, not as bad as the cop was hurting! She collected the groceries that spilled from the bag and then, without another backward glance, turned and dashed into the woods, expecting to hear the sharp report of gunfire behind her.

Until she was concealed by the foliage, she was careful to avoid the place where Hocker was waiting. Only after she was deep in the woods did she turn and start backtracking. She intended to circle around town, find Hocker, and tell him they had to pack up their gear and run away.

What was the name of the town? she wondered as she ran. Dyer? It didn't matter. They had to be miles from here by evening!

# PART TWO

"Night falls like fire; the heavy lights run low, And as they drop, my blood and body so Shake as the flame shakes . . ." —Swinburn

# CHAPTER FOUR
## "A Visit to the Home"

## I

"I noticed you were limping coming up the walkway," Dale said as he swung open the front door. He stepped back, and Winfield forced a thin smile as he entered Mrs. Appleby's house.

"Aww — nothing serious," Winfield said gruffly. "Just bumped into the edge of my desk. Hurt my leg a bit— that's all." To add weight to his lie, he rubbed the top of his thigh.

Lil poked her head out from the kitchen and waved. "Good afternoon, Jeff. The two of you make yourselves comfortable. I'll be right in with coffee and a little something to eat.

Winfield looked at Dale and said, under his breath, "If I know Lillian Appleby, her little something will be fresh, apple pie topped with home-made vanilla ice cream."

"She fed us a supper last night that would put to shame most people's Thanksgiving meals," Dale said.

Winfield grunted as he limped painfully into the library and lowered himself into the chair nearest the fireplace. He let out a sigh of relief, grateful that those yellow spots had finally stopped spiraling in front of his eyes. It had been a while since he had been in this house, but it was exactly as he remembered it: clean, warm, homey and secure.

An awkward silence descended, broken only by the throaty tick-tock of the grandfather clock in the entryway, but that sounded natural in such a quiet room. Dale was yearning to ask Winfield what he had fond out from Rodgers at the funeral home, but he bided his time, realizing he had just met Winfield that morning, and there was no reason for either of them to implicitly trust the other. What he wanted to overcome was the edge of suspicion he felt from Winfield whenever Winfield looked at him.

While Dale considered ways to gain Winfield's trust, Lillian arrived with a large serving tray loaded with goodies. Winfield had been wrong about the apple pie, though: it was blueberry. But he had bit it right with the home-made ice cream, and there were fresh-baked chocolate chip cookies and raisin bars to make up for any disappointment he might feel about not getting apple pie.

"Some things never change," Winfield said as he snatched up one of the raisin bars. "I swear, you're trying to fatten me up for the kill, Lillian. You should see the treats she comes up with for the Congregational Church Fair." He looked at Dale and shook his head. "She practically sends the whole town into a sugar coma."

Lillian chuckled, almost spilling the coffee as she poured. "That's not true at all, Jeff," she said. "Lately I've been trying all sorts of desserts with less sugar."

Dale took the cup Lillian was holding out to him, then picked up a plate with a wedge of pie. Thick, purple juice ran from the edges as soon as he cut into it with his fork. He popped the pie into his mouth and closed his eyes with pleasure at the burst of flavor.

"I've got no complaints," he said. "We'll be leaving day after tomorrow, right after the funeral," he added, hoping mention of the funeral would prompt Winfield to fill him in on what he had found out.

Lillian sensed something was up. After all, Jeff Win-field didn't make a habit of dropping in for social calls. She put the coffee pot down on the tray and sat down. She was burning to know what was going on, but she reassured herself with the knowledge that, in a town like Dyer, word would get around soon enough.

Winfield revealed nothing the whole time they sat pleasantly chatting in the living room. He and Lillian caught up on the latest local gossip, and Dale had a chance to tell them about himself. At one point, Win-field asked where Lisa was. Dale told him she had gone downtown with his daughter Angie. The policeman stiffened.

"You have a teenage daughter?" he asked, leaning forward in his chair. His first thought was, I wonder if that's the girl I met earlier today? The one who gave me the shot to the balls!

"Yeah. Her name's Angie. She and Larry were pretty close," Dale said. "I thought it would be important for her to come to the funeral, too. You see, when her mother died, she was only four years old. I don't think she knew what was going on. I mean, all of a sudden, Mommy wasn't there any more, but she wasn't old enough to experience real grief. I talked with a psychologist about it at the time, but he said I shouldn't worry unless she started showing any unusual behavior. You know, really morbid thoughts or whatever. Anyway, I think she still has some ... I guess you'd call them hang-ups about death and feeling deserted and all. It's nothing serious, but I wanted to make sure she worked through those feelings this time."

"I can understand why," Winfield said, nodding his head. "It must he terrible, losing your mother at such a young age." His voice softened, but he kept an intense gaze focused on Dale, as though he was measuring him.

"It's terrible at any age," Lillian said. "But from what I've seen of her, she's a perfectly wonderful girl. It's obvious you've done a marvelous job raising her, Dale."

She had been avoiding the temptation of her own treats for the better part of half an hour, but now she snatched up a chocolate chip cookie and took a bite.

Dale shrugged, feeling uncomfortable under Winfield's scrutiny. "It hasn't been easy."

"Do you happen to have a picture of her?" Winfield asked. The question popped out of him, and its suddenness seemed as disruptive as a gunshot.

"What kind of father would I be if I didn't have a picture of my kid?" Dale said. He punctuated his question with a small laugh, but his hand was trembling as he hiked forward, fished his wallet from his hip pocket, and flipped it open. "This is her class picture from last year. Her hair's a lot longer now."

Winfield took the photo from Dale and looked at it for a second before handing it back to him. For all the interest he had suddenly shown in Angie, he didn't seem to care much once he saw the photo. Dale slid the picture back between the credit cards in his wallet, wondering what the hell was going on.

Winfield's mood changed after that. He and Lillian batted gossip back and forth, commenting on a dozen different situations and incidents around town. But as he sipped his coffee and ate his pie, Dale felt on edge. He was poised in his chair, leaning forward, as though waiting for a starting gun to go off. He just wanted to go with Winfield to the funeral home and ask the funeral director if he could view the body. Nothing wrong with that! A bit morbid to consider, but not wrong!

So why, he wondered, do I feel this wound-up? His stomach felt like the coil in a mattress, twisted up, ready to go *sproing* and shoot out through the tatting. Winfield's sudden shifts in mood didn't help either.

"Well, I'd better get things cleaned up in the kitchen," Lillian said. She stood up and started collecting the now-empty pie plates on the tray. In a clatter of cups, plates, and silverware, she disappeared into the kitchen, leaving the two men alone.

"Did you get a chance to talk with Rodgers?" Dale asked. He hoped that by speaking honestly about what was bothering him, he could diffuse the tension he sensed building between him and Winfield.

Winfield nodded and got up, rubbing his hands over his bulging stomach. Then he shifted his gun belt into place. Not wanting to let Harmon know too much, he decided to bend the truth a bit and not say that he had spoken with

Rodgers. "I talked with his receptionist and made it clear we'd be by this afternoon. Maybe a little later than I'd wanted to, but I 'spect he'll still be there."

"Did you?" Dale started to say, then paused, unsure exactly how to phrase his question. "Did you tell her why we'll be stopping by?"

Winfield snorted a short laugh. "Why? Hell, no! Larry ain't going anywhere." He limped as he walked over to the kitchen door and, leaning through the doorway, called out his thanks to Mrs. Appleby.

"Don't make yourself such a stranger," Lillian said, her voice muffled by distance and the loud clatter of dishes as she loaded the dishwasher. "It doesn't take an official visit for you to be welcome here."

Winfield laughed again, louder. "I'm gonna have to punch a new hole in my belt tonight 'cause of what I just ate," he replied. But his eyes weren't smiling when he glanced back at Dale. As they went out the door and down the walkway to Winfield's cruiser, they were both wondering how much Lillian Appleby knew about how official his visit had been. In the backs of their minds, they both wondered how much either of them knew what in the hell was going on!

# II

Rodgers' Funeral Home sat on a gently rising hill well back from the road, its spacious lawn and wide circular driveway— *wide enough to get quite a funeral cortege lined up,* Dale thought with a shiver—embraced on both sides by curving arms of deep forest. The funeral home itself was palatial by Aroostook County —or any—standards. Its white-pillared front with black door and shutters made it look more like the home of a successful politician than a funeral home. Sunlight slanted through the trees, etching the eaves with a golden warmth.

The theme song from "Mr. Rogers' Neighborhood" sprang into Dale's mind, but he didn't allow himself even the slightest of chuckles when it registered that the *next* cortege was going to be Larry Cole's!

As Winfield pulled to a stop and cut the cruiser's engine, Dale realized that he had been holding his breath. He let it out in a long, whistling sigh. Several tiny specks of white light zigzagged across his vision, and he forced himself to breathe evenly.

"Funeral homes always give me the willies," he said, glancing at Winfield.

Winfield opened his door and, stepping out onto the driveway, shook his head. "Can't say they're exactly my favorite place, either."

They went up the stairway to the business entrance at the side, range the bell, and stepped into the entryway. Soft organ music floated through the too-warm room, thick with the cloying smell of flowers. The furniture in the waiting room was a collection of beautifully refinished Victorian antiques: no industrial cloth and metal frames here. Everything was perfectly restored, and Dale had the fleeting thought that maybe Rodgers jacked the furniture up with embalming fluid to make it look so well-preserved.

Margaret Sprague, the receptionist, looked up and stiffened when she saw Winfield. She was a middle-aged woman with graying hair and dull brown eyes. Her complexion was pale and pasty, and Dale's first thought was that she needed to spend more time outside.

"Afternoon, Maggie," Winfield said, giving her a half-hearted salute as he strode over to her desk with Dale in tow. "I'd like you to meet Dale Harmon. He's up from Augusta for Larry Cole's funeral."

"Pleased to meet you," Maggie said, standing up and extending her hand over her desk for Dale to shake. It was surprisingly warm and firm. "I'll page Mr. Rodgers and tell him you're here."

"That won't be necessary," a voice, deep and resonant said from behind. Maggie and Dale both were startled, but Winfield calmly turned around as the funeral director came over to them from the hallway door.

He was at least six feet tall and dressed in a beautifully tailored blue suit with matching dotted tie and handkerchief. His light brown hair was combed straight back, exposing a wide, pale forehead. When he spoke, his teeth appeared to be slightly too large for his mouth, and his thin lips added to the illusion.

"Nice to see you, Jeff," Rodgers said, extending his hand to the policeman. Then turning to Dale, he said, "I'm Franklin Rodgers."

"Dale Harmon," Dale managed to say, even though his throat felt lined with sandpaper.

His first impression of Rodgers was that his handshake was just what a funeral director's should be: cool and moist, a gentle grip, but with a hint of restrained strength that made his fingers vibrate with energy. Hell! Dale thought, trying desperately to keep at bay the memories of the last time he had dealt with a funeral director when Natalie had died. You'd have to be strong to work with corpses every day.

"Officer Winfield spoke with me earlier and said you'd be coming over," Rodgers said, his voice low and soothing.

Dale glanced at Winfield. His raised eyebrows silently asked, "Why didn't you say so?"

"I must tell you how sorry 1 am about Larry's un- timely death," Rodgers said. "I've been in this business for . . . going on ten years, now, and I still can't accept it when the young die. So tragic ... so tragic."

Then Dale got his second clear impression of Franklin Rodgers. It hit him so fast and so hard, he was surprised it didn't register like a flashing neon sign on his face. Right from the moment Dale had first seen Rodgers. Walking toward them from the darkened hall doorway, there had been something . . . something *weird* about his looks. It wasn't just his pale, thin face, or the shadows from the dimly lit room, or the atmosphere of gloom and mourning that wrapped around him like a dark cloak. It was something about his eyes.

... His *eyes!*

It was damned near impossible for Dale to focus on Rodgers' face until he realized what it was: the man's right eye was absolutely normal, a perfectly average brown eye, but his left eye looked damaged. The white had a sickly yellowish tinge; the iris was pale blue, like a chip of ice and the pupil was almost fully dilated, a swelling black hole that glistened so brightly, Dale was convinced that, up close, it would reflect the room like highly polished onyx.

"Please," Rodgers said, stepping to one side and directing Winfield and Dale down the hallway.

At the far end, a door stood ajar, and they could see Rodgers' office. Doors on both sides opened onto large rooms with dark wood paneling. Dale felt a sudden dash of chills when he saw that the room to the left was "occupied." Wall sconces lit with dim, flame-shaped light bulbs illuminated a mound of floral arrangements that surrounded a coffin. The coffin lid was open, and an elderly woman lay with her hands folded across her chest. The organ music in the room was just a notch louder, and the smell of the flowers was almost choking.

Dale pushed aside the thought that beneath those folded hands, stuffed into the cavity of that old woman's chest, was her brain, removed from her skull and placed there by Rodgers, just as artificially as the pink flush on her cheeks and the plastic cups that held firm the rounded edges of her closed eyelids. Dale didn't know what they did with the removed eyeballs. They were probably stuffed into her chest along with her brain. He shivered, remembering how, during Natalie's funeral service, she had looked merely asleep and he had been *positive* he had seen her chest heave up and down as she breathed.

She's not dead! his mind had screamed, time and time again throughout the service and for weeks after that. She isn't really dead!

But he knew it was nothing more than an illusion and a credit to the mortician's art. He wished he didn't have to think about it now as he silently followed Winfield and Rodgers into the office. Once he and Winfield were comfortably seated in a plush leather chair, Rodgers shut the door and took his seat at his desk.

"To get directly to the point, I understand, Mr. Harmon, you have been shall we say concerned about Mr. Cole's body since the night of the accident."

Dale shifted nervously in the chair. When he glanced at Winfield and saw no support in his expression, he cleared his throat and said, "You have to understand, Mr. Rodgers — "

"Won't you be my neighbor?" Indeed! Dale was angry with himself for allowing such a sick parallel to enter his mind.

"Larry Cole and I were close friends. The shock of his death has been . . ." His voice trailed off, and he swallowed with difficulty.

In his line of work, Rodgers must face people who, out of grief and anguish, are unable to speak. He quickly rose and filled a cone-shaped paper cup with water from a cooler and handed it to Dale with a sympathetic nod.

"Thanks," Dale said, still not quite wanting--or daring—to look squarely at Rodgers' strange eye. He quickly drained the cup before it became a soggy mess in his hand, took a deep breath and continued.

"I went to visit Larry's mother last night, you see, and she, well, actually, Roberta, her sister, expressed some concern that they hadn't been allowed to view the body. You must understand that, in order to get through the grief surrounding a death, it is sometimes necessary actually to see the body. That's part of the healing process: to see and verify that a person is really—gone."

"I understand your concern entirely, Mr. Harmon," Rodgers said. "And I understand Mildred Cole's depth of grief, perhaps more than you do. Now, you may not have spoken with Mildred directly, but I have, and I can assure you of a couple of things. Officer Winfield was the policeman on the scene that night. I'm sure he's mentioned the condition of Mr. Cole to you."

Dale nodded, wondering why water coolers always used such damned small cups. His throat still felt constricted, and he still didn't dare to look directly at Rodgers' dilated pupil.

"After receiving the body—well, in cases such as this, it is my determination whether or not I could possibly allow the next of kin to see the body. You're correct on one point, Mr. Harmon. In most situations, viewing the body is a necessary part of the healing process. But think of the other side of it. Imagine if you will, as in Larry Cole's case, that the body is severely mutilated in an accident. It not only does not help the grieving process. It can destroy it if a close friend or relative should see the deceased in such a mutilated condition."

Dale felt chills like knife blades of ice run up and down his spine. He realized Rodgers was talking about his best friend, Larry, but all the while Dale's mind was picturing Natalie lying in a closed casket somewhere in the basement of this funeral home, her twisted and torn flesh as cold as stone.

"In such cases," Rodgers said, nodding in Winfield's direction, "I, along with the approval of the police, will not allow the family to see the deceased. The psychological damage could be much worse than any amount of grief could inflict."

"Were you in on this decision?" Dale asked, turning to Winfield. If he had been, Dale thought, then why the hell was he going along with all of this with him?

Before Winfield could speak, Rodgers said, "No, he wasn't." His voice maintained an even strength, but the way he responded surprised Dale and even seemed to surprise Winfield. "In fact, his mother requested the closed casket, based on my advice. I would suspect what we have here is simply a case of misunderstanding. Perhaps, in her grief, she's forgotten her original request. More likely, her sister is projecting some of her own anxiety into the situation. In any event, it was Mildred Cole who specifically asked that Larry's coffin be closed."

Dale was disappointed that he didn't gain even a small bit of ground in this confrontation. Oh, yes! It was a confrontation, all right. He didn't know all the

dynamics of the situation. Hell, he'd probably have to live in Dyer for years before he picked up on all the subtle power structures. But there was *something* going on here. If it didn't include the death of his best friend, he would just let it
all drop. But it did include Larry. Dale realized that as soon as he had entered
the Rodgers' Funeral Home, he had been on the defensive—

Why? he wondered. What in the sweet name of Christ was going on here?

Crumpling the paper cup, Dale twisted in his chair and shot the cup toward
the plastic-lined wastebasket beside the cooler. Good for two! he thought when
the cup hit the mark. Then, folding his hands together, he leaned forward and
looked directly at Rodgers.

*Dilated pupil be damned!*

"I guess, then, for my own satisfaction, I want to ask you if I could see
Larry's body before the funeral," Dale said. He tried to keep his voice as low
and even as Rodgers'. "Even if I can't reassure Mrs. Cole about it, I'd like to
know that, if nothing else, I've seen him."

"I'm sorry, Mr. Harmon, but I can't allow that," Rodgers said. The firm control in his voice slipped just a bit, and it looked as though his pupil dilated even
further, leaving just the tiniest ring of surrounding blue.

"I'm afraid I don't understand why not," Dale said softly.

He glanced again at Winfield, wishing he, too, would jump in and press the
attack. Yes! Dale thought, attack is the right word! But Winfield sat there,
slouched in his chair, silently regarding the toe of his shoe as he stroked his
cheek with one hand. The other hand rested on his gun belt, but Dale didn't
think that was significant. The attack couldn't possibly get that serious!

"I can spare you perhaps some possibly complicated explanations and state
simply that, because you are not the next of kin, you have no legal right to view
the body." Rodgers held his hands out toward Dale, as if to plead with him to
see reason, but there was a harsh, commanding tension in him that suggested
power beyond such a simple thing as being in control in the security of his own
office.

It's his damned eye! Dale thought. Don't let something like that get to you!

"I just don't understand your hesitation," Dale said. He meant to continue,
but Rodgers cut him off sharply.

"I'm not hesitating, Mr. Harmon. I'm refusing your request, flat out." He
shifted back in his chair and prepared to stand up, thus signaling that their conversation was concluded.

Dale was looking for support from Winfield, but the policeman appeared to
be satisfied. He was already up and heading toward the door.

The first thought in Dale's mind was to investigate the possible legal implica-
tions here; he'd like to look up a lawyer in town and see if there was any legal
way he could demand to see Larry's body. What would a lawyer ask for? Prob-
able cause or some such nonsense. Dale didn't have any concrete evidence to

suspect Rodgers except his unnerving left eye. But he was convinced that there was something very strange about all of this.

"Good day, Mr. Harmon," Rodgers said, extending his hand over the desk and giving Dale's another cold, moist handshake. "Officer Winfield . . ."

Dale followed Winfield down the hallway, back to the entryway, where Maggie Sprague sat, crocheting at her desk. Dale passed up the opportunity to ask if business was slow this time of year, and with a friendly smile and nod, went out into the parking lot, where Winfield waited beside the cruiser.

"Well, there you have it," Winfield said once they were sitting in the car. He started it up by giving the gas a few heavy pumps. "You've met Mr. Franklin Rodgers. What do you think?"

Dale regarded the policeman for several seconds before answering. He couldn't understand why he would bother to take him out here in the first place, and then, once he insisted on viewing the body, why Winfield wouldn't offer even a word of support.

Bottom line, Dale thought, Winfield probably doesn't give a shit! He's the guy, remember, who had to scrape Larry up off the road. Probably a good chance he just didn't want to see anything to remind him of that night.

Let it drop, a voice whispered in his mind. This is just your half-assed way of not admitting that Larry's dead!

"I don't know what I think about him," Dale said, squinting as he looked at Winfield, desperately trying to read him. One thing you had to say about Winfield, though—he was a damned good cop. He never let what he was thinking show on his face. The man certainly didn't need a pair of mirrored shades!

Winfield stretched out his arm and glanced at his wristwatch. "Well, I'll tell you what I think," he said as he turned the key and started up the engine. "I think it's damned close enough to the end of my shift so I can call it a day."

The driveway was big enough to turn around by making a wide circle before pulling onto Mayall Road. As they drove slowly toward Main Street, he whistled an off-key tune between his teeth and casually glanced at the scenery, apparently without a care in the world.

When they stopped in front of Appleby's, Dale hesitated before getting out. He figured he should just say "thank you," get out, go up to the house, and forget all about it until the funeral tomorrow afternoon.

Let it drop, the voice in his mind said again. Let it go! Larry's dead, and that's that!

"Tell you what," Winfield said. "Give me 'bout an hour to go back to the station and clean up a few things. I'll meet you downstairs at Kellerman's at six o'clock. All right?"

Dale nodded his tentative agreement, but he couldn't help but wonder at the sudden change in attitude.

"Good," Winfield said, nodding as Dale got out of the cruiser. "Maybe we can split a pizza and beer. You'll gain too much weight if you eat at Lillian's every night, anyway."

"Sounds good," Dale said, leaning in through the open door. "Should I bring Angie along?"

Winfield considered that for a moment before shaking his head. "No, I don't think so." His voice was hushed and hesitant. "You know, I'll tell yah. Something about Rodgers' attitude today really got to me. Something stinks and stinks *bad!*"

He revved the engine, and Dale shut the cruiser door, backing away as Winfield pulled out onto Main Street and left. Then he went quickly up the walkway to the house. He had time for a long, hot shower before meeting Winfield at Kellerman's, and that's what he needed because he felt a bone-deep chill that had nothing to do with the oncoming autumn.

# III

As soon as Dale and Winfield left his office, Rodgers went over to his door and shut it. His pale hand trembled as he turned the bolt to lock the door. His forehead was slick with sweat, and he allowed himself a moment to lean it against the cool, polished wood. His breathing came in shallow gulps, as if he were drinking water.

He stood this way for several seconds, then straightened up and walked back to his desk. His leather chair creaked under his weight as he sat down and picked up the telephone. He punched the intercom button, and Maggie answered.

"Yes, sir?"

After a deep, shuddering breath, Rodgers said softly, "I have a few phone calls to make. See that I'm not disturbed."

"Yes, sir," Maggie replied, and the line went dead.

First things first, Rodgers thought, and then said it aloud. "First things first."

Keeping the receiver to his ear, he dialed a number from memory, waited for four rings until a voice on the other end said, "Hello?"

"Higgins?" Rodgers said. That was all.

That was enough, though, because the voice at the other end suddenly tightened. "Yes, sir. What can I do for you?"

"It's what I can do for you," Rodgers said. "I have Mr. Cole almost ready for you."

"Have there been any problems?" the man named Higgins asked. His voice sounded hesitant and filled with concern. "The last time, there were a few complications that I-"

Rodgers laughed softly, cutting him off. "Nothing I can't take care of at this end."

"Well, you know what happened last time."

"What happened last time was merely a fluke," Rodgers snapped. His warm breath moistened the receiver mouthpiece. "It was a simple mistake of dosage amounts that will not happen again."

"I hope not, sir," Higgins said. "It wouldn't pay to — "

"You just let me handle the details on this end, all right?" Rodgers said. "What happens once I deliver is not my concern. It's yours, correct?"

"Yes, but I . . ."

"But you nothing!" Rodgers shouted, cupping his hand over the receiver in case Maggie had gotten curious and was outside his door, listening. Not likely, but it paid to be careful. "I told you he'll be ready by tomorrow night."

"Tomorrow?" Higgins said, "You told me it would be tonight!"

Rodgers sighed, as though he was carrying the weight of the world. "The funeral isn't until tomorrow, so now I'm telling you—tomorrow night!" '

The last thing he needed, he thought, was to let Higgins know about the visit he had had this afternoon. Sure, Winfield had sat there, silent and stupid as a stone the whole time, but just the fact that he had been by with that man Harmon. It didn't bode well. There was no sense taking any risks. He just wanted to play it safe. C.Y.A., as they say: "Cover your ass!"

"Then tomorrow night it will be," Higgins said. There was disappointment in his voice, but also a note of resignation.

"Any time after dark," Rodgers said, and without another word, he cut the connection off by gently cradling the receiver. After a few seconds of staring at the phone, quietly enjoying the panic and anger he knew Higgins was feeling, he leaned back in his chair, slid his hand into his pants pocket, and withdrew his key chain. He selected a small, flat key, then unlocked and pulled open the top middle drawer of his desk.

Reaching inside, he found the small wooden box at the back of the drawer. The box was covered with tiny carved figures. Only close examination would reveal that the figures were something straight out of a vision of Dante's Inferno or a Bosch painting. Dozens of nude men and women were tangled up in grotesque postures that suggested either bizarre sexual positions or contortions of extreme physical agony. Ecstasy or suffering, they're always in the eye of the beholder.

The trembling in his hands intensified as Rodgers fumbled for another, smaller key on his key ring to unlock the little hasp lock on the box. The box contained a single vial half-filled with a dark liquid. The bottle was capped with the rubber end of an eyedropper. Rodgers leaned back in his chair and, for the first time since Winfield and Dale had left, breathed evenly and deeply.

Holding the bottle up to the light and giving it a quick shake, he inspected the thick liquid, so darkly purple it actually looked black. He felt the corners of his mouth twitch into something close to a smile as, first, he loosened the cap and then gave the rubber bulb a couple of firm squeezes to fill the dropper completely with liquid. After removing the dropper, he leaned his headway back and brought it over his left eye. He had done this so many times, now, he didn't need to hold his eye open. He stared blankly at the ceiling as he brought the dropper closer until it was just above his eye. Then, with a sudden tensing of his fingers, he squeezed the bulb.

The liquid spurted out in a thick glob that landed in the center of Rodgers' pupil. For an instant, a chill like the stab of a metallic sliver jabbed his eye. Nerve impulses shot along his optic nerve and were interpreted by his brain as "vision." Fiery-edged shapes shot across his retina, but then, as a deep warmth spread out, gradually embracing the whole of his eye, the visual impulses faded, leaving only dim, glowing after-images.

As always, Rodgers became intensely aware of the roundness of his eye as the liquid generated heat that flowed into veins and capillaries. He was still leaning back, still staring up at the ceiling of his office, as he anticipated what would come next. His pupil, he knew, was now dilated wide enough to receive light. Quickly, he screwed the cap back on the bottle and put it down on his desk top. No sense spilling it by mistake, he thought as his anticipation spiraled upward.

Then it happened. The textured ceiling tiles began to sparkle like fresh-fallen snow seen in the glare of direct sunlight. Winking points of light exploded into watery concentric circles as the drug entered his system. The warmth that had embraced his left eye now spread out long, dark fingers that reached out and massaged every convoluted fold of his brain, the fingers pulsed with warm, dark strength as they reached deep inside his brain.

"Eyes! The windows of the soul," Rodgers said, his voice a papery rattle in his throat. A low laughter rumbled in his chest as the light patterns on the ceilings intensified, exploding into shimmering rainbow sprays. On the edge of his awareness, he heard distant and muffled voices.

What he saw and heard, Rodgers knew, was merely the electrical impulses traveling along his optic nerve to his brain. But there was more. What was really happening was that the liquid, shot into one eye, gave him a special kind of vision. It was a vision that allowed him actually to see and hear things from other worlds and other dimensions.

In the years since he had first discovered this liquid and its variations, he had tried many experiments, some successful, some not. At least the unsuccessful ones hadn't been done on himself! One of the simplest experiments compared the vision of each eye, once immediately after he had "taken a squirt" (as he called it) and then after the drug had lost its intense effects. The physical discoloration of the left pupil didn't surprise him in the least, and he learned to accept it as the price he paid for his "visions."

Obviously the dilated pupil made it very difficult to be in direct sunlight without sunglasses. That was why he preferred to have the funeral home so dimly lit all of the time. Looking directly at merely a candle flame could be painful, but after years of practice, he had gotten used to hiding the pain sudden, direct light caused his left eye.

And there was the reverse side of things that made it all worthwhile. The pupil of the left eye was permanently open, but so, also, was his night vision vastly improved. As a matter of fact, Rodgers suspected the changes had occurred so slowly over so many years he didn't really appreciate how good his night vision was. When he thought about it, he believed he could see at night almost as well as any cat or owl.

In a real sense the drug opened up a new world to him. He could see in two different worlds, and that was the basis of all his other experiments with this liquid. Years ago, when he first encountered the liquid as a Harvard graduate student studying botany in Haiti, he had suspected the potential for this liquid: taken in proper dosages, it could open up whole new dimensions of awareness.

As the drug flowed through his system, he chuckled again, loudly, not caring now if Maggie Sprague or anyone heard him. Christ! he thought, his mind suddenly feeling like a honed razor, Maggie was such a tight-assed bitch! What she needed was a squirt of this!

"Right up the old cooze!" he said aloud, and his laughter got even louder as colors and lights pinwheeled through his brain. The voices he heard grew louder and louder, until he could understand what they were saying in their low, sing-song chant. He closed his eyes and leaned back, listening and watching while the liquid carried him far, far away . . .

# IV

"It stinks," Winfield said, sitting back from the table and sipping on his beer. "It stinks to high heaven."

Winfield off-duty, Dale thought, looked exactly like Winfield on-duty. Only the uniform had changed. He still kept his thoughts and feelings locked tightly inside him. Dale had his own lingering doubts because of what had occurred at the funeral home, but he realized Win-field wouldn't take him fully into his confidence until he trusted him. Until that time, Dale would have to trust what Winfield said and take it as the truth.

Kellerman's on an early Sunday evening was practically deserted. Five regulars, who had all greeted Winfield by his first name, were gathered around the pool table at the back of the restaurant exchanging shots. An Emmylou Harris tearjerker drifted from the jukebox, whose only concessions to rock were a few Beatles oldies and the latest from Bruce Springsteen. If you favored country-western or Fifties rock, it was a gold mine.

The pizza, Dale discovered, was good, but all you could get on tap was Budweiser. It would take a while for Sam Adams beer to make inroads up here. All that remained on the paper plate in front of them were a few uneaten crusts—what Angie used to call "pizza bones" when she was little.

"I can't really say I'm glad to hear you say that," Dale said, after glancing over his shoulder to make sure he wouldn't be overheard by the pool players. "But I guess I am. I think it stinks, too."

Winfield took another sip of beer and sat back, rubbing his hand under his nose as he shook his head.

"So," he said, "what do you figure's going on?"

Dale considered the question then shrugged. "This is your town, not mine. Until this afternoon, I'd never heard of Franklin Rodgers. My first reaction was that he's . . . it's like he's hiding something."

"I just can't figure it," Winfield said.

Dale took a swig of beer. "Well then, maybe you can start by telling me what you know about Rodgers. Maybe I can figure out some angle that doesn't make sense until we put together what we've got."

"There's not much to tell about Rodgers. Not really."

"Is he from around here?" Dale asked. "Meeting him today, I'd say he fits in here about as well as you or I would in Harlem."

"Naw." Winfield drank some more. He picked up a small piece of pizza crust, but then dropped it back on the plate. "He moved into town about ten years ago. maybe fifteen. Said he was from Massachusetts."

"How'd he get started in the undertaking business?"

It was Winfield's turn to shrug. "He took over the funeral home from Bill Porter's family, right after Bill died. 'S far as I know, he was an undertaker in Massachusetts. I know he's got a Ph.D. in botany from Harvard. You might have noticed it hanging on the wall in his office."

"No I didn't," Dale said. "But what the hell is a botanist doing running a funeral home?"

Winfield snorted with laughter when he thought of a reply. "Maybe it helps him pick the right flowers for the service," he said. "How does *anyone* become an undertaker? It ain't exactly the kind of job you want your kid to say he wants to be when he grows up, is it? I'd start worrying if he did! Christ, Bill Porter used to run the funeral home and deliver oil. Least that's what he did when he was first starting out."

"Yeah," Dale said, "I hate to sound so damned narrow-minded about this, but Rodgers seems so perfect for the job. He looks like a goddamned corpse himself."

"And that eye of his!" Winfield said, drawing out the last word as he leaned forward.

Dale was shaking his head, but he glanced over at the pool table when there was a sudden explosion of laughter. Emmylou had been replaced by Waylon Jennings on the jukebox.

"That left eye sure does make it hard to look straight at him," Dale said. "I think he uses that to intimidate people. It is pretty unnerving, but I don't think that's all that's weird about him. There's more, maybe a lot more."

Winfield drank some more, and smacking his lips, said, "Nothing I've noticed until today. Maybe there ain't anything else. I've just been listening to you too much. You've got to expect that someone who goes in for that line of work has got to be typecast. Maybe you're just seeing all of this because of what happened to Larry."

Dale took a sip of beer and stared at the wall for a few seconds, letting his thoughts tumble over one another. He knew Winfield might be right. Hell, denial was a very real, a very human response to the death of someone close to you. He knew it was possible that he might be blaming Rodgers for what happened to Larry.

Could it be something as simple as that? he wondered.

In Rodgers' office, Dale had become convinced that Rodgers was hiding something. Just the way he had denied Mildred's request to see her son's body, ignoring what he said about her request for a closed casket and the way he had so cleanly cut off, on legal grounds, Dale's request seemed almost as if he wanted *to keep the body for himself!*

The words jumped into Dale's mind, and when they did, he couldn't repress the shiver that raced up his spine to the base of his skull.

"Maybe that's where we should start," he said. "We should start by going out to the accident site. Maybe there's something there that will give us a clue to what's going on."

Winfield laughed and shook his head. "Now you're starting to sound like one of the Hardy Boys," he said. "There aren't any clues to dig up. Look, Larry Cole is dead, and that's final! I was the guy who pulled his body out of the wreck. Why can't you just let it drop?"

Dale heaved a shuddering sigh and sank back against his chair. He took a sip of beer, but it was warm and flat.

Winfield's right, he thought. Let it drop for Christ's sake! Go to the funeral. Bury Larry. Then take Angie back to Thomaston and try to go on living!

"Will you show me where the accident happened?" Dale asked, even though his better judgment was telling him to shut up, order another beer and lighten up. Let it drop!

Winfield regarded him silently for a moment, trying to fathom him. Since his initial meeting with Dale this morning until now, he still couldn't quite nail him down. He didn't think Dale was hiding anything. He *certainly* didn't suspect Dale was the pyromaniac mentioned in the telex; but he had a driven quality about him. It was a pushiness that just wouldn't quit. In spite of that, though,

Winfield genuinely liked this guy. If only he would let all this nonsense about seeing Larry's body drop!

"I don't really have time to do something like that," Winfield said after a moment's consideration. What he wanted to say was that, as the policeman on the scene, he didn't think he had the right to start poking around. The accident report had been filed, the death certificate was filled out and right after the gravediggers shoveled in a few scoops of dirt, that would be that.

"Could you at least tell me where it happened? I'd like to go out there by myself," Dale said. "I want to see where it happened."

"No problem," Winfield said. He would have been surprised if Dale hadn't asked that question. "Head south on 2A. About four miles out of town there's a bend in the road, a sharp right. Around here, it's called Casey's Curve."

"Why's that?"

"On the side of the road is a large boulder. The high school kids spray painted it with all sorts of shit. My favorite's the big skull and crossbones. Anyway, back in the sixties, during a blizzard, a school bus driver named Henry Casey drove the basketball team from Houlton straight into that rock one night heading for a game in Mattawamkeag. Seventeen kids and the driver died instantly. Quite a few of the others were hurtin' troopers for a long time."

"If I'm not mistaken," Dale said, "that's one of the stretches of roads Larry was surveying. The state was going to improve that road."

"It's a killer, all right," Winfield said. "Casey isn't the only one to make an acquaintance with that boulder."

"Kind of ironic, though, don't you think?" Dale said. "Larry is killed on the same road he's checking out so there won't be as many accidents."

Winfield snorted and signaled for two more beers. The waitress nodded and went to the tap to fill the mugs.

"As I was saying, Larry didn't quite make the turn. His car glanced off the boulder and overturned several times. You can see where it went into the woods. Plowed quite a path through the brush."

Dale looked up when the waitress came over and put the beers on the table. "You all done with this?" she asked as she picked up the paper plate with the remains of the pizza.

Winfield nodded and watched her as she walked away without another word, carrying the plates and their empty beer mugs.

"You don't suspect that Larry had been drinking or anything, do you?" Dale asked. "I know he didn't do any drugs."

Winfield was shaking his head. "No. They did an autopsy, and there was no alcohol or drugs found in his blood. 'S far as we could determine, it was a simple case of the turn coming up too fast. He was driving late at night, and maybe wasn't as alert as he should have been. He just didn't react in time."

"Jesus," Dale said, sipping from his fresh beer.

"Hey!" Winfield suddenly shouted. He stood up and waved his arm over his head. Dale looked and saw a young woman standing in the doorway. She was casually dressed in a plaid shirt and faded jeans. Her eyes were lively and bright and they got even brighter when she saw who was waving to her.

"A good friend of mine," Winfield said to Dale. "I haven't seen her in years." Then Winfield shouted, "Hey! Donna. C'mon over!" His smile widened as the woman started toward their table. Dale watched the men stop their pool game long enough to check her out, giving each other little nudges.

"How you doing, Jeff?" the woman said. She gave Winfield a quick hug and a kiss on the cheek. Her smile exposed a row of wide teeth, and Dale noticed that, up close, her blue eyes looked warm and friendly.

"Have a seat. Have a seat," Winfield said as he sat back down and scooted over to make room for her at the table. "I heard you were back in town and figured it was just a matter of time before I saw you."

"I knew I'd find you here if you were off-duty," the woman said. She followed with a laugh that immediately enchanted Dale.

"Dale Harmon," Winfield said, holding his hands up in the air, "I'd like you to meet one of my best friends and secret lover," he said with a wink. "Donna LaPierre. Donna, this is Dale."

"Pleased to meet you," Donna said, nodding her head slightly and then taking a long, steady look at Dale. The look made him uncomfortable.

"Same here," Dale said. His hand circled his beer glass while his thumb rubbed away the condensation. He found it difficult to make eye contact with Donna because he wondered if Winfield had really meant it about her being his "secret lover." Probably not, he figured, because of the age difference. What business was it of his anyway? "So," Donna said, once she was settled in her seat and lit a cigarette, "What in God's name brings you to a town like Dyer, Mr. Harmon? I still have family and friends — "

"And lovers," Winfield added, chuckling like a lecher.

Donna shook her head, making it obvious Winfield was making a joke. "Right. And lovers. What's your excuse, Mr. Harmon?"

"Call me Dale."

"All right, Dale. What are you doing in a backwater town like Dyer if you don't mind my asking." She rolled the tip of her cigarette in the ashtray; then, after studying it for a second, she ground it out, her face wrinkling with distaste.

"Actually," Dale said, feeling his fingers tighten on the beer glass, "I came here for the funeral of a friend of mine, Larry Cole."

Donna's smile melted, and her eyes dropped. "Oh, yeah. Wasn't that horrible?"

"Hey, let's not get all bummed out, okay? It's great to see you," Winfield said, trying desperately to lighten the mood at the table. But for the rest of the evening, while the three of them drank at Kellerman's, things were never the same after Dale mentioned his reason for coming to Dyer.

# V

It took Tasha longer than she thought it should to make her way back to where Hocker was supposed to be waiting. By the time she got there, she was covered with scratches and bruises from stomping through the woods. Her hair was a tangled mess, and some thorns had ripped a hole in her shorts. The bag of groceries was ripped, spilling everything onto the ground for a second time, but by using the front of her shirt as a temporary basket, she had made it back just as the sun was setting. She wasn't sure if she was happy or pissed to see that Hocker wasn't anywhere around.

"It Goddamn figures," she hissed as she knelt down and let the groceries tumble to the ground. Everything was dented and squished, but edible except for the store-bought bread. But what could you expect from a loaf of bread that could be squeezed into a ball the size of a marble?

She found Hocker's backpack where he had stowed it and took the time to divide the food up and portion it out, making sure to put the heavier cans into Hocker's pack. Then, brushing her knees, she stood up and looked around.

The woods were silent, perhaps a bit *too* silent, she thought as she scanned as far as she could see in the fading light. This late in the season, there weren't many insects chirring in the dusk. The only sound was a low, gusty wind that rattled the dead and dying leaves on the ground and the branches overhead. Tasha shivered, then opened her backpack, took out her sweater and put it on.

"Hock?" she called out, more whisper than shout.

The wind moaned, sending a spray of leaves swirling like a flurry of bats against the pale sky. Off to the east, the fat, round face of a nearly full moon was cross-hatched by the tree branches that looked like scars across the golden disk.

"Hey! Hocker!" she called, a bit louder as she began pacing back and forth in the small clearing.

She tried not to let herself think what she was thinking, but she couldn't keep the thoughts at bay. The cops got him, her mind whispered, and the gusting wind seemed almost to laugh. After what happened down- town, they came looking for her and found Hocker. They've hauled him off to jail, and right now they're running a check on him and finding out about the stolen truck, and the old man . . .

"Oh, shit," she hissed, pacing faster and rubbing her hands over her shoulders to fight the chill. "Oh, *shit!*"

Of course, she wasn't worried about what had happened to Hocker so much as she wondered what the hell she was going to do! She realized she didn't have the slightest idea how to build a campfire. And even if she did, it was already too dark to collect enough wood and get the tent pitched. So what was she going to do, sleep out under the stars? Alone? She wished that she had stayed in town, leaving Hocker on his own. She wondered why she kept coming back to him. It plain didn't make sense!

"Come on, you prick!" Tasha hissed as she stamped her feet on the ground. "Where the fuck are you?"

"Right here," said a voice, so suddenly she couldn't even tell from which direction it came. She wheeled around and raised her fists high for protection. The darkening woods filled with a deep, rumbling laughter. Tasha felt pressure build in her bladder. She wasn't even sure that it was Hocker.

"Who's there?" she yelled. Her voice echoed back. "I'm warning you. I've got a gun!"

The laughter came again in a swelling wave, then it abruptly stopped. The bushes behind her rustled and a figure stepped out into the clearing.

"You asshole!" she yelled as soon as she recognized who it was. "What the hell are you doing sneaking up on me like that?"

Hocker raised a wad of spit from his throat and shot it off into the woods. "I ain't sneaking up on you, you jerk," he said. "And I heard what you called me: *come on, you prick!* Nice talk for a girl!"

"I was getting scared," Tasha said, letting her voice trail off into a whine. "And I ... I had a little trouble in town."

Hocker rummaged through the backpacks and was emptying the food she had carefully stocked away. He grunted and rammed the canned goods back into the packs.

"The grub looks like you used it for a football," he said angrily.

"That was part of the trouble I had," Tasha said, looking down at the ground. "I had a run-in with the cops."

She was surprised that he didn't freak out right away. His first response was simply to raise another ball of spit, and this one he sent flying in her direction. It plopped on the ground in front of her.

"You're shittin' me," he said, slowly rising from a crouch and taking a step toward her. In the dusk, she could see his fists clench tightly at his sides.

"I'm not," she answered. "A cop chased me down this alleyway. I kicked him in the balls to get away. And I made sure it looked like I was heading south. If they decide to come after us, they'll start looking in the wrong direction."

Hocker snorted. "Good thinking. But it was pretty damned stupid to get caught in the first place."

"He saw me and started following me. I did what I had to do to get away. First thing in the morning, we've gotta get as far away from here as we can."

Hocker shook his head viciously. "No way! Not yet. I found a place where we can hole up for a while."

It was Tasha's turn to shake her head. "No way! That cop would recognize me in a second. There's no way I wanna be arrested for assaulting a police officer."

"That's the least of our fuckin' worries," Hocker said. "But wait'll you see this place. It's a farmhouse! You're gonna love it! Come on. Follow me. I'll show you where it is now."

"In the dark?" Tasha said, not willing to budge an inch. "We'll never find our way back here."

Hocker went over to the packs, grabbed Tasha's, and slung it at her. It slammed into her ankles, sending a jolt of pain up to her knees. He hoisted his onto his back and said, "Come on, then. For tonight, we'll sleep in the woods out behind the house to make sure no one lives there. We'll take up occupancy tomorrow morning."

Tasha shook her head as she bent over and picked up the pack. "Is it far?" she asked, knowing that, once his mind was made up, there was no way to get him to change it. "I've been walking all goddamned afternoon. My legs are useless."

"Over the river and through the woods," Hocker sang, his voice flat and off-key. He turned the words into a whistle as he started off into the darkened forest. His heavy footsteps rustled leaves and snapped branches as he went.

Tasha knew she'd spend the night alone if she hesitated, so she lit out after him. His shrill whistle led her on through the darkness. Branches slapped her in the face and pulled at her jacket sleeves as she went, but she knew it was useless to complain.

"You're goddamned crazy, you know that?" she said at one point.

From up ahead, Hocker suddenly stopped whistling and shouted, as loud as he could, "You're goddamned right I am! I'm crazy as hell!"

# VI

"Well," Donna said, letting amusement warble her voice, "that about does it. You've seen all the night life Dyer, Maine, has to offer."

She and Dale were sitting in Dale's car, parked at the top of the hill in Brook Lawn Cemetery. It was the best place around town she knew to go "parking." Right now, there were no other cars there. They joked about how kids these days probably couldn't be bothered by the discomfort of trying to get a little sex in the backseat of their car. Say good-bye to a great American tradition lost because of small, imported cars!

The cemetery hill overlooked the whole town. Over the cityscape of tombstones, they saw the lighted windows of homes, most of which flickered with the pulsating light of a television. A fat, round moon was rising in the east, casting long shadows from the tombstones. Stars sprinkled the sky, and for the first time in a long time, Dale noticed how the Milky Way actually resembled a streak of milk in the sky.

For a while they played the radio, but every signal was weak. The radio rose and faded with an irritating static, so they turned it off and talked. To cut the chill in the air, Dale kept starting up the car and turning on the heater for short bursts. Donna opened her side window a crack before lighting a cigarette but only smoked half of it before crushing it out. Dale told her she should try to limit her smoking; for the first time in a long time, he felt tempted to start smoking again.

What they talked about ranged over a whole variety of subjects, starting with what they remembered about Larry Cole and then leading around to aspects of their own lives. After a while, both of them found they were revealing pieces of their lives they normally kept concealed.

Dale told Donna about Natalie's death, and about the turmoil and questions and doubts that nagged at him over the years, and about how he had finally got over his grief. When Donna asked him point-blank if he had started dating yet, he told her no. She fell silent, finding it unnecessary to point out that his grieving wouldn't truly be over until he started dating again. He didn't tell her that being with her for—what? Only a couple of hours now? —made him think for the first time that he could once again feel something for someone else. It unnerved him that he felt instantly and intensely drawn to her; It also felt good.

Donna, for her part, told Dale all about Brad Phillips, and how he dumped her to go back to his wife. She had felt such anger, betrayal, and hatred then. And as she told him about the parties and the yacht cruises and the weekends in fancy hotels and restaurants, it all for the first time actually started to sound shallow. She began to see herself in a way she didn't like, as a jaded and superficial bitch. When she said so out loud, Dale surprised them both by cupping her chin with his hands and kissing her firmly on the mouth.

That kiss led to what they later jokingly referred to as some "heavy petting," and if it hadn't been for the cramped quarters of the car and the chill on the grass, they would have "gone all the way!" They had to settle for hugging and kissing, and the desperate grasping of two people whose lives seemed to be swirling in the back-eddies of a river totally out of their control.

At one point, locked in a deep kiss, Donna suddenly jerked away, and her eyes widened with fear. "What was that?" she said as she sat up and looked around.

"What was what?"

"I heard something," she said. Her voice edged up the register. "A thump sound."

Dale pulled back and casually glanced out his side window. "I think I might've kicked the floor. God!" He laughed and straightened up in his seat.

"You're acting like a nervous high school girl, afraid the cops or your parents are going to catch you necking."

Donna looked at him but didn't laugh. Her face was grim as she peered out the side window over the moonlit landscape. "No, it sounded like something hit the side of the car."

"Well, I'm not about to get out and check," Dale said. He put a false nervous edge to his voice and widened his eyes as he looked out over the cemetery. "I don't want to meet up with The Hook!" He made a sudden, lunging grab at Donna, who held him back at arm's length.

"Maybe we'd better leave," Donna said, still not laughing.

"Before we go too far? Is that what you're afraid of?" Dale said, leering at her. He knew his humor wasn't getting to her, so he started up the car and backed around. He had just shifted into forward when both of them heard—and felt a solid thump on the side of the car. The shock absorbers gave a high-pitched squeak, but that was soon lost beneath Donna's shrill scream.

"What the …?" Dale muttered, looking around quickly. He reached past Donna and snapped down her door lock, then his own. He stepped on the brakes so the red taillights would illuminate whatever was behind them. "Maybe I bumped one of the gravestones, backing up," he said. But he knew *it* wasn't a gravestone. The bump on the side of the car had sounded soft, as though he had hit a person. The impact had that solid, yet yielding sound. It was the same sound he remembered when, last spring, he had hit a skunk in the middle of the road.

"I don't see anything," he said, searching the red-lit grass. Looking ahead, at the far reach of the headlights, he could see a mound of fresh-dug dirt, and he realized that was where the cemetery workers had excavated Larry's grave. A cold chill splashed his stomach.

"Let's get going," Donna said, her voice a nervous warble.

Dale took his foot off the brake, but then, as the car started moving forward, they heard the sound again. It was a solid "thwonk," and this time it definitely came from under the car.

"Maybe I've got a flat tire," Dale said. He was about to shift the car into park when Donna screamed and practically jumped into his lap, between him and the steering wheel. Dale's eyes widened when he saw, looming out of the darkness and into the headlights, the slouching figure of a man.

"I didn't hit him, did I?" Dale shouted.

Donna ignored him. She was too busy shaking his arm, trying to get him to drive away.

The man looked at them, staring straight into the harsh light. His figure was sharply lit against the black backdrop of the night. The light bleached his face to a snowy white, and his eyes stared wide open. What struck Dale as really weird were the man's pupil's. Even in the full force of the high beams, they were almost fully dilated, twin bullet-holes of black, glaring at them. The man's thin, pale lips were moving, but nothing intelligible came out, only a muffled garble as he raised his arms and lunged forward at the car.

"Drive! *Drive!*" Donna shouted as the man made a grab for the car. He stumbled and fell forward, glancing off the side of the car. "He isn't hurt!" Donna cried. "Come on! Let's get the hell out of here!"

Dale shook her away from him, gripped the steering wheel tightly, and turned hard to one side; then he stomped the accelerator. The tires screeched, kicking up dirt and grass that splattered against the underside of the car as it fishtailed left and right, then straightened out. The brightly illuminated man, struggling to stand upright, disappeared off to the side, winking out in the darkness as suddenly as he had appeared.

Glancing in the rearview mirror for just an instant, Dale's breath caught in his throat. In the glow of his taillights, he could saw a dark, bulky shape lying in the middle of the road.

It was another person! his mind screamed. Had there been someone else behind them? He pushed that thought aside and concentrated on his driving.

It wasn't a person back there, lying in the road! he told himself. It couldn't have been! He hit one of the trashcans that line the cemetery road, or maybe backed over a large floral display that had been left on a grave. It couldn't have been another person!

Dale's foot barely tapped on the brake pedal as he pulled out of the cemetery and onto Main Street. His pulse was hammering so hard in his ears, his vision bounced back and forth with each beat. He realized he was holding his breath, and as he slowed down, he let it out with a long, whistling sigh.

"Who in the name of Christ was that?" he said, glancing over at Donna, who sat huddled by her door with one hand covering her mouth. Her eyes were two wide orbs, glistening in the light from the dashboard.

Shaking her head abruptly, she looked at Dale, her mouth struggling to form words. "I have no idea," she said. Her voice was low and gravelly.

"Well, we must've disturbed someone. Maybe it was someone sleeping out there in the cemetery," Dale said, as his pulse gradually dropped and he regained his self-control. "Probably a drunk or something," he added lamely.

"I don't know," Donna said, her voice still shaking. "I didn't recognize him. But it all happened so fast."

Dale nodded. "Yeah, well, I guess that'll teach us to go parking in the cemetery." He decided it best not to mention to her what he had seen in the rear view mirror. It couldn't have been a person!

Donna forced a little laugh and said, "You bet. I'm gonna be a good girl from now on!"

This was obviously the climax to the night, and any thoughts of inviting Donna back to Mrs. Appleby's with him had dried up and blown away. They said very little as he drove back to the parking lot behind Kellerman's where Donna had left her car.

"Do you want me to follow you back to your sister's?" Dale asked. "You know, just to make sure you get home okay?"

Donna had the car door open, one foot already out on the asphalt. She still felt a tingling all over and, quite honestly, wouldn't have minded not only having Dale follow her back, but also having him slide in between the old sheets with her, too. She knew he'd have a great time explaining that to Angie in the morning!

"I'll be all right," she said. She leaned across the seat and planted a warm kiss on his lips. "Don't worry."

Dale smiled tightly and nodded. "Yeah, well—umm, give me a call in the morning, all right?"

"Sure," Donna said.

"Oh, and another thing," Dale said. "You said you were thinking about going to go to Larry's funeral. Are you?"

"Sure," Donna said. "We can talk tomorrow and make plans."

"I was wondering if after the funeral, you might do me a favor."

"That depends," Donna said, smiling slightly.

Dale was glad to see her sense of humor return after the scare in the cemetery, but what he had to ask made him feel somber. "I was wondering if you'd come with me out to the accident site out at Casey's Curve."

At first, Donna didn't say anything as her eyes flickered back and forth, looking out at the parking lot illuminated by Dale's headlights. She had to fight hard to control the flood of panic that rose in her whenever she recalled that man's face, looming at them out of the darkness. She shivered and hugged her shoulders tightly.

"It's not exactly my idea of a fun time, you know," she said, her voice lowered almost to a growl.

"I know, I know," Dale said, "but I just—I feel as though I owe it to Larry to take a look around. Somebody's got to do at least that much for him."

Donna's lips tightened into a hard line, but she slowly nodded her head. "Yeah. Okay, I guess. Tell you what. I'll give you a buzz in the morning."

"Night," Dale said, as Donna got out and shut the car door. He waited, his car idling, while she got her car started. As she drove away, they gave each other quick little beeps on their horns. Feeling an odd mixture of elation and sadness, he drove back to Mrs. Appleby's house, wondering how and why, when he was in this town for the funeral of his closest friend, he had found someone who had made him feel deep stirrings that he hadn't felt since Natalie died. They were feelings he had thought he would never feel again.

Funny, he thought, how life can be like that.

# VII

It surprised Tasha how fast the woods got completely dark. Not even the light of the nearly full moon was enough to light up her way. Even Hocker's whistling up ahead began to get lost to her sense of direction, and at times, in a fit of near panic, she had the sensation that the shrill notes were coming from behind her, from the left, from the right from all around her! The bouncing of her backpack in the small of her back didn't help her attitude any, either, but she struggled ahead through the undergrowth, hoping it would come to an end soon.

Suddenly, Hocker stopped in his tracks. Tasha didn't know this until she walked smack into him, almost knocking him over.

"For Christ's sake!" she wailed after regaining her balance. "Will you at least give me a warning?"

"Sorry," Hocker said. The unusually subdued tone of his voice tipped Tasha off that something was wrong.

"Wha—what's the matter?" she whispered, groping in the dark until she found his arm and squeezed it tightly.

"Shit!" Hocker said, and she could hear him stomp his foot heavily on the ground. "Goddamn!"

"Don't tell me you're lost," Tasha said, feeling tension winding up in her gut.

"Just a little bit off the mark, I guess," Hocker said sullenly. "I think I must've gone too far to the left. We should've come to it by now."

Tasha glanced around, trying to see how he could know where he was. All she could see were the stark limbs of trees overhead and the dusty, coal sky beyond that. A chilly breeze raced through the pine boughs, making soft, hissing sounds that reminded Tasha of a snake.

"Real good," she said, not letting go of her grip on his arm. "You make one hell of an Indian scout!"

"No sweat, no sweat," Hocker said, shaking his arm loose from her. "We ain't more than a coupla' hundred yards off, one way or another."

"Yeah, but which way?"

Hocker deliberated for just a second, then pointed to the right. "This way, I think. Come on."

Tasha sighed deeply, wishing they would just spread out their sleeping bags here for the night. Hell, even sleeping without a tent would be better than thrashing around in the friggin' darkness, she thought.

But she followed, and it wasn't long before she heard Hocker swear softly under his breath. It didn't take her long to realize what had gotten him angry, either. Up ahead, through the screen of trees, they could see the warm, yellow glow of light.

"If that's the farmhouse I found," Hocker said softly, "I guess it ain't unoccupied like I thought. Come on, let's go see."

"Let's just spread out the bags here," Tasha said, trying to keep the pleading whine out of her voice. "I'm hungry, cold, and tired. All I want to do is—"

"Shh! *Quiet!*" Hocker hissed. He slapped at her in the darkness and connected a glancing blow to her arm. "I can hear voices. Stay behind me and be
real quiet!"

For what seemed like the hundredth time today, Tasha wished to God she
had the courage to dump Hocker and head out by herself. Is that what she
lacked, courage? What would have been the worst that could happen? She'd
hitch a ride with some horny old businessman and she'd end up in his bed for
the night. Would that be so bad? At least the bed would be in a warm motel
room somewhere, with clean sheets and blankets, and a shower in the morning.
Better than *this* by a damned sight!

But she did what Hocker said and kept her mouth closed as she crept forward through the black-drenched woods, keeping as close as she could to him.

The woods abruptly ended, and before them stretched a wide field. Dusty
moonlight cast rippling shadows over the furrows where the tangled vines of
potatoes grew. The land sloped gently upward, and at the crest of the hill stood
a large barn. The light they saw came from a single bare light bulb, hanging
from a wire in the center of the barn.

"What the fuck's going on up there?" Hocker whispered as he knelt at the
edge of the woods, staring up at the barn.

Tasha surely didn't know, and furthermore, she didn't care. It looked to her
like some kind of meeting—just a bunch of farmers, by the looks; but if it was
some kind of gathering, the group of men up there didn't look like they were
having a good time.

"Can you see what they've got there?" Hocker asked. "It looks like some
kind of big vat or something."

"I don't know," Tasha said. "And I don't really care. Come on. Let's get the
hell out of here. I'm exhausted!"

"Hold your ass," Hocker hissed.

He watched intently as the men, maybe twenty or twenty-five in all, stood
motionlessly inside the barn while one man, the best-dressed of the lot, stood
near a large black kettle. He seemed to be addressing the men, who were lined
up in a ragged line. Because of the distance, Hocker couldn't make out their
faces very well, but they all seemed uninterested in what the well-dressed man was
saying. While he spoke, he held a large ladle in one hand and stirred something
in the kettle.

"That's probably some home-made kooch," Hocker said, smacking his lips.

Tasha moaned softly and said, "I just want to get some sleep."

"Just a second," Hocker said firmly. "I wanna check this out. Then we'll see
if I can find that farmhouse. I think it's down that way." In the dim light, she
could see him pointing off to the right.

Hocker figured the men were migrant workers, in the area for the potato
harvest. They didn't move as the well-dressed man spoke with them. After stirring the kettle a while longer, he knocked the ladle on the edge of the kettle,

and the men began to crowd around closer. For the first time, Hocker noticed that each of them held a cup of some kind in one hand; as they drew up to the kettle, the well-dressed man doled them out a small amount of liquid. In the harsh light of the naked bulb, the liquid looked dark, a deep purple.

"Hot damn! That's what it is!" Hocker said excitedly. "They've got some kind of home brew."

"Good for them," Tasha said sourly.

Hocker stayed crouching as he watched each man receive his portion and then walk away to sit down in a corner of the barn, and quickly drink it down. It was one drink per customer, no refills. That made Hocker think it must be some potent, son-of-a-bitching drink!

He also thought how great the barn would look with flames licking out of its loft windows and angry red sparks spiraling skyward beneath a heavy belly of smoke.

Yes-sir-ee bob-cat! he thought, feeling a tingling in his groin, the same tingling he felt whenever he contemplated torching a building. His hands began to tremble with excitement at the thought as the funny tingling spread up into his belly. Hell! It felt better, by far, than what he had felt the few times he had played with himself and the sticky white stuff had shot out of him. That felt good, too, but it didn't come close to what he knew he'd feel if, once those men left for the night, he went back there and checked to see if there was enough hay in the loft, maybe even some *gasoline!*—to get things really going.

"Look, Hock. If it's something to drink you want, you can head to town and score a six-pack. If it's the damned barn you're so psyched up about, I found another one while I was slugging my way through the woods after the cop nabbed me. This one definitely ain't being used. It was all overgrown with trees around it. Actually, we could have made our camp there for the night if I'd gotten back sooner."

"Another barn?" Hocker said.

"Umm. On the other side of town. Do you want to try to make it there tonight?"

Hocker shook his head, still keeping his eyes fixed on the men in the barn. The well-dressed man had finished dispensing the liquid, and it nearly broke Hocker's heart to see him grab the edge of the kettle and overturn it, spilling the remainder of the dark liquid onto the ground.

"Naw," he said, his voice rasping. "We can camp like I said, in the woods behind that abandoned farm house. If no one shows up, we'll check it out in the morning. Maybe we can play house there for a few days."

"Sounds like fun," Tasha said, convinced that Hocker wouldn't catch her sarcasm.

"But before we bug out of this town," he said, "you have to show me where that other old barn is, okay?" He smiled widely as he pictured the black skeleton of the barn burning as raging tongues of orange flame roared into the night sky.

# VIII

The first Tasha knew there was any trouble was when a booted foot slammed into her side, jolting her out of a deep sleep.

Cops! she thought as she doubled up in pain, not knowing whether to hide deep in her sleeping bag or scramble to her feet and fight like hell. As she rolled over, she opened her mouth to scream and got nothing for her effort but a mouthful of dry leaves, dirt, and pine needles.

"Hock!" she sputtered, but the cry was lost as she spit to clean out her mouth.

The small campfire they had built before going to sleep had burned down to orange coals, but the moon, now high in the trees, shed enough light to see by. She wasn't sure if Hocker was still tangled in his sleeping bag or if he was one of the four figures she could see silhouetted against the sky. When one of the figures swung wildly at another, though, she had her answer.

Bitter panic rose from her stomach to her throat, choking her as she beat aside the sleeping bag. One of the silhouettes loomed over her, as tall as a tower, threatening to crash down on her. The foot came out of nowhere, catching her on the underside of the ribs. She doubled up in pain just as a crushing weight fell down on her.

Her screams caught in her chest, and the only sound that came from her mouth was a strangled grunt as she clawed desperately at the face pressing down on her. By simple luck, her finger wrapped around the man's throat, and she held him back long enough to see his face, lined in harsh relief by the moonlight. The memory of that leering, grinning face, more skull-like than living flesh, etched itself like acid into her brain. Wide, staring eyes, swirling whirlpools of black thicker than the night,— gazed deeply into her eyes, ripping like a wild animal into her soul. A sickly, sour breath washed over her face like a spray of vomit.

With a strength charged by adrenalin, she loosened the grip with one hand and raked her fingernails across those eyes. The effect, even in her panic, was stunning; the man seemed barely to notice! His dead weight still pressed her down, crushing the breath out of her! The face loomed closer, and when the man opened his mouth and viciously chomped his teeth several times, drawing closer to her face, Tasha was positive she would spin backward into unconsciousness, a faint from which she would never awaken.

But then, just as suddenly, there was a loud explosion and a flash of light close to her ear. The weight of the man lifted off her. She looked up, horrified, to see that the man's entire head was blown away from his shoulders. His head-

less corpse lurched up, staggering once in the pale moonlight, and then crumpled to the ground, where it twitched spasmodically before lying still.

A whining buzz filled her ears as she looked, horrified, at the dead man.

*Jesus Christ! Where did you get a gun?* she wanted to yell to Hocker, but he had
already turned to face the two other attackers. Tasha extricated herself from the
sleeping bag and groped about on the forest floor, seeking something she could
use to protect herself. She found a wrist-thick branch and, giving it a testing
heft, stood up to help Hocker.

Hocker was circling the small clearing where they had camped. The gun waved
menacingly in his hand, glinting in the moonlight.

"Come on, you fuckin' scumbags," he growled. "Come *on!* You want it? I'll
*give* it to you!"

The whole situation didn't make sense, but what happened next made the
least sense of all. In any conflict, Tasha would have bet good money that, even
two men, faced with a gun, would back down. Maybe because they knew one of
their group was already dead, they wanted revenge. Maybe they were escaped
convicts, desperate men on the run with nothing to lose. (Like us, Tasha
thought.) Whatever it was, first one man then the other coiled back. Then, with
gut-deep grunts, they launched themselves at Hocker.

The gun blasted twice. Tasha barely registered seeing one of the two go
down, but even on the ground, he clawed at the mulchy soil to propel himself
forward. His feet scrambled wildly on the ground, like he was trying to burrow
into the soil. The other man slammed into Hocker like a run-away bull, pushing him back in a flurry of arms and legs into the brush. The sound of them
thrashing in the woods filled the night.

Tasha moved forward, thinking she might be able to help, but as she
stepped over the fallen man, she felt a clamp-like hand wrap around her ankle.
She squealed and, instinctively raised the stick up high and brought it down hard
on the man's head. Once, twice, three times! She pounded as hard as she could.
Each blow made a sickening hollow "thump" that made her believe she was beating on a pumpkin instead of a real person's head. She had a fleeting image of
the man's head splitting open, and what spilled out was not brains, but rotten
pumpkin fiber.

Worst of all, though, was when she vividly imagined the man's face and
those eyes glaring up at her.

They were *dead man's eyes!* The image terrified her; and charged her with
even more frantic energy. Again and again, she slammed the stick down where
she knew that face was. She wanted to smash the skull until it was pulp; she
wanted to knock that black, hypnotic gaze out of his eyes. She didn't stop hitting even after the grip had loosened on her leg and let go. Tears blurred the sil-
very-lit clearing as she slammed, and slammed, and slammed!

What brought her back to reality was the sound of gunfire, muffled in the
distance. She looked over to the bushes where Hocker and the other man had

disappeared, but now, except for a faint rustling, all was quiet. Silence settled back down on the night like a heavy blanket. Even the wind seemed to have stopped. Moonlight washed the clearing with dull silvery light.

"Hocker?" she called out feebly. The sound of her voice, twisted and strained, intruded unnaturally on the night. Again, she heard a rustling of leaves, and the only thought that filled her now was: Hocker's dead! Now that guy's coming for me!

Her grip on the stick tightened until the palms of her hands hurt, but she waited in the clearing, figuring either Hocker would come out of the brush, or *that* man.

This is it! she thought as tears flooded her eyes, making it almost impossible to see. I'm gonna *die!*

If the man had killed Hocker and now had the gun, she could expect at any second to see a bright flash of light and feel a bullet rip out her chest. She waited, her legs trembling, her stomach filled with ice. Waited, now, for the end.

"For Christ's fuckin' sake, will you come over here and help me?"

It was Hocker's voice, calling to her from the dark woods. Never before in her life had she been so relieved to hear his throaty growl. As soon as she tried one step forward, though, her legs gave out beneath her, and she crumpled to the ground. When she awoke, the sun was cutting through the morning mist in the trees, and Hocker was crouched by a small campfire, heating up a can of baked beans.

Tasha looked at him through narrowed eyes. When the horrors of the night rushed back to her, she jolted into a sitting position. The night's events had the gauzy overcast of a dream, but as soon as she moved, the knife-like pain under her ribs convinced her it had been real.

"What the . . . ?"

"Don't worry," Hocker said, smiling as he stirred the beans with his spoon. "Everything's taken care of."

"What do you mean?" she said, although it was difficult, practically *impossible* to speak. She was positive she had screamed several layers from inside her throat, and just taking a tiny breath hurt like hell!

"Over there, pretty well hidden," Hocker said, nodding to one side. Through the screen of brush, she could see three rectangles of fresh-turned earth.

"All three were dead?" Tasha asked. Her body was wracked by a wave of shivers that felt like they would never stop.

"They are now, for sure," Hocker said. He raised up a wad of mucous and spit in the direction of the three new graves. "I don't want to sound superstitious or anything," he added. He tested the beans with his finger and licked his fingertip clean. "But just to make sure they stay dead, I cut off their heads before I buried 'em. Pretty wild, huh?"

# CHAPTER FIVE
## "FUNERAL-TIME"

## I

"I'm surprised she even remembered me," Donna said as she and Dale left Mrs. Appleby's and walked out to her car, parked down by the curb. "She must have had hundreds of students over the years, and she really did remember me."

Dale chuckled and shook his head, "Well, you must admit, that little 'accident' you had would have been pretty memorable. What a riot!"

"I didn't think it was very funny back then," Donna said. Her face turned several shades of red, remembering what had happened to her when she was a fourth-grader in Mrs. Appleby's class. She hadn't even remembered the name of the boy responsible, but Mrs. Appleby did: it had been Tommy Anderson.

One day, as a practical joke, Tommy had secretly taken the hem of Donna's dress, (she remembered the dress vividly; it had had a yellow and white check design, and a tiny black poodle sewn on the left shoulder puff) and tied it in several knots around the back support bar of her chair. Apparently he had tied it a little too good. When Mrs. Appleby called on Donna to do a multiplication problem at the blackboard, she stood up. With a sudden, sharp hiss, the whole bottom half of her dress ripped away, and she was left standing in the middle of the room with her skinny legs sticking out from her frilly underpants.

"I think that was Tommy's way of trying to get me to pay attention to him," Donna said, still embarrassed. "But it didn't work. I never even remembered his name until today."

"Well, something like that would make an impression on a teacher," Dale said.

When they got to the car, Dale opened the driver's door for Donna before he got in. They decided to take a drive into Houlton that morning, before the funeral, so Donna could buy an appropriately dark dress. That was what started Mrs. Appleby reminiscing about the famous "yellow and white check dress" story.

School started in mid-August earlier than the southern part of Maine, but let out during the several weeks of harvest. Angie decided to stay at the house and hang out with Lisa. Dale thought he detected a slight jealousy now that Donna had wedged herself between them so fast. If that was the case, however, he felt he'd have no problem reassuring her that this was "nothing serious." He smiled to himself, though, as Donna started up the car and pulled away from the curb. It was significant, he thought, that this was the first time since Natalie died, that there was even a question of any relationship with a woman becoming serious.

When they passed Brooklawn Cemetery, they exchanged nervous glances, not having to voice their thoughts about what had happened in the cemetery last night. Dale was still haunted by the thought that it had not been a trash can or a floral arrangement he had hit as he backed around out of there. What if the man they had seen had had a buddy out there with him? Maybe a couple of old friends had gone out to the cemetery, as he and Donna did to enjoy the peace and quiet and the view of the town, as they shared a bottle of Ripple. And what if Dale had run the man down? What if he was up there, right now, dead in the road, waiting to be discovered? Maybe to be discovered by the cemetery workers who were coming to work today to bury Larry?

He tried to push those and other thoughts away as Donna drove by the first cemetery gate without a backward glance.

If that's what happened, he thought bitterly, then, that's what happened. He'd have to turn himself in!

When he saw a second gateway to the cemetery up ahead, he tapped Donna on the arm and pointed to the black, wrought iron entrance.

"Just zip in there for a minute, will you?" he asked, hoping the tension wasn't noticeable in his voice.

Donna forced a smile despite the memory of that man's face looming in front of them out of the darkness. "Want to see if our buddy's still up there?" she asked.

Dale nodded. "Just checking."

Donna slowed and took the turn. Once inside the cemetery, they followed the twisting, twin-rutted dirt road to where they had parked the night before. Donna put the car into park and waited behind the wheel while Dale got out and carefully inspected the ground. His first sensation was of relief; there was no corpse in the road. If there had been one, wouldn't there be police lines and cruisers all over the place?

The criminal always comes back to the scene of the crime, his mind whispered softly.

After his initial relief at not finding a dead man there, Dale took a few seconds to look around for any sign of the man they had seen. The ground all around was well-trimmed and there were, as far as he could tell, no signs of anyone having been there. There were no footprints, no empty Ripple bottles leaning against the tombstones: nothing. Not even a trace of what had happened last night.

"Satisfied?" Donna called through her open window.

Dale nodded as he circled the area one last time, making a wide swing that included the road where he thought he had seen something. An icy tingle ran through him when he saw a small dark splotch in the middle of the dirt road.

*Could it be blood?* he wondered. Maybe the guy they saw hauled his friend's body away himself, leaving nothing behind but a small puddle of his dead friend's blood!

Dale shook his head and knelt, slowly extending his fingers to touch the dark damp spot. It made his hands sticky, but the more he looked at it, the more he became convinced it was oil or something else ... It was certainly not *blood!*

"Yeah," he said, standing up and wiping his fingers on his pants leg as he walked back to the car. "I guess there's nothing here."

He got in but couldn't resist taking one last glance over his shoulder as they pulled away. The events of last night took on a strange, unreal cast, like a dream, only partially, but vividly remembered.

"Oh, damn, you know what?" Donna said as she pulled to a stop at the cemetery exit. "I think I left my other keys behind." She slammed the car into park and picked up her pocketbook. After a minute of frantically pawing through the contents, she let out a sharp breath that angled up over her face, making the hair on her forehead bounce.

"A problem?" Dale asked.

"The keys to my folks' house," she said, grimacing as she continued her futile search. "I went out to the house yesterday, and I must've left the keys there. They're probably right there in the door."

"Is it far from here?" Dale asked. He knew they wouldn't be back from Houlton in time for the funeral service unless they left now. His detour to the cemetery had eaten up enough time as it was.

Donna looked at him, a shadow of worry wrinkling her brow. "It's not far," she said, "and I really should check to see if they're there. I wouldn't want anyone getting in there."

Dale shrugged. "We won't make it to Houlton in time if we take much longer."

Donna shook her head, angry at herself for being so thoughtless. It wasn't like her to be so absent-minded, but when she remembered the thoughts, the feelings, the emotions that had flooded her yesterday at the house, she wasn't all that surprised that she had left the keys. She would consider herself lucky if that was the worst that happened.

"I suppose I can wear something I brought with me," she said, scratching her cheek. "That will cut a lot of the hurry out of the day. We can take our time not rush-rush-rush."

"That's one thing I like about this town," Dale said. "The whole feeling that life is somehow unnatural if it goes at a very fast pace."

Donna smiled in agreement. "That's why I wanted to get out of here so much when I graduated. I wanted to live in Boston or New York City or someplace, and get away from the really small minds around here. It's only now after I've lived that kind of life" —and seen what it can do to a person! she added in her mind —"that I can sort of appreciate it."

"Let's go out to the house, then," Dale said decisively. "You can give me a guided tour down memory lane." He paused, then added, "Maybe I can dig out a few more embarrassing stories about you."

Donna smiled as she looked him straight in the eye. "I'll trade your embarrassing stories, one for one. By my count, you already owe me one!"

# II

Tasha couldn't stand the thought of being near where three bodies were buried, so it didn't take much convincing on Hocker's part to get her to agree to check out the abandoned farmhouse he had found the day before. After sharing the can of warmed-up beans, they covered their fire, packed up their camping gear, and left. Just the thought of those three freshly dug graves back there in the woods sent shivers coursing through her body.

"I can't understand how you can just ... just walk away from what you did last night," Tasha said as they started across the field. In the distance, they could hear the deep-throated rumble of farm machinery, tractors, probably, digging potatoes.

"Not just what I did," Hocker said, looking at her with a twisted smile that was scary and ridiculous at the same time. "What *we* did! I only killed two of them, remember? You battered the other one's head until there was almost nothing left. So if you start thinking this is just *my* problem, you better think again. We're in this thing together, baby."

His words stripped her nerves raw, and in her mind she saw the whole rest of her life as a long, narrow black tube. I actually killed a person! her mind repeated over and over, until it became a numbing litany. I actually *killed* a person! Stealing the truck down south, even if Hocker had murdered that old man, at least she hadn't done anything; but now . . . *now* . . .

*I actually killed a person!*

She knew she would have to live with that thought for the rest of her life, and nothing she could ever do would free her from it.

"You actually think three geeks like that will ever be missed?" Hocker said. He spit onto the ground for emphasis. "I mean, did you catch a whiff of those guys?"

Tasha grunted, thinking, Boy, he should talk about 'catching a whiff! She couldn't maintain eye contact with him for fear of seeing herself reflected in his crazy eyes.

The old farmhouse was at the bottom of a long, downward slope. Crouching low, Hocker studied the worn-out barn and the empty driveway. Everything looked quiet and peaceful and there was no evidence that there was anyone around. So they made their way to the house, approaching cautiously in case there was someone inside. The closer they got, the more Hocker became convinced the farmhouse was deserted and free for the taking.

"When that last one tackled me and rolled me into the bushes, I thought the smell alone would kill me. It was like that guy had been swimming in sewerage! Gawd!" He waved his hand in front of his nose as if to fan away any lingering traces.

"They were human beings," Tasha said simply.

"Not any more, they aren't!"

They arrived at the steps that led up to the back porch, and stood, looking up at the weather-beaten house. Hocker strained to hear any trace of activity inside the house, but all he could hear was the distant rumble of a tractor, somewhere off in the distance.

The windows reflected a distorted view of the sunlit fields stretching behind them up to the horizon. Tasha wanted to cry when she saw herself: a small, nearly transparent reflection, standing next to this monster!

The word "monster" echoed in her head, almost drowning out the words as Hocker said, "Come on, let's check it out."

She followed him, walking mechanically up the steps, her fingers gliding over the chipped paint railing. When they were out of the sun, beneath the shade of the porch, Tasha shivered as though she had jumped into cold water.

Hocker looked into the kitchen, his breath fogging the glass that, only moments before, had reflected them. "Well, I guess we don't have to worry 'bout anyone being around." He told Tasha. "This place is deserted."

"Don't you think—" Tasha started to say, but then she cut her words off, looking frantically over her shoulder as the sound of farm machinery got suddenly louder. A tractor, it's harrow raised and gleaming in the sun, chugged its way across the field in the distance.

Hocker ignored her and went around the corner toward the front of the house, and Tasha followed silently. The screen door spring let out a rusty "twang" as he opened the door and tried the doorknob. He looked back at her, his mouth a rounded O when the knob clicked, and the door swung inward.

"I'll be damned!" Hocker said before stepping into the musty cool of the house. Diffused sunlight from outside barely made it through the grimy windows. It looked as though the house was filled with a thin haze of smoke.

With another nervous backward glance (something I'll be doing the rest of my life! Tasha thought) she followed him in, making sure to shut the inside door and throw the bolt just as the rusty spring pulled the screen door shut with a bang. In the entryway, Hocker was bouncing on his toes, obviously satisfied with their discovery. "Ahh, this'll be great," he said. "Absolutely perfect!" He suddenly turned back to Tasha and frowned. "You were saying?"

Tasha shook her head, confused.

"You started to say, 'Don't you think?' Think what?"

Tasha still couldn't look him squarely in the eyes, so she pretended interest in checking out the house as she spoke. "I was saying, I think it might not be such a smart idea to hang around this town even for one more night."

Hocker snorted and waved his hand at her. "Why? Because of those three guys?"

"I mean it," Tasha said, irritated that her voice was approaching a whine. "You, I mean, *we* . . ." Her voice choked at the word. "We killed them. If someone finds their bodies, it isn't going to take a whole hell of a lot of brain power to connect it to us."

"Don't sweat it," Hocker said as he walked into the living room, looking around. "No one's gonna find 'em."

"I don't know," Tasha said, feeling swept up in a spiral of fear. "When hunting season comes, some guy's gonna be out in the woods with his dog, and the dog's gonna catch a whiff. 'N as soon as he starts digging there, he's gonna find them!"

As she talked, she looked at the closed door, thinking the last thing she wanted on the face of this earth was to be trapped in this house with someone like Hocker! She had to squint her eyes hard to keep from crying. I've been a complete jerk not to dump this creep sooner, she thought. Her eyes were burning, but she didn't cry.

Then another, even uglier thought rose in her mind, and try as she might to hold it back, it whispered in a voice as dry and harsh as dead leaves being crushed underfoot.

*He'll hold it over you, you know,* . . . the voice hissed. *He'll hold it over you and use it to control you! And the only way you'll ever be free of him will be to . . .*

"No!" Tasha said, not even sure if it was aloud or not. Tiny tear drops squeezed between each tightly pressed lid.

*. . . Kill him!*

She turned away from Hocker and ran her jacket sleeve over her eyes. The fabric felt like sandpaper, and made her eyes water all the more.

*You will, though,* the voice whispered, nearly a cackle. *You know it, so you might as well get used to the idea. You may have to beat* his *brains in like you did to that guy last night!*

Her memory filled with the moon-lit image of the man's head, splitting open and oozing not brains, but tangled, rotten fibers as she slammed the stick down again and again and again!

"I think we'll be comfortable here for a day or two," Hocker said. "And it sure as hell will be warmer than sleeping in the woods." He wandered from the dining room to the kitchen while Tasha stood there in the entry-way, but his voice seemed to be coming from miles away.

Tasha's mind was lost, spinning backward in a widening black gulf, hearing Hocker as though his voice was coming over a radio with a torn speaker. She was so bound up in her mounting fear that she hadn't heard the car when it pulled into the driveway. She became aware of it when she heard two car doors open and slam shut.

"Oh, fuck!" she muttered. Through the tattered lace curtain in the side lights she saw a man and a woman coming up the walkway.

"Hock!" she hissed, moving swiftly on tiptoes to the kitchen and clapping her hand over his mouth before he shouted something.

"Someone's here," she whispered close to his ear.

Hocker shook himself free, and leaned his head into the dining room as the front door knob turned and the door jiggled. One of the windows in the side light vibrated.

"Out the back door?" Tasha asked, but Hocker shook his head and jabbed his finger at the door in the kitchen. "That's the cellar door. Get down there. Quick!"

Tasha didn't have time to elaborate on all the reasons why she didn't want to go down there. She thought they were too obvious, but she didn't resist when Hocker swung open the door and pushed her toward the stairway. Tasha stumbled down the stairs, but her hand snagged the railing, and she righted herself. The cool, damp air of the cellar surrounded her, and she felt as though she was sinking down, over her head into murky water.

Hocker eased the cellar door shut and came down the stairs right behind her. Sunlight barely pierced the milky-glazed cellar windows, but the view was clear enough for them to see when two people walked by, heading around the house to the back door.

Hocker gripped her by the arm and squeezed hard. "You have all your stuff, don't you? You didn't leave anything upstairs?"

Hocker shut up when he heard footsteps on the back porch, and the sound of the back door jiggling in the jamb. A woman's voice on the outside said something to the other person, but the words were distorted and unintelligible.

"Hide in there," Hocker said, pointing toward the slatted walls of an old coal bin. Without complaint, Tasha hiked herself over the wall and crouched on the floor. Her motion sent billows of coal dust swirling into her face like a cloud of mosquitoes. She sneezed, but silenced it in the crook of her arm.

Hocker, meanwhile, was looking frantically around the cellar for some left-behind tool he could use as a weapon in case these people came in and found them. He considered using his gun, but he knew the difference between three bums in the woods and two people out looking at a house in broad daylight. A rusted shovel was the best he could find. Clutching the shovel, he leaped over the coal bin wall and joined Tasha, who was huddled on the floor in the darkness.

"I sure as shit don't want any more trouble," Hocker said, his breath a warm wash over Tasha's face. "But if they come down here, I'm gonna have to waste 'em!"

# III

"There they are," Dale said. He pressed his face against the window and looked into the empty kitchen while Donna tried the back door. She hadn't used it yesterday, so she would have been surprised to find it open.

"You're kidding," she said, joining him at the window. But there was her ring of keys, lying on the edge of the countertop. "Damn! I must've just put them down unconsciously while I was going through the house yesterday. What an idiot!"

Dale smiled and shrugged as he straightened up. "Hey, it's not the first time," he said.

But Donna was angry with herself. All her life she had prided herself on not being absent-minded. Other people, not Donna LaPierre, left their keys lying around, and of all the stupid places to leave them!

"Does you sister have spares?" Dale asked.

Donna nodded, biting her lower lip in frustration.

"Well then, you've got two choices as I see it. We either go back to your sister's to get the spare, then drive back to pick up the ones you left inside, or we break a window and get them now."

Donna's frown deepened. "If you think you could get a window open without breaking it, I'd rather do that now than get Barbara's spare. We've had more than our share of arguments about the house, and I don't want her thinking I'd be so damned stupid as to do something like this."

Dale laughed as he leaned close to the kitchen window, inspecting the lock. It had been made back in the days when you didn't need high-tech security. This was a simple window with a hasp lock, and if anything, the age of the house would probably make getting in easier because the sashes were old and rotten.

"Yeah, I might be able to do something," Dale said. He took out his wallet and removed his Visa card. It was easy enough to get the card edge up under the sash, but it took a bit of effort to get the edge to catch onto the lock. After several passes, though, the card knocked the lock aside enough so, with a little upward pressure, it eventually gave.

Dale felt foolish when he hoisted himself up onto the sill and scrambled to get a knee up. Dried paint and crumbling putty dug into his elbows and hands as he pulled himself up and in. Once he finally grabbed the counter edge, the rest was easy.

Inside the house, he pulled himself across the dust-laden counter top and then dropped to the floor. After brushing himself off, he picked up the keys and went to the back door to let Donna in.

"Thanks," she said when he dropped the culprit keys into her open hand. She made a point of putting them directly into her purse and snapping the purse shut.

"So," Dale said, scanning the peeling wallpaper of the kitchen, "this is home sweet home, huh?" It took quite a stretch of imagination to see how the place would have looked with fresh paint and paper.

Donna felt a wave of embarrassment as Dale looked around, and she was surprised how, ever since yesterday's nostalgic trip through her childhood, the house now seemed so much smaller, dingier, and uglier.

"It, uhh, it was a lot nicer when I was a kid," she said. "It's funny how small places from your childhood seem when you're older."

"I think it's just great," Dale said, not entirely convincingly as he wandered from the kitchen to the dining room to the living room. "It must have been cozy."

They spent the next half hour wandering through the house, upstairs and down. Once she got started, Donna related story after story about things she, Barbara and their friends had done, some funny, some sad. Once they returned to the kitchen, Dale leaned over the kitchen sink and looked out at the distant fields.

"Looks like the harvest has started for some folks," he said, standing back so Donna could take a look.

Off in the distance, a tractor was making slow passes along row after row of potatoes. Everything was silhouetted against the pale blue sky, and because the closed window muffled the sound, the view had a peculiar dreaminess. Trucks, moving faster than the tractor, sliced back and forth across the field, dropping off empty barrels and picking up full ones.

"Once it starts," Donna said, her eyes glazing with memory as she watched, "practically everyone in town joins in. If it wasn't for potatoes, I think a lot of Aroostock County would just dry up and blow away."

Dale grunted as he watched the workers. They followed in the wake of the tractor, bending over to pick up the potatoes the tractor had loosened from the soil and then putting them in near-by barrels for the truck crew to pick up. They moved slowly, backs bent, their arms mechanically picking up. The sheer drudgery they must feel was obvious as they worked, usually from sunrise to dark, always with one more row to clear.

"God, that looks tedious," Dale said. It took an effort of will to realize this was not a film, running in dreamy slow motion. These were real people out there, doing backbreaking labor simply to survive!

Donna let out a long sigh. The memory of potato digging made her shoulders and the small of her back begin to throb.

"It's wicked hard work," she said, lapsing for a moment into the Maine accent she had worked so hard to lose over the years. "I picked plenty of potatoes all through high school. The work is hard, and the pay is crap. Why do you think so many kids from the County want to go away to college and never come back? I made a vow when I got out of here that I'd beg on the streets before I'd dig potatoes." She nodded toward the window. "That's no way to live!"

Dale stretched out his arm and glanced at his watch. "Hey! If we don't get a move on, we're going to be late. Where's this lead?"

He swung open the door and saw that it led down to the cellar.

"You don't need to see down there!" Donna said. She crossed the floor and started to swing to door shut, but then something caught her eye and brought her up short. "What the-"

Dale glanced in the direction she was looking but didn't see anything unusual. It was a rickety stairway leading down into a gloomy cellar. Nothing extraordinary.

Donna swung the cellar down shut and gave the doorknob a firm shake to make sure it was closed. It wasn't until they were back in the car and driving away that she turned to Dale and said, "Did you see what I saw in there?"

Confused, Dale shook his head. "It's your house, not mine. I couldn't tell if there was anything out of the ordinary."

"On the cellar steps," Donna said, but her voice choked off momentarily when she remembered the old man's face, looming out at her from the darkness of the cemetery, looking almost as if he were *dead.*

"What?" Dale said, glancing anxiously up at the house unsure of what he was supposed to see.

"When I came out here yesterday, I never went down there, but just now I saw fresh dirt on the steps. It looked like someone had been down there recently."

Dale stiffened and scanned the house, but it looked as silent and deserted as it had been when they drove up. "Are you sure you didn't imagine it? Maybe the dirt wasn't fresh."

Donna looked at him with a grim set to her jaw. "I saw what I saw," she said, her voice low and steady. "I think someone else has been in there. Maybe they're still there!"

Dale twisted around and put his arm over her shoulder, trying to draw her close. "Look, you're just getting a little carried away what with last night and all.

I'm sure having to go to Larry's funeral isn't helping. Your imagination's working overtime, that's all."

Donna shook her head tightly as she put the car into gear and backed around, heading toward the road. When she started forward, she stepped too hard on the gas, and her tires spun out with a scraping hiss.

"Hey, if you're worried about it," Dale said, "give your buddy Winfield a call. Have him come out and take a look around. He's supposed to be keeping an eye on the place, isn't he?"

"I suppose so," Donna said, her voice lacking in conviction as she stared into the rearview mirror at the receding image of her family home.

# IV

Angie looked stunning in her dark navy blue dress; and Dale, in his imagination could picture her attending a wedding rather than a funeral that afternoon. When she dressed up, it pained Dale to see how much she resembled Natalie.

When he looked at her face, into her eyes, he could see the depth of the pain she was feeling. She was disappointed when Lisa said she wasn't going to go to the funeral with her, but Dale suspected Angie preferred to be alone with her sadness. It was natural for her to feel lonely, especially now that her father was "seeing Donna," as Dale phrased it.

The afternoon was crisp and cold as they walked out to their car in the driveway. Overhead, tumbling white clouds moved slowly to the south, and the sun, at one o'clock, already slanted toward the horizon. Angie shivered and snuggled into the collar of her coat, but she pulled away when her father tried to put his arm around her shoulder.

In silence, they drove out to Donna's sister's house. Donna was ready when they arrived, and came running out to the car before Dale reached the door. She scored an immediate point with Angie when, without pause, she climbed into the backseat.

"Did you give Winfield a call?" Dale asked before backing out of the driveway.

Donna nodded. She didn't want to say much in front of Angie, so simply said, "He told me he'd swing by today and take a look around."

"Good."

No one spoke as they drove out to Rodgers' Funeral Home, where the service would take place. They arrived early, but there were quite a few cars already lined up in the wide driveway when they drove up. A young man, shivering in a summer-weight jacket and tie, directed them to a parking spot out back. Dale found a spot right next to the long, black hearse, which was backed down a sloping ramp to the rear door.

So this is where they load and unload the bodies, Dale thought, unable to suppress a shiver as he got out of the car and pocketed the keys. He went around the car, opened the doors for Angie and Donna, and cocked out both arms for each to hold on as they walked to the front of the funeral home.

"Quite a turnout," Dale said to Donna.

"In a town like Dyer, everyone knows everyone," Donna said. She saw several people she hadn't bumped into since coming back, but now was not the time to catch up, so she nodded cursory greetings and followed Dale inside.

As soon as they entered the home, a smell hit Dale, setting his memory reeling. It wasn't just the cloying aroma of flowers, thick as fog in the still air; it was a smell beneath that, the sting of formaldehyde. The smell reminded Dale of specimens from biology class: twisted dead frogs, floating in a thin, brownish liquid. When he closed his eyes for a moment, to drive that sickening thoughts away, he saw, more vividly, faces, human faces floating wide-eyed in huge vats of the stuff. When his imagination made one of those faces Natalie's, his hands involuntarily tightened, and Angie and Donna looked at him, questioningly.

"You okay Dad?" Angie asked.

Dale gritted his teeth and nodded his head, afraid to speak because what might come out would be a long, wailing scream. The mental image of Natalie, floating in a sea of formaldehyde, began to fade, but not before he thought that he had seen her open her eyes and raise one hand, beckoning to him!

They signed the guest register and went into the dark paneled room where, only yesterday, Dale had seen the corpse of an elderly woman. Now, among a mass of bouquets, stood a closed white casket. Dale's knees weakened as he walked down the aisle a short way and then stepped back to allow Angie to sit first. He took the next seat, leaving Donna on the aisle. Soft strains of organ music mingled with the sounds of grief coming from the front of the room where Larry's family was already seated. Dale immediately recognized Roberta and the woman he assumed was Mildred, Larry's mother.

Before long, the room was full, and the minister entered and began the service. There were several eulogies from people who had known Larry, and three young girls, from Mildred's church, Dale guessed, sang *Abide With Me*. Dale was glad he hadn't been asked to say anything; he was sure his voice would have shattered even worse than those who did speak.

Not long into the service, though, Dale felt the uncomfortable sensation that someone was watching him. At first he figured it was his self-consciousness. He felt like an outsider here. This was Larry's town, and these were Larry's people. They had raised him, educated him, sent him off to college and a job. They were the ones who deserved to be here, sharing their sorrow, not *him!*

But as the service continued, the sensation grew stronger that someone was behind him, boring into his skull with a harsh, hostile gaze. Dale shifted in his seat and, pretending to reach into his pants pocket for his handkerchief, snuck a look around behind him. A dash of ice water ran through his veins when he saw Franklin Rodgers leaning against the wall in the farthest corner of the room. One of the candle sconces was next to his head, and a sliver of light caught his dilated left eye, making the pale blue pupil glow with vibrant intensity.

Dale flushed as he stiffly turned back around. He raised his arm and hugged Donna's shoulders, drawing her closer to him. She glanced up at him, her eyes brimming with tears.

The minister asked everyone to join in prayer for Larry's soul, but Dale only half-heard the words. Just knowing Rodgers was standing there, staring at him rattled Dale.

It's that *evil eye!* his mind shouted, and even though he knew such things were superstitious bullshit, he couldn't repress a shiver.

*What's the protection from the evil eye?* he wondered almost but not quite—smiling. He fought hard to pay attention to the words the minister was saying, but it felt like there was a dentist's drill boring into the back of his skull.

It wasn't until the service was over, and everyone stood to walk past the coffin to pay their last respects that he dared to look back at Rodgers.

Why is he watching me? Dale wondered

The funeral director hadn't moved. As far as Dale could tell, he hadn't even *breathed.* The light still glinted from his left eye, and the piercing blue speared out at him. Rodgers' lips were pulled back tightly, exposing his wide, flat teeth, and when their eyes met, he smiled at Dale, as if to say "I'm on to you."

But why was Rodgers acting so suspiciously, Dale wondered. Was he simply angry that he had bothered him yesterday with his request to view the body? Did he think Dale knew something he wasn't supposed to know? Was Dale close to something he wasn't supposed to find out?

*What the hell was going on?,* a voice inside Dale asked.

Dale's legs were stiff as he followed Donna out into the aisle and then waited to let Angie lead the way up to the front. Her face was streaked with tears, and no amount of tissue was going to stop the flood. She was sniffing and blowing her nose as she walked slowly forward. Dale and Donna held hands, but he kept one hand firmly on Angie's shoulder, ready to catch her just in case she fainted. That was about the only good thing about the closed-casket service that he could think of: at least Angie would be spared seeing Larry's death-waxed face, resting, forever in that satin-lined box.

They made their way past the family. Dale nodded a silent expression of sympathy to Mildred and Roberta, then followed Angie and Donna past the coffin. Angie paused and said something, but her voice was too hushed and strained from crying for him to hear what.

"Goodbye, Lar," Dale whispered as he reached out to let his fingers brush lightly over the polished wood. "I'm gonna miss yah." He imagined he could feel a faint trembling of energy vibrating the coffin. Angie was trembling with sorrow, so Dale clasped her tightly to his side and walked on by with Donna on his other side.

As they came back down the aisle, Dale saw to his relief that Rodgers was no longer standing there, waiting to lance him with his blue eye. Of course, now that the service was over, Rodgers would have business to attend to. He needed to get the casket loaded into the hearse and drive it out to Brooklawn, where, after a few more words from the minister, Larry would be lowered into the ground, never to be seen again.

The sunlight stung Dale's eyes as they went outside to get into the car and join the procession to the cemetery. He started up the car and came around to the front of the funeral home, then put the car into *park* while he waited. He drove mechanically, though, his mind blank and his heart feeling . . . hollow. He couldn't stop wondering how much of the numbness he felt was from Larry's death and how much was from Rodgers' cold stare.

"I just can't—can't get used to the idea that I'll.... I'll never *see* him again," Angie wailed. She turned and crumbled forward, burying her face into her father's chest.

"There, there," he cooed. "Just cry it out. It's the only way you'll feel better." He patted her on the back and drew her close, surprised by how small and frail she seemed. For so long, now, he had been thinking of her as a big girl, but this had reduced her to a little girl again. He could picture her at four years of age, trying to understand why her mother wasn't coming home anymore.

Natalie! Dale's mind echoed, the name receding into a whisper that blended with Angie's deep sobs. His own eyes were stinging, but he held back his tears, making himself strong for Angie's sake.

Donna leaned forward over the backseat and whispered softly, "If you think it'd be better for you two to be alone, I can walk home from here."

"Oh, you don't have to do that."

"It isn't very far," Donna said. She stroked Angie's hair and smiled sympathetically. "And actually, I think I wouldn't mind having a little time by myself."

Dale knew Donna had never considered Larry a close friend. They had grown up together in a small town, had been junior high school sweethearts for all of a week— and they couldn't help but bump into each other now and again; but Donna had run with a different crowd. She had forgotten Larry just as she had tried to forget everyone and everything else in Dyer. He appreciated her offer, though, and smiled his thanks.

"You're sure you don't want a ride?" he asked.

Donna shook her head, firmly *no*.

"I'll give you a call later this afternoon, then," he said, as Donna opened the back door and got out of the car.

"Sure," she said. Shutting the door gently, she started down the walkway toward the street.

The funeral procession took a few minutes to get organized. Dale kept hugging Angie close to him, trying to comfort her, but all the while his mind was filled with just one image: that of Franklin Rodgers' dilated blue eye, staring unblinkingly at him; and one thought kept springing into his mind: What is it that Rodgers doesn't want me to know?

It was as simple as that! Slightly paranoid, perhaps, but simple!

As they drove out to Brooklawn Cemetery, where the deep, rectangular hole waited to receive Larry's coffin, Dale became even more convinced that, with or without Winfield's help, he was going to check deeper into Larry's death; and he knew the first thing to do, right after he dropped Angie off at Mrs. Appleby's, was to drive out to the accident site and have a look around.

# V

The burial took less than fifteen minutes, and for that, Dale was grateful. Between the loss he and Angie were feeling, and the disturbing sensation that Rodgers was watching him, Dale wanted nothing more than to be done with the funeral. But he had also wanted to say a few words to Larry's mother, so after the minister had said another prayer and sprinkled a handful of dirt over the coffin, Dale lingered while the immediate family gathered, heads bowed, around the freshly-dug grave.

The afternoon sky grew pale—as pale as Rodgers' left eye, Dale thought with a shiver as a strong wind from the west sent autumn leaves flying. Some leaves blew into the open grave and gathered, like brown snowdrifts, in the lee of the mound of flowers surrounding Larry's casket.

Dale kept looking back over his shoulder, positive that Rodgers, sitting in the hearse unseen behind the glare on the windshield, was watching and waiting for the family to depart before supervising the final covering of the grave. The back of Dale's neck prickled when he imagined those cold, blue eye, boring into him from behind.

What's the magical protection against the evil eye? he wondered more than half-seriously.

Mildred Cole suddenly collapsed and would have fallen to the ground if her sister hadn't caught her. Dale heard her as she wailed, "My baby! *My baby!*"

The minister came over to her and, gently but firmly guided her to one of the waiting cars. They passed close to Dale, but Mildred seemed not even to notice him. Her eyes were brimming with tears, and she had the vague, unfocused stare of someone who is heavily medicated.

"Mrs. Cole?" Dale said, his voice catching in his throat.

She paused, looked at him for a second, and then continued her stiff-legged walk toward the waiting car. Dale took a shuddering breath, cast one last look at

Larry Cole's casket, and then, realizing words were futile went down to where Angie waited for him in the car.

# VI

An hour after the funeral, especially after he had changed out of his suit, Dale felt a slight measure of relief; and when he picked up Donna at her sister's house, he felt even better. She was wearing jeans and a mint green sweater that did very little to hide the curves of her body. Without makeup, her face radiated a clean, natural beauty that, despite knowing her for so short a time, filled him with a bubbly, light-headed feeling.

"I hope Angie's feeling all right," Donna said as she slid into the front seat. She leaned forward and gave him a quick kiss on the cheek. It was not as steamy as last night's "heavy petting," but Dale was just as glad to let things slow down ... a little bit.

"I feel a little guilty, leaving her alone now," Dale said, smiling weakly.

"We don't have to do anything today," Donna said quickly. "If you think you should spend the time with her, you should."

Dale grunted and shook his head. "Well, I don't know. She said she was feeling better. And Lisa and she were planning on going to a movie in Houlton. Mrs. Appleby was going to drive them. So—I guess she'll be in good hands. She has to be out doing things to get her mind off it."

"Getting over something like this takes a lot of time," Donna said. She had her own thoughts about things that she had to get over. Thinking about Brad Phillips made her envy Angie and her grief in at least one respect: they both had to overcome the pain of losing someone they once loved but at least Angie didn't have to get over the black poison of resentment!

Her smile was warm and sympathetic, and it made Dale like her all the more. He told himself he wasn't in love but when he was honest with himself, he admitted that he felt good with her. Time spent with Donna was good and comfortable, as if they had known each other much longer than one day.

"She'll do fine," he said as his gaze drifted out toward the vault of the sky, and he really believed Angie would be fine eventually. But he honestly wondered if he himself would be fine again. The funeral had stirred up thoughts and feelings he had buried long ago. Memories of Natalie rose in his mind like dark fragments swirling in a ghastly stew.

And it certainly struck him as ironic, that he would meet someone like Donna when he least expected to. He had gotten used to living with his memories and his loss, and now here was Donna! He had no idea what her plans were; he knew she didn't want to stay in Dyer for very long, but beyond that, she was evasive. On top of everything else, he felt like such a fool for even thinking about such things.

"I've already shown you all of Dyer's hot spots," Donna said. "What did you have in mind?"

For a moment, for the sake of levity, Dale almost said "Let's drive out to the No-Tell Motel, rent a room, and screw until we're raw!" But when he considered what he really intended to do, a sudden wave of darkness clouded his mind.

"You said yesterday you'd drive with me out to Casey's Curve."

Donna heaved a deep sigh as she looked him squarely in the eyes. "Don't you think you might be . . ." She paused and drew another breath, choosing her words carefully. "Maybe pushing this a little too far?"

"What do you mean?"

They were driving down Burnt Mill Road, with the afternoon sun behind them, lighting up the town with a soft, golden light. Except for Sparky, still manning his post by the gas pumps, the town seemed all but deserted. The windows in the town building reflected back the sky like slabs of cool, black marble.

"I mean," Donna said as Dale signaled and turned left onto Main Street, "that I'm beginning to worry about you just a little bit," she hurriedly added.

"Because I want to go out there and have a look around?"

She nodded. "You don't just want to, you *have* to!" she said, an edge of irritation creeping into her voice. "Why don't you just forget about it? I mean, Larry's dead and buried, and that's that! Let him rest in peace."

"Yeah, but that's just it," Dale said. "There are still a couple of things bothering me. And it's not me alone; it's Larry's mother, too. I won't rest easy until I check it out. I just think we might find something. I don't know what! I just want to have a look around."

As they approached the edge of town, Dale stepped down on the accelerator. Soon they were cruising south along Route 2A, his car negotiating the curves with solid ease.

Donna was silent for a while, having decided to let Dale have his way. She figured this was one way he had of laying Larry's ghost to rest once and for all, so maybe after he did that, it would be over and they could get on with . . .

*"With what?"* she wondered as she looked out at the wall of pine trees flashing past the window. What the hell exactly was happening between them? He certainly wasn't any Brad Phillips, but you could never tell.

"It's coming right up," Donna said.

Dale eased up on the gas, and realized he had been lost in his own thoughts, completely unmindful of why he was driving out here. Maybe, he thought, it has something to do with the winding road. It does sort of hypnotize you.

"Just over this crest. There on the left."

Dale checked his rear view mirror to make sure there were no cars behind him before pulling over to the left side of the road and stopping right in front of the rock that marked Casey's Curve. He killed the engine, and he and Donna got out.

Dale noticed that here, so short a distance out of town, the forest began to reassert itself. Dyer was surrounded to the north and west by large expanses of potato fields, but to the south and east, towards Canada, it was all heavy forest, primarily towering spruce and pine. The wind swayed the tall tops of the trees which hissed like steam. The slanting sun had almost no chance of cutting through the thick growth, and everything was cast in deep shadow.

As they walked from the car toward the rock, three crows took flight from the pile of litter where they had been picking. Cawing rough protests at being disturbed, they wheeled overhead once and then vanished into the woods.

"Great omen," Dale said. He was a bit surprised at himself for sounding so superstitious—first Rodgers and his evil eye, and now three crows! Good way to end up in the funny farm, he told himself.

The boulder on the side of the road was much larger than Dale had imagined it from Winfield's description. It was twelve feet tall and covered an area of ground larger than three full-sized dump trucks. Rusted beer and soda cans, along with candy wrappers and empty potato chip bags, which the crows had been picking ranged the base of the rock like a filthy necklace.

Dale whistled between his teeth as he looked up at the rock. "Looks like the kids in these parts like to party out there," he said.

Donna nodded. "It was the same back when I was in school. They like to sit up at the top at night, drinking beer or smoking pot, waiting to see if there'd be an accident."

"They're not ambulance chasers; they let the ambulance come to them. Sounds like great fun!" Dale said, kicking up a clump of crumpled, sun-bleached litter.

Winfield had been right about one thing, though; the kids from surrounding towns had had a field day, spray-painting messages and pictures on the face of the rock. *Terry luvs Debbie*—(The "luvs" had been X-ed over and replaced with "rubs"), *Houlton Hornets Suck Shit, Eat The Rich; You can take away my Gusto, just keep your hands off my Busch,* along with the symbols of several high school fraternities and sororities and what Dale guessed were the logos of some current heavy metal bands. One particular drawing caught his eye: a scaly white snake, swallowing its own tail.

"I guess you couldn't miss this in the dark," Dale said, glancing at Donna.

She was lost in her own memories, thinking about the time, long ago, when Ralph Hutchins had painted *Ralph Loves Donna* on the rock. He had used Latex paint, and the message didn't even survive one winter. But that was longer than the romance had lasted, she thought with a laugh.

"The thing is, it comes up kind of fast on you because of the crest back there," she said, hiking her thumb back the way they had come.

Dale wandered around the rock, stumbling over the torn open bag of garbage that was the departed crows' supper. When he saw the swath Larry's car had carved out of the woods, a thick lump formed in his throat and almost choked him. One edge of the rock looked freshly chipped, and at a sharp angle from there, a seven-foot wide strip cut more than twenty feet into the brush. The trees that had finally stopped Larry's progress had fresh gashes, like trail blazes left by a vicious woodsman.

"Goddamn!" Dale said when Donna came up behind him and slid her arm around his waist. "He must've been going sixty or seventy miles an hour to do this kind of damage."

Donna said nothing; she simply stood there, shaking her head. Dale broke away from her and carefully walked the length of the clearing made by Larry's car. Smaller trees were flattened, and the mulchy ground had twin runnels, several layers deep where the tires had skidded. He could see the deep tire imprints where the tow truck must have backed in to haul out Larry's car.

For the next few minutes, Dale walked back and forth across the cleared area, bending low and carefully observing the ground. He really didn't know what he was looking for; it certainly looked as though the police had done a thorough job of cleaning up. The woods would take its own time to heal the rest of the wounds.

"You know, one thing just keeps coming back to me," Dale said when he rejoined Donna, who was still waiting at the edge of the road.

"What's that?"

"How really God-damned pitiful it is that the reason Larry was up in this area in the first place was the reason he died. It was roads like this that the state wants to improve. We've certainly had enough complaints to warrant some improvements up here."

Donna nodded. "Yeah, but I don't think it's just the curves in the road that cause accidents. If you've ever driven a long stretch of this road, you'd know it's the monotony that gets you more than anything else. Just trees, and trees, and more trees! It can all sort of lull you, until you come to a sharp curve. Sometimes on a straightaway, a logging truck will pull out on to the road from some timber road, and *whammo!* That's it. You're history. Of course, some people sort of add to it."

"What do you mean?"

Donna shrugged and looked fearfully down the dark stretch of road. "Lots of people insist this stretch of road is haunted. You've got to admit, it *is* kind of creepy."

"I suppose so," Dale said, nodding agreement. He stood there silently for a moment, his chin in his hand, contemplating. At last, with a deep sigh, he said, "Yeah, but Larry was just heading out of town. He'd been on the road for what? a few minutes. He didn't have time to get 'highway-hypnotized.' "

"It was late at night," Donna said. "Maybe he was overtired and shouldn't have been driving."

Dale shook his head. "Another thing I wonder is, why was he going so damned fast? I knew Larry. He wasn't a hot-rodder. As a matter of fact, when he would drive me out to a construction site or something, I'd get frustrated at how slow he went. I always said he drove like an old lady. It just wasn't like him to speed."

"Yeah, but you're forgetting how fast this turn comes up on you after that crest back there," Donna said.

"And you're forgetting that Larry grew up here. He knew this curve and this rock were here just as well as you did! You were in the same class as Larry, right?"

Donna nodded.

"How old were you when Casey totaled the school bus here?"

"I don't know, maybe five or six."

"But old enough to remember it, right?" Dale said.

"Oh, sure."

"So," Dale said, clapping his hands to his sides. "Larry wasn't a dummy. He knew the curve and the rock were here. So why . . . why wasn't he more care-ful? Unless maybe he was being followed. Or maybe chased?"

"Right," Donna said, snorting with laughter. "He was —I've got it; he was running drugs from Canada, and the Mounties were after him. He died in the crash, and they confiscated the drugs, so there was a big cover-up. Starting with Jeff Winfield, who was getting a kick-back from some Canadian drug-lord. Right?"

Dale's frown let her know immediately that he wasn't amused. "I was thinking more along the lines of Franklin Rodgers," he said. He tried, but wasn't success-ful in keeping the image of Rodgers' blue eye and dilated pupil from rising in his mind.

"Oh, yeah. Sure," Donna went on, "Rodgers was in on the drugs. Larry was so pumped up, the last thing the authorities wanted was an autopsy, so Rodgers forced the closed casket on Mildred to hush everyone up."

"That isn't close to funny!" Dale shouted, suddenly turning on Donna with a blast of anger. "My best friend *died* here! And if you're going to stand there making jokes about it, you can . . . you can . . ."

"Hey! Come on," Donna said. She came up close to him and slid both arms around his waist. "I was just trying to make you see how silly it is for you to be getting all worked up about this." She pulled his face down toward hers and gave him a long, slow kiss. Her tongue darted into his mouth, and she made a soft moaning sound as she hugged him closer.

"There, is that better?" she asked when they finally broke off the kiss.

Dale nodded, but she could tell by the tension in his body that it wasn't bet-ter, not by a long shot!

"I was thinking, one thing we could do is pick up where we left off last night," she said, her voice low and husky close to his ear. "I don't want to sound too easy, but I'm willing to 'go all the way."

Dale looked at her, and her eyes were sparkling with humor at her use of such an old-fashioned phrase; but beneath the humor, there was a smoldering longing, a need to be loved. His heart thumped heavily in his chest.

"One thing before we go," he said, backing away from her. "I want to walk up to the crest there and take a look around."

Donna sighed deeply, and as he turned to go, reached out and snagged him by the arm. "And after that, you'll let it drop?"

Dale looked her squarely in the eyes and said, "After that I will. I promise."

Donna smiled and nodded. "Well, then, while you do that, I think I'll just wait in the car and have a cigarette if it's all right with you."

"Just make sure you open the window," Dale said, frowning.

# VII

The hospital doors slammed open, and the Medcu emergency team quickly rolled the stretcher into the emergency room.

"Get someone here. Stat!" one of the men shouted when the desk nurse came over toward them. But before she could respond, a thin man with black hair and thick glasses came out of the doctors' station. The name on his badge read: *Steven Wayne—Physician's Assistant.*

"Steve!" one of the Medcu team shouted as soon as he saw him.

"What have you got?" Steve said as he quickly scanned the man lying on the stretcher. He was young, probably around thirty years old, had sandy hair and a fairly hefty build. Right now, Steve saw, he was alive and conscious, but obviously in a great deal of pain. "Did you get vitals?"

The Medcu man nodded. "Pulse and B.P. are all right. His name's Reginald Perry, from Mars Hill. He was out harvesting on a farm along Bates Ridge. He stumbled and fell, and a tractor ran over his chest. From what I could gather, he was damned lucky. He fell in between two rows, and the tractor tire sort of pressed him into the ground. It was soft where it had just been dug. Otherwise, we could've just slipped him under the door at Rodgers'."

"Oh—gee," the man on the stretcher said, gasping loudly. "Thanks for the—" He coughed, high and tight, and his voice cut off with a gasp.

"Don't worry, Mr. Perry," Steve said. "You're going to be just fine." He peeled back each eyelid in turn and held a penlight close to check pupil dilation. Then he took an ear scope and checked for bleeding inside the ears. After a quick stethoscope check, Steve nodded to the Medcu team.

"We're looking okay," he said. "No cuts or serious contusions. Get him down to X-ray right away. My only concern right now is any lung punctures. There's probably a cracked rib or two."

"It—hurts—like—*hell*—to breathe," Perry said. His eyes were tiny slits; when he tried to cough again, the best he could make was a watery rattling sound.

"Let's get him down to X-ray," Steve said. He backed away as the Medcu team and two nurses shifted Perry onto a hospital stretcher.

"My insurance—card is—in my—wallet," Perry gasped.

"We'll take care of everything. Don't worry," Steve said as watched Perry get wheeled away. "I want to see him as soon as he's through in X-ray," he called out just as the stretcher rounded the corner and was gone. The Medcu team turned and rolled their stretcher back out to the van; then one of them came back to fill in the necessary emergency forms.

An hour later, with a tube stuck down his throat to keep his throat clear, an I.V. line jabbed into the back of his hand, an oxygen mask over his nose, and a strong jolt of pain-killer doing cartwheels in his system, Reginald Perry resting about as comfortably as possible, considering the internal damage he had suffered. The room where he was sleeping was silent except for the steady beep of the monitors that registered his pulse and other vital functions. Late afternoon sunlight, sliced into thin bars by the closed Venetian blinds, reached across the floor and up onto his bed. Perry wasn't sleeping deeply, merely hovering somewhere in a drugged haze of pain.

The door to Perry's room, Room 217, swung slowly open. Steve Wayne quickly entered and hushed the door shut behind himself. For a few seconds, he stood there motionless, watching his sleeping patient and listening to the steady beep of the monitors. He had his left hand in the pocket of his white doctor's jacket; his other hand repeatedly swiped at the sheen of sweat that glistened like dew on his forehead and upper lip.

Prison bars, he thought as his eyes focused on the narrow bands of light crossing the bed. Great . . . just great . . .

He took the padded chair from the corner of the room and slid it over in front of the door, bracing it so the top was jammed up under the handle. He gave the door a hefty tug to make sure it would stay shut, then went over to the bed.

Reginald Perry's breathing was short and shallow, and Steve could hear a slurping sound from deep inside the breathing tube. With his left hand still in his jacket pocket, he gingerly peeled back the blanket covering the sleeping man. The thickly-muscled arm, tanned a deep brown, lay heavily on the clean, white sheet. Twisting blue veins twined over the inside of Perry's forearm.

"I promise you," Steve whispered hoarsely, "this won't hurt you at all."

Saying that, he gave the sleeping man's arm a squeeze just below the biceps, probing until he found the artery he wanted. Then he withdrew his left hand from his jacket pocket and held an empty syringe up to the light. The clear barrel caught a ray of sunlight and reflected it. As Steve slowly drew back the plunger, the needle tip made a thin whistling sound. Steve froze when Perry stirred on the bed, but the man's eyes remained shut, and his breathing remained shallow.

"Almost ready," Steve said softly. He held the needle poised and then slid it into Perry's arm with a quick jab.

"Auggh!" Perry cried, his eyes snapping open and widening with fright as Steve pressed in the plunger and shot a bubble of air into Perry's brachial artery.

Steve reached over and turned the monitor volume down, but not off. That would look suspicious. He stood back, a thin smile playing across his lips while he waited for the effect he knew was due within seconds. The bubble of air, no larger than a B-B pellet, would rush to Reginald Perry's brain and *pop!* one dead emergency room patient!

Steve quickly pocketed the blood-tipped syringe, pushed the chair back into the corner of the room, and, calmly as he could, walked out into the hospital corridor. He let go a hissing sigh of relief when he saw that the corridor was deserted; no one had seen him either enter or, more importantly, leave Perry's room.

So far, so good, he thought as he walked briskly down the corridor. Just beside the waiting room was a bank of pay phones. Dr. Joseph Foster, the emergency room director, had made it clear on several occasions that he didn't want the personnel using the hospital phones for personal use, so he knew it wouldn't look unusual when he entered one of the booths and swung the door shut. He wanted to be sure he could make this call without being overheard!

His fingers were shaking as he fished change out of his pocket, counted out two dimes, and dropped them into the slot. As soon as he heard the dial tone, he punched the buttons for a number he had dialed more times than he cared to remember. While he waited for the other party to answer the phone, he thought, again, of the bars of light slicing across the bed in Room 217.

Prison bars! he thought ... If they ever find out about this, that's what I'll be looking at.

"Hello?" a gruff voice said on the other end of the line.

"Hello. This is Steve Wayne, up at Northern Med."

"Yesss . . ." The voice drew the single word out in a long sibilant.

"I've got a fresh one for you," Steve said, cupping the mouthpiece with his hand. His eyes kept flicking out in to the corridor every time someone walked past the phone booth. Already, the booth was heating up, filled with the sticky stench of sweat.

"Oh? You do?" the voice said, almost purring.

"Just came in a little while ago," Steve said, glancing nervously at his watch. It had been almost three hours since they had wheeled Reginald Perry into the Emergency Room; less than five minutes since the air bubble had popped into his artery. By now, there should be a nice, solid flat line on his monitors.

A sudden flurry of activity outside the phone booth caught his attention, and Steve watched, almost smiling, as two nurses hurried down the corridor. He opened the phone booth just a crack, and then smiled when he heard a voice on the public address say, "Code nine. Room 217. Code nine. Room 217."

"They just found him," Steve whispered into the receiver. His left hand was tucked down into his jacket pocket, clenched around the smooth barrel of the hypodermic needle. He knew he had to get rid of that soon; he wouldn't want to be found holding onto an empty, blood-tipped needle, especially not when the blood matched that of the recently deceased.

"Well, then," the voice on the phone said softly, "I suppose I should hang up, now. I assume I will be getting a call soon from the hospital."

"Uhh —" Steve said quickly as a doctor walked briskly past the booth, heading toward Room 217. "Before you hang up. About my payment . . ."

"Don't worry," the voice said. "You'll be taken care of soon."

Steve's smile widened. "I know this might not be the time to mention it, but I've been thinking lately that since *I'm* the one who's taking most of the risk here, I think I ought to be getting maybe a little more than usual."

"We've already established a price," the voice said, and there was more than a hint of iron in the tone.

Steve took a shallow breath and held it. "Yeah, well, I think the price just went up," he said, fighting to keep control of his voice. "Just wait 'till you see this one. He's a good one."

There was a long pause at the other end of the line, and Steve could hear the other party take a deep, rasping breath. "Tell you what, Mr. Wayne. I'll wait until I actually see this one, and I'll consider whether or not you're due for an increase. Is that fair?"

"Look, I've got to go," he said. "I guess—yeah that sounds all right."

"We'll be in touch," the voice said, and there was a soft click on the phone, followed by dead air. Steve slowly cradled the receiver and, casting a furtive glance each way, left the phone booth. First he'd dump the hypodermic needle; then he'd rush on up to Room 217 and see what the commotion was all about. He occupied his mind with thoughts of what he was going to do with the money once he got it.

# VIII

The loneliness of the road, now that Donna was waiting for him in the car, intensified as Dale walked along the dirt-rutted shoulder, scanning his eyes back and forth. The sun was close to the horizon, so what few beams of light made it through the trees cast long shadows. Night came fast in the woods, but Dale wanted to survey the road, and the fatal turn, from the crest of the hill. He had to see what was surely the last thing Larry Cole saw!

He walked slowly, keeping his eyes to the ground until he was at least a hundred yards from his parked car. Then he stopped and turned around. The spray-painted graffiti on the rock stood out as though it was lit in neon, but Dale had to remind himself that Larry had been driving late at night. All he would have had to see by were his headlights.

Would they have been enough? he wondered as he looked back along the last hundred yards of road his best friend ever got to drive. He kept telling himself: Larry had grown up here ... He knew the turn and the rock were here! So why in the hell was he driving fast enough to plow so far into the woods?

Dale's eyes started to sting as he looked back along the road in the fading light. The quiet and loneliness ate at his nerves. He could almost imagine Larry's ghost, still shocked at the suddenness of his death, hovering in the mist-shrouded trees, its face a ghastly, bloody mess. The finality of it all jabbed through him like a spear, and he didn't bother to wipe away the tears that now flowed freely down his cheeks.

He could see the dim silhouette of Donna's head, the pale blue cigarette smoke drifting out of her window as she waited for him in the car. Along with his questions about Larry, several dozen questions shot into his mind about her, too.

*How much do I feel for her?* he wondered. *What do I actually feel?*

In some perverse way, Dale felt like he was still working out his feelings for Natalie in his attraction to Donna. He had been so strongly and so immediately drawn to her, he couldn't help but think she might be little more than an emotional lifeline for him, the first available anchor he could grab to help him deal with this fresh loss.

Am I being fair to her? Dale thought. Am I stringing her along so she could be my emotional crutch for the next few days? Maybe I see her subconsciously as a surrogate for Natalie, just to help get over losing Larry.

And here they were, acting like long-term lovers, talking as casually as people did before AIDS about finding a motel and shacking up! It wasn't just crazy. It was *insane!* He didn't know her at all. Emotional commitments take time!

"*God-fucking-damn* it!" he whispered hoarsely as he drew his jacket cuff roughly across his eyes. He kicked his feet viciously at the ground, sending a wake of leaves flying into the air. They drifted down in a rattling shower, and it was only on the fringe of his mind that it registered that he had kicked something other than leaves. He distractedly looked for the object he had kicked when he glanced down at the ground, but when he saw what was there, his heart almost stopped.

"Holy Mother of—" he whispered as he knelt and looked at the object. The light was dimming so fast, and he realized with a dash of chills that maybe even a minute or two later, it would have been too dark for him to see it. He might have missed it! His hands were shaking as he knelt down and reached out tentatively to pick up the object.

He had recognized the tape recorder instantly! He and Angie had picked it out for Larry as a Christmas gift three years ago. It was a Sony-Micro voice-activated dictating machine. For years, Larry had complained to Dale (and everyone else in the office) that he hated taking notes and typing them into a report. The dictating machine had been Angie's idea, and Larry had loved it.

"Holy Mother of God!" Dale repeated. As soon as he said it, there was a faint click, and the tape spools began to turn. "Testing, one—two—three," Dale said, looking at the slowly turning tape.

He stood up slowly, examining the machine, found the rewind button, and snapped it. The tape spun sluggishly for a few seconds, then stopped with a jerky drag. When Dale pressed play, the tape began to turn, but the voice that came from the small speaker was tinny and distorted.

". . . mother ... of God . . . Testing . . . one—two — three . . ."

Dale didn't think it sounded at all like his voice. He pressed stop/eject, and the transparent lid clicked open. He removed the micro-cassette and held it up to the fading light in the sky. Everything looked fine on the tape, but the recorder itself was another story. The outside was scuffed, and one corner had chipped off, probably from the impact when it had hit the road.

"But why was it *here?*" Dale said out loud, glancing the length of road from where he stood to the rock and the cleared swath where Larry's car had gone off the road. "Why this far away from the crash?"

He heard the car door open, and saw Donna stand up. Leaning over the car roof, she called to him, "Hey! It's getting kind of lonely down here, you know."

"Yeah . . . yeah," Dale shouted back. His voice echoed with a strange reverberation that, oddly, reminded him of how it had sounded over Larry's damaged recorder.

Had Larry tossed the tape recorder out of the car window, knowing he was about to hit the rock at Casey's Curve? Dale wondered. He was trying frantically to picture what might have happened out here last Friday night, but his mind kept coming up blank.

Had someone else, maybe one of the policemen investigating the scene, found it and then later dropped it?

Had there been someone else, either driving with or following Larry? Someone who Larry wanted to keep from finding the tape?

The answer might be right here, Dale thought, slapping the cassette into the palm of his hand. The first thing to do was to listen to the whole tape. Maybe the answer he was looking for was right in Larry's own words!

Donna was still leaning over the car roof, watching him as he walked back to the car. The darkening loneliness of the road sent a wave of shivers up her back, and she wished to God he would hurry up so they could get the hell out of there.

As he walked, Dale popped the tape back into the machine and, squinting to find it in the dark, pressed the rewind button again. The tape spun slowly in fits and starts, and it was obvious there wasn't enough power left in the batteries to keep it going. After spinning for a few seconds, the tape stopped abruptly. A small red light with the word *Battery* printed below it winked on like a tiny, angry eye.

"Shit!"

"What'd you find?" Donna asked when she saw he had something in his hand.

Dale showed her by pressing eject and holding the small cassette tape out to her.

"Larry always had the habit of dictating his notes while he was on the road," Dale said. "I found this way the hell back there, almost at the crest of the hill."

Donna looked up the road, then back at Dale.

"The batteries are just about dead, though," he said, pointing to the red warning light. He flipped the recorder over, found the battery lid, and slipped it open. "Looks like we need four double-A's."

Donna shook her head and said, "Well, we're not going to find them out here. Let's drive back into town and see if they have some at the Mill Store. Wait a sec. Don't you have a cassette player in the car?"

Dale shook his head. "Wrong size tape. These are the small ones that are used just for dictating."

They got into the car, and Dale had just started the engine when a pair of bright headlights suddenly came up on them from behind. The glare in the rearview mirror stabbed his eyes. He switched the mirror to night-view and then paused, staring at the headlights. After a moment, he realized the headlights weren't getting any closer to them.

"What the — ?" he muttered as he craned his neck around and looked back. The trees on both sides of the road narrowed down into a sharp *V* with the bright set of lights at the bottom point.

The vehicle sat there at the crest of the hill, its lights washing down on Dale's car and illuminating the large rock in harsh relief. Dale waved his hand, signaling for the driver to take off his high beams, at least, but nothing happened. The car just idled there at the crest of the hill.

Dale had the sudden, sinking feeling that the car behind them was a hawk, and he and Donna were the rabbits that should have sought shelter. His breath caught in his throat when he turned to Donna and said, "I don't like this!"

"Neither do I," Donna said. "Let's get the hell out of here."

Dale eased the car into reverse and backed out onto the road. As soon as he started to turn, heading his car back toward town, the headlights suddenly shot forward.

"Shit!" Dale shouted as he jammed the car into first, pressed the accelerator to the floor, and let the clutch pop out. The tires kicked up dirt and gravel, sounding like tearing paper as the car leaped forward with a loud squeal. Larry's recorder fell off the dashboard to the floor, but Dale held tightly onto the tape.

As his car shot forward, Dale clicked on his own headlights, flicking his eyes back and forth between the road ahead and the headlights that were suddenly very close to his rear bumper and closing in on him fast!

"What the Christ is this?" he said, glancing at Donna as he slammed through the gears and negotiated the curving road ahead.

Donna's face looked sheet-white as she put her elbow up on the back of the seat and watched the car behind them. She grimaced, and a low moan escaped from her throat.

"I have no idea who it could be," she said. Her voice twisted tightly every time the headlights loomed closer.

"Well, it sure looks like they don't want us on the road here," Dale said. He pressed down on the accelerator as hard as he dared, but the twisting road kept throwing its own surprises at him. He could feel a knotted tension winding up into his shoulders, and the back of his head began to tingle.

"It sure as hell isn't the cops," Donna said, still staring back at the car. "They'd have their blue lights going if they wanted you to pull over."

"If it was official, I guess they would," Dale said. "It's a big car. I can tell by how far the headlights are spaced." He jerked his hand back and forth, taking the curves as tightly as he could, hoping that his smaller car could out-maneuver the big car behind them.

"I think it's —I don't know," Donna said, straining to see behind the glare of light. "It looks like some kind of limo or something."

As they started rounding a particularly sharp curve, the car behind them suddenly pulled up close to their rear bumper, so close, in fact, Dale muttered something about they would be touching if his bumper had one more coat of chrome. The headlights behind them suddenly started flashing rapidly on and off, creating a strobe-light effect inside the car and on the road ahead. A wave of dizziness swept over Dale as he focused as hard as he could on the scrolling road ahead. He suddenly realized that whoever it was behind them, doing this was probably the same person who had done exactly the same thing to Larry!

A numb pain started to spread up the back of his hand holding the cassette tape, and Dale kept telling himself that, if they survived this, he would learn everything he needed to know once he got new batteries and played Larry's tape.

Larry had known something and whatever it was, it was so important that someone had arranged for Larry to die at Casey's Curve.

"But I've got the tape, you bastard!" Dale suddenly shouted, shaking his hand that held the cassette. "I've got this, and I'll be goddamned if *you're* going to get it!"

Donna's eyes were two large ovals of fear, glowing with the reflected light of the car close on their tail. Her soft whimpering had grown louder, but it was barely audible above the racing whine of the car's engine.

"What's the road like up ahead?" Dale asked suddenly.

He was managing to keep a slight lead on the pursuing car, so he was beginning to relax. As far as Dale was concerned, he could race like this all night. Still, he didn't want to get caught by surprise if there was a dangerous stretch of road ahead.

Donna shook her head furiously. "I don't know, I don't know. I mean, Christ, I haven't lived around here in years! I can't remember!"

"We're heading into Haynesville, right?"

"Yeah."

"Well . . . What's the road like?"

"Christ if I know!"

The headlights suddenly darted up close again, and the driver started flashing the high beams, but Dale kept his jaw firmly set and his eyes on the road, ignoring the distraction. They passed a few houses along the side of the road, but so far, there was no sign of a cop anywhere.

They were rounding a gradual curve at a high speed, and Dale was confident he had control of the car, but then the unexpected happened: A deer shot out of woods, and when it saw the oncoming cars, with lights flashing madly, it froze stock-still in the middle of the road.

"Ahh, shit!" was all Dale had time to shout. Donna let out a long, warbling scream that was buried when Dale laid his hand down on the horn and didn't let up on it as the car fishtailed around the curve. When the tires swerved onto gravel on the right side of the road, he thought he was going to lose control. He had a vivid instant of looking into the deer's eyes, two wide, glistening pools, reflecting cold, green light, and he braced himself, waiting for the impact.

Donna's scream slid smoothly up the scale until it was nothing more than a high-pitched screech. Dale ground his teeth together, waiting for one of two things to happen: he would either smash his car against a deer, or the car behind him would give him that extra little nudge he needed to carve his own trail into the woods. No doubt, that trail would end with a thick-boled tree where the deer ought to be, and he and Donna would sail face-first through the front windshield.

But neither of those two things happened. By some miracle, Dale swung around the deer, and as his right foot gently pumped the brakes and he fought for control of the car, he suddenly became aware that the lights had winked out of his rearview mirror.

"Mother-humper!" he hissed between clenched teeth as he downshifted and brought the car to a skidding stop. Dust swirled like fog up around the car, but with barely a pause, he slammed the car into reverse and spun the wheel around. He gasped when he looked back along the road.

The deer was gone, had disappeared like smoke into the woods. The car that had been trailing them was also gone, vanished without a trace. One second it was there, right on his bumper, and now . . . puff! Gone! The surrounding woods were as silent as the forest before dawn.

Dale slouched back in the seat and let out a deep sigh. "You okay?" he asked, turning to Donna, who was on the floor beside him.

She looked up at him with scared-rabbit eyes. Straightening up, she ran her hands down her sides, as though checking to make sure she was all there. She took a deep, shuddering breath and let it out slowly, then reached for a cigarette and lit it.

"Where the Christ did he go?" Dale asked. He suddenly felt like Ichabod Crane must have felt when he crossed the bridge and the Headless Horseman had suddenly disappeared. How could it be over so quickly, so completely? And they weren't dead!

Donna shook her head and blew out a thin stream of smoke. She was simply marveling that she was alive and not wrapped around a pine tree, bleeding to death.

Dale suddenly leaned close to her, his face contorted. "What were you saying? Something about this stretch of road being *haunted?*"

Donna shrugged, still finding it impossible to speak.

"It's weird," Dale continued, more to himself than to her, "how it just isn't there. Like it didn't really happen or something."

"It was real, all right," Donna said, her voice breaking as if someone had his hands wrapped around her throat. "A little too real!"

"Oh, I don't doubt that," Dale said. "And this is real, too," he added, juggling the micro-cassette into his open palm. "And I've got a feeling, whoever that was behind us just now also had something to do with Larry's death."

"Dale," Donna said, but her voice suddenly cut off before she could say more. Without thinking, she flicked the ash of her cigarette onto the floor. "I mean it," he said, still staring wide-eyed up at the empty, night-blackened road. "And I sure as shit aim to find out what's on this tape, right after we have a little chat with Officer Winfield."

# CHAPTER SIX
## "LARRY TALKS"

# I

The afternoon following Larry's funeral, Angie and Lisa spent most of the time riding bicycles all around town. Lisa allowed Angie to use the new pink Schwinn she had gotten for her last birthday while she dragged her rusted, purple Huffy out of the cellar and used that. The tires were bald, and the frame was bent, but she managed with it for the afternoon. After filling themselves with candy at Sparky's store, Lisa took Angie out on Ridge Road, so she could show her where she went to school.

Angie wasn't very impressed by the Tarr Memorial Junior High School, but she tried not to let it show as she politely followed Lisa around the building while Lisa chattered on about what went on in each room. After the grand tour, Angie started thinking it might not be a bad idea to head on home. She still got goose bumps whenever she remembered what had happened—and *almost* happened—to them out at Lisa's "secret place," and she didn't want to roam too far from home.

They were heading out of the school parking lot when Lisa told Angie that Larry's mother lived only two houses away from the school. Casting a fearful glance at the sky and at the sun sunk low on the horizon, she felt tempted to cruise by the house, if only to see where Larry had grown up; but she also didn't want to be outside after dark. Not when there was a chance those hobos might be around town.

"How far is it to your 'secret place' from here?" Angie asked her, hoping the tension she felt wasn't revealed by her voice.

Lisa seemed to stiffen as she twitched her head over in the direction of the tennis courts. "Through those woods there, I guess," she said. "I never really went there from anywhere but my backyard."

"Do you . . . ?" Angie started to ask, but she cut herself short before she finished her question.

Think those men are still out there? her mind completed the question for her. Goosebumps darted up both of her arms, and her teeth made a rapid little chattering sound.

"Come on," Lisa said as she swung her leg over the seat. "We can just ride by Larry's mom's house and then head home."

"Okay," Angie said as she mounted her bike, not thinking it was the best of ideas. They pedaled off together, with Lisa in the lead. Under the shading branches of tall pine trees, they sped down the road, their bike tires whistling in the wind.

"That's it there," Lisa said, twisting around and pointing at a house on the left side of the road.

Angie looked up at the modest home, somewhat surprised that it looked so simple. Somehow, she had expected Larry's home to be—well, different. Certainly, she never thought he had been raised in a mansion or anything, but this house looked too ordinary.

The driveway was filled with cars, and Angie knew Larry's family was probably gathered after the funeral to share a meal, to renew acquaintances, and to reassure themselves that they were still here. Through lighted windows, the girls could see people moving from room to room.

Angie slowed down and stopped beneath a spreading maple tree on the side of the road opposite Larry's house. Lisa kept going until she noticed Angie was no longer behind her. She slowed and turned around in a wide circle, rejoining her friend as she skidded to a stop underneath the maple. Still thick with leaves, the tree cast a dark shadow over the girls' faces as they both looked up at the house.

"Why don't we go back home now?" Lisa said softly. She could sense that Angie was making herself feel worse, staring up at the house. What she didn't like seeing was the tears running down her friend's cheeks.

"Yeah," Angie said, her voice hitching in her chest. But she didn't move. She wanted to reach out with her feelings, to touch a part of Larry one last time, and she honestly felt that she could do that if she were close to the place where he had grown up. She imagined that one of those silhouettes on the window shades was Larry's; she could go up the walkway, ring the doorbell, and Larry, smiling his silly, warm and wide grin, would hold his arms out to her and give her one of his famous bear hugs.

*Not anymore,* her mind whispered. *Not anymore!*

"If we don't get a move on, it'll be dark before we get home," Lisa said with sudden agitation. "I think my gram'll be mad at us if we don't get a-moving."

"Yeah, sure," Angie said, sniffing loudly and wiping her eyes with the back of her hand. But before she started to pedal away, with one last look at the house, she was filled with a sudden image that nearly stunned her in its awfulness. For a flickering moment, she felt certain that Larry really was up there in the house. He was there, with his family, and he and everyone else up there was . . . *dead!* Those shadows weren't cast by real living flesh and blood people. They were the shadows of *dead* people!

A twisted, tortured moan began to build in Angie's chest. She placed her foot on the pedal and leaned her weight forward, but her foot slipped, and her shin scraped roughly against the pedal. But the pain was overshadowed by a panic that flared up within her like a fire urged on by a dousing with gasoline. With a worried glance over her shoulder at Lisa, she started pedaling, and was soon sailing down the street with the wind streaming her hair back.

The tires of her borrowed bicycle hissed on the asphalt as her legs pumped furiously. Even when Lisa called out to her from behind, Angie didn't bother to look back. She was suddenly very certain that the same men who had been out at the abandoned barn now were in the woods all around them, and if she didn't get back to Mrs. Appleby's immediately, something awful was going to happen!

What would it be? she wondered frantically. What would happen? Larry wasn't up there! He couldn't be! She watched him get buried just that morning.

Her legs pumped the bicycle even faster, fueled by a raging fear that even now those men were in the fringes of the woods, watching her ride by at full tilt.

You'll be dead, a small voice, like the wind, whispered -. her ear. You'll be dead just like Larry if those men find you!

"Angie! . . . Angie! Wait up!" a voice called out from behind. In her panic, it took several seconds for it to register that Lisa was calling her. All day Lisa had struggled valiantly with the rattling frame, the rusted chain, and the slick tires of her old bike. Lisa pumped her legs as hard as she could, but she couldn't keep up with Angie, flying like the wind.

"Come on, Angie! . . . *Wait up!"* Lisa shouted, her voice a thin, warbling echo from the gathering darkness. -That's not fair!"

Her friend's complaint did, finally, cut through to her, and as Angie neared the corner of Ridge Road and Main Street, she stopped pedaling and, gently squeezing the hand brakes, coasted into the parking lot of Grace Baptist.

I'll be safe near a church, she thought as she glided in a wide circle. She came to a stop in the shadow of the steeple.

"Angie!" Lisa shouted as she came speeding down the street. "I'm gonna tell your father!" She had her head bent down, and was grimacing as she pumped on the pedals. Even from a distance, Lisa could see the strain registered on Angie's face.

Angie swung around again in a wide arc, thinking Lisa had seen her; but when she glanced back over her shoulder, all she saw was Lisa's back, hunched over the low handlebars of her bike. Her rapidly moving legs were a blur as she rounded the corner onto Main Street.

Angie realized Lisa either hadn't seen her or, more likely, had seen her and was giving her a taste of her own medicine. With one quick, worried look up at the white steeple pointing at the oncoming night sky, Angie pushed off again, confident she could easily catch up with her friend.

They raced down Main Street, the gap between them rapidly closing. Store fronts and houses whizzed past them. The town's streetlights had come on, but Angie took small comfort in their small pools of light. On the stretches between telephone poles, she felt vulnerable, wondering who or what might be lurking there in the darkness, just out of sight: . . . those men from the barn? ... or maybe Larry and his dead family?

"Hey!" she gasped as she came up quickly behind Lisa. "Why don't you wait up yourself?"

As soon as she spoke, Angie saw the front tire of Lisa's bike wobble. Her friend turned around with a wide-eyed, frantic expression that silently asked: where the hell did you come from? Angie was still looking ahead, so she saw the danger first. It was only after Lisa's front tire started scraping along the curb that she sensed trouble as well.

What happened next happened so fast, it seemed to be over before it began. Lisa's bicycle crashed into the curb at an angle which, at that speed, spelled big trouble. There was a loud screech as Lisa stepped back on the pedals, futilely applying the brakes. But the brakes were old and rusty, and they slipped. The impact tore the handlebars from her hands, and with a scream of fright, Lisa flew head first up and over the handlebars.

Angie squeezed both hand brakes when she saw Lisa's bike fly, "ass-over-tea kettle," as her grandfather used to say. She saw Lisa flip up into the air, her toes pointing skyward before she plummeted downward. If Lisa had just a bit more space to fall through, she might have okay. As it was, her forehead came down onto the sidewalk with a resounding crack, and the momentum carried her in an awkward, twisting flip. Her legs and back tumbled over and hit the sidewalk hard.

Angie was nearly blind with panic as she stopped the Tike and let it fall to the ground. She ran over to her friend, positive that Lisa was dead; and with a horrifying jolt, realized that she was the one who had made it happen!

"Oh, God! Oh, Jesus!" she wailed as she ran up to where Lisa lay, face up on the sidewalk, her legs splayed awkwardly. A passing car had seen the accident but had not stopped.

Tears streaked Angie's face as she knelt down beside Lisa, her hands fluttering wildly in the air, frantic for something to do. There was a street light nearby, and in its yellowish glow, Angie could see a small, dark pool of red.

*Blood!* her mind screamed. I've killed her! Oh my God, I killed her!

She was so lost in a whirlwind of panic, she only vaguely noticed a stirring on the ground in front of her. What brought her to was a low, bubbly moan from her friend as she opened her eyes and tried to sit up. Finally, with a near-superhuman effort, she did sit up.

"What the hell *happened?*" Lisa said. She had her head bowed and was shaking it slowly from side to side. Pinwheels of light cut like meteors across her vision, and there was a ringing sound in her left ear that modulated wildly up and down the scale.

"You're not dead!" Angie shouted, unable to believe what she was seeing. For a panicky moment, she was filled by the blinding fear that Lisa was dead, she just didn't know it yet.

Lisa gradually straightened up, moving stiffly and trying each limb, one by one, to make sure everything was still working. Thick ribbons of blood were gushing from Lisa's forehead, painting her face with wide, dark red stripes.

"You've cut yourself," Angie managed to say, as soon as the initial shock started to fade. "It looks pretty bad."

Frowning, Lisa put her hand up tentatively to her forehead, and when her fingers came away sticky with blood, her eyes rolled up to the back of her head, and she fainted. Luckily, Angie caught her before her head hit the sidewalk a second time. It was just then that a passing motorist saw the girls and stopped to help. All Angie could think was, Thank God for good Samaritans!

# II

Dale and Donna felt as though they had lucked out in at least one regard: when they got to the police station, Winfield's shift had already ended, but he was still at his desk, shooting the breeze with one of the other policemen.

"Have you got a minute?" Dale asked, interrupting a roaring gale of laughter inside the office.

Winfield, still shaking with laughter, looked up. His expression immediately sobered when he saw Dale in the doorway.

"Uh, yeah, sure," he said, getting up from his desk and coming over to the door. The other policeman nodded to Dale and Donna, then exited without another word.

"We're not bothering you, are we?" Dale asked as he stepped aside for Donna. They entered the office and Dale shut the door behind him. They sat down in the chairs next to the desk.

"No, not at all," Winfield said, as he sat back down at his desk. "Ernie, there, was just telling me a joke he heard. What can I do for you? Is this an official visit?"

Dale nodded. "Yeah, sort of." His hand went to his jacket pocket, where his fingers glided over the micro-cassette. Right after visiting Winfield, they planned to go buy some fresh batteries so they could play the tape.

"Well, I see you two have hit it off," Winfield said, still chuckling. "You're not here to ask me to give the bride away, are you?"

Donna flushed, and Dale cleared his throat. Winfield coughed with embarrassment and started twiddling with the pen on his desk.

"Oh, and by the way," Winfield said, "I haven't had a chance yet to go out to your folks' house and have a look around. I'm off-duty now but I could swing by before heading home."

Donna shrugged. With all the excitement out by Casey's Corner, she had forgotten all about the suspected problem out at her old home.

"I guess it could wait 'till tomorrow," she said.

Winfield nodded. "I may take a spin by tonight, anyway. So, what can I do for you?"

"Actually, we've got a complaint and a question for you," Dale said. "We had a little run-in with someone out on Route 2-A."

"What do you mean, a run-in?" Winfield asked. His voice suddenly tensed, and he sat forward in his chair. The grip he had on his pen tightened.

Dale quickly told Winfield what they had done after Larry's funeral, how they had gone out to Casey's Corner and then been chased by someone. Winfield listened attentively. It looked like he was taking notes, but in actuality he was merely doodling as he listened.

"You never got a good look at the car though, huh?" he said when Dale was finished.

Dale shook his head. "No, but it was big and bulky."

"What I could see of it," Donna added, "it looked like it might be a black, or dark blue, limousine. The headlights were wide apart; and when we first saw it, it wasn't quite night, but the car was a dark color, real dark."

Winfield leaned back in his chair, scratching underneath his chin as he looked up at the ceiling. "And you think this someone in a black limousine was out there to stop you from looking around at the crash site?"

"Have you got a better explanation?" Dale asked sharply. He hadn't mentioned finding Larry's dictating recorder yet; he wanted to listen to it first, before Winfield or anyone else heard what was on the tape.

Winfield shrugged. "No. Not really." His eyebrows were furrowed, casting his eyes into shadow as he pondered.

"So," Dale said after the silence had grown uncomfortably long. "Who do you know around town here who drives a black limo?"

Winfield opened his mouth, about to say something, then clamped his lips shut and sat back. He sighed shallowly, shook his head, and brought the back of his hand to his mouth.

"I, umm," he hesitated. Winfield fell silent for a moment before continuing. "The only person I know is someone you know, too," he said at last. When he saw Dale react, he quickly leaned forward, tapping his forefinger on his desk. "I don't want you to go jumping to any premature conclusions, now," Winfield said, his voice harsh, commanding.

"Rodgers," Dale concluded. There was a note of conviction in his voice that told Winfield he had already suspected it was Rodgers, and that he had just been waiting for confirmation.

"Well, it's pretty thin ice, if you ask me," Winfield said. "We're talking about very flimsy circumstantial evidence."

"That car, no matter who owns it, almost ran us off the damned road!" Donna said. In her voice, there was still an echo of the stark fear she had felt.

"But I can't very well go arresting someone just because you think it was a dark limousine, now, can I?" Winfield said. He was thinking, if it had just been Dale Harmon alone, he might have been less likely even to listen; but he had known Donna her whole life, and he liked and respected her. If she confirmed it, that put a whole new light on the matter!

"Is there anyone else in town who you might think would do something like this?" Dale asked intensely.

"I'm not saying there is or there isn't," Winfield replied. "Granted, I may not be Rodgers' biggest fan in town, but I certainly don't intend to go over to his house and ask him where he was this afternoon. You have no evidence."

"Why?" Dale asked. "Why can't you just question him?" He paused, and in the awkward silence that followed, quickly added, "You could probe a little deeper than you did yesterday."

Winfield tossed both hands into the air. "Because I happen to know where Rodgers was the same time you say you were out on the road."

"Oh?" Dale said. He couldn't deny a wave of disappointment that Rodgers might somehow wriggle off the hook.

Winfield was nodding his head with assurance. "Yes sir. There was a harvesting accident up on Bates Ridge this afternoon, and a fellow named Reginald Perry was taken into the hospital in Houlton. After he was treated for his injuries, he seemed to be doing all right, but sometime late this afternoon, he got a blood embolism and died. I think it was just around sunset that Franklin Rodgers drove to the Houlton hospital and picked up the body."

# III

Mrs. Appleby nearly fainted when she saw Lisa, Angie, and a woman she didn't immediately recognize coming up the walkway to the house. The blood on Lisa's face had dried to thin, brick-red flakes, but she still looked more dead than alive.

"You have to keep in mind that head wounds look a lot worse than they really are," said Joyce Carter, the person who had been driving by and had stopped to help. "There are a lot of blood vessels in the scalp, so there's going to be a lot of bleeding."

Mrs. Appleby thanked her profusely for helping the girls get back home. When she left, Angie left with her to unload the bicycles from her trunk, where they had stuffed them for the short drive up Main Street.

The night was cool, almost down-right cold. Overhead, the stars glittered with a sharpness Angie had never seen before, and directly over the house, the rippling glow of the Northern Lights swung like heavy curtains. She felt cold and alone and miserable as she wheeled the bikes up to the garage one at a time. She wished her father was around so she could talk to him, but lately, since Larry died, she had found him distant. She thought it was because he was spending so much time with the woman he had met, Donna LaPierre.

Back in the house, Mrs. Appleby sat Lisa on a chair in the middle of the kitchen floor beneath the harsh glare of the overhead light as she gently washed Lisa's head wound with warm, soapy water.

"I think Mrs. Carter was right. These look a lot worse than they are," Mrs. Appleby told Angie once she had rejoined them in the kitchen. She was standing, tensed, in the kitchen doorway, feeling rotten that she had made something like this happen!

Lisa winced every now and then as her grandmother's fingers probed the patch of scraped skin. A few scratches started bleeding again, and blood tickled her when one thin stream ran down beside her eye.

"What in the dickens were you two doing, anyway?" Mrs. Appleby said angrily. "You're both grown-up girls. You should know better than to fool around like this!"

"It was my fault," Angie started to say, but Lisa quickly cut her off.

"It was an accident! I should never have taken that junky old bike out in the first place!"

"Well, we'll make sure it goes out with the trash on Wednesday morning, if it's all the same to you," Mrs. Appleby said with finality.

Lisa nodded agreement, then winced when the motion of her head made her grandmother pull another cut open.

"Other than the cuts, are you feeling all right?" Mrs. Appleby asked. Head wounds may bleed easily, but she also knew that bumps to the head could be quite serious. Her own brother had fallen when he was a boy, and ever since then, due to some kind of scrambling to his brain's wiring, he had suffered with epilepsy. Head injuries Mrs. Appleby knew, were nothing to fool around with.

Lisa closed her eyes, taking a silent physical inventory. Although the ringing in her ear was very faint and seemed to be fading, it was still there; it rose in volume now and then, sometimes actually masking what her grandmother was saying to her.

"I—umm," she started to say, then fell silent when she glanced over at Angie, who still stood in the doorway, nervously biting her lower lip.

Lisa gave her head a tentative shake, and winced with the pain that bolted up the back of her neck. "I think I could use some aspirin or something," she said as her eyes began to water from the pain.

"If it's really bad," Mrs. Appleby said, "we could drive up to the hospital in Houlton. Maybe we should have it X-rayed."

Lisa protested and shook her head gently, so the pain wouldn't rocket through her.

"I think I'll give Doctor LaChance a call. He'll make a house call if I ask him, I'm sure. I know he has that young man from Houlton working for him now, too. One of them should be able to come out to the house."

"I don't think that'll be necessary," Lisa said. "I think if we get the cuts bandaged up, and I take a couple of aspirin, I'll be just fine in the morning."

"Well," Mrs. Appleby said, giving her granddaughter a kiss on the cheek, "you make sure you let me know if it starts hurting any worse. I don't want to take any chances." She couldn't dispel the image of her brother during one of his seizures: eyes rolled back, body stiffened, blood-flecked foam running down his chin. Please God, she prayed silently, don't make me have to deal with it again!

Lisa promised she would let her know if she started feeling any worse, but when she looked at how guilty-looking Angie seemed, Lisa resolved that she wouldn't say anything that might get either of them any deeper into trouble, no matter what. In a couple of days, she was sure, the pain would recede and maybe even that high-pitched ringing in her ear would go away.

# IV

If there was one thing Winfield prided himself on, it was the goodness of his given word; so as soon as Dale and Donna left the police station, he got into his cruiser to drive out to the old LaPierre house and have a look around. He knew, that with the harvesting just getting started, it was entirely likely that someone had decided to get free housing for a few weeks, to save on renting a room in town. He decided it would be smart to keep his pistol handy, just in case Donna had been right about the prowler.

Once he turned onto Mayall Road from Main Street, the dark night seemed to come crashing in on him. It always struck him as remarkable how, with the town lights lost behind a single curve in the road, the darkness thickened and the stars got intensely brighter. He liked to imagine how the world looked to the Indians who had lived here before Europeans settled the land. He shivered, thinking how stark and lonely it must have been, out beneath the star-sprinkled stretch of sky with nothing more than a campfire to push back the darkness.

For reassurance, he patted the metal tube of his flashlight on the seat beside him. Although he knew it had three fresh batteries, he gave the button a quick flick anyway and grunted satisfaction at the bright yellow oval that lit up the side panel of the door. Even with the security of a powerful flashlight in his hand and his service revolver at his side, though, he couldn't repress a shiver when he pulled into the driveway of the abandoned LaPierre farmhouse and looked up at the cold, moon-washed siding.

Winfield flicked the switch on his alley light from inside the car, and aimed the strong beam at the house. Wherever the light went, it lit up the house brighter than daylight, but from the outside, there was no indication of any trouble. There were no broken windows, and the front door wasn't hanging off its hinges. The screen on the outside door was torn, but it had been like that for a year or more. The house looked secure to him, desolate and lonely as hell, but secure.

Taking a deep breath, he got out of the car and eased the door shut. A peculiar loneliness swept over him as he started up toward the house, his feet crunching the gravel of the walkway sounded like crackling ice. Winter was on its way, he knew, and the weird feeling he had about this place, he told himself, was just that—the quiet, cold, early autumn night.

When he reached the steps leading up to the front door, Winfield snapped on his flashlight, flooding the entryway with a harsh, yellow glare. His right hand drifted slowly down to his revolver, undid the snap, and firmly grasped the handgrip. It was reassuring, but not much. There might be something wrong here. He could *sense* it.

"Yeah," he said, under his breath as he went up the steps, "that and a quarter will get you a cup of coffee."

The stairs creaked underfoot, and as he stepped under the shadow of the porch roof, a small gust of wind sprang up. It whistled shrilly in the gutter overhead, sounding like someone calling to a dog from far away.

Winfield's oval of light darted around the front door, then swept both lengths of the house, pausing to make a quick circle around each window. The windows seemed to suck up and hold, rather than reflect, the light, making them look as though they were made of black marble slabs instead of glass. The land around the house was washed with powdery, gray light as Winfield went slowly down the length of the porch and rounded the corner to the back of the house.

As he was walking past the kitchen window, he thought he saw something moving out in the field, over by the woods to the left. He froze in mid-step and stared, wishing to God he had waited until daylight, to come out here. For a second, he considered going back to the cruiser to radio his location; he could ask Ernie to drive on out, so he'd have a little back-up, just in case . . .

Gettin' old or somethin'? Winfield thought angrily to himself. Startin' to let the ole imagination run away on you!

But still he didn't move as he looked out across the field toward the woods, waiting to see if something else moved.

"Oh, boy," he muttered when he saw something: it looked like two or three people, walking up the length of the field, away from the house. They kept to the fringe of the woods and moved slowly, so Winfield couldn't be sure if they had seen him. If they had broken into the house, though, they might plan on returning. Then again, he had driven up in the driveway and walked up to the house with his flashlight on, in clear view. If they had seen him coming, they sure as hell would leave. And if they had half a brain, Winfield thought, they would keep away.

Winfield slowly stood to his full height and clicked the safety off his revolver. Pointing it off to the side, he shone his flashlight on the moving figures.

"This is the police!" he shouted, his voice echoing back from the woods with a hollow distortion. "Stop or I'll shoot!"

The night swallowed up his light, so it never reached the people at the distance they were away from him. He cursed softly under his breath, knowing that what he had done was foolish. Who the hell, with that kind of lead, was going to stop for one lone cop? But what the hell! He figured they had seen him coming, anyway, so it was worth a try. He also figured — *what the hell?—take* the next step, too.

He slowly squeezed the trigger. His revolver kicked in his hand as it spit a splinter of orange flame and a lead bullet into the night. The explosion of the gunshot made his ears ring, and he watched in frustration as the figures continued up the hill. They didn't even increase their pace, so confident were they of the lead they had on him, and that made Winfield all the madder.

He leaped over the railing to the ground as if to follow them, but he knew it was futile to try. They were already cresting the hill, and then the night swallowed them up without a sound. Winfield was left with the impression that they had never really been there, that he had let the night shadows trick his eyes, but he knew better. Donna had said she was sure *someone* had broken into the house, and that was the proof, disappearing over the hill.

"Might 's well take a quick look around," he said as he went up the back steps to the porch. He knew from what Donna had told him that there weren't any valuables in the house, at most, some left-behind old furniture and a bunch of rusted old tools in the cellar. Still, he figured he'd better take a look around inside to see if they had done any damage before leaving.

He reached for the doorknob to the back door, and was surprised when it turned in his hand and the door swung slowly open, squeaking loudly on rusted hinges. Again, just before he entered the darkened kitchen, a gust of wind hooted in the eaves. His grip on the flashlight handle tightened when he took one last look up the slope to where those people had disappeared.

*Maybe,* he thought, *they'll come back when they think it's safe.*

Winfield stepped into the kitchen, letting his flashlight beam sweep the room like a hungry animal. He saw only a few signs that someone had been here: one edge of the rug by the door was flipped over, and there were a few clumps of dirt on the floor. No damage, though, at least not here in the kitchen.

The short hallway to his right led to the living room. As he started in that direction, he suddenly became aware of a shifting noise from behind him. He was just turning around when the closet door beside him slammed open. A dark figure shot out like a Jack-in-the-box, but Winfield never saw the lead pipe that came swooping down at him. In the next split-second, he felt a sudden explosion of pain that started from his forehead but instantly crashed through every nerve in his body in burning, white splinters.

His last hazy thought was really a question: was that loud explosion the sound of his gun going off in his hand as his fingers clenched from the pain, or was it his head, smashing the floor as he fell? He wouldn't have his answer until three hours later, when he woke up, bound and gagged, in the old coal bin in the cellar of the La-Pierre house.

# V

Hocker and Tasha were sitting cross-legged on their spread-out sleeping bags on the living room floor when the cruiser pulled into the driveway. They had spent most of the day rummaging through the house and the barn out back; and now, after a light supper, they were taking it easy before retiring early for the night. Hocker had found a few things worth hanging onto, but the house had been pretty much cleaned out before now.

As soon as they heard the car's engine at the foot of the driveway, they crept to the front windows and crouched, watching as the cruiser's high beams swept across the back yard before coming to a stop, pointing up at the house. The headlights winked out, and they heard the engine shut off.

"Get upstairs quick!" Hocker whispered to Tasha.

She could see, in silhouette, the siren and beacon lights on the roof of the car, and she froze like a jacked deer. This is the same cop I nailed yesterday afternoon! she thought. He knows I'm here, and he's coming to get me! Her hands turned cold and clammy as she gripped the edge of the window. She felt an urgent need to urinate.

Other, even scarier, thoughts flooded into her mind with a rush that sounded like the wind in her ears:

—The old man Hocker had slugged and whose truck they had stolen and now we're both wanted for questioning!

—Maybe, all along the way from Georgia, Hocker has been killing people! I'm on a cross-country murder spree, and I don't even know it!

—The truck Hocker had sent over the cliff in a ball of flames had started a major forest fire, and now they want us for arson!

No matter what she thought, it was all bad, so the small part of her mind that had wanted to kiss Hocker's ass goodbye and be gone barely had a voice. She knew that no matter what happened, she wouldn't let the cops get her!

"Get the fuck down!" Hocker yelled, slapping her shoulder hard when the spotlight on the side of the cruiser suddenly came on and started waving back and forth across the front of the house. Whenever the beam came through one of the windows, it cast hard bars of light onto the back walls. The light had a laser intensity that, Tasha was convinced, could start a fire if it was focused long enough on one spot.

"We're gonna get nailed!" Tasha said, her voice a twisted whine. Tears had formed in her eyes and shattered the sweeping light into thousands of diamond-sharp pieces.

"Just be cool," Hocker said. He was crouched under the window by the front door, his hand wrapped around a piece of lead pipe he had picked up in the cellar. "I've handled stuff worse than this before."

*I'll bet you have,* Tasha thought, unable to keep from her mind the memory of that old man, unconscious and crumpled on the ground.

"Just get your skinny little ass upstairs," Hocker whispered. "And don't come down 'till I tell you it's all right."

Tasha knew she didn't really have a choice. She silently gnawed at her lower lip as she watched the floodlight wash the room, but she didn't move.

But when she heard the cruiser door open and slam shut, Tasha sprang up and scurried as fast as she could up the stairs. In the dark, she tripped on the top flight and went sprawling onto her face, but she felt for the wall, regained her bearings, and hurried down the hallway to one of the empty bedrooms. She went over to the far wall by the closet, and crouched there, listening in the dark. The only sound she made was a mouse-like squeak when she heard a gun shot go off. It sounded like it was outside, behind the house.

Hocker, meanwhile, had crept over to the stairwell and flattened himself against the wall as he listened, tense, as the cop came up the front steps. A less intense beam of light came in through the front door window and wormed its way back and forth; then the heavy, clumping of footsteps went around the side of the house to the back.

Hocker quickly darted back through the living room and into the kitchen, pausing for only a moment to see what the cop was doing out there. He could see the man poised, caught in mid-step as he stared out over the field behind the house. When the man outside shouted, "This is the police! Stop or I'll shoot!" Hocker thought for a moment that the cop had seen him inside the house, but a quick glance out the kitchen window showed him that wasn't the case. The cop still had his back to the house and was looking into the back yard.

Hocker's mind rapidly snapped off the possibilities: who the hell else might be out there? he wondered.

In the hallway between the kitchen and living room, he looked around for the best place to be if the cop came inside. Without thinking, he clicked open the closet door and slipped inside, pulling it closed, leaving a small space open. If this worked, he thought, fine; if not, the cop would just go away and that would be it.

When the gun went off, Hocker thought the cop was shooting the door lock to get inside, but that struck Hocker as ridiculous; no cop would do something like that!

Unless, of course, it wasn't a cop after all.

*Naw,* Hocker thought. The guy shouted out "This is the police!" So what the hell was he doing? Was there really someone else out there?

The pulse in Hocker's ears was as loud as a drum when he heard the hinges squeal as the kitchen door slowly opened. He tensed, waiting in the darkness, try-ing to judge exactly where the cop was in the darkened kitchen.

That dumb cunt left the door unlocked! Stupid bitch!

The floorboards creaked underfoot as the cop walked across the kitchen floor. The crack underneath the closet door glowed with yellow light as the cop swept his flashlight beam back and forth. Then the footsteps got closer and closer. Hocker held his breath, hoping to Christ he timed this right because if he didn't, he was going to be in a world of hurt!

The beam of light bobbed closer, swinging silently from side to side. The floorboards creaked, and Hocker could hear the heavy breathing of the man. Hocker sensed, more than saw, the bulk of the man passing the closet door. Thankfully, the cop didn't think to check in the closet before starting for the living room.

Hocker took a quick, shallow breath and, heaving his weight forward, sud-denly swung the door open, raised the lead pipe up, and brought it swiftly down. He knew he would never be able to describe his satisfaction when he heard the soft thump the pipe made when it connected with the top of the cop's head. The cop's revolver dropped to the floor as the cop did a slow, spinning fall, bumping his head on the closet door as he dropped to the floor.

Hocker's jaw almost hurt from the wide smile that widened across his face. He leaned over and picked up the cop's flashlight, taking a moment to scan the unconscious man's face. The lead pipe had hit a glancing blow, lifting up a wide patch of skin that now was beaded with blood. By the look of it, Hocker knew this man was going to have one hell of a headache, but he also knew, like the old fart he had iced to steal his truck, this cop was going to wake up eventually. By then, of course, Hocker would have to have him safely "iced," unless he de-cided to permanently ice him.

He'd wait and see, but for now, he had to get this jerk out of the way.

Hocker picked up the cop's service revolver and inspected it in the glow of the flashlight. It was a solid little handgun, much better than the one he already had, so after clicking the safety back on, he tucked it into his belt and went over to the stairwell.

"Hey! You can come down now!" he shouted. His voice echoed in the stairwell.

From upstairs, he heard a faint shuffling as Tasha made her way cautiously down the hallway. Hocker shined the light up the stairs as she rounded the corner, and she held her arm up to shield her eyes from the sudden glare.

"What happened?" she said as she started slowly down the stairs. "I heard a gun go off. You didn't kill him, did you?"

Hocker spit a thick gob of mucous onto the wall. "Naw! The asshole never even saw me coming. He was shooting at something out back."

"He didn't leave, though," Tasha said nervously. "I didn't hear his car start up."

"Don't sweat it," Hocker said, laughing. "He's right down here, safe and sound. Before I haul his ass down to the cellar, I want you to take a look at him. See if he's the one you kicked in the nuts today." Tasha followed Hocker into the kitchen. She let out a faint gasp when she saw the unconscious man. Broken blood vessels under his skin were spreading a plum-purple bruise over the side of his forehead. The little bit of bleeding had already stopped, leaving little claw marks of blood streaks running into his hair. "You're getting pretty handy at knocking people cold, aren't you?" Tasha said, unable to disguise the trembling in her voice. "You know, when the other cops around town notice this guy's missing, they're gonna be swarming over the countryside, looking for him."

"Hell, he's probably the whole department. And if he isn't, well fuck them!" Hocker said, and he spit again on the floor. "By the time they get their shit together, well be long gone. No problem."

Tasha shook her head quickly from side to side. "I don't know, Hock. I mean, hitting an old man is one thing, but when you start screwing with the cops, it's getting serious!"

"The only thing serious right now is dragging this useless sack of shit down into the cellar. I saw some rope down there, though I'd bet it ain't the strongest stuff. We can use his handcuffs to make sure he don't get away."

"What are you gonna do, just leave him down there?" Tasha said. "You can't do that! He'll die!"

"You think I give a shit? Have you all of a sudden developed a fondness for cops?"

Tasha turned away, looking down at the floor, but her eyes came to rest on the fallen cop, she shivered. It's incredible, she thought, how being with Hocker, things just keep going from shitty to shittier!

"Come on," Hocker said. "Make yourself useful." He bent down and, grasping the cop by the utility belt, lifted him off the floor a bit and rolled him over onto his side. "Grab his handcuffs."

Tasha did what she was told because she didn't dare defy Hocker; she had enough evidence to convince her that he wouldn't hesitate to do the same to her if he got mad enough. He had said as much before, and she believed it now. He was nuts, really *dangerous* nuts!

After they had wrestled the cop's dead-weight around and gotten his hands safely cuffed behind his back, Hocker made a brief inventory of everything in the man's utility belt and pockets. He dropped his heavy key ring into his own pocket, then rifled through the cop's wallet.

"Well, you might be pleased to know his name is Jeffrey Winfield." Hocker said, glancing at the identification cards in the wallet. There were three twenties in the billfold. Hocker snickered as he slid them into his own pocket. "Officer Winfield," he said, his voice taking on a sudden dangerous tone. "I'd like to introduce you to Tasha Stewart. Tasha, this is Officer Winfield,"

Tasha stood there, staring blankly at Winfield's closed eyes. He looks so peaceful she thought. So peaceful he could almost be *dead!*

"Say 'hello' to Officer Winfield, Tasha," Hocker said, his voice harshly edged and high-strung. "You're not being very polite to our guest!"

Before she could check herself, Tasha muttered a low, "Hello."

"And you, Officer Winfield? Aren't you going to say 'hello' to Tasha?" He suddenly reached down, grabbed Winfield by the lapels, and lifted him while giving him a rough shake. "You're not being very polite!" he shouted, and with that, he let go of the policeman's coat. Win-field's head fell back onto the floor with a sickening, dull thump. Tasha had to turn away when she felt her stomach constrict and begin to rise.

"Well, you can stay here with our unsociable friend," Hocker said. "I think I'll do something about that police cruiser in the driveway, first. Wouldn't be too smart of us to leave it out there in plain sight, now, would it?"

Tasha didn't say a word as Hocker, swinging the key ring around his finger, started for the front door.

"If he wakes up, make sure he doesn't get into any trouble, all right?" Hocker said.

Tasha heard him swing open the front door and walk outside. She knew Hocker was feeling good because she heard him bring up some mucous from deep in his chest and spit violently into the night.

# VI

Kellerman's was a lot busier on a Monday night than on a Sunday. Dale figured, like any other workingman's bar, the customers felt they needed a break after facing another Monday. He and Donna were sitting at the bar, working their way slowly through a loaded pizza and a pitcher of Pabst.

After leaving Winfield's office, he called Mrs. Appleby's to see if Angie and Lisa wanted to join them for pizza, but Angie said no. At first she didn't want to tell him why they couldn't join them, but Dale noticed her nervousness, so she told him about Lisa's accident with the bike. It had taken Mrs. Appleby a while to reassure him that the injury was very minor: no, they didn't need to drive to the hospital in Houlton; no, he didn't need to cancel his date with Donna; yes, Mrs. Appleby had everything under control; yes, she was fine and would watch out for herself.

What Angie didn't tell him about was the morass of self-guilt she was feeling about the accident. That could wait until later she figured. It seemed to her like just yesterday that she could tell her father anything but now, she wasn't quite so sure.

The same country-western music was playing on the juke box, and, it looked to Dale, the same group of guys were slamming away at the pool table. He felt unnerved by the scrutiny he and Donna had gotten when they walked in. He wasn't sure if they were wondering who in the hell he was, or if they were busy checking out Donna. Either way, it wasn't very comfortable.

Dale and Donna carefully steered their supper conversation away from what had been happening to them recently. The strain of what had happened out on the Haynesville Road was taking its toll on Donna. Her face looked drawn, and her eyes looked tired; whenever there was a sudden outburst of laughter from somewhere in the bar, she jumped and looked around.

Dale, too, was beginning to feel wrung out from everything he had had to absorb since Nichols' early morning call, informing him of Larry's death. A good part of his mind, the sensible part, he told himself, told him to let it all drop. Larry was dead and buried, and that was the end of it.

"So was Natalie," a small part of his mind whispered, as softly as a cobweb fluttering in a dark corner.

The incident out on the road had no connection with Larry's death or any secret he was close to uncovering, he told himself. It was just some hot-shot in a fancy car who probably had a bumper sticker that read: Excuse me, but I do happen to own the road!

Then again, there was the cassette tape! He hadn't had a chance yet to pick up some double-A batteries so he could play it. Demands of the stomach had superseded that, but now that they were almost through eating, and the beer pitcher was just about empty, Dale was getting anxious to buy some batteries and hear whatever was on that tape. He didn't want to mention it to Donna, though; he was hoping she would bring the subject up first.

While they sat at the bar, making small talk, a heavy-set man, wearing a plaid, wool jacket and a fluorescent orange cap, strolled into the bar and hoisted himself up on a stool three seats down from where Dale and Donna sat. He glanced at Donna, and a faint expression of recognition passed across his face as he tilted his cap in her direction. Donna flushed and looked down at the bar.

"How yah doin' tonight, Pat?" the man in the orange cap asked as Kellerman came over and slid a frosty beer mug to him.

As the man leaned back and took several generous gulps of beer, Kellerman shrugged. "All right, I s'poze. You hear any more on how Perry's doin'?"

The man in the orange cap put his half-empty beer mug down on the bar and wiped his mouth thoughtfully with the back of his hand. "You ain't heard?" he said. He spoke with great effort, and it struck Dale almost as funny that such a large man would appear so shaken!

Kellerman shook his head, and the men at the pool table got suddenly quiet and looked toward the bar.

"Reggie didn't make it," the man in the orange cap said softly, but still loud enough to be heard over the sounds of Dolly Parton. "He died at the hospital a cou-pla' hours ago."

"No shit?" Kellerman said, his face paling as his eyes flicked nervously from face to familiar face. He looked like he wanted to say more, but instead, his mouth just kept making small motions that made him look like a fish.

"I don't fuckin' understand it, pardon the French, miss," the man said, glancing at Donna who was looking just as stunned as the rest of the people in the bar. Dolly's song finished, and for the moment no one put in another quarter. The bar filled with an ominous silence.

"I'd heard he was doin' all right," one of the men at the pool table said. He placed his cue stick on the table and knocked a ball out of position, but no one seemed to notice or care.

"Yeah," another said. "My brother was out on Bates Ridge when it happened, 'n' he said when the Medcu guys picked him up, they said they didn't think it was anything serious."

The man in the orange cap took another series of gulps, draining the glass. Then, placing his empty glass gently on the bar, he nodded at Kellerman, who instantly drew him a refill.

"All I know is what I was told at the hospital when I went up to see him," he said. It was obvious to Dale and everyone else that this man was under a great deal of strain, and Dale couldn't help but wonder if he was the dead man's brother or something.

"I'll be damned," someone at the back of the bar said softly, and nearly everyone grunted their agreement.

"I didn't even hear about it 'till late in the afternoon, so I went up to Houlton right after work. Didn't even bother to clean myself up." He held his hands up so everyone could see he was still wearing his work-stained shirt and pants. "The nurse at the front desk said something about a ... an eubolism or embulusion ... somethin' like that."

"Embolism," Dale offered, and the man's eye flickered in his direction.

"Yeah, that's it," the man said, almost brightening for a moment. "They said it was probably 'cause he got a lung punctured, and some air got into his blood. When it hit his brain, he . . . he . . ." Rather than let his voice choke off, he grabbed the full beer glass Kellerman had placed in front of him and did some serious damage to its contents.

"I'll be damned," the voice at the back of the bar repeated. "You know what I think it is? I think it's them clowns who work the ambulances. They ain't real doctors. I think they don't know what the Christ they're doin'!"

Kellerman was shaking his head sadly from side to side, obviously almost as upset as the man with the orange cap. "It ain't that," he said, a tone of firm command in his voice. "Those people are trained to handle all sorts of situations,"

"Well then, it's them fools they call doctors these days," someone else offered.

The man in the orange cap shook his head slowly and with his eyes closed, as though there was a pain far in the back of his skull.

'They told me he was fine when they brought him in. He'd been checked all over, and was all full of tubes. They were pretty sure his lung was punctured. That's why he had a breathing tube shoved down his throat. I guess it's something they can't always prevent."

His voice broke again, but he forced himself to continue. "I was there when Rodgers came with his goddamned hearse to pick him up. Jesus Christ!"

He suddenly raised his fist above his head and brought it down, forcefully onto the bar. His hand grazed his beer glass and flipped it over, but he didn't seem to notice. Beer flowed in a foamy sheet across the bar. Covering his eyes with the heels of his hands, the man leaned his elbows right in the spilled beer and sobbed.

Kellerman reached over the bar and clapped him firmly on the shoulder. "Just take it easy, Will," he said. "Take it easy. I know how you must feel."

The man looked up, his eyes glistening as he nailed Kellerman with an icy stare. "No, you don't! You have no fucking idea how I feel! He was my brother!"

"You're forgetting, Will. I lost a brother in Korea," Kellerman said mildly. He started to sop up the spilled beer with a heavy towel. Everyone else in the bar was silent, just standing there, nervously shifting from foot to foot, as they stared at the large man, bawling his eyes out.

"That was different," Will said, his voice rising up the register. He pushed his orange cap back and viciously rubbed his face with both hands. "That, at least, made some kind of sense. This! This! I mean, he was in the hospital, all checked over, supposedly doing just fine and blam! The fucking undertaker's wheeling him out the door! You haven't got the slightest goddamned idea what I'm feeling!"

With that, he pushed himself away from the bar and walked slowly toward the door. Two of the pool players caught up with him before he left and tried to say something, but he shrugged them off and strode out into the night, leaving the clientele at Kellerman's wrapped in an awkward silence that took quite a while to break.

Dale, though, had listened to the whole exchange with an odd tingling in his stomach. That tingling had blossomed into a flush of fear as soon as the name 'Rodgers' was mentioned. He nailed Donna with a wide-eyed, questioning look, but her expression had been impossible to read.

*Was it just another coincidence?* he wondered. *When you thought about it, who would be most likely to drive a big, dark limousine? It would be the perfect choice. Not a limo, but a hearse!*

"You done?" Dale asked as he drained the last bit of beer from his glass.

Donna nodded stiffly, and when Dale started to say something else, she raised her forefinger and placed it gently over his lips.

"Don't say a word, all right?" she whispered. "I know what you're thinking." She fished a cigarette from the pack in her purse, but rather than lighting it, simply rolled it between her fingers. "If Sparky doesn't have the batteries we need, I'm sure LaVerdier's across the street will."

With that, Dale stood, took a ten dollar bill from his wallet, and left it on the bar top with the bill. They left, side by side, and when they stepped out into the night, Dale had to remind himself that it was just the cool of the evening that sent a wave of shivers up both of his arms, the evening chill and nothing more than that!

# VII

Earlier, Hocker had popped out one of the windows in the side door of the barn to get it open. Now, he had to use a crow bar to rip off the boards that held the front door shut. It would have been easier to do in the daylight when he could see what he was doing, but it would have been foolish to leave the police cruiser out where someone might see it and begin to wonder. By the time Hocker got the double doors swung outward, he was sweaty and angry as hell.

He couldn't resist the rush he felt, though, sitting behind the steering wheel of the cruiser and starting up the engine. He pressed the accelerator down, hard, letting the engine whine. He could feel the cruiser's power, straining to shoot forward in a burst of speed. It took an immense amount of self-control not to flick on the flashing lights and siren, and then drive crazy circles around the abandoned farmhouse.

Once he got the cruiser into the barn, he swung the door closed and, using the boards and bent-over nails he had removed earlier, nailed the doors shut. He realized that the doors might not be as secure as before, but it was good enough for his purposes. He didn't care if anyone broke into the barn and found the cruiser, so long as he and Tasha were long gone by then.

Hocker then spent the next hour or so with Winfield's flashlight in hand, going through the cruiser from the trunk to the glove compartment. There was a small first aid box in the front, which Hocker realized he and Tasha could use. He put that and a small, backup flashlight on the barn floor and went to the back of the cruiser.

The trunk had the most interesting stuff, and Hocker found it increasingly frustrating when he realized he was going to have to leave most of this equipment behind. There was a pillow, blanket, oxygen tank, and a few other medical emergency supplies, as well as assorted tools and weapons. What struck Hocker's fancy the most was the riot gun. His own gun, and even Winfield's service revolver, had no power compared to the stopping force of this baby. Hocker fondled the rifle like a ten-year old who had just gotten his first Daisy pump-action B-B gun for Christmas.

"You beautiful mother fucker!" he exclaimed, his breath warm on the rifle butt as he pressed the heel into his shoulder and sighted along the smooth metal barrel. His finger tensed, burning to flip the safety off and squeeze the trigger all the way back to see what this baby could do to the wall of the barn. But, there was no telling who might be within hearing range. Gunshots in the night, even during hunting season, would certainly warrant a call to the police from curious neighbors.

Hocker put the rifle on the ground with the first aid box and spare flashlight, figuring he had to get something for all his trouble. He spent a little more time shuffling through the contents of the trunk, but everything else looked like useless shit to him. If there was an easy way to carry it, he would have taken more; but they had made it this far with out much gear, they could do without. He threw most of it onto the barn floor and slammed the trunk lid shut.

Back in the front seat of the cruiser, Hocker directed his flashlight beam onto the police radio. A small red light was glowing, so Hocker assumed it was *on* and ready to use. He thought how funny it would be to switch on the radio and call the station. Maybe he could pretend to be Officer Winfield. Again, though, he passed on the idea because it would be damned foolish to alert any other cops that Winfield was in trouble.

"Yeah," Hocker said as he spit out the car door onto the floor. "He's in deep trouble, all right."

Suddenly, the radio hissed and a voice crackled from the receiver.

"One-niner! . . . One-niner! Do you copy? Over."

Hocker's tensed, wondering if Winfield was "One-niner." If he was, and he didn't answer, then headquarters would know he was in trouble, Hocker's eyes darted from the radio to the small doorway leading back up to the house. His hand was shaking as he reached out, ready to pick up the microphone and talk if he really *had* to.

The message was repeated and then, much to Hocker's relief, another voice came on, this one so full of static he couldn't make out any of the words. He could tell, though, from what the voice said, that "One-niner" had responded.

Hocker eased back in the cruiser's seat and ran his forearm over his brow. His heart was thumping softly in his chest, and there was a warm dampness in his armpits. In the glow of the flashlight, he leaned forward and studied the radio for a moment. At last, he found the *on/off* switch and pushed it with his thumb. The tiny red bulb on the upper left corner of the radio winked off, and Hocker felt even more relieved.

After a fruitless second search of the glove compartment, Hocker eased out of the driver's seat. He carefully balanced the flashlight on an old barrel near the barn wall so its beam shone straight into the cruiser. Then Hocker picked up the riot gun, snapped off the safety, and took aim at the black box of the police radio. The rifle slammed into his shoulder when he squeezed off two shots in rapid succession. There was a snap and a sizzle of electricity, as shards of plastic splattered the floor of the car.

"That'll shut *you* the fuck up, *one-mother-humpin-niner!*"

He held the rifle across his chest, only vaguely aware that he was panting with excitement. Now that he had started, though, there swelled inside him, like a noxious, black cloud, a compulsion to do more damage. Gripping the rifle by the barrel, he cocked his arms back and swung the rifle around as if he was swinging for the "green monster" in Fenway Park. One of the blue bubble lights on the cruiser's roof shattered, sending fragments of plastic flying into the darkness.

Without a moment's pause, Hocker kicked the cruiser door shut and then slammed the rifle butt into the side window. A spider web of cracks, sickly white in the flashlight's glow, spread across the window. Hocker saw a brief flash of his own face reflected in the window, a mosaic of wild eyes and wide grin. A low laughter sounded like distant thunder in his chest.

For the next several minutes, Hocker completely lost all sense of where he was and what he was doing. His mind felt like a raging red fire consuming everything it touched as he hammered and pounded the rifle butt against the police cruiser. Mirrors and sirens and lights and windows were smashed into useless junk; everywhere on the car fist-sized dents appeared like twisted flowers. And all the while, Hocker was laughing wildly.

The frenzy stopped almost as fast as it had begun. Hocker let the rifle drop to the barn floor as he leaned over with his hands on his knees. He was panting like a racehorse. Sweat ran down from his brow and stung his eyes. He didn't notice tiny cuts on his hands from flying glass and metal. Staggering backward, he slammed into the barn wall and almost fell down as he inspected the damage he had done. In just minutes, the cruiser had become a totally wreck. Oh, he had no doubt the engine would still start up and he could drive that sucker out of here; but this baby was going to be a long time in the body shop!

"All right," he muttered as he rubbed his arm across his mouth. The unnoticed cuts left smeary blood streaks on his cheeks. His jacket sleeve came away foamy with pink-streaked saliva. Through his exhaustion, he felt a great satisfaction, a tremendous relief almost, as if he had just seen the cruiser get swept up in a raging sheet of flame!

Now wouldn't that be something? he thought.

That was what he really wanted! More than wanted ... he *needed* to see towering sheets of orange flame sucked skyward beneath a heavy belly of black smoke! He wanted to see a windstorm of sparks cork-screwing into the night, taking the cruiser, the barn, and the whole fucking house with it!

His first instinct was to siphon gasoline from the cruiser, and—yes, he remembered seeing a reserve tank of gasoline in the cruiser's trunk! He could get five, maybe ten gallons of gas even if the cruiser was low on fuel. But these cops always keep their tanks full, don't they? With that much gasoline, he could easily splash enough around the barn so he could get a ripping good blaze going before the town's firefighters had time to respond. His fingers itched, and his mind burned to do it; just as he had not allowed himself the luxury of letting the cop's siren whine, he knew that a fire would attract unwelcome attention.

If this urge became unbearable, Hocker thought, there was always the potato barn they had seen last night, where the men had been drinking together. There was also that ancient barn Tasha had told him she had found when she was making her way back from her "ball-kicking" encounter with the cops. Oh, there were plenty of opportunities around this town for things to go *whoosh!*

All it came down to was a question of "what" and "when." Right now, he was exhausted from wrecking Winfield's cruiser. The next thing to do was to make sure Winfield himself, once he came to, was in no position to cause him any trouble. So, with the riot gun under his arm, he gathered up the flashlight, first aid kit, extra ammunition for the rifle and went back to the house.

"We'll take care of our guest first," he said aloud, snickering to himself. "Then we'll see what other opportunities might come our way." He whistled jauntily as he went up to the back door of the farmhouse and called out, "Hey, Looo-sy, I'm home!"

# VIII

Dale couldn't stop his hands from shaking as he sat in the front seat of his car, trying to break open the blister pack that held four brand new double-A batteries. He and Donna were parked in front of the local LaVerdier's. The street light was shining down on them with a cold, blue light.

"There's a diagram here showing which way they go in," Donna said as she held the miniature cassette recorder up to the light.

Dale grunted and swore softly under his breath when his fingers fumbled, and the package stayed sealed.

"I have a nail file you can use," Donna said. She picked up her purse and started rifling through it.

"No, no," Dale said. His voice was distorted by the edge of the package in his mouth. "I think I've got it." He gave the battery pack a quick pull, and the batteries shook out and fell to the floor. He swore softly as he leaned over and fished around, trying to find the batteries in the dark. Once he found them, he took the recorder from Donna and, squinting to read the directions, slid the batteries in, one by one. He felt like he was loading bullets into a gun. Snapping the cover back on, he sat back in the seat and let out a long, whistling exhalation.

"You've still got the tape, I hope," Donna said.

Dale quickly slapped his jacket pockets, then his shirt pocket. Panic flooded him when he didn't feel the tape, but when he reached inside his jacket, he found it in his shirt pocket, where it had been all the time.

"Are you ready for this?" he said, snapping open the plastic hood and sliding the tape into position.

"Never been more ready," Donna said with a trembling in her voice.

"I feel like I'm prying into someone's private diary," Dale said. He grimaced as he turned the recorder over in his hand, found the play button, and pressed it. For the next three minutes he and Donna listened as the voice of Dale's closest friend, dead for three days now, filled the car.

". . . Testing . . . testing . . ."

There was the shrill sound of whistling, and faintly, below that, the rumble of a car engine.

*"All right, seems to be working. I don't know where to start really. The date, the date, yeah. It's Friday, August, August. . .* Damn! *I can't remember! The twenty-something! I've gotta think. Let's see. It's after midnight, I know that much 'cause I was at the home between eleven and eleven thirty. So, okay, after midnight. I've gotta keep my head straight about this, but Jesus Christ! Who could? Fuck!"*

"He sounds really upset," Donna said, glancing at Dale. Her eyes were dark hollows in the blue glow of the street light.

"Understatement of the year," Dale said, hushing her with a wave of his hand as the tape played.

*"I'm driving south, on Route 2-A, out of Dyer, heading toward Haynesville. What I've seen and learned in the last few days will. . . would make anyone think they were crazy!"*

There was a long pause, filled only by the sound of the car's engine.

*"No one will ever believe what I'm going to say. Maybe I'm doing this to —to keep my own sanity . . . to say it out loud so I can . . . can . . ."*

Larry's voice suddenly broke off into a wild laughter that quickly shot up the scale until it cracked.

*"Gotta get a grip on myself and talk . . . talk fast 'cause I think they're . . . oh, shit! Who's that behind me? Headlight! I think they're after me. Okay, talk fast. What I know,*

*what I've found out, is basically so simple it's . . , it's crazy! The roads up here have always been a problem . . . mostly 'cause they were built along old wagon trails that were never designed for motor vehicles. So, okay—that makes sense. But for years, now, we've been trying to improve some of these roads up in the County. 'Cause of the logging trucks and other stuff, there have been a lot of fatalities. I . . . shit! . . ."*

There was a loud smashing sound, and, faintly, the squeal of tires.

*"It is them! They know I'm on to them!"*

"Stop it a second," Donna said, as she gave Dale's arm a quick shake.

Dale snapped the recorder off and looked at her. His whole body had gone cold as soon as he had heard Larry say that *someone* was following him. There was no doubt that Larry had recorded this message just before he died.

"I don't think we should listen to any more of this until we play it for Winfield," Donna said. Her voice was shaking so much her teeth chattered. Her breathing came in short hitches. Dale knew she'd be lighting a cigarette soon.

"I've got to hear the rest of it first," Dale said. He popped the play button, and Larry's frantic voice filled the car again.

*"I don't know the details of all of this, but I do know that there are reasons certain people don't want any road improvements up here. They want people to keep having accidents and dying on the roads! They need them!"*

Larry's voice kept fading in and out on the recorder, and Dale had the impression Larry was frantically dividing his attention between dictating his report and watching whoever was following behind him. In his mind, Dale saw the flashing headlights that had threatened to run him and Donna off the road. There was no doubt it was the same person, but who was it?

*"What's been going on up here, for, . . . I have no fuckin' idea how long . . . It's . . . I've been checking into it since the day I got up here. I don't want to say who my first contact was 'cause if they ever get this tape, I don't want them . . ."*

Again, the squealing of tires hissed from the tape.

*"I know who's doing it, though. There's an undertaker in town, named Franklin Rodgers. What little I could find out about him tells a lot. He studied botany and did some field work in Haiti on different drugs used in voodoo potions. What seems to be going on is this guy, with help from the local hospitals or something, is getting bodies from accident victims and using these drugs on them. The basic drug seems to be some kind of extract from potato plants. I discovered that the potato is a species of deadly nightshade, and it's been used for witchcraft for years. They're taking dead people and turning them into . . . into . . . zombies!"*

Once again, Larry's voice broke off into cackling, hysterical laughter; and this time, it didn't just rise and fall, it kept building higher and higher until it vibrated the tiny speaker of the recorder.

"Please turn it off," Donna said. Her hand clutched Dale's forearm, and through the fabric of his jacket, he could feel her fingernails pressing into his skin. "I can't listen any more!"

Dale stopped the recorder, cutting off Larry's insane laughter abruptly. He held a fisted hand up to his mouth and bit down hard on his thumb joint as tears stung his eyes and ran down his cheeks. Donna was breathing shallowly, as she stared blankly out at the front of the car.

"I can't listen to it any more," she said again, weakly. "That's *crazy!* He's talking, like . . . like he's lost his mind!"

"I know," Dale said. He nodded his head and slowly wiped his eyes with the back of his hand. His breath felt like it had condensed into a hot coal caught somewhere deep in his chest. "But it does kind of fit in with what we suspected."

"What? Are you nuts, too?" Donna shouted, her voice harsh and insistent. She turned and looked at him, asking herself what kind of man she'd hooked up with this time. "You don't mean to tell me you believe any of this!"

Dale took as deep a breath as he could and, running his fingers through his hair, let it out slowly.

"I don't know what I believe," he said. He turned and gave Donna a harsh stare. "But I do know a few things. I know Larry's dead, and I know I wasn't allowed to see his body, prevented by the same man Larry says was doing something with dead bodies."

"But *zombies!*" Donna said incredulously. Her voice never even approached the laughter she felt certain was building up inside of her. She took a cigarette and lit it, not even trying to blow the smoke out the window.

This is how you'll end up if you believe this! her mind whispered. You'll be laughing insanely, like Larry on the tape.

"All right," Dale said, slapping the steering wheel with the flat of his hand. "Maybe not zombies, but something sure as hell is weird around this town. Come on, Donna. Think for a minute. What did Sherlock Holmes used to say? 'Eliminate the impossible, and whatever remains, however improbable, is the truth.' Right?"

"You're talking *zombies,* for God's sake! 'Night of the Living Dead' comes to Aroostock County!" Donna wailed. "What will we call this, 'Night of the Living Spud?' Come on, Dale. This is real life, not some crazy movie! Stuff like that just isn't real!"

"And how do you know that?" Dale said, keeping his voice low and level only by great effort. "How do you know there isn't some kind of drug that can do that? Maybe Rodgers found something in Haiti: or the basis of something that he adapted for use up here. What Larry said about the potato being in the nightshade family, is that true?"

Donna shrugged. "I don't know. I think I remember reading something about tomatoes being in that group of plants, and that people thought they were poisonous until, like a century ago."

"So maybe there's something to it!" Dale said, hitting the steering wheel again, harder. "Rodgers is concocting something from the potato plants and experimenting on people. He's got the perfect opportunity here, being an undertaker. I mean, how much does anyone around here know about him? Where'd he come from? Why'd he set up his business way up north here? Winfield didn't seem to know a whole hell of a lot about him. So who would? Who'd check this guy out?"

Donna shrugged again. "Hey, people die everywhere. Even up in the County, they need an undertaker or two."

"Yeah, but there's something about Rodgers that I just don't trust."

"You told me so yourself," Donna said. "It's his weird eye that bugs you. Look, Dale, I still think you're creating some paranoid fantasy out of all of this because you just can't accept that Larry's dead." She suddenly cut herself off and lowered her gaze.

"And because I still can't accept that Natalie's dead, too. Isn't that what you were going to say?"

Donna took a drag of her cigarette and exhaled a transparent stream of smoke. Looking at him, her heart ached. She admitted to herself that she liked this guy a lot! But this business he was wrapping himself up in was so incredibly *insane!*

"I didn't want to say that," she said, huskily, "because I don't want to hurt you, but yeah. I think you still haven't really gotten over your grief."

Dale was shaking his head. "No, it's not that simple," he said. "Was that car that tried to run us off the road part of my paranoid fantasy? Was it?"

He suddenly froze when his mind recalled the old man they had seen in the cemetery the night before. Suddenly, it was very clear to him why the man had seemed so empty! He pictured how the man had moved so slowly, as if he had no will of his own.

And if he was already dead, Dale's mind whispered, that would explain how even if I did run him over with the car, he wouldn't have been there in the morning! He would have gotten up and walked away, because he was already *dead!*

"What?" Donna asked. The concern she felt for him bubbled up like a warm gush of water. She crushed her cigarette out in the ashtray and shifted closer to him.

"I was just ... no!" Dale said, shaking his head. "Nothing. Just let me hear the rest of the tape. If you really don't think you can handle it, why don't you go back to the drug store? I'll come and get you when I've finished."

Donna considered for a moment, then she shook her head. "No," she said, taking a deep breath. "I think I can handle the rest of it now."

Dale nodded and pressed reverse for a second, then play. After a second or two of Larry's crazy laughter, he started to speak again.

*"They're turning them into zombies and then he's selling them to a couple of the local landowners who use them for harvesting. Brilliant, huh? Cheap labor that doesn't need to sleep or eat or anything. Just mindlessly work out there in the fields, day and night, when you have to get the harvest in. I don't know for a fact, but I suspect they send them south to rake*

*blueberries in July and August, and to pick apples before the potato harvest. It's just so ... so fucking wild! I can't believe it myself, . . . but my contact says he's positive of it, and . . . oh,* shit!"

Larry's voice suddenly cut off. The car's engine whined, and there was a dull thump that rattled the speaker. After a blast of static, there was a loud crashing sound.

"That must be when he dropped the tape recorder out the car window," Donna said.

"Or *threw* it out," Dale said softly. "More likely, he pitched it out the window, hoping someone would find it in case he didn't survive."

"You think he knew he was going to die?" Donna asked.

Dale looked at her and frowned. "Come on, Donna. If the same car that chased us was chasing him, then, yeah! I think he knew he had to get away but if he couldn't at least to try to save his report so someone might find it."

Donna's teeth were a pearly white as she ran them over her lower lip. She jumped when the static on the tape suddenly cleared, and they heard a tremendous explosion. Dale quickly spun the volume down.

"That—" he said, but his voice choked off.

"—Was the car, hitting the rock on Casey's Curve," Donna finished for him.

They had no doubt they had heard the fatal crash, but as the tape played, they suddenly became aware of some other sounds on the tape. Though faint with distance, Dale and Donna clearly heard another car, the car that had been chasing Larry and caused the accident, skid to a stop. There was a harsh, skidding sound as the tires ran off the road into the gravel. Then they heard the sound of three car doors opening and slamming shut.

*"Hold it there! Not so fast!"*

The voice spoke on the tape recorder so clearly Dale had the fleeting impression there was someone else in the car with them. "Tell me that didn't sound like Rodgers!" Dale said, nailing Donna with a glance.

Faintly, they could hear the sound of heavy, trudging footsteps sounding like several people walking away from the tape recorder, dragging their feet in the roadside gravel with long, shuffling strides.

*"Don't touch him! I have . . ."*

There was a low, mean-sounding laugh that faded with distance. And sounding even further away, a chorus of heavy, grunting noise was audible sounding like something out of one of those horror movies Donna had mentioned not so long ago. The throaty growls rose sharply in intensity, filling the car with unworldly noise and sending waves of chills through both Dale and

Donna. But the voice, assumed a deep, commanding shout. It had to be Rodgers, Dale was sure.

*"Don't touch him. You can feed later! I have a special little treat in store for this one!"*

The small speaker in the tape recorder rattled with the rush of sounds that split the lonely quiet of the night like a hatchet blade. Insane hoots and guttural grunts, wild, winding laughter and low, animal snorts, issued from the tape recorder. Then the noises moved away from the microphone.

What do these sounds mean? Dale wondered. Anger? Joy? Pain? Fear?

He closed his eyes, trying to imagine himself there, on that stretch of road last Friday night: Larry's car is crumpled in the woods more than thirty feet off the road. Larry, probably already dead from the impact, but maybe . . . just maybe still alive, is hanging through his smashed front window, his body tattered and bleeding. Smoke is rising from the crumpled hood; diamonds of glass are scattered all over the ground, sparkling in the bright headlights; and six or more hulking figures are chattering and gibbering as they shamble toward Larry's lifeless body. Their arms are raised stiffly as their cold, dead fingers reach for him, eager to peel him off the car's hood and tear him apart!

This isn't *real!* his mind screamed, and he looked frantically at Donna for some kind of anchor to pull him back to reality. This couldn't really have happened!

"It is real," he whispered, his voice so constricted it sounded like someone was speaking from outside the car.

Donna was as freaked out as Dale was, and she looked at him with a silent pleading to say something to make everything just go away, to make it all a dream. We can wake up now— *please.* What she wanted was for them to have a chance to see if what had started could develop into the kind of relationship she hadn't expected ever to find again.

Dale stiffened. The fingers of his hand holding the tape recorder were starting to ache. He took a long, shuddering breath and eased back into the car seat, bringing one hand up to his forehead. He was slick with sweat.

"I know what we've got to do," he said hoarsely.

Donna looked at him, pleading silently that he couldn't say what she most feared.

"Did you pick up what Larry said earlier in the tape?" he rewound the tape and played it. Larry's voice on the tape would soon be lost in insane laughter, and then, seconds later, be silenced forever. As the tape played, Larry's frantic tone chilled the interior of the car.

". . . 'cause I was at the home between eleven and eleven thirty"

Dale pressed stop and looked at Donna, waiting for her reaction. His breath was rasping as loud as metal scraping metal.

"I know what we have to do," she said after a moment of silence. "We have to take this tape to the police. Turn it over to Winfield."

"And tell him what?" Dale said angrily. "What are the cops gonna do?"

"Maybe it'll be enough for them to —I don't know, start an investigation or something. What do they do in a situation like this? Christ, Dale, I'm just a friggin' secretary! I don't want to get involved in anything like this!"

"So you believe at least some of it? Enough so you're scared, right?"

"Of course I'm scared. Christ! Who wouldn't be?" Donna pounded her clenched fist on the dashboard. "There's something weird going on, all right, but I don't think we should get involved any deeper than we already are. This is something for the cops to handle."

Dale snorted and shook his head. "You just don't get it, do you? For all we know, the cops, Winfield and all of 'em, for miles around here, are up to their fucking eyebrows in this! Rodgers, if he is doing something with these dead people, even if it isn't turning them into zombies, he's gotta be getting help from some other people. Larry said as much on the tape! If we go to the cops with this, we could both end up like Larry."

Donna shivered as she looked over her shoulder out on the cold night. The yellow traffic light in the center of town winked on and off. A silence seemed to fill the town. A *dead* town! Wasn't that what she had called it ever since she could remember? A God-forsaken, wasted, dead town! And it didn't take too much of a stretch of her imagination to picture dozens of workers from the potato fields, their eyes and brains dead, shuffling down the streets, looking for ...?

"What do zombies eat, supposedly?" she asked, her voice wound wire-tight. "That voice on the tape said 'you can *feed* later."

Dale snorted. "If I remember correctly, they eat the . . . brains of living people," he said, his eyes shifting to follow Donna's gaze up the dark, deserted street.

After a short pause, Donna shook her head and said, "I really think we could trust Jeff with this. I've known him all my life. He wouldn't get hooked up in anything like this!"

Dale shook his head. "You haven't known Rodgers all your life, though. You didn't listen to what Larry said, did you? He said 'I was at the home' . . . *the* home! Not home, as in his mother's house. *The* home, as in, maybe, the *funeral* home!"

"Oh, Christ, Dale. Let's just drop it. Look, I could move down to Augusta. I'm sure I could find a job there. We could be together. We could go pick up Angie, swing by my sister's and get my stuff, and be a hundred miles away from here within two hours."

"Donna . . ."

"It's just—just that, I don't want any part of this! It's not our problem. And if it's like you think, really organized, it's way too big for us. Why can't we just leave it behind?"

"You think you could do that?" Dale asked, his voice low and intense.

Donna shook her head. "No, not really," she whispered. "But I know I'm not going to like what you're going to say."

Dale forced a tight smile across his face and nodded. "That's right, babe. I think we should take a drive out to Mr. Franklin Rodgers' Funeral Home and see if we can get in there and take a look around."

Donna sighed, her breath a long sputter. "I think we're making a mistake. I think we should talk to Jeff first."

"After we have a little look around out at Rodgers'," Dale said firmly. He popped the cassette out of the recorder, slipped it into his pocket, and started up the car.

# PART THREE

"... graves have yawn'd; and yielded up their dead; ... and ghosts did shriek and squeal about the streets." — Shakespeare

# CHAPTER SEVEN
## "BACK TO THE HOME"

### I

All during supper and television time afterward, Lisa was unusually quiet. Her appetite, even for cheeseburgers and fries, just wasn't there, and her grandmother repeatedly asked her if she was feeling all right. She lied every time, telling her she still had an ache where she had banged her forehead on the pavement. In truth, there was a steady pounding in her head that felt as though someone was pounding the back of her skull with a jack-hammer.

"I've still got some home made vanilla ice cream in the freezer," Mrs. Appleby said, looking up from her knitting as the closing credits of "Alf" rolled.

Angie was up like a shot and already halfway to the kitchen before she turned and saw that Lisa was still sitting in the beanbag chair in front of the television.

"You want some ice cream?" Angie asked. She once had a beanbag chair and had never liked it because it made her feel like such a clod whenever she tried to get out of it.

Lisa looked over her shoulder at Angie, and when she did, a white stab of pain jabbed her behind the eyes. She wasn't sure if it was the pain that stunned her or if it really had been a visual effect. For a flickering second, the entire living room looked as bright as if it were flooded by spotlights—million watt spotlights.

"You all right, dear?" Mrs. Appleby said, her voice edged with concern.

Angie waited, leaning on the kitchen doorway. She was still wallowing in the guilt of having caused her new friend such pain, and it sickened her to see Lisa looking so drawn and pale.

"Of course I am," Lisa said as she bravely struggled to get to her feet. The hammering in the back of her head puzzled and scared her.

*Why in the back?* she wondered. *I hit the front of my head.*

Then she unexpectedly fell forward, reaching blindly with her hands to break her fall. Her knees hit the floor first, then her hands. She was indistinctly aware of the impact because the sparkling pain in her head was so demanding.

*"Lisa!"* Mrs. Appleby said, louder and more anxious.

"Must've slipped on the rug," Lisa said as she got her feet under herself and stood up. She had to move slower than she wanted to prove to her grandmother that she was all right; but no matter how slowly she moved, the pain pierced through her body.

Angie waited in the doorway, feeling as helpless now as she had when Lisa had fallen on the street. She wished — earnestly that it had been her, instead of Lisa, who had taken the fall. But she realized that there was an element of selfishness in that thought: if she had been the one hurt, at least then she would have something concrete to deal with. She wouldn't have to stand by, watching helplessly.

Lisa was standing up straight, smiling widely in spite of the pain in her head. But then, just as she turned to follow Angie in the kitchen, the white light came again, and this time, there was no doubt about it: it was as though a brilliant white bolt of lightning flashed across the room right in front of her. She staggered, turned, and walked straight into the wall.

The impact shook the wall and knocked one of her grandmother's oil paintings askew. Lisa bounced off the wall like a basketball and, arms waving wildly, fell backwards. Luckily, she landed on her back in the beanbag chair, but she didn't know it. All she knew was that the insides of her eyes stung from the jolt of light, and her ears were ringing as though a concussion of thunder had erupted right beside her.

"Oh my God!" Mrs. Appleby said, throwing her knitting aside and rushing over to Lisa. Crouching beside her, she felt her granddaughter's face. It was cold and clammy, almost like touching someone's who's . . . Mrs. Appleby couldn't finish the thought.

"Angie!" she shouted as she wiggled her hand under Lisa's head and cradled it gently. "Call the doctor. The number is next to the phone!"

Only for another split-second was Angie frozen in horror and guilt as she looked at her friend. Then she rushed to the antique phone and dialed the emergency number, waiting for an eternity the old-fashioned black rotary dial to spin around.

Mrs. Appleby, meanwhile, was leaning over Lisa, looking down at her face. Lisa wasn't unconscious; her eyes were open, and there was *even—still smiling, God love her!—* a faint smile on her lips. But her face was so pasty white, Mrs. Appleby had the impression there was a thin layer of translucent wax over it.

Lisa's eyes looked like glazed sky-blue pottery as she looked up at her grand-mother. She opened her mouth and tried to speak, but her grandmother hushed her and gently stroked her cheek.

In her mind, Mrs. Appleby was doing two things: she was reciting every prayer she had ever learned or said in church, and she was thinking about all the loved ones she had seen die: her mother, her father, two uncles and an aunt, her husband, and worst of all, one of her own children. She tried to turn away from those thoughts, and only send her ardent prayers upward, but the light in Lisa's eyes looked as though it was fading. She seemed to be trying to focus on her grandmother's face, but her pupils kept rolling back and forth with a sludgy motion. The whites were sharply veined with red.

"You just relax, honey," Mrs. Appleby cooed, not even sure if Lisa was hearing her nor not. "You just relax and take it easy. The doctor's on his way."

Angie suddenly appeared in the living room. She came and knelt down on the other side of Lisa. Her hands were folded in her lap, and she was squeezing her hands so hard, the knuckles were aching and turning white.

"Is she okay?" Angie said.

"She'll be fine, I'm sure," Mrs. Appleby said, although really she felt no such assurance. "Did you reach the doctor's office?"

Angie nodded. "Doctor LaChance wasn't in, but he has a helper working for him. He said he was a physician's associate or assistant, something like that. Anyway, his name's Stephen Wayne, and he said he'd be right over."

"Good," Mrs. Appleby said, never bothering to look up from her grand-daughter's waxy, pale face. "The doctor's helper is coming, honey. He'll take care of you."

# II

"There's a place we can leave the car, in the woods just past the funeral home. At least it was there when I was a kid," Donna said as Dale took the right turn onto Mayall Road. "It's on the left, a place that's always been called Coffin Bog locally."

"Any connection with the funeral home across the street from it?" Dale asked, but even to his own ears his attempted joke sounded flat.

He made a conscious effort not to slow down and stare at the funeral home as they drove past it. He did notice there was a light on around back, and two of the cellar windows glowed with dull yellow.

"It's getting past nine o'clock," Donna said. "Any traffic on Main Street af-ter nine o'clock will probably be noticed."

"Especially if Rodgers knows we're on to him, huh?" Dale added.

Donna shivered. "I don't like to think about it," she said tightly. "And I still say we should just go find Win-field and tell him what we think. We shouldn't be fooling around like this!"

"I'm not fooling," Dale said as he shook his head and slowed to turn off into the narrow dirt road Donna had pointed out to him up ahead. He was beginning to think like a true paranoid, he noted, with only slight amusement, as he doused the headlights and turned the car around so he could back into the road.

"Wait a second," Donna said. "Let me get out and direct you in. There's no sense scraping up your car."

Dale smiled, thinking if all they got tonight was a few scratches on his car, they'd be lucky . . . *damned* lucky!

"So, what do we do now?" Donna asked once Dale shut off the engine. Through the screen of trees, they could still make out the lights in Rodgers' Funeral Home. Dale sat there, drumming his fingers on the steering wheel as he tried to remember what he had seen of the home when he went there with Winfield. He hadn't had the chance to see much more than the front office and visiting rooms.

He was also running over in his mind how Winfield had acted during that visit. The more he considered it, the more he thought the policeman hadn't been very aggressive in asking Rodgers about why they couldn't view Larry's body. As he recalled now, Winfield had just sat there and let him do all the talking. If he had any doubts, he sure as hell didn't express them!

Did that mean Winfield might be in with Rodgers on whatever the hell was going on? Dale wasn't sure.

Maybe the little bit he had already told Winfield had already gotten back to Rodgers. Maybe Winfield knew damned right well that it was Rodgers' limo that had tried to force them off the road. Christ! Maybe Winfield had been driving the damn car! He sure seemed anxious to give them Rodgers' alibi for the time when they were being chased.

If you think about it like this, he warned himself, you will end up totally paranoid!

"This is your town," Dale said, taking a deep breath. "What do you know about what's around the house here."

Donna shrugged. "I don't know. I mean, Dyer isn't exactly the development capital of the world. I think things have stayed pretty much the same since I was a kid. I think this stretch of woods runs up beside the house on the left as we look at it. It may even curve around behind it. I never really played around here as a kid but I do remember there used to be an old barn somewhere out there—" She pointed towards the woods. "The kids used to hang out there, drinking and stuff."

"Is that all kids do around here, drink and fool around?"

Donna shrugged. "Well, if you're not into high school basketball, there's not much else going on."

Dale grunted and turned to look again at Rodgers' Funeral Home. "Well, I suppose, as long as we keep to the woods, we can try to get a look around the whole yard. We should be safe. Maybe we'll see something out back that'll tell us what we want."

"And what exactly do we want?" Donna asked. She had her hand on the door latch but couldn't quite get up the nerve to open the door.

"Beats the shit out of me," Dale said.

He pocketed the car keys and opened his door. As soon as he stepped out into the cool night, he ran his jacket zipper right up under his chin. His breath came out in small white puffs, and he couldn't help but think it wasn't this damned close to autumn back home — Thomaston!

Donna got out and came around the car, standing close to him and winding one arm around his waist. Pulling him close, she whispered into his ear, "Don't you think this is just a bit ridiculous? I mean, we're two grown adults, right?"

"Theoretically," Dale said with a half-chuckle.

"And here we are, out on a cold night, about to go spying around a funeral home to see if the funeral director is turning the townspeople in zombies. Doesn't that strike you as just a bit over the edge?"

Dale smiled and almost laughed aloud, but before he could stop it, the voice of Larry Cole, speaking into his dictating recorder, spoke as clearly in his mind as if he was standing on the other side of him.

" . . *He's turning them into zombies!*"

And then, almost as clearly, but with an icy tone that sent shock waves of chills up his spine, Dale remembered another voice, that of Franklin Rodgers, caught unawares by the Sony as it lay in the dirt by the side of the road, still running.

*"Don't touch this one. I have something special planned for him!"*

"I just want to have a look around," Dale said, his voice tight and sounding as if he was talking with his mouth closed. "Do you remember Rodgers having a security fence around his house?"

Donna shook her head. "How the hell should I know? I make it a point not to come home unless I have to. And when I was a kid, Rodgers didn't even own the place."

Dale pulled her close, wishing her warmth could drive away the chill he felt winding like cold, dead fingers around his heart. "Yes," he said, "and for two of those trips home, you had funerals to attend."

He could feel Donna tense in his embrace.

"Did either of those funerals take place here?" he asked, indicating Rodgers' Funeral Home with a wave of his free arm.

"Both," she said, sounding as if someone had tight fingers around her throat.

Dale didn't say the obvious: what if even back then he was experimenting? What if he did something to your parents, too? What if they aren't even in those caskets you saw lowered into the ground?

They stood in the dark woods for several seconds, considering how best they might approach the house, but at last, as amateur spies, Dale opted for the simplest approach.

"Look," he said, holding Donna back at arm's length, "we'll just stroll up along the margin of the woods, making sure we keep our eyes and ears open for anything that might indicate Rodgers is on to us. If we see anything like a burglar alarm or hear guard dogs or anything, we'll just turn around and get the hell out of here. All right?"

Donna nodded. She thought it best not to say what she was thinking, that as soon as they crossed the street they would hear a chorus of barking, and she and Dale would just pivot on their heels and get back into the car and drive the hell away from there.

"And then we'll go find Winfield, okay? I know we can trust him," she said as she followed Dale across the street and into the woods beside Rodgers' Funeral Home.

*Damn!* she thought as Dale's dark silhouette was swallowed by the dark shadows under the trees. *No dogs yet!*

# III

"She's resting pretty well now," Steve Wayne said, looking at Mrs. Appleby across the bed where Lisa lay sleeping. The bedside lamp cast a dim, warm yellow light over the quilted bedspread that was tucked right up under Lisa's chin. Her face looked relaxed, and a warm, living color had returned to her cheeks.

"Do you think we should take her into the hospital for a check?" Mrs. Appleby asked. Her heart was fluttering in her chest, and she was concerned that her anxiety for Lisa's health might actually endanger her own.

Steve shook his head as he dropped his stethoscope into the small black medical bag on the bed. It had warmed Mrs. Appleby's heart to no end to see that someone was training to carry on Doctor LaChance's tradition of making house calls. These were the days, she knew, of heartless emergency rooms and quick-care medical centers in the cities. She hoped this Stephen Wayne intended to fill Doc LaChance's shoes once he was gone.

Lisa stirred on the bed. Her eyelids fluttered but didn't open. Steve nodded toward the door and followed Mrs. Appleby out into the hallway. He looked back at his black medical bag on the bed as he eased the door shut.

"I don't think there's anything to worry about," he said, his voice a harsh whisper that, try as she did to ignore it, grated on Mrs. Appleby's nerves and made her like him a little less.

"I was afraid, though, that she may have fractured her skull. Wouldn't that account for the dizziness? If she has . . ." She couldn't bring herself to say the words, *brain damage.*

Steve waved his hand in front of her and clicked his tongue.

"The bump on her head looks bad, but I don't see where it's serious," he said. "If she had been complaining of any headaches, or if there was some ringing in her ears of if she complained of bright light hurting her eyes, I'd be more concerned. I think the best thing to do is let her rest and to regain her strength. If she's still not feeling better in a day or two, you might want to bring her into the hospital for an X-ray."

He started to turn toward the door when they heard a low moan issue from Lisa's room. Easing the door open a crack, his eyes immediately came to rest on his black bag. He smiled slightly to himself, thinking, I may have another one here! That would make three since Friday . . . Not bad for a weekend's work!

"My goodness," Mrs. Appleby said, her voice tightening up as if it was a screw someone was twisting deeply into wood. "You can't imagine how frightening it was, to see her hit the wall and fall like that! Lucky for her that beanbag chair was where it was."

Steve nodded. "True. Another blow to the head, and I would definitely have taken her directly to the hospital. I think, though, that she'll be just fine come morning. Just let me give her another shot for the pain," he said, pushing the bedroom door open. Looking back at Mrs. Appleby, he added, "You might want to wait outside for this one."

Mrs. Appleby nodded agreement and went downstairs.

All this time, Angie was in her room, lying on her bed with her hands clasped behind her head, staring up at the ceiling. She was mulling over, not just what had happened today, but everything that had happened since she and her father had come to Dyer. She felt all twisted up inside, like there were things happening to her that she wasn't ready to accept or ready to absorb.

The incident out at Lisa's "secret place" still danced like foxfire on the fringes of her mind. It was overshadowed by her concern for Lisa, but now, staring at the ceiling like she had the night after that crazy man had punched through the trap door and tried to grab her, it all came crashing back. She wondered what the man and those others down there with him would have done to her and Lisa if they had caught them. Would the man have killed them? Or done something *worse?* She shivered and scrunched her eyes tightly, trying to stop the flood of fear that threatened to sweep her away. She rolled onto her belly and stuffed a corner of her pillow into her mouth to keep from screaming out loud.

From the hallway, she could hear Mrs. Appleby and Doctor Wayne speaking in hushed voices. No, it wasn't "Doctor" she reminded herself. When Mrs. Appleby had called him "doctor," he had repeatedly insisted that he was not a doctor! "Just a physician's assistant," he had said, and Angie hadn't missed the edge of hostility in his voice.

Other thoughts flickered through her mind: Larry's funeral; her father's meeting this woman named Donna; her own crazy fear that those same men from Lisa's "secret place" were stalking her, still looking for her so they could finish what they had started. But most of all, she wallowed in the regret that she had caused Lisa's accident! That, even more that Larry being dead, was something she was going to have to live with forever!

Outside her closed door, she heard footsteps tread slowly down the stairs. She wasn't sure but thought it sounded like both Mrs. Appleby and Mrs. Wayne had gone. With a quick kick, she rolled off the bed and went to her door, pausing for just a moment to listen, but she didn't hear any voices from downstairs.

She sucked in her breath and held it as she tiptoed out of her room and down the hallway to Lisa's bedroom door. The door was open just a crack, and as she stood outside, she could hear Lisa's deep, heavy breathing.

"Lisa?" she called softly as she creaked open the door.

She let out a little squeak just as Mr. Wayne looked up and saw her. Surprise registered on his face, and he let out a startled grunt. He had been leaning over Lisa, and his hands jerked upward. Angie saw a quick flash of the glass of a hypodermic needle, as it spun out of his hand and flew end over end. It disappeared behind the bed, but she knew what had happened to it by the sound of breaking glass.

"What the hell?" Steve Wayne shouted, looking up at her with anger flashing like fire in his eyes.

"I thought you left," Angie said meekly as she hesitated in the doorway, not knowing whether to stay or leave.

Steve's hands shook as he looked back down at his patient. A small bead of blood was slowly growing larger on the inside of Lisa's arm where he had suddenly yanked out the needle. When he saw the spray of thick, purple liquid on the bed sheets, he realized his fingers must have involuntarily squeezed the plunger as he was pulling the needle out. A ball of anxiety swelled in his gut when he looked down at the floor and saw there, too, a small, spreading puddle of purple liquid.

How much did I get into her? his mind screamed, even though he knew there was no way to estimate from the splatters on the sheets and floor.

"Look what you made me do!" he shouted at Angie, his face contorted with rage. He had just one dose in his medical bag. It didn't pay for a physician's assistant to be carrying around any excess of an unknown drug, in case of an accident.

But now what? his mind shouted.

How much is in her? What will a partial dose do?

He forced his hands to stop shaking as he knelt down and hurriedly collected the fragments of his syringe. The puddle on the floor was simple enough to clean up, but what about the stain on the bed sheets? How was he going to explain that?

"I'm really sorry I made you jump like that," Angie said as she came around the side of the bed and squatted down to help him clean up the broken pieces.

"I can handle this," Steve said tightly, pushing her away. "Why don't you get some paper towels or something I can put this broken glass into?"

Angie hurried out of the room and raced downstairs, where she snapped several paper towels from the dispenser and then grabbed the brook and dustpan. As she was heading upstairs, Mrs. Appleby came out of the living room and asked her what was going on.

"Oh, nothing," she said, feeling torn between not wanting to get into Mrs. Appleby's disfavor and not quite trusting what she had seen going on in Lisa's bedroom.

Why, she wondered, was this doctor guy acting so jittery? He had looked at her guilty-like, as though she had caught him doing something wrong.

"Mr. Wayne dropped something, and I was just going to help him clean it up. It's nothing," Angie said, and with that she ran up the stairs, taking them two at a time.

Mrs. Appleby sighed deeply and started up slowly behind Angie.

Back in Lisa's room, Steve Wayne had scooped up all of the broken glass and dumped it into his medical bag. He opened up several sterilized gauze pads and was busily dabbing at the stains on the bed sheets with rubbing alcohol. The stains had turned a pale shade of blue like blueberry stains, or faded ink stains, but he was afraid they would be there even after washing. As Angie watched him, the only thought running through her mind was, what kind of medicine looks like that?

By the time Mrs. Appleby entered the room, Steve had pretty much cleaned up everything, so he felt confident there wouldn't be any questions asked.

"Clumsy me," he said, smiling as he looked at Mrs. Appleby. "I dropped the medication." He had already daubed away the bead of blood from Lisa's arm.

Angie noticed the softening of his manner when he spoke with Mrs. Appleby, almost as though he was trying to hide something.

"I have to admit it," Angie said, looking at Mrs. Appleby and then squinting as she watched Mr. Wayne for his reaction. "I thought you both had gone downstairs, and I came bursting in here and made him drop whatever it was he was going to give her."

Mrs. Appleby gave her a harsh stare, but it took only a moment for it to soften; the last thing she wanted was for this little girl to worry herself sick about Lisa's condition. No, she thought sympathetically, let me do the worrying for both of us.

"I was giving her another injection to help her rest. She got some of it." Steve said. His voice still had a trembling edge to it that Angie didn't like one bit.

Mrs. Appleby frowned as she looked down at her sleeping granddaughter. "Well, she seems to be peaceful enough," she said.

Steve nodded. "Oh, she's fine, I'm sure. We'll just have to hope it was enough to do the trick."

# IV

As it turned out, there weren't any dogs guarding Rodgers' Funeral Home. There wasn't even a fence, so unless Rodgers had one of those state-of-the-art laser alarm systems, the man was arrogant enough to think he' didn't need to hide what he was doing. Or maybe he was just what he appeared to be: an undertaker with a peculiar eye. His eye was disconcerting, but it certainly wasn't grounds for criminal accusations. As he and Donna made their way through the woods around to the back of the house, Dale felt like quite a fool.

They made noise as they tromped through the heavy underbrush in the dark. Fallen leaves and branches crinkled and snapped underfoot, and they kept getting snagged on unseen limbs. What little moonlight filtered through the trees was weak, and it threw them off by casting deep shadows and distorting their perception.

Once they were at the back of the funeral home, they both crouched and studied the building. The driveway sloped down to a sublevel double-wide doorway. Certainly that made sense, if only for "shipping and receiving." Dale shivered when he considered what precisely Rodgers "shipped" and "received." There were several spotlights shooting cones of light across the parking lot behind the house. The basement windows glowed with dull yellow light, but the doorway was cast in thick shadows. Dale couldn't tell if it was opened or closed.

"Do you think we can get any closer?" Dale whispered, his mouth close to Donna's ear. His breath was warm on her face, but that didn't drive away the chill by a long shot.

"Who'd want to?" she whispered back. She briefly toyed with the idea of sticking her tongue into his ear in an attempt to seduce him away from this crazy quest, as if they could accomplish anything, crouched out here in the cold and dark!

"Well." Dale said, scanning the silent parking lot, "the house is pretty dark except for the cellar. Don't you think it's a bit late to be working?"

Donna shrugged and shifted her weight from one to the other leg. "I wouldn't think so, not if he has a body to get ready for a funeral tomorrow."

"Come on," Dale said, standing up. "Let's see what's going on."

Saying that, he ran out of the woods and across the lawn, not stopping until he had flattened himself against the corner of the house. Donna was still crouched in the woods, her breath caught in her chest like a lead weight. She was wondering if her damned legs would suddenly turn to rubber halfway across the lawn, and she'd go sprawling onto her face.

Dale's silhouette was nothing more than a black blob against the side of the house. He was waving his arm for her to come, so overcoming her better judgment, Donna dashed out of the woods to join Dale at the corner of the house.

"Just like commandoes, huh?" Dale said, still huffing from his run.

Donna frowned, but it was lost in the darkness. All she wanted about now was a big cup of cocoa and a cigarette. "It's not exactly my idea of fun."

"Let's see if we can see anything in any of these windows," Dale said. "Then we'll split." He started edging his way along the side of the house, careful not to trip on anything and alert whoever was in the house to their presence.

At the first illuminated window, Dale peeked his face slowly around the frame to spy inside. But if Dale had been expecting a view into a mad scientist's secret lab, he was sorely disappointed. All he saw was a brightly lit waiting room, with overstuffed chairs, coffee tables spread with magazines and religious material, and a coat rack in the corner by the entrance. At the far end of the room was another open door, and from what little Dale could see, he thought it might be a showroom for coffins. He stiffened when he remembered sitting in the private waiting room in another funeral home, just prior to picking out a casket for Natalie.

Donna was still waiting at the corner of the house, thinking "this is his gig . . . let him do the snooping." She was content to tag along. Hopefully they wouldn't be arrested for whatever the hell they could charge you with for sneaking around someone's house at night.

Dale left the first window and approached the embankment that dropped off into the sub-level doorway. He was just about to look over the edge when headlights swept around the driveway. A car pulled into the back parking lot from the street.

With a panicked glance back to where Donna was, he saw with relief that she had already ducked out of sight. Dale fell flat on the ground, praying that the embankment would shield him from the sight of whoever was arriving.

He lay flat on his face, inhaling deeply of the fresh earth smell as the hiss of car tires did a long, slow turn in the driveway. Then, like a search light in a prisoner-of-war escape movie, the back of the house lit up brilliantly as the car came forward toward the doublewide doorway. Any second, now, Dale expected to hear the warbling wall of sirens. The car's engine rumbled with a deep, throaty power, and Dale was burning to take one quick peek to see if it was a long, black limo.

As the car moved slowly down the ramp to the doorway, there was no sound of a door being opened, so Dale at least had one question answered: the door had been open, as if Rodgers had been expecting someone!

The car braked to a stop, its red brake lights lighting up the inside of the embankment like fire. The engine revved up once, then stopped. This was followed by the sound of a car door opening and slamming shut. Footsteps echoed hollowly up from the basement as the unknown person walked deeper into Rodgers' basement.

"Good evening, Sam," said a voice, unmistakably Rodgers'. So far, so good, Dale thought, we haven't gotten caught yet.

"Is he ready?" the man called Sam said gruffly. "I want to see him before you get your money this time."

Rodgers made some reply, but it was lost as their footsteps retreated deeper into the basement. Again, there was no sound of the heavy door being run back down, so Dale figured Sam wasn't planning on staying long.

Dale craned his neck around and looked back to where Donna had last been. For all he knew, she had panicked and run all the way back to the car as soon as she had seen the headlights. But no, he saw a dark blur of motion, and then she peeked out around the corner.

She was hissing softly and waving at him. It was obvious to Dale that she did want to bug out, but he slowly raised himself and then, in a crouch, signaled for her to join him. It was a duel of wills for a moment, but Dale won. Crouching low, Donna tiptoed across the lawn and knelt down beside him.

"Let's get the Christ out of here," she said, her voice trembling. Her eyes were twin, pale saucers in the darkness, and Dale could feel her whole body shaking.

"There's something really strange going on here," Dale hissed in her ear. "Who around town here's named Sam?"

Donna scrunched up her face for a moment and shook her head. "I don't know! Christ! There are *plenty* of Sams. There's Sam Talbot, Sam Hardy, he runs the little barbershop on Main Street. 'Course, there's Sam Higgins."

"Who's he?"

"He and his family have lived here I think since the area was first settled. Sam's one of the biggest land owners; makes most of his money farming."

"Potatoes?"

Donna snickered. "What the hell else do you think?"

"Remember what Larry said on the tape?" Dale asked. He kept his eyes riveted to the doorway, expecting at any second to hear Sam's car start up and back on out of there. "Larry said Rodgers was selling these zombies he was making to use during the potato harvest."

"Do you realize how crazy you sound?" Donna asked. All she wanted to do was get the hell out of there. Never in her life, even more than after graduation, had she wanted to leave town and never come back.

"I know something's up," Dale said. "And I aim to find out what." With that he swung his leg up over the embankment, positioned his hands, and silently vaulted to the sloped driveway below. He landed and caught his balance, then quickly signaled for Donna to follow. Clinging to the shadows, he edged his way down to the doorway. A wave of disappointment hit him when he saw Sam's car and immediately realized that it probably hadn't been the car that had tried to force them off the road. A few more steps inside, though, and he saw something that made his breath catch in his throat: it was obviously Rodgers' car parked further inside. It was a long, sleek—and *black*—limousine.

Donna crept up silently behind him, and almost bumped into him in the dark when he stopped to run his hand along the side of the car.

"Does this car strike you as familiar?" he whispered.

Donna sniffed, afraid that if she opened her mouth, nothing would come out except a lung-ripping scream. She sure as shit did recognize this car!

Dale quickly went to the front of the car. Feeling around blindly, his fingers traced the smooth, polished chrome, but then something snagged his fingers. He couldn't be sure without seeing it in the light, but it felt like a deep dent in the front fender. From ramming a car? he wondered as a chill spread through his veins.

"I think they went down there," Dale whispered, pointing along a corridor that ran the length of the house. "Let's go into this room over here. Maybe we can hear what's going on through the walls and not get caught."

Donna was shaking her head. The thought that filled her mind was that she and Dale were both going to end up on marble slabs down in this basement if Rodgers caught them.

The door to the waiting room was unlocked. After a quick peek to make sure the room was empty, they tiptoed inside, pulling the door shut behind them. Dale wiggled the doorknob, making sure they weren't just locking them-selves in as they went.

"Do you think this could be a set-up?" Donna whispered as they crossed the room and headed toward the casket display room.

Dale turned and looked at her, his mouth a firm, harsh line. "What do you mean?"

"I mean the door's wide open to this place at night. Does that make sense to you? I would think an undertaker, even if he wasn't doing something strange, would have some kind of security system. Wouldn't it be, like, a state law or something? So people wouldn't be breaking in and ... I don't know, steal bodies and stuff?"

Dale shrugged as he leaned on the doorjamb and looked in on the long lines of caskets. There were at least thirty different varieties in this vast room, ranging from little more than an unpolished box with cheap satin liner and pillow to what had to be the Rolls Royce of caskets, heavy, ornate, and expensive. The only thing missing was a gold-inlay and diamond-studded coffin!

Dale was chilled by his own memories as he looked at row after row of coffins. All but two of them had their half lids opened to reveal the plush interiors. He tried to keep away the mental image of Natalie, lying there in her soft puff of pink satin, her fingers laced stiffly across her chest, her face and lips looking so lifelike.

Enough so you almost expected her to get up!

There were two other doors leading into this display room. One, double-wide, like the outside doorway, obviously led directly to the basement and the ramp up. The other door, at the far end of the room, just as obviously led to Rodgers' laboratory where he eviscerated the deceased, and gave them their jolt of embalming fluid. It was where he applied make-up and other cosmetics, so the living could admire the dead, muttering softly as they proceeded by, "Oh, he looks just like himself!"

In the back of his mind, he again heard Larry Cole's frantic, nearly insane voice say:

*. . . taking dead people and turning them into . . . into . . . zombies!*

Dale stepped into the display room with Donna close at his heels. He could faintly hear the buzzing of voices through the wall, and he was thinking he could maybe learn all he needed to know if he could just hear what Rodgers and Sam were saying. They were half-way across the floor, though, when the door from the laboratory started to swing open. With a barely suppressed shout, Dale shoved Donna in between two of the caskets and quickly ducked in behind her. Crouching low, they scurried to the far end of the room as footsteps approached and the voices got louder.

"Oh," Rodgers said, his voice swelling with pride, "just wait until you see him. This is, without a doubt, my best work. Here, see for yourself."

Dale and Donna tensed when the footsteps stopped beside one of the caskets. Was that one of the closed ones? Dale wondered frantically. Peering under the tables that supported the caskets, all he could see were two pairs of legs from the knees down.

"You open the lid," Rodgers' voice boomed, "and see for yourself."

Dale cast an anxious glance back at Donna, who was shivering as she crouched beneath the casket display. She had one hand clapped over her mouth, and her eyes were opened so wide Dale could see white all around the pupils. She took her hand away to whisper something to him, but he shushed her with a wave of his hand.

From where Rodgers and Sam were standing, there was a soft click, and then someone, probably Sam, grunted as he raised the casket lid, as Rodgers had directed.

"My goodness," Sam said, his voice hushed with awe. "That certainly is incredible!"

"Like I said, he's definitely my best yet," Rodgers said.

Dale was burning to know what or who they were looking at. They certainly weren't admiring the wood finish on one of the coffins.

*What in the name of Christ is going on?* he wondered as he considered what they should do next. The options were definitely limited: he either had to maneuver so he could see what they were looking at, or he and Donna were going to get the hell out of there and convince Win-field he had to investigate. Playing the tape for him might convince him!

Maybe now, Dale thought they could or should trust Winfield and if they were going to, now wouldn't be such a bad time to get him out here. But getting Win-field out here first required that they get out.

Dale's hands were slick with sweat as he crouched on the carpeted floor, wondering which way to turn. The door back into the waiting room, at least for now, was out of the question; Rodgers would easily see them as soon as they made a break. But if they waited for Rodgers and Sam to leave . . . hell, they might be here all night. And if either Rodgers or Sam for any reason happened to lean over, they would easily spot them.

"And watch how well he obeys," Rodgers said.

Dale tensed, and the next words her heard rang in his ears like the heavy pounding of a hammer on metal.

"Larry," Rodgers said, his voice deep and commanding, "I want you to get up now."

In the tingling silence that followed the command, the only sound in the room was the heavy rustling of something shifting weight on slick satin. Someone groaned deeply, and the sound reminded Dale of a heavy oak door, swinging slowly open.

Donna was cringing back against one of the table legs, shaking her head slowly back and forth, a though what she had heard couldn't he real! Whatever was happening over there, she wanted absolutely no part of it!

Dale knew he had to see with his own eyes before he would truly believe what he feared was happening in the casket. He tried unsuccessfully to block out the images that rushed into his mind as he quietly edged his face around the side of one of the caskets. He felt a flicker of relief when he saw that both Rodgers and Sam were standing back to him, but what he saw made the blood stop in his veins.

He was staring straight into the dead eyes of *Larry Cole!* His face was a tangle of dark, rotten meat, showing strips of sick-looking pink beneath, and he was slowly *rising from his coffin.* One side of his head was sheared clean of hair, giving him an odd, lopsided look. Either his lips were skinned back in a grimace, or they were gone, possibly burned off in the car crash. His teeth were chattering from the effort of movement, and the hollow *clicking* sounds they made reminded Dale of Mrs. Appleby's ever-present knitting needles. Larry's eyelids were peeled back, exposing sickly, yellow orbs; and the pupils had swollen to the size of twin black marbles that looked blankly ahead, directly at Dale, where he crouched.

Like Rodgers' left eye! Dale's mind screamed, his breath catching in his throat like a tangle of briars.

As Larry sat up stiffly in the casket, Rodgers and Sam each took a few involuntary steps backwards. Then they turned, looked at each other, and, nodded.

"You see," Rodgers said, stroking his chin, "I had to continually modify the ingredients of the compound. The important thing, I'm sure you'll agree, is control. The drug cannot be effective unless it completely reduces the individual's will and his sense of purpose."

"Don't tell me about control," Sam said sharply. "Considering the problems we had with those last two you sold me."

"It was a mistake, I'll admit. But all the ones before those two are still fine, correct?"

Sam nodded.

"And I assure you it won't happen again with this one or any others. The drug is perfectly balanced now, and, although I'm quite sure the individual is still dimly aware that he is or was living, there's no motivation to do anything except what he's told to do."

"And what about the other problems?" Sam said. He turned sideways to face Rodgers, and when he did, Dale got a good look at his face. Quickly signaling Donna he slid back behind the casket so she could sneak a look.

"Is that Higgins?" Dale whispered at her ear.

After only a split-second look, Donna ducked back down. Her mouth was set in a grim line as she nodded her head yes.

"The deterioration rate, yes," Rodgers said. "Well, when you consider all the factors, we're lucky they last as long as they do. Repeated doses of the drug in liquid form will maintain this state for ... well, what's the longest time you've had one last?"

Higgins scratched behind his ear. "I think I had a couple that lasted nearly two years before they . . . well, you know what happens."

Rodgers cleared his throat and cast a glance at Larry, who was now sitting bolt-upright in the casket, his eyes vacantly focused straight ahead. "I've told you, I'm sure," he said, "what my studies in Haiti indicated."

Higgins nodded.

"Unless you can think of some way to provide a steady diet of human brains, your workers will inevitably deteriorate with time. There's really no way I know of yet, to stop the body's decomposition. I'm working on it."

Higgins shook his head vigorously from side to side. "No I don't want to get into *that*" he said, his voice raking on a trembling edge. "I mean, what we're doing with these is bad enough. I'm not going to start murdering people just to feed these things."

Rodgers tossed his hands up into the air and then clapped them to his side. "Well, you certainly can't have it both ways. Besides, it's not as though we haven't on occasion *arranged,* shall we say, a bit of an accident for someone who's perhaps a little too close to our project."

"Look!" Higgins said, suddenly turning on Rodgers and jabbing a forefinger at him. "I pay you to do what you do, and for now it works out just fine for both of us. I get cheap labor, and you get to 'experiment' with your drugs and potions. At least so far, by moving them around frequently, and not being too obvious, we've been able to keep the police and people around town here from getting suspicious. Let's just leave it at that, all right?"

"I mean nothing by it," Rodgers said placidly. He took Higgins by the arm and turned him toward the door. Dale just had time to snap down behind the casket, and as the footsteps approached, he and Donna wriggled under the table to the other side.

"Do you want to take this one with you tonight?" Rodgers asked.

Higgins huffed. "You said you had another one that will be ready by tomorrow night?"

"Yes," Rodgers said. Dale could see their legs as they stopped by the waiting room door. "That poor chap, Mr. Perry, who died this afternoon in the hospital. He's in the lab now, but after the fuss that friend of this one made about the closed casket, I'm going to have to wait until after the ceremony to get him out of the coffin and give him the final dose."

"I suppose, then, that I could wait until tomorrow night to pick them up," Higgins said as he walked out into the waiting room.

Dale saw this as his chance to escape, and pointing toward the door that led to the laboratory, told Donna to get going. Higgins and Rodgers were through the doorway when Dale and Donna stood up and made a dash for the door. If there was an exit from the lab they would be safe; if not . . .

Donna was at the door, fumbling to turn the knob; and Dale was just a few paces behind her when from behind them, they heard a loud, gurgling moan that froze them both. Glancing over his shoulder, Dale saw Larry's wide, black, empty eyes fixed unblinkingly on him. His arms were raised, reaching out toward him as though in greeting.

Does he recognize me? Dale thought, his heart all but bursting from his chest.

Again, the moan issued, this time louder, from Larry's dead throat. Satin hissed and dry ligaments crackled like ice underfoot as Larry struggled to kick his legs free of the confining coffin.

"Come on!" Dale whispered harshly to Donna, who stood there, unable to turn the doorknob clenched in her hand as she watched, fascinated with horror.

"Open the fucking door!"

*"You!"* Rodgers' voice suddenly boomed in the room as his face peered around the door jamb.

Dale and Rodgers locked eyes for a frozen instant, then Dale shouldered Donna aside, turned the doorknob, and slammed the lab door open. The harsh smell of formaldehyde was like a solid wall in the room, and Dale had the instant impression that he had suddenly plunged under water. Pulling Donna in behind him, he started to swing the door shut; but when he chanced one last glance over his shoulder, he saw something that took all of the nerve from him.

Rodgers had moved back into the display room, but he hadn't begun pursuit. Instead, he was standing with his finger pointing to the lab door. His voice like iron when he riveted his eyes on Larry Cole, sitting up in his coffin, and shouted, "Get *them!*"

# V

Lisa woke up about an hour after everyone had left her room. She had some vague sense of people milling around her bed, but she had been lost, spinning backward into a dizzying—yet, in a strange sort of way, *fun*— darkness. The feeling was cold, tingling every nerve in her body, but it also had a measure of reassurance, as though she had somehow been transported out of her body.

When her eyes flickered open, though, she knew something was dreadfully wrong! The lamp beside her bed was still on, but the light it shed burned her eyes, making the edges of everything dance with a ripple of vibrating red. She squinted her eyes tightly shut, but the after-images remained, dancing and weaving with light that for some reason had a sense of *touch* to it.

How can you feel light? she wondered, as a low whimper struggled inside her for release.

She couldn't tell how long she lay there, lost in darkness spiked with points of hard light. She tried to will herself out of her body again, to get back to the pleasant darkness but something held her down, as if hundreds of tiny fish hooks had pierced her flesh and pinned her to the bed, not letting her escape.

Sweat streamed down her face, mixing with the tears that seeped from underneath her closed eyelids. Her hair was plastered against her forehead. She was distantly aware of all of this, but worse than that, she felt as though her very *bones* were being tormented into different shapes. Her skin and muscles twitched with wet, snake-like ripples, and a distant corner of her mind filled with the fear that she was somehow going to slough off her skin, as a snake does, or worse that her skin was going to crawl away from her on its own accord.

With a sudden, gut-wrenching shout, she sat up in her bed, forcing her eyes to open in spite of the pain that dropped down on her in one heavy, smothering load.

Her bedroom was alive with energy. The dark rectangle of the window was dancing with fingers of blue light, slow-motion lightning touched her bed and bureau and reading chair. It touched everything in a slow, sinuous dance. Colors ran and melted into each other, twisting like bubbly plastic, and everywhere light fragmented into bright prisms.

A sound like thunder rumbled behind her. Turning, she looked in horror as two *things* lurched in through her door and came slowly toward the bed. The light from the hallway behind them poured like a waterfall into the room and seemed to sweep these *things* up and carry them toward her. There were dark spirals where then-faces should have been, and long, tangled fingers reached out of the spirals, grabbing for her throat.

"No! . . . No!" Lisa screamed. Her words reverberated and got increasing louder, rather than fading. In her mind, every syllable she spoke became a different colored foam.

The two dark shapes loomed over her, and Lisa was sure that, within seconds, she would feel a crashing weight flatten the life out of her. She flailed wildly, kicking free of her covers that held her like claws as she scrambled away from the onrushing creatures.

"*What's . . . the . . . matter . . . Lisa?*" a voice as cold as death booked. It was so close to her ears it hurt. Each word was drawn out with sludgy, thunder-rolling slowness.

Lisa stood up as tall as she could, stretching to challenge these beings before they got her.

"Go away! Leave me alone!" she wailed, as she battered at them in a flurry of fists.

"*It's . . . me . . . Lisa!*" ... the voice droned.

"Go away! *Go away!*"

The waterfall of light, sparkling silver like a river in the sun, caught her eye. Coiling up all of her strength, Lisa ran past the figures; she dove into the light and, as though her legs belonged to someone else, was transported down the stairs and toward the front door.

"*Lisa . . . wait!*" the voice boomed from up stairs, but Lisa plunged through the door and into the night. Her fleeing footsteps rang hollowly on the walkway, like hammers on stones. All around her, the night jumped and sparkled with trembling purple light. At first it briefly hurt her eyes to look around as she ran as fast as she could from the house. Everywhere she turned, though, it didn't look like night at all or day, for that matter. The world was suffused with rippling violet light, and now that the threat of those creatures that had tried to destroy her was past, Lisa's mind was fixed on one thought on her mind . . .

She was *hungry!*

# VI

Dale watched as Larry swung his legs out of the coffin and dropped to the floor. For just an instant, his legs sagged, and, like the scarecrow in "The Wizard of Oz," he looked as though he was going to collapse; but then came Rodgers' harsh command: "I said *get* them!"

"Come on, Dale! Run!" Donna shouted as she tugged on his arm.

Dale suddenly snapped to and shouldered the door shut. His fingers fumbled to throw the dead bolt lock; but if he hadn't been leaning against the door, it would have flung open when something slammed into it with a heavy thud.

"There's a door to get out of here!" Donna shouted from the far side of the lab.

Dale was still leaning against the door, afraid that thing out there would smash through the door as if it were balsa wood. *It's no longer Larry!* he thought. *It's a dead thing!* He tried not to imagine those rotted hands, reaching through the splintered door and grabbing him by the throat.

"Come on!" Donna shouted.

Dale found the courage to lean away from the door, but when he turned to run, his eyes finally registered what was all around him. There were three marble slabs, arranged side by side, each one illuminated by a powerful stainless steel overhead work light. Neatly arranged on the slabs and in several hand carts was a wide assortment of tools that looked like surgical instruments. Dale tried hard not to imagine what they were used for. In one corner of the lab there was a large plastic-lined trashcan. Sticking up over the rim were two shriveled human arms.

On each slab there was a human corpse, two men and one woman. Each was in a different state of decomposition. The freshest looking one, a young man, was strapped down. As Dale looked at it, he was positive he saw the muscles working against the restraint of the straps.

"Do you see what's going on in this place?" he shouted, stripping his throat raw, "Look at this!"

Donna was fumbling with one hand to undo the lock and banging the door with her other hand. "I don't want to see! I don't want to know!" she wailed.

Dale tore his eyes from the ghoulish specimens spread out on the slabs and dashed over to the door. He practically tore the lock off and, flinging the door open wide, ran out into the night, dragging Donna along behind him. Just as they left the room, they heard the locked door burst open with a loud shattering of wood.

"Run like a bastard!" Dale shouted as he and Donna started off across the lawn toward the woods. Their minds were filled with images of Larry Cole, stumbling after them in the darkness with his dead arms reaching out, his senseless fingers burning to crush their throats. And Dale couldn't forget what he had heard Rodgers tell Higgins . . .

*"It's not as though we haven't, on occasion, arranged a bit of an accident. . ."*

Suddenly the whole of Rodgers' back yard was flooded with light as every spotlight winked on. Dale and Donna cast long, wavering shadows as they ran, not daring to look back to see how close the pursuing *thing* that had been Larry was getting.

"You'll regret this, Mr. Harmon!" a voice suddenly shouted, cutting through the night and echoing all around. "You'll regret this dearly!"

Dale's lungs were burning, and his mind was numb with terror and grief over what had become of Larry Cole; but as they ran, he managed to say to Donna, "Don't worry! . . . He's just trying to scare us!"

"He's doing a . . . damned . . . good job," she said, breathlessly.

They made it down to the road and ran furiously back to the parked car. Dale's hands were shaking wildly as he fumbled to get the keys from his pants pocket and into the door lock. "Hell of a time to worry about locking the car doors!" he shouted at himself.

"Hurry! Hurry!" Donna yelled. She was looking back at the house, now all lit up as brightly as if for Christmas. Around one side of the house, she saw a dark, stumbling figure heading toward the road with lurching strides. When the figure stepped out into the light, she gasped.

Dale finally got the key into the slot, popped the lock, and swung the door open. One hand reached to open Donna's door as the other fumbled the key into the ignition.

"Don't choke it out," Donna said as she dropped onto her seat and slammed her door shut. She locked it, although she was convinced it would do her little good if that *thing* ever caught up with them. She could see it getting closer to the road, but it seemed to be running with little purpose, darting this way and that, like a bloodhound searching for a scent.

Dale stepped down hard on the accelerator as he cranked the key, and the car mercifully started right up. The engine whined as he floored the gas and popped the clutch. In a shower of dirt and leaves, the car spun out onto the road, its tires squealing as they left twin streaks of black rubber on the tar.

Both Dale and Donna were panting, their lungs burning and their legs aching from their sudden dash. Dale's relief at getting away was so overwhelming as he sped down Mayall Road toward Main Street that it all suddenly struck him as extremely funny.

*What they had seen in Rodgers' Funeral Home was . . . funny!*

*What was happening to the people of Dyer was . . . funny!*

*These people couldn't even die and make an end of it.*

*Instead, as in life, they ended up still working in the potato fields . . . forever! And that was . . . simply hilarious!*

"Dale . . ." Donna's voice said, cutting into his thoughts like a rusty razor blade.

"Huh? What?" He shook his head and tore his eyes away from the road ahead. Curled around the steering wheel, his fingers felt as though they would never straighten out. That, too, struck Dale as funny.

I'm losing it! his mind screamed. I'm heading straight off the deep end!

"I said I think we'd better try to find Winfield," Donna said, her voice trembling almost to the breaking point. "Rodgers knows it was us, and unless you want both of us to end up like Larry . . ." She cut herself short, and Dale saw her tremble with the thought.

"I know, I know," he said, forcing his mind to calm down. Take it easy! he told himself. Let what you've seen absorb slowly, and then maybe it will start to make sense.

He automatically snapped on his turn signal for the turn by the town hall to the police station. Just as he made the turn, he saw a small figure, dart into a doorway, away from the sweep of headlights.

"Hey!" Donna said, twisting to look behind them. "Didn't that look like Lisa Grant? Mrs. Appleby's granddaughter?"

Dale shook his head quickly. "No. What would she be doing out this time of night? I just hope to hell Win-field's at the station!"

# VII

"I'm sorry," the desk officer said. The name plate on the front of the desk read: "Officer on Duty—Sgt. Ernie Brooks." He was speaking into the telephone and nodded a greeting when Dale and Donna burst into the police station. Donna didn't recognize his name from when she was growing up, but she figured he was probably one of the Brooks boys whose family lived out on Pole Hill Road. Most likely, he had been a few years behind her in school.

"I understand that," Officer Brooks continued, "but you have to understand that I'm a bit short-handed. I can't send anyone out to look for her until the patrol officer gets back from the call he's on presently." He paused to look at Donna and Dale, rolling his eyes ceiling-ward. "I understand that you're upset, ... I know, but I can't leave the station unattended, now, just to go ... I understand. Yes, I will. Thank you."

With that, he hung up and, rubbing his forehead with the flat of his hand, said, "Damn! For a slow Monday night, things sure as hell are jumping. What can I do for you?"

Dale raked his fingers through his hair and hurriedly tried to compose himself. If Donna's looks were any gauge, they must look like quite the pair, Dale thought standing there disheveled and panting, with sweat glistening on their faces.

"I was hoping Jeff might be on duty tonight," Dale said. He had to fight the urge to burst out laughing when he considered what Winfield's reaction would be when they told him what they discovered at Rodgers' or that *Larry Cole* had attacked them! At least he still had the tape, the only concrete evidence that this all wasn't some wild hallucination or nightmare.

Brooks shook his head and took a sip of coffee.

"Jeffs on days this week," he said. "Is there anything I can help you with?"

Dale opened his mouth, about to spill the entire story in a rush; but then he felt Donna's hand tighten on his, so instead he shook his head. "Uh . . . No, I guess not. We had some personal business with him."

They started to turn for the door when Brooks stood up behind the desk. "You're sure I can't help you?" he asked.

The expression on his face was sincere, but Dale thought right away there was no way he would be able to convince this man what they had seen was real. He and Donna simultaneously shook their heads.

"Well, when he left here," Brooks said, "he said he was going to head out to check . . . Damn! I can't recall where it was he said he was going . . . out to check somebody's house. If he was on-duty, I'd have logged it, but. . . Anyway, after that, I figure he'd head on home if he didn't stop at Kellerman's for supper, first."

"Could you call him at home?" Donna asked.

Brooks shrugged, picked up the phone, and quickly dialed the number from memory. He waited what seemed like an awfully long time to Dale, then with another shrug, hung up the receiver.

"No answer. Your best bet is to check down to Keller-man's. You can tell whether or not he's there 'cause his cruiser'll be parked out front."

"Thanks a lot," Dale said as he turned on his heel and left. Donna followed close behind him. At the exit, as a precaution, they both stopped cold and peered out into the darkness. They were expecting at any moment to see a dark figure shamble toward them across the parking lot.

Dale opened the door a crack and looked along both sides of the building. "Looks okay to me," he said.

"You folks all right?" Brooks shouted from down the hallway.

Dale glanced to the right and saw a water fountain. "Just getting a drink, officer." To convince him, Dale flipped the fountain on and off a few times. "You ready?" he asked, looking at Donna.

She was standing at the door, her face pressed against the glass as she looked out on the night. With a quick nod, she knocked the door open with her hip, and they both hurried across the parking lot to Dale's car. The station door slammed shut behind them with a loud "clang."

Dale chanced a quick glance over his shoulder, and he saw a flurry of motion in the darkness near the side of the building; but he wasn't about to go over and check it out. He glanced quickly into the back seat, saw that it was empty, then unlocked Donna's door and went around to the driver's side. Just as he was sliding in behind the steering wheel, he saw something move up the stairs by the station door. A shifting reflection made it look as though the glass door had swung open and shut again. He started up the car and cut a tight circle and drove around toward the front of the building.

"So . . ." Dale said as he slowed for the left onto Main Street. "Where do we go from here?"

Donna was silent for a moment, and when she responded, it was with nothing more than a tight squeak. Dale turned to her and immediately saw what the problem was. Heading straight toward the side of the car was a pair of glaring headlights.

"Mother-*humper!*" Dale shouted as he slammed the accelerator to the floor. The on-coming car darted out at them from the Baptist Church parking lot with cobra-like swiftness. With a squeal of tires, Dale's car shot forward just before impact, and as he gained speed going down Main Street, he saw, in the rear view mirror, the long, black car swerve and straighten out.

"He's after us," Dale saw, setting his mouth in a firm line as he sped down Main Street. His mind clicked faster than the cylinders of this car . . .

Where the hell are the cops now, when you need them? Dale thought bitterly. As a matter of fact, where the hell was *anyone?* The entire town looked deserted, and it was only eleven o'clock. Had Rodgers known they were at the station and had just waited there for this chance? Or had he just been out cruising, waiting to, literally, bump into them?

"This is your neck of the woods," he said to Donna. "Where the hell can I go where I can shake him off our tail?"

Donna grunted and pointed to the blinking yellow light up ahead. "Turn left there. Maybe we can out distance him there. The road's going to get a bit rough, but it doesn't have the twists and turns Route 2-A has."

Dale took the turn fast, and he felt a swelling of satisfaction that his car held the road firmly. When he glanced at the gas gauge, though, his heart skipped a beat. There was only a quarter of a tank left; if this turned into a long chase, they were going to end up sputtering to a pitiful conclusion somewhere on a dark, deserted road.

"Where does this take us?" Dale asked. His heart thumped in his chest when he saw two circles of yellow light swing around the corner behind them. It was difficult to judge the distance, but it sure as hell looked as though those head-lights were closing the distance . . . *fast!*

"This is Burnt Hill Road," Donna said breathlessly. "After a stretch of houses and a few farms, it gets pretty woodsy. After about—I don't know, ten or fifteen miles it connects with Town Line Road. We can either circle back around toward town or go south."

"Go south," Dale said with a grim laugh. "I think maybe I should have taken your advice about leaving when I could have."

"Just fucking *drive!*" Donna said, still looking back at the following car.

"I've got a good lead, now if I can just shake him."

Donna made a deep-throated sound and shook her head as she watched the car behind them. It looked to her as though it was slowly but steadily closing the distance. She tried to block from her mind the image of herself, stretched out on one of Rodgers' marble slabs while he injected her veins. "No!" she said, closing her eyes and clenching her fists tightly.

Dale was having a hell of a time, keeping his eyes focused on the road as if unfolded in front of his headlights. The houses and open fields, just as Donna had said, soon gave out, and they were enfolded by the thick, black walls of forest on both sides of the road. Donna was also right about the road; although it was relatively straight, the pot-holes and bumps made Dale's teeth rattle. The only comforting thought was that the road was probably doing more damage to the heavier-bodied limo.

"Can you go any faster?" Donna asked, her voice so tight she didn't sound like herself.

"Not if I'm going to keep us on the road."

As soon as he said that, Donna again saw in her mind what she wished to God she could forget: Larry Cole's dead, smiling face as he looked up from his coffin and started coming after them!

Dale expertly negotiated the road, taking each curve with a smooth, steady twist of the steering wheel. If he wasn't exactly leaving the limo in the dust, it at least wasn't running them down like an eighteen-wheeler over a rabbit. The only problem he saw was the gas! He glanced at the speedometer with trepidation: Sixty-six, sixty-seven, sixty-eight miles per hour! These roads weren't designed for this kind of speed, he thought.

Both cars sliced through the darkness as though sucked forward by their cones of yellow light. Just as he was rounding a curve, Dale saw headlights coming at him. His first thought was that Rodgers had signaled ahead, and this was someone aiming to cut them off. But as he whizzed past the on-coming car, he gasped with surprise when he saw the black and white designs of a cop's cruiser.

"Rodgers can't touch us now," Dale said. He considered slowing, when he saw the cruiser's brake lights flash as the cop slowed for his own turn. By the time he had started his turn, though, Rodgers' limo had also streaked past him. Dale knew that was their only chance. The cop would take Rodgers first. The devil take the hindmost! he thought. All the cop had to do was delay Rodgers only a few seconds; then they'd were home free.

"He's got him!" Dale said joyfully when he saw the cop's blue lights winking off and on in his rear view mirror.

"Oh, Jesus!" Donna said with a gasp.

"Huh?" Dale said. He still wasn't sure how this was ail going to end, but the situation was improving.

"That cop back there," Donna said, her throat as raw as sandpaper. "If he stops Rodgers, he's . . ."

"Oh, shit," Dale said as the full import sunk in. "The only way Rodgers is going to get out of explaining what he's doing, driving like this on back roads at night, is to ..."

"Do to *him* what he did to Larry!" Donna finished for him.

"But we're safe for now," Dale said, finding little joy in the thought that the cop back there, whoever he was, was going to be dead soon *(sort of dead,* he thought with a shiver), just so they could live. And that didn't take care of anything!

Rodgers still wasn't going to be found out!

He and Donna were still in serious trouble!

And where was Winfield? Once Winfield heard the tape, he might be convinced. But all of this was turning into some insane nightmare, and they still had no way of getting out of it without ending up dead ... or *worse!*

"We've got to check out at your parents' house, first," Dale said. He rounded a curve and the cop's blue light disappeared. A frigid chill hit his stomach as he imagined what would happen next back there on that lonely stretch of road.

Probably what happened to Larry last Friday night, he thought.

"There's a dirt road up ahead. I don't think we passed it yet. That'll take us over to Mayall Road, just above Beaver Brook Lake," Donna said. "We might be able to tell if Winfield's been out to the house yet."

"It's as good an idea as any," Dale said tightly. A large part of his mind was screaming at him to turn around and go back to where they had left the cop. By now, Rodgers had probably been pulled over, shown his license and car registration, was now explaining, in his honey-smooth radio announcer's voice, that he was driving to pick up a body. Because the car ahead of him had been going so fast, he had just sort of not paid attention to his speed."

*"Sixty-five, officer? Really? Isn't it funny how sometimes it just doesn't seem like you're going that fast?"* And then what?

As the cop was putting his registration back into the glove compartment, Rodgers would pull out a gun or perhaps a scalpel. It would all happen so fast, the cop would be caught completely by surprise. He'd be crumpling to the pavement, his life seeping from him, before he could begin to react or think. "He'd look up at the towering black trees surrounding the road, and he'd simply slip away into nothing. And then . . . *then,* what?

Rodgers would take his body back to the funeral home. The cop would become something he would have thought impossible. His lifeless body would be filled with a drug that, while not restoring the true fire of life, would bring back the semblance of life. And in his death-clouded brain, would there be a spark left of the person he had been? Would he *know* that he had once been warm, living flesh and blood? Or would he simply, mindlessly lurch, like a puppet on strings, to do what his master Franklin Rodgers commanded him to do?

Dale shuddered at the thought, and it was only with supreme effort that he didn't scream his lungs out. The road and the surrounding night-stained trees became little more than blurs as he drove ahead, trying to block from his mind what had probably, by now, already happened back there.

# VIII

When Officer Brooks heard the front door shake and then open, he assumed that the man and woman who had just been there had decided, after all, that it wasn't a personal matter; he could help them just as easily as Winfield could. He stood up and came around the corner of his desk, a smile on his face as he called out, "Yoh!"

He took a step back, though, when he saw that it wasn't the man and woman returning. At first, he didn't recognize her. Her face was so pale, and her eyes were opened wide as she looked up at him. The ceiling lights reflected on the glistening curves of her eyes. Her teeth were chattering, and it took Brooks several seconds to realize that this was Lisa Grant. He couldn't imagine why she was out on a cold night like this, wearing only thin pajamas. She was bare-footed, and her feet had left streaked, muddy splotches on the tiled floor.

"For cryin' out loud, Lisa," he said as he took only a few steps closer to her. "Do you know how much trouble you've caused me tonight?"

Lisa looked at him in spite of the bright lights. His face distorted, as though it was made of plastic that had gotten too close to the heat. To Lisa, his nose was large, bubbly smear, and everything around him shimmered with pieces of light, pieces that were as real and sharp as wood splinters.

"Your grandmother has been calling me every two minutes." Brooks said as he slowly approached Lisa, his hands held out reassuringly. "She even threatened to report me to Chief Bates and have me fired." He chuckled, but the laughter didn't come from his gut; it sounded forced and unnatural.

Lisa didn't say a word as she stood there, shivering. Her hands slowly flexed until her fists were iron-tight balls. She could feel her fingernails pressing into the palms of her hands as the muscles in her shoulders knotted tighter and tighter.

"Come on in here," Brooks said as he as he swung open one of the office doors. "I'll get you a blanket. How about a cup of tea? I don't think we have any hot chocolate. Knowing Winfield, he probably drank it all."

A low sound came from deep within Lisa's chest, but Brooks wasn't sure if she meant yes or no. He took a rough gray woolen blanket from the supply closet and shook it open. On one corner was stitched the words "Property of Dyer Police." He went over to Lisa and handed it to her.

"Do you want to talk about anything?" Brooks asked. "I mean, did you have an argument or something with your gram? Is that why you ran away?" He couldn't get over how terrible she looked. It was as though she had been lost in the woods for a week without sleep.

Lisa held the blanket loosely in one hand. She trembled so hard Brooks was sure she would drop the blanket before she could get it around her shoulders. When he reached over to help her, he was surprised by the steel-tight grip that suddenly clamped his wrist. He looked at Lisa, shocked by the sudden wild fury that was blazing in her eyes.

"I'm . . . hun . . . gry," she said, her voice a tortured rasp. Her eyes held his with a smoldering rage that instantly flashed the policeman a warning: *She's crazy! She's nuts!*

"Let me get you warmed up," he said as he tried, gently, to break her hold on his arm. "I can see if anyone left anything in the refrigerator." She was twisting her hand with his every effort, and her fingers just wouldn't let go of his wrist. It was as if she had more strength than he had. But, he thought, he didn't want to do anything that might hurt her; he couldn't very well go beating up on a kid.

"I'm . . . *hungry!*" she said again, and when Brooks looked down, he saw something that made his breath catch in his throat. She was leaning forward, her mouth open wide.

Lisa brought her teeth down hard on his arm. For a split second surprise cancelled the pain; then it slammed up his arm to his shoulder like an electric shock, numbing and hard. Brooks felt momentarily detached from everything, as though he was watching this happen to someone else, but then his brain registered it all: the pain, the warm gush of blood, the grinding sounding of teeth on bone. *His* bone!

With a twisted shout, he jerked his arm back with all of his strength, but that only made the hole in his arm worse. Blood cascaded down his arm, and all he could hear was the gurgling sound of *drinking!*

She's drinking my fucking blood! his mind screamed as he struggled to free himself.

But Lisa's grip was tight, and she clung to him like a hawk to a rabbit. His panic and shock only aided her as her teeth ground back and forth, shearing through skin and muscle. Then there was a rough grinding sound that told Brooks she had gone clean through to the bone. He couldn't even feel his fingers, just the gushing warm rush of blood, pouring from his arm.

"Jesus Christ!" he wailed, backing up and trying to shake her off. *"Jesus Fucking Christ!"*

He could hear a heavy plopping sound, and he knew the sound that was his blood dripping to the floor as Lisa's mouth filled and overflowed. He could hear her swallow, and he tried not to think that his own flesh was going down her throat! She was *eating* him!

With a sudden burst of frenzy, he shouted aloud as he slammed his arm first backwards and then forward. Lisa's feet skittered beneath her, and then, mercifully, the pressure on his arm eased up. With one more vicious shove, he sent her reeling backwards. Her feet got tangled on each other, and she fell. Her head made a hollow, coconut sound when she hit the wall and then slid to the floor, ending up sitting with her legs awkwardly splayed. Her eyes were still open, but they were crossed and unfocused.

Brooks doubled up in pain and almost vomited when he looked down at his arm. There was a ragged hole about the size of a baseball. Thick red blood pumped up out of the wound and flowed in thick streamers down his arm to the floor. He had seen enough accidents in his years on the Dyer Police to know that the pearly white he saw was exposed bone, but he had never thought he'd ever see his own exposed bone!

With stumbling, lurching steps, he went over to where Lisa sat against the wall. Thick gobs of his flesh hung from her mouth, and her pajama front was saturated with blood. It clung heavily to her heaving chest.

Brooks had just enough presence of mind to take his hand cuffs from his belt and clap Lisa's wrists together before staggering back to the front desk and dialing the rescue unit. By the time the Medcu crew got there, Brooks was unconscious on the floor behind the desk. They at first overlooked him; and once they had found him, it took them some time to figure out who was the more seriously injured. Finally, though, they loaded both Brooks and Lisa onto the ambulance and, siren wailing and red lights flashing, drove to the hospital in Houlton.

# CHAPTER EIGHT
## "Trapped"

# I

"Let's take it a little easy, okay?" Donna said as Dale slowed the car for the turn into the driveway of her old home.

Dale nodded quickly and took a deep breath. "Yeah, I think I've had enough excitement for one night."

The moon was riding high above a band of clouds. It cast a cold, eerie blue light over the landscape, making it look snow-covered. The house appeared about as forlorn as a house could look, sitting up on the gentle rise of land bordered by the woods. Judging from the outside, everything looked peaceful and quiet.

But you could say the whole damned town looked peaceful and safe, Dale thought; what he had found out so far tonight easily put the lie to *that* idea!

He realized he had been holding his breath as he looked up at the house; he let the air out slowly between his teeth as the car jolted up to the top of the dirt driveway.

"I don't see Winfield's cruiser," Dale said. He had a sudden thought that sent a ripple of panic through him: What if that was Winfield who stopped Rodgers back there?

It didn't strike him until just now that it could have been Winfield, driving back to town after checking the farmhouse; seeing two cars speeding down the road, even though he was off-duty, he might have given chase. Dale had assumed it had been someone else, some other poor soul who probably right now was on his way to Rodgers' Funeral Home. If it had been Winfield, then the thin possibility an ally in all of this had just disappeared.

Dale didn't tell Donna what he was thinking as he pulled to a stop. He left the engine running and the headlights fixed squarely on the front door.

"Looks okay to me," he said. "Think we ought to take a look around?"

Donna sat with her shoulder hunched forward. She was silent as she stared at the house. The black shadows cast under the eaves looked thick and solid.

"Why don't you stay here? I'll take a peek inside," Dale said. He opened the door and stepped out onto the driveway. The car was still running, and the lights illuminated the walkway. What's there to worry about, he thought, but he couldn't deny the chill that gripped him as he started up toward the house.

He quickly mounted the porch steps and, leaning forward, cupped his hands to the front door window and looked inside. Only a small square of light from the car reached the living room, and Dale couldn't tell a damned thing from that. It wasn't until he turned to head back to the car, convinced that Winfield hadn't been there yet, that he saw a clump of mud on the top step.

"Oh, shit," he muttered as he knelt to inspect the mud. He probed it with the tip of his finger. It was fresh, still wet; whoever had made it, had made it recently. Maybe it had been Winfield. Maybe not.

Looking up, straight into his glaring headlights, he smiled and waved quickly to Donna. Someone had been here, and not too long ago. But were they still here? Maybe it had been *Rodgers!* He would have had the time. He might have checked the house first while they were at the police station. Hell, if Winfield and Rodgers were in on this together, Winfield might have told him to come here, and this was nothing but an elaborate trap to lure them here.

When a floorboard creaked behind him, Dale spun around, expecting someone to lurch out of the darkness under the porch roof and close off his throat with icy, dead hands. He waited, breath held until it burned in his lungs, but nothing came.

He went quickly down the steps, but then in the distance, he saw a car approaching.

"Jesus!" he shouted, waving his arms wildly over his head. "Donna! Get out of the car!"

The headlights were low and widely spaced like a limousine's. Dale crouched on the front lawn and waited to see Donna's door open. There was no mistake: someone had turned off the road and was starting up the driveway fast! There was a slight chance it was Winfield, finally finding time to check on the house, Dale hoped.

"Come on!" he shouted, waving his arm to spur Donna on. The headlights bounced up and down over the rutted driveway. Dale could hear the steady whine as the car tried to gain even more speed.

*"Come on!"* he yelled. He took several steps forward, but then was relieved to see Donna's door swing open. She was no more than a dark blur against the headlights as she ran toward the house. Dale could hear the frightened wail in her voice as she called to him.

"What'll we *do?*"

"Run!" he yelled. "Run like a bastard!"

The car raced up the driveway, but the bumps held it back, so it didn't get the speed it needed. As Donna fell forward, collapsing into Dale's arms, they both saw the black limo slam into the side of Dale's car. The sound of breaking glass and bending metal filled the night as the heavy limo strafed along the side of the car, folding in the driver's door. The car sagged to the side, threatening to roll over.

"Quick!" Dale snapped. "Up on the porch!"

He waited while Donna quickly scaled the steps, then, without taking his eyes off the limo's headlights, he followed her. They stood side by side at the railing and watched as the limo backed up. Dale knew it had to be just his imagination, but he was positive the limo's headlights glowed with an eerie red.

"Who's my insurance?" Dale said, forcing a laugh as he turned to Donna. "Why, John Hancock, of course!"

The limo's engine whined as it raced faster and faster. Then, with a sudden roar, it sped forward, spewing dirt and gravel out from under its rear wheels. Dale's car took the hit squarely on the driver's door this time. The car shifted to the side as the wheels bent on the axles. One of the limo's headlights went out, but the driver slammed the car into reverse and pulled back for another hit.

But he didn't aim for the car again. As the limo backed up, the front wheels turned and aimed directly at the front porch.

"Jesus Christ," Donna whispered. "He isn't going to. . ."

"I think he is," Dale said, pushing her back toward the corner of the house. The limo's single headlight swung around, nailing both of them as they cringed on the porch. Dale was surprised to notice how cleanly and sharply the light illuminated everything. Maybe your senses sharpen just before you die, he thought as his arm blindly sought out Donna and pulled her to him.

"The man's lost his goddamned mind!" Donna said softly. "He can't get away with this!"

"Be ready to jump to your left as soon as he hits the porch, all right?"

Donna nodded.

The night suddenly filled with the revving sound of the limo's engine; it can-celled out every other sound except the steady arterial thump Dale heard hammering in his ears. He tried not to picture his body, broken and lifeless, twisted across the hood of that limo.

Then the limo started forward, its tires churning up clots of grass as it charged toward the house. Dale imagined the car was a raging bull, ready to gore them both, but when it actually hit the porch, the impact wasn't quite as bad as he had expected. The car bounced up over the steps. The front bumper tore into the porch rail-leaving behind a gaping hole. Handrails splintered and scattered everywhere, clattering like bowling pins. The top rail was knocked loose and slammed into the side of the house.

At the instant of impact, Dale and Donna both jumped to the side, clear of any danger. The limo's engine raced wildly as the rear wheels sought purchase to press on further. A loud, insect-like whine filled the night. Held in check by the stairs, the rear wheels spun uselessly, spewing out the sickening smell of burning rubber. At last the limousine sagged backward and, swerving from side to side, pulled back down the driveway.

"Fuck you, you bastard!" Dale shouted. He picked up one of the broken porch pieces and brandished it like a club. "Come on, you prick!" he yelled, so loud he thought his throat would tear. "Come on! I fucking *dare* you to come up here, one on one!"

In response, the limo sat there, its engine suddenly dropping to idle with a steady rumble. The single headlight glowed like an angry eye.

It reminded Dale of Rodgers' left eye and the thought sapped him a bit of both strength and anger.

"We can't stay here all night, fighting him," Donna said.

"You feel like walking down the road there?" Dale said. He felt curiously detached from what was happening, as though he had suddenly realized he was dreaming. But the choking smell of burning rubber was too real, as was the cold knot of fear tightening in his stomach.

"So what are we supposed to do?"

"It's his move. Let's wait and see. He'll run out of gas if he sits there too long," Dale said.

His grip on the loose handrail relaxed, but he didn't drop it yet. If Rodgers made another charge at the house, he wanted to charge the car and smash the windshield if he could. It sickened him, but Dale savored how sweet it would be to take that piece of railing and pound Rodgers' face to a pulp.

He's the man who killed Larry! Dale told himself.

The night hushed as the limo waited, idling. The darkness telescoped down into a narrow tube. But then, suddenly, the engine roared and the car bolted forward, its tires squealing. Dale pushed Donna behind him, cocked the handrail back, and positioned himself as the headlight came rushing forward.

The limousine didn't aim for them where they stood on the side corner of the porch. Instead it roared up the walkway and catapulted up the front steps. It knocked down both porch columns, and the porch roof sagged downward as the limo slammed like a battering ram into the front door. The door buckled inward with a loud snap.

Glass and wood exploded into the house as Dale darted forward, the handrail high over his head. In the light reflecting from the house, he could discern Rodgers hunched at the wheel. His face was perfectly composed, certainly not the insane maniac Dale had expected to see. In a blinding instant, Dale brought the railing down as hard as he could onto the window, shouting his anger over the screaming engine.

"You rotten *bastard!*" he wailed as the wood glanced off the windshield. A numbing tingle shot up his arm. It was enough to make him lose his grip, and the piece of handrail flew off into the darkness. It landed somewhere in the darkness as Dale ran back to the corner of the house where Donna watched in horror.

The limo's rear tires sent up thick clouds of vile-smelling smoke as it tried to climb further up onto the porch. The car labored and lurched like a heavy animal, trying to force its way into the house. Below the ear-splitting whine of the engine, Dale heard the splintering of wood as the porch started to crumble.

Dale watched helplessly as the dark edge of the porch roof fell lower, closing down on the limo like a huge mouth.

Maybe it will swallow him, he thought hopefully.

But the limo suddenly jolted backward and, miraculously, escaped just as the roof folded downward. Dale's rage bubbled like lava as he watched the limo skid across the lawn. The underside of the chassis glanced off the walkway, sending out a spray of bright sparks. Back on the driveway, the limo waited, its engine purring.

"And who's *your* insurance company?" Dale said, glancing quickly at Donna. The whole situation struck him as ludicrous, and he wanted to burst out laughing.

Donna was silent as she stared at the single headlight of the limo as it idled there, watching and waiting. The night seemed to hum and crackle with anticipation.

"The man's obviously lost his mind," Donna said softly. She was mulling over in her own mind their best chance to get out of this. If they went into the house, they'd be trapped there. Rodgers could set fire to the house, wait until they made a run for it, and then easily run them down. On the other hand, if they made a break for it, which way could they run? Would they be safer in the woods, or would Rodgers send some of his dead creatures after them?

Dale was shielding his eyes and watching the single headlight, nothing more than a watery smudge in his vision. The sound of the limo's engine cut through to him. It reminded him of an angry beast, growling as it waited for its prey to bolt.

"If he had a gun, don't you think he'd have used it by now?" Donna asked.

Dale shrugged. "I don't know, I suppose so."

"We could try to make it into the woods around back," she said softly. "His car wouldn't get too far into that."

"And then where do we go? Where do we run?" Dale shouted, turning and glaring at her as if this was her fault. "How do we know he doesn't have some of those *things* in the car with him? He could send them after us. I, for one, don't want to get caught in the dark by one of them!"

"Do you want to get caught right here by one of these guys?" Donna snapped. So far, she felt she and Dale had handled the events of the night fairly well, at least considering what they were dealing with. But if the threat continued for much longer . . . well, she felt confident in how *she'd* handle things, but there was no telling how he'd react. Even just a second ago, his gale of laughter had unnerved her. If he was going to lose control, she might be better off not sticking with him.

"We could go into the house," Dale said softly, still staring at the headlight as he wiped his eyes with the back of his hand. "I think we've got to wait until dawn before we make a break for it. How close is the nearest house?"

Donna shrugged. "More than a mile to the Larsen's."

"How fast could you run it?" Dale asked.

"With *that* on my ass?" she asked, nodding toward the idling limo. "I could probably make it in about thirty seconds."

"Right," Dale said. He edged over to the smashed in front door, inspecting the damage in the halo of light from the car. His heart was hammering hard in his chest, and in spite of the cold night air, his face glistened with sweat. He pushed on the broken door, and it gave way enough for them to get easily inside.

*And then what?* Dale wondered.

Would Rodgers wait out there all night? Or would he leave, maybe to come back with some of his *creatures* to finish them off?

"Come on," Dale said, waving Donna over to him. "We can keep an eye on him from inside the house. I don't think he's going to get that car any further up onto the porch tonight."

Donna peered into the dark opening of the door. She was filled with a rush of memories as the old, familiar smell inside the house reached out to her. She could hardly believe that this is how it would all end at the old home. She had always assumed she and Barbara would eventually sell the place, split the money, and that would be an end to it. But not *this!* Not to be held at bay by a madman who was threatening to kill them. It was too insane!

"How do we know he's even in the car?" Donna asked. Her eyes glowed like a frightened animal in the light from the headlight.

As if in answer, though, the car's engine revved up. Suddenly darting forward, the limo scattered a shower of dirt behind it as it started a third time toward the house. Dale tensed, expecting that Rodgers was going to make one last attempt to nail them, now that they were standing in the wreckage in front. But then the car turned sharply to the left. The tires churned large clots of the lawn as it raced around the side of the house. After a few seconds, it reappeared from around the other side of the house, still speeding and swerving crazily.

Dale didn't know whether he wanted to laugh hysterically or shout with anger. All he knew was that Rodgers was toying with them, as if he had them under his complete control and would dispense with them when he felt like it. He suddenly knew what a mouse felt like, trapped beneath a cat's playful paws.

"One on one!" Dale shouted, shaking his fists in the air as the car passed by close to the fallen porch.

After another circuit of the house, the limo cut back across the lawn. It must have been moving at least fifty miles an hour by the time it shot down the driveway and, without even a flicker of brake lights, onto Mayall Road, heading back toward town. Dale and Donna both let out long sighs of relief as they listened to the sound of the engine, rapidly fading into the night. The quiet of the darkness settled over them like a heavy blanket.

"You okay?" Dale asked. He took hold of her by the shoulders and looked at her squarely. In the darkness, her face wasn't much more than an indistinct blur, but she smiled and nodded.

"I think so," she said huskily. "And you?"

Dale grunted, still holding onto her.

"I thought you were losing it for a while there," Donna said. "When you started laughing like that."

Again, Dale snorted. "Well, you've got to admit this has been one hell of a night!"

Donna suddenly leaned forward, collapsing into his arms. Dale ran his hands up and down her back, trying to quiet the subtle trembling he felt in her shoulders.

"Where do you think Rodgers is going?" Donna asked after a moment lost in the comfort of his embrace. She pulled back and looked up at Dale. "Do you think it'd be safe for us to try to get back to town?"

Dale shrugged. Looking out at his wrecked car, he said, "Well, we certainly aren't going to drive. I don't know about . . . holy shit!"

"What?"

"What the Christ is *wrong* with me?" Dale said, his voice threatening to break. "All this time, and I haven't even thought about Angie! What if that's where he's going?"

Donna's stomach did a quick flip, and the tension she felt was made worse by the thought that if that was where Rodgers was heading, they were helpless to stop him.

"No," Donna said, her voice tight with fear. "I mean, he may have seen her with you at the funeral today. But he doesn't know where you're staying. She'll be all right."

"You think where I'm is some kind of secret? Come on, Donna, this is your hometown. You know damned well he knows where I'm staying." If Winfield was in cahoots with Rodgers, Dale realized, Angie was as good as dead already!

Dale looked out at the dusty light of the moon brushing the lawn with a cool blue. The sound of the limo had I long since faded, leaving nothing but the hissing quiet of the night. The driveway and road unwound like a smoky ribbon, leading to town. And to *what horrors?* he wondered. *What horrors did Rodgers—and possibly Win-field—have in store for this little town?*

"There isn't a chance the phone's still connected in the house, is there?" Dale asked.

Donna shook her head quickly.

"I didn't think so," he said, pressing his fist to his mouth. Worry and fear were gnawing at his gut like tiny, hungry animals. *If that bastard does anything to hurt Angie . . . !*

"So . . . ?" Donna said. She took a step toward the broken door but tripped on something in the dark and almost fell. Dale reached out and steadied her. His features were lost in the shadows under the porch, but she could tell his face was creased with worry about his daughter.

"I really want to get back to town, to make sure Angie's all right," Dale said tightly. "But I just don't think we should try it in the dark. I know he'll be out looking for us. At least here we have some protection."

"Not if he returns with some of his . . . Jesus, even trying to say it sounds so goddamned stupid!"

"His *zombies!* What, you still can't admit the truth? You saw one of them," Dale said evenly. "Just tonight, you saw what Rodgers did to my best friend." His voice broke at the memory of Larry's cold, death-glazed eyes staring at him as he lumbered, stiff-limbed, after them, his hands flexing to tear the life from them.

"So you think we should wait here until dawn, huh?" Donna said. "And what if he knows we're staying here? He wrecked your car. He knows we won't chance the woods in the dark. If he comes back here with any of those *things,* we're as good as dead."

"I know, I know," Dale said. "We're stuck between the proverbial 'rock and hard place.'"

"I guess you're right, though," Donna said, sighing as she looked again at the smashed-in front door. The whole night still seemed like a bad dream she hoped would end soon.

"I've got a flashlight in the car," Dale said. "Wait here."

He leaped over the tangle of splintered wood and ran down to his demolished car. The driver's door was hammered in so badly the door handle was flat against the panel. He couldn't even get his fingertip under the door trigger. Both front and back wheels on the driver's side stuck out at sharp angles from the wheel wells. The axles were bent way out of shape, and he was positive this car would never see road service again!

On the passenger's side, though, he could open door. The dome light didn't come on when he opened the door, but that was no surprise. After fishing around blindly on the floor for a few seconds, he found the little penlight he kept for reading maps at night.

As he started back up to the house, he looked at the damage the limo had done to the front lawn. Everywhere, there were deep trenches and skid marks. Moonlight cast them in black shadows, making them look deeper than they really were. The front of the house, Dale thought, looked as though a bomb had gone off. Behind a large section of fallen roof, there was a gaping black hole where once the front door had been.

"Come on," Donna said, her voice coming from the blackness under the fallen porch, seemingly disembodied. "Hurry it up."

Dale ran up the walkway and, once back beside Donna, snapped on his penlight. The beam was weak and threw a feeble circle of light onto the caved-in door.

"That's it?" Donna said, watching with a trace of amusement as the little yellow oval darted over the smashed wood.

Dale grunted. "Fraid so," he said. "Come on, let's get inside. Maybe we can get some wood from the barn and brace the door back up. At least we won't be stumbling around in the dark all night."

He held the light so it shined into the opening, and stood back as Donna entered the house. He followed her in, taking one last look out onto the silent, cold night. That Rodgers would return, he had no doubt, the only real question was *when?* Dale was determined that, when he did, Rodgers wouldn't catch them off their guard. Not *ever* again!

# II

Mrs. Appleby and Angie left for the hospital in Houlton seconds after the call that Lisa and a police officer had been taken there by ambulance. They left a note on the kitchen table, telling Dale where they had gone and not to worry, that everything was under control.

In the ambulance on the drive to the hospital, Officer Brooks had regained consciousness and identified Lisa. He had gotten increasingly agitated about being anywhere near her, and had gotten so upset, one of the Medcu crew had to give him a shot to sedate him. They were both unconscious when they were wheeled into the emergency room.

Lisa was still asleep when her grandmother and Angie entered her room. She had been washed up, and her blood-soaked pajamas had been exchanged for a fresh hospital johnny. She was hooked up to an intravenous tube, but the on-duty nurse repeatedly assured Mrs. Appleby that, so far as they could tell, Lisa was just fine. There were no signs of any internal or external injury at all except for the large bruise on her forehead.

Mrs. Appleby went to speak with the nurse at Admissions, and there she gave the full details of Lisa's bicycle accident and what Stephen Wayne had done for her when he came out to the house.

Angie, meanwhile, sat in the most comfortable chair in the room and watched as her friend slept peacefully. She couldn't get out of her mind the expression she had seen on Lisa's face when she had swung at them and then run downstairs and out the door. In some odd way, she felt Lisa's pale face and bugging eyes were somehow connected to those strange men they had encountered out at Lisa's "secret place." She had seemed to be filled with the same fury that seemed to possess the man who had smashed his fist through the trap door and had grabbed at her. Lisa seemed to have been driven by the same strength and frenzy.

As the minutes stretched out and the hospital room got warmer, a gentle weariness came over Angie. She tried to keep her eyes open, but the stress of everything that had happened weighed down on her like lead. Her eyelids fluttered, and the dim light of the room wavered as she sank down deeper into the soft chair. She kicked off her shoes and put her stockinged feet on the edge of Lisa's bed. Within minutes she was asleep, breathing heavily.

One of the night-shift nurses had called in sick that evening, so her replacement, who had been on duty the previous shift, grabbed a quick nap at the nurses' station. No one noticed when Lisa's eyes snapped open. For just a moment, she lay there, staring up at the hospital ceiling. Her eyes blinked rapidly as she tried unsuccessfully to figure out where she was.

"Grammy. . . ?" she called, sitting up stiffly in bed to look around. "Grammy? . . . I'm *hungry.*"

She finally realized that she was in the hospital, but that didn't surprise her. Since that spill off her bike, though, she had been having some pretty strange dreams. When did her grandmother bring her here? How long had she been here? What the heck time was it? The only certainty she had was that her stomach felt like she hadn't eaten in weeks.

She swung her legs out from under the covers, careful not to wake up Angie, and put her feet to the floor. A chill raced up the backs of her legs, but looking down, she saw a pair of cheap, paper hospital slippers. She leaned forward and slipped them onto her feet and, with a low groan and stretch, stood up. The IV impeded her for only a second. She ripped the adhesive tape off and pulled the needle out, then walked unfettered to the door.

She wasn't exactly sure where she was going as she opened the door and peered out into the deserted corridor. All she knew was that she was hungry . . . *really* hungry.

"Where d'yah get food around this place?" she asked herself silently as she started down the hallway.

The lights in the ceiling glowed with a strange brilliance. The plastic rectangles covering the bulbs were dim, but the glow all around them was vibrating with green and blue spikes. In the corner of her eye, she could see bright colors, swirling and spinning on the walls, but she could never see them directly when she turned to look; the sparkles always shifted away from her as she turned her head back and forth.

Lisa started down the corridor, moving with a curious stiffness, as though her knee and hip joints had rusted. The sound her paper slippers made on the freshly waxed floor was as harsh and abrasive as sandpaper; it hurt her ears. She had no idea where she was going, but hoped to find someone who could tell her where she could get some food. What she craved—*right* now—was something like a thick, juicy hamburger!

Back in Lisa's room, Angie awoke with a start; and when she saw Lisa's bed empty, a cold fist punched her stomach and made her sit bolt up-right.

*She had trouble in the night*, Angie thought in a flood of panic as she stood up and looked around the room, frantic with fear. *She died, and they've taken her away!*

Glancing at her watch, Angie saw that she couldn't have been asleep more than ten minutes. Mrs. Appleby should have been back from Admissions by now. And where was the duty nurse? What had happened to Lisa? Angie stumbled into the corridor as she tore the door open.

Two nurses coming back to the nurses' station saw Angie stumble out of the room. Words were tumbling from her mouth so fast they couldn't tell what she was talking about.

"What have you done with her? Is she all right? I must've just fallen asleep for a minute or two, 'n when I woke up she wasn't there. Why can't you tell me what happened?"

Both nurses quickly came over to her. They were as confused as Angie was when they went back to Lisa's room and saw that her bed was empty. One of them immediately called security. The other nurse forced Angie to sit down with her and drink a glass of juice until she calmed down. She told her, over and over, that nothing had happened to Lisa. It would take them only a few minutes to find her; she couldn't have gotten far, the nurse said and certainly she couldn't have left the hospital.

As it turned out, it took five nurses, four security guards, and two janitors almost thirty minutes to find her; and when they did, they couldn't believe what they saw.

Lisa had gotten into the hospital kitchen unobserved. The door to the walk-in refrigerator was wide open, and she was sitting, cross-legged, in the middle of the floor, completely indifferent to the cold. In both hands, she held thick clumps of raw hamburger. Brown streaks of meat juice were running down both arms and dripping onto the floor, and thick chunks squeezed between her fingers. Her hospital johnny was splattered with red, and her fists were clenched. Hamburger was oozing out between her fingers. Her mouth and chin were smeared with pieces of raw meat.

"Sorry. . ." she said, looking up at them and avidly chewing a mouthful. "I couldn't help myself. I was *wicked* hungry!"

# III

When Winfield opened his eyes, he wasn't even sure he *had* opened them. Darkness so thick he could feel it pressing against his skin like a weight surrounded him. It was that sensation and a tight pressure on his arms and legs, that convinced him he wasn't really dead.

As he struggled to awareness, he felt like a spent swimmer whose lungs are burning as he looks up at the rippling light of the surface so far away, straining and struggling to make it up to the light, back to the air.

Time meant nothing to him in this well of blackness, but the longer he thought about it, the more he remembered what had happened. There was a crashing pain on the back of his head, and where that had come from he had no way of knowing; it came like a freight train out of the dark.

*Kitchen.* The word sprang into his mind, and he remembered, yes, he had been in someone's kitchen. It had been dark; he remembered holding a flashlight as he checked through the house.

*Whose house?* he wondered, *and what in the name of God was that pressure on his arms and legs?*

He expected the pressure to disappear as he came more fully conscious, but it was still there, binding his arms and legs.

He tried to bring one hand to the back of his head to feel if he had been shot—or cut.

But his arm wouldn't move. He tugged, first gently and then as hard as he could, but all he felt was something biting deeply into his wrists. The blood flow was restricted, and his hands prickled with pins-and-needles.

"What in the name of Christ ...?" he muttered.

He leaned his head back, and felt cold stone, gritty with age, rub against his scalp. His eyes had been open long enough for them to have adjusted to any light, if there had been any; but wherever he was, it was as dark as a pit.

Winfield decided, if his eyes wouldn't help, that he would stretch out with his hearing. It was an effort to fight back the waves of panic that threatened to sweep him away, but he took several deep, even breaths and listened.

At first, there was nothing but silence as thick and solid as the darkness. But after a moment—*how long,* he wondered, having no sense of time passing—he heard a low creaking sound. It reminded him of the sound his grandmother's rocking chair used to make when he was a little boy, and she used to read to him. It was the slow, steady thread of footsteps.

Someone was walking on an old, creaky floor above him!

Winfield concentrated on bringing the sound closer, but then the sound simply vanished. As soon as it was gone, he wondered when he had heard it? How long ago? There was no time in this thick darkness. Maybe I am dead! he thought, wishing he could move just an arm or a leg to prove he wasn't dead.

He was getting closer to remembering, but the pain on the back of his head pounded rhythmically like a horse's hoof beats.

"Caught from behind," he said out loud, his voice no more than a choked whisper. And suddenly a much larger piece of memory snapped into awareness. He had been going through the old LaPierre house, checking on a complaint Donna LaPierre had made that someone might have broken into the house.

Winfield snickered softly in the darkness, surprised by the odd, disembodied sound. Well, there *had* been *someone* in the house. No doubt on *that* score. But who? He could hear soft, shifting sounds in the surrounding darkness.

Was there someone there in the dark with him? Winfield worried. He let out a low whimper as he imagined he wasn't the only one down here.

"Hello?" he called out softly.

His answer came just a few seconds later. A door opened up at the top of the stairway, and a sliver of light darted down. (Yes, *down,* he thought feeling a flood of relief; I must be in the cellar!) The light hit him squarely in the eyes, hurting as if it had been a bullet; it slammed into his eyes, and with a pained shout, he turned his head away as footsteps hurried down the stairs.

The beam of light got stronger as it came closer, and Winfield saw a man and a woman, hurry toward where he sat, propped against the stone wall in what looked like an old coal bin. The man and woman were huffing with the effort of carrying a load of unrolled sleeping bags and camping gear.

Winfield got dizzy, trying to follow the light as it darted back and forth. The man approached him and shined the light directly into his face. Winfield turned away from the lance of pain, but in the glow, he recognized his own service revolver aimed directly at his forehead.

"Listen, asshole," the man said in a harsh whisper. "We got some more company upstairs. If I hear one tiny little peep out of you, I'm gonna splatter your brains, however few, all over this wall. You understand me?"

Even though it pained him to move, Winfield nodded his head, mindful not to make a sound.

"Get over here," the man said to the woman. He handed her a second flashlight and a smaller gun. Not for a moment did he take his eyes or his flashlight beam off the cop.

"He's tied nice and secure," the man said. Turning to Winfield, he added, "Don't you like the fit of those handcuffs? You should. They're your own!" Then to the woman, he said, "What I want you to do is sit here. Keep the light off, but if he makes the tiniest sound, turn on the light and shoot him."

The woman shook her head slowly. "I can't do that," she said. "You can't expect me to kill someone in cold blood."

The man laughed with a deep, hollow sound. "I'd say it's either him or you at this point. Don't fuck it up."

With that, the man shielded his own flashlight in the cup of his hand and went back up the stairs. The girl kept her light on for a few seconds, and then snapped it off, plunging the room back into the darkness. The silence fell back into place like a lock, only now it was broken by the shallow sound of the girl's breathing.

Winfield began to speak.

"Shush," the girl said, her voice trembling. "I don't want to have to kill you. But I will. I'll *have* to if you make any noise." She sniffed loudly. Winfield wasn't sure if she was crying or simply trying to catch her breath.

"You know," she said after a short pause, "I'm sorry I had to kick you like that today."

"It was *you?*" Winfield said with a laugh. That pain had been all but forgotten in the wash of pain he felt now in his arms, legs, and the back of his head.

"Sorry," the girl said. She was about to say more, but there came a loud noise from upstairs. Tasha and Winfield fell quiet and listened in silence, trying to figure out what was going on upstairs. There was the sound of feet on the porch, and then the roar of a car's engine followed by a shattering crash. It sounded as though it was happening directly above them. The girl cried out softly and, covering her flashlight lens with her hand, snapped on the light to make sure they weren't about to be crushed to death.

For the next several minutes the sounds of shattering wood and breaking glass, the racing whine of the car, and muffled shouts filled the cold black of the cellar.

"You know," Winfield said, fighting to keep the desperation out of his voice. "I have a spare key to the cuffs in my left shoe."

"Quiet," the girl said, pointing the gun at him. It wavered, but not much.

"If you cut these ropes and unlock the cuffs, I promise I'll get you out of this. I can tell you're hooked up with a very bad guy here. I can tell you're too smart to be his girlfriend. If you let me go, I'll make sure you get out of this. What do you say?"

She obviously was considering it because as minutes passed, she didn't say "no" and she certainly didn't shoot him.

"Come on. What's your name, by the way?"

"Tasha . . . Tasha Stewart," she said softly.

"Well listen here, Tasha. I can tell you've made a few mistakes along the way. My guess would be that you've run away from home, right?"

Tasha nodded.

"And my next guess would be that, since you've teamed up with what's his name?"

"His real name's Roy Moulton," she said, "but I call him Hocker 'cause he spits so much." She chuckled to herself.

Winfield chuckled too, but not so much at the joke but to relax her even more, to get her to lower her guard. He knew, once he got her comfortable and talking, it might all come out: the rotten home life; no friends at school; maybe a little experimenting with drugs and sex, out of rebellion more than interest; the "dreams" that life would be better anywhere but where she was. It was the typical pattern for a runaway.

But try as Winfield might to put her at ease, the sounds coming from upstairs were distracting and downright scary, and she seemed to be paying more attention to the noise than to what he was saying. It sounded like Hocker and someone else were tearing the goddamned place apart!

"I mean it, Tasha," Winfield said, trying to keep the pleading out of his voice. "The key's in my left shoe. Do it, and I'll help get you straightened around."

"I don't need to be *straightened* around," she said, suddenly flaring with anger. Winfield was positive he had unwittingly used a catch phrase her mother or, more likely, her father had used on her once too often, and he was pissed at himself. He could sense the steel coming back into her resolve.

"And if you keep talking," she said, low and dangerous, "I will shoot."

"No you won't," Winfield said calmly. "Because I know, no matter what you and this Hocker character have done, you sure as hell don't want to add murder of a policeman to your list. Do you?"

"Just be quiet!" she demanded. She jabbed the gun in his direction.

"You know, that name . . . Roy Moulton. Seems to be I've seen it somewhere before. Do you happen to know if he's wanted for any thing?"

Tasha was silent, but Winfield was relieved to see the muzzle of the revolver drop.

"I'd swear I saw his name on a Teletype or something. Isn't he the . . . I've got it!" If his hands had been free, he would have slapped them on his thighs. "We got an APB on him a couple of weeks ago. I remember it because it struck me kind of funny when I read it. He escaped from a mental hospital somewhere down South. Alabama was it? No, Georgia. Yeah, Georgia. And I remember thinking why the hell would someone, even someone from a mental hospital be heading up this way? With winter coming on, you'd *have* to be nuts to come to Aroostock County this time of year!"

"Knock it off, will you?" Tasha said. She didn't brandish the gun or shine the light in his eyes to intimidate him, so Winfield knew what he was saying was working on her—at least a little. Now, if he could get her to free him before that commotion upstairs stopped and Hocker rejoined them!

Judging by the noise upstairs, things up there were getting worse. The car seemed to be making circuits of the house. It sounded to Winfield like a heavy bodied, big engine thing. Maybe it was the limousine that guy Harmon had mentioned? The racing sound rose and fell, hitting high frequencies and then fading as it moved around. Finally, Winfield thought he heard the car speed off into the distance, and the night plunged back into silence.

"It's still not too late," Winfield whispered as he and Tasha craned their necks to hear what was going on Up there. The silence coming from upstairs had an ominous edge to it, like a well-honed knife.

Tasha's biggest fear was that Hocker had been discovered and she would be next; everything this cop had said about helping her out would fly out the window, and she'd end up doing a jail sentence. The things they had done since they crossed the Maine state line would be good for at least twenty years in the slammer. If that old man had died, she figured she'd be in for life!

Through the floorboards, Winfield heard the stealthy sound of footsteps, and then the sound of other, heavier feet. The voices of two people were muffled by the floor and sounded like nothing more than tantalizing buzzings. Winfield watched Tasha, trying to guess if she knew what was going on up there. He was frantically debating whether or not to yell. Even if he ended up dead, maybe those people upstairs would get away before Hocker caught them.

Suddenly, the cellar door flew open, and two people, one practically dragging the other, came down the stairs quickly. Hocker's face was wild with fury as he shoved a woman to where Winfield was bound. She fell face-down on the floor, her arms and legs splayed.

"Take this and tie her," Hocker shouted. *"Quick!"* He flung a coil of rope at Tasha, who quickly scooped it up and went over to where the woman lay. She rolled her onto her back and ran several loops around the woman's wrists. She made two knots and leaned back, pulling them tightly.

As soon as Tasha had rolled the woman onto her back, Winfield gasped with surprise to see Donna LaPierre. He started to say something, but as soon as a syllable came from his mouth, he was looking at the unblinking black eye of the revolver's bore.

"Go ahead," Hocker said, low and evenly. "Just *one* fucking word!"

Winfield shook his head and sagged back against the cellar wall, watching helplessly as Tasha began binding Donna's legs.

"Still got a little business to do upstairs," Hocker said, and for the first time, Winfield saw him live up to his name; he spit viciously into the dirt beside Donna's face, missing her by less than an inch.

"You keep these assholes quiet while I go up and get the last little member of our party. He's gonna have an Excedrin headache like you got, copper." Hocker said, laughing and shaking his head from side to side. "Christ! This is turning out to be busier than Grand-Fucking Central Station!"

# IV

As soon as they had entered the house, Dale had said, "Just wait here in the kitchen. I want to take a look in the barn. See if there's anything we can use to shore up the front door. I won't be a minute."

Donna wanted to protest. As far as she was concerned, when Rodgers returned, a few planks nailed over the door weren't going to stop him. Their best chance, she thought, was to make a run for it. Whether they stayed to the road or chanced the forest at night, they had to get out of here. Rodgers knew where they were, and there was no sense waiting around, giving him all the options.

"We can't be as surprised in the daylight," Dale said as he swung open the kitchen door and glanced out at the barn. "So if we can hold him off for the night, we should be all right." For all he knew, the barn itself could be swarming with Rodgers' creatures. He might walk out there, bold as can be, and they'd be ripping his arms and legs off before he could say *ouch!*

The woods and surrounding yard were quiet, almost peaceful, if he ignored the trenches carved in the lawn by Rodgers' limo. The moon cast a long, pointed shadow from the peak of the barn. Only the brightest stars twinkled through the hazy glow in the sky. He glanced at his watch, surprised to see that it was still only a few minutes before midnight. He felt as though the night had stretched out like soft taffy, dragging minutes into hours.

"Just be cool," he said to himself as he stepped into the night. Dale quickly crossed the dooryard to the barn, hesitating for only a second at the barn door before pushing it inward. His penlight was nothing more than a feeble splinter of light in the darkness, but as soon as he saw what was inside the barn, he knew he and Donna were in serious trouble.

For just a moment, as he looked at the smashed cruiser, he considered going straight back to the house for her. Something was *seriously* wrong.

Maybe Donna was right, he thought. Maybe they should take a chance on the woods.

If he had gone back right then, he might have changed everything because, as soon as he was out the door and the door closed shut behind him, Hocker had stepped out of the stairwell where he had been hiding and clapped his rough hand over Donna's mouth. She tried to scream, but the sound died quickly in her throat when she saw the heavy revolver come around in front of her and press like cold lips against the side of her head.

But Dale didn't go back to the house right away; he took a few minutes to inspect the damage to the car. Headlights and flashing lights were nothing but broken glass and plastic. Huge, baseball-sized dents pocked the side panels, hood, and roof and especially on the town police insignia on the side doors. The trunk was open, obviously already looted for anything useful

Dale's first thought was to see if the radio was working, but as soon as he looked into the trashed front seat, he saw the radio's guts spilled all over the cruiser floor.

"Son of a bitch," he muttered, as his thin beam of light danced over the interior of the car. His mind was rapidly clicking off the possibilities here.

—*If Winfield's cruiser was here—in this condition — where and in what condition was the policeman?*

—*Had Rodgers—or some of his creatures—done this while they were held at bay on the porch? Or before they had even gotten there?*

*— Or was Donna right? Was there a prowler out at the house who had done this? . . . and right now was he waiting for them back there in the dark house?*

Panic flooded Dale as he straightened up and looked back out the barn door at the house. Was that Donna's face in the window? He couldn't tell for sure because of the glare of moonlight on the window panes. As he exited the barn, though, just for his own security, he waved a greeting in case that was her.

He approached the house, and as the angle to the window changed, he breathed a sigh of relief. It *was* Donna standing by the window; he could clearly see her dark silhouette outlined in the moonlight. He hurried across the dooryard, his hand eager to swing open the door and his arms eager to hug her close.

Maybe things were over for a little while, he thought as he entered the kitchen, a joyful greeting all set to spill out of his mouth. But then Dale saw, not Donna but a man, standing by the kitchen sink. A sliver of moonlight through the window gleamed on the polished surface of the gun he was aiming at him.

"Welcome to the party," the man said, followed by a low chuckle as he waved the pistol back and forth, its muzzle pointing squarely at Dale's chest.

"Who the Christ are you? . . . And where's Donna?" Dale shouted.

"You mean your lady friend? Why, she's nice and comfortable. You can see for yourself."

"If you've hurt her, I'll . . ." Dale darted forward, but the kitchen suddenly filled with an orange flash and a thunderous explosion. Dale heard the bullet whiz past his ear.

"You make another move like that, and you'll have a nice big piece of your face blown off," the man said. There was no tremor in his voice, nor the slightest indication of nervousness, so Dale knew he meant it. "Now there won't be any trouble if you just follow the bouncing ball down cellar." Saying that, he snapped on a flashlight and illuminated the stairway, leading down.

Dale had no doubt that this was the man who had left the dirty footprints they had seen in the house earlier that day. There was also no doubt that this man was *dangerously* crazy!

"Just remember," the man said as Dale started toward the steps, "I've got this pea-shooter pointed right at the back of your head. You make a single move that even looks like you're gonna try to take me out, and you're fucking dead. You understand?"

Dale grunted. His ears were still ringing from the sudden explosion of the shot, and the last thing he wanted to do was anything to set this jerk off.

The impact of the gun slamming on his head came as a total surprise, but it didn't knock him out. He staggered forward, slamming into the wall. As much as he wanted to turn on this man and fight him, though, Dale knew he'd be risking a bullet in his skull before he could blink

"That's just to remind you to fucking behave," the man said, his voice low, twisted, and dangerous. "So you just do what I tell you!"

Dale grunted an acknowledgment of the order. The back of his head was throbbing as he started down the steps, slowly and carefully. His legs wanted to fold up underneath him, but he kept telling himself he had to maintain; he had to be strong if he was going to get himself and Donna out of this.

When he reached the bottom of the stairs and looked over by the coal bin, his mouth dropped open in surprise. Sitting on the floor, trussed up with their backs to the wall of the coal bin, were Donna and Winfield! There was also a young-looking girl, squatting across from them, holding a pistol in one hand and a flashlight in the other.

"Donna? You all right?" Dale asked, his voice almost breaking when he saw how scared and tired her eyes looked. The steady thump of pain where he had been hit on the head receded in a surge of anger at this creep who had done this to them.

Donna nodded her head but said nothing. The helplessness in her eyes cut him to the core.

"We're all doing just fine," Winfield said, smiling broadly. His teeth looked unusually large and shiny in the dim light of the flashlight.

"All of you just shut the fuck up, all right?" the man barked. "Tash, there's some more rope in the kitchen closet. Get it for me."

Without a word, the girl stood and ran quickly up the stairs, her flashlight beam bobbing at her feet in front of her. But Dale noticed the curious exchange of glances between the girl and Winfield just before she left. He tried not to let himself think that there was something "agreed-upon" between them.

"Sit your ass down right over there," the man said, shining his light onto the wall next to Donna. "Soon as Tasha returns, I'll make you nice and comfortable. You just might be here a while." "Not for the rest of my life, I hope," Dale said firmly. Hocker laughed, coughed up a wad of spit, and shot it straight at Dale.

# V

"You screwed the whole thing up," Rodgers said. He was silhouetted by the streetlight behind him, which gave his head and shoulders a hazy gold outline. He had one hand resting on the top of his sleek blue Volvo. The black limo, dented and missing one headlight, was parked in the basement garage back at the funeral home.

"I really don't think so, Mr. Rodgers," Steve Wayne said nervously. He was clutching the thick envelope Rodgers had just given him, but the security of knowing he had another two thousand dollars didn't help the rubbery feeling in his legs; he was afraid he would crumple to the ground if he had to stand there under Rodgers' stare for very much longer.

"First of all," Rodgers said, ticking off the count with his fingers. "You called me and left me that half-assed, frantic message on my telephone recorder, my business telephone! Second." He ticked off another finger. "On your own initiative, you attempted to give this girl . . . What's her name?"

"Lisa Grant," Steve said softly. "Her grandmother, Lillian Appleby, has that boarding house."

"I *know* who Lillian Appleby is, for God's sake!" Rodgers said. He kept his voice low and tight, even though he wanted to shout; but here in the hospital parking lot, the very last thing he needed was to draw attention to himself. "And then three . . ." Still ticking off his fingers. "You botched the injection! You left traces of the drug on her bed sheets at her home, and I suppose you still have the broken hypodermic needle in your personal medical bag! Am I right?" He shook his head, exasperated. "Do you realize how simple it would be to trace this all back to *me?*"

"It's all under control," Steve said, but the quiver in his voice betrayed him.

"No it's not!" Rodgers said, clenching and shaking his fists with repressed rage. "It most certainly is not under control. This man Dale Harmon, the friend of Larry Cole's, has been asking far too many embarrassing questions around town. He even had the police out to my house, asking if he could see Cole's body before the burial! It's not under control at all, and any little screw-up now can unravel the whole damned thing!"

Steve glanced around the parking lot, earnestly wishing to see anyone nearby so he could talk loud enough to be noticed; but this late at night the lot wasn't even half-full of cars, and there was no one around. The solitary guard, watching TV in the parking lot attendant's booth, was around the corner, clearly out of sight and hearing range.

"You get paid good money to do one thing," Rodgers said, holding up his index finger and taking a step closer to Steve. "You 'arrange' for certain individuals to die of complications in the hospital. That's *all!*" He made a quick, chopping motion with the edge of his hand. "The people I do this work for don't want you getting involved with any experiments on your own. Do you understand? When I gave you that sample of the drug, I wanted you to run a few experiments with it using the hospital lab equipment and that was all! I certainly didn't intend for you to try anything on your own."

"Look, I'm sorry, Mr. Rodgers, honest," Steve said. He looked longingly across the lot to where his own car, a beat-to-shit Mustang, sat in the thick shadow cast by the hospital. "I'll admit I might have screwed it up a little, but, hey!" He stretched out his arm and looked at the glowing face of his wrist watch. "I'm due at work now." He started to turn to leave, but Rodgers' voice froze him.

"You'll leave when I say you can leave!" Rodgers bellowed.

Steve turned and faced him, feeling his heart thump like a cold knot in his throat.

"Look, it's not going to be any problem to finish the job," he said. He was holding tightly onto the envelope Rodgers had given him, slapping it repeatedly into the palm of his hand. "From what I saw, she has a fairly serious bruise on her forehead. It's not going to be any problem to slip into her room sometime during the early morning and pop an air bubble into her. No sweat."

"And you honestly think you can do it right this time?" Rodgers said, his voice steely and commanding.

"'Course I can," Steve said. He wanted to laugh out loud but his throat still felt constricted, as though Rodgers physically had his fingers gently laced around his neck and was squeezing, ever so slowly.

"I don't think you can," Rodgers said. He put one hand to his mouth, seeming to consider for a moment, but as soon as Steve shifted on his feet, letting his guard down, Rodgers' fist shot out of the darkness and connected solidly with Steve's jaw. There was an explosion of bright light behind Steve's eyes, and he was only vaguely aware that his legs had finally given in to that rubbery feeling; he dropped to his knees on the asphalt. He would have fallen face-first onto the parking lot if Rodgers hadn't caught him

With a quick glance around to see if they had been noticed, Rodgers grabbed Steve under the armpits and turned him around so his back was leaning against the side of his car. It took considerable effort to prop him there, but once he had him set so he wouldn't keel over, Rodgers withdrew a small leather case from the glove compartment and leaned over Steve.

"You said you experimented on the Grand girl because you were curious, huh?" Rodgers said, addressing the unconscious man. He snapped open the leather case and withdrew a hypodermic needle. Holding the needle up to the street light, he pressed on the plunger until the dark liquid in the barrel filled the needle tip.

He rolled back the right sleeve of Steve's coat and then jabbed the needle into Steve's exposed forearm.

"I'll show you how to do it *right!*" Rodgers hissed. "You said you were curious to see what effect the drug would have on someone who was still living." He laughed softly as he pressed the plunger and the needle drained into Steve's veins. "I've taken small doses of this stuff for years, but I often wondered what a generous dosage would do. Would it simply kill you so you'd end up like all the others? Or would the drug have a different effect when it went to work on *living* tissue?" He snorted with laughter as he withdrew the needle and put it back into the leather case.

"Well, Stephen old boy, maybe *if* you regain consciousness, you can tell me all about it! Satisfy my curiosity as well as your own!"

Rodgers leaned Steve's inert form forward, opened the back door of his car, and, with effort, dragged him around and pushed him onto the floor in the back seat. He took the blanket and casually draped it over the silent form.

Then he got into the car and drove out of the parking lot, waving cheerfully to the elderly man in the guard booth.

"Good night," he said, brightly, all the while thinking I'll probably be seeing you soon, too!

He drove slowly down back to Dyer, not wanting to chance being stopped and asked questions by any more cops tonight. The one who had stopped him earlier that night, while he was pursuing Dale Harmon, had let him off quite easy. Rodgers' first thought had been that he would have to kill the man and dispose of him. But as it turned out, he worked for the Haynesville Police Department. As soon as Rodgers had flashed his identification, the kid had let him go with a verbal warning to "watch your speed on these back roads, 'specially at night!"

Rodgers wanted to get Steve's body back to the funeral home quickly because there were still so many things he had to take care of before dawn. Now that he knew how much Dale Harmon and that woman knew (which was too much; otherwise they wouldn't have gone straight to the cops after what they had seen happen to Larry Cole) and where they were now, the most pressing problem was exactly what he was going to do to silence them. He smiled to himself, glancing in the rear view mirror every now and then to catch the merry gleam in his eyes.

Oh, he wasn't worried; he'd think of something very special for both of them, of that he was sure. It was just a matter of time.

# CHAPTER NINE
## "Under Attack"

## I

The thin light of dawn was no more than a diffuse gray wash in the cellar and it brought little cheer to Dale, Donna, or Winfield. After a night spent bound and unable to move, each of them suffered sore joints and aching muscles that, no matter how much they shifted their positions, wouldn't get better until they could stand up and move.

Throughout the night, Hocker or Tasha came down to the cellar to check on them and make sure they hadn't worked free of their bonds. The first time Tasha had shown up, Winfield had whispered, "The left shoe," but she had checked the ropes and left without a word. The biggest surprise and most encouraging sign to Winfield was that she didn't tell Hocker about the hidden key, or take it away herself; maybe she didn't believe him, or thought he was just trying to get her close enough so he could catch her. In the time between checks by their captors, Dale and Donna filled Winfield in on what they had found out and what they suspected.

The gray light had grown bright enough to see by the time they finished telling everything. "I know it's pretty difficult to believe," Dale said.

"Difficult?" Winfield said, snorting with laughter. "It's damned near impossible!"

"If I could just have had a chance to play that tape for you," he said, dipping his head downward to indicate the pile of shattered plastic strewn on the floor. Light brown audiotape was unspooled into a tangled mess. Hocker had patted him down before binding him up— removing the bills and credit cards in his wallet; when he found the cassette, he had laughed as he ground it into the dirt floor of the cellar with his boot heel.

"I didn't really conceive anything like this could happen until I heard it in Larry's own voice — " He choked with memory of his dead friend, sitting up in his coffin and *looking* at him with eyes as glazed and flat as marble slabs. "Even *then,* it took me a while to believe it. Hell, I probably can't really accept it even now. But if you had seen what we saw out at Rodgers' house last night." He shivered, and not just from the damp cold of the cellar.

Winfield looked over at Donna, whose face looked pale and much thinner than he ever remembered it. Was this the face of someone who had seen things she couldn't accept? he wondered. Or had she, somehow, been drawn into the insane delusions of this man?

"You said you could hear what Rodgers was doing out there last night, trying to run us down," Dale said. "This man is very afraid his time's run out and that he's going to take the fall on this soon. He's desperate, and he knows we're here. If he can silence us, well, things might continue the way they have been for quite a while up here. It's going to take a lot of persistence on the part of someone to find an answer to where we've disappeared."

Winfield sighed and sagged back against the wall. Chill be damned! If he couldn't get Tasha to help them, they were screwed!

"I know it sounds crazy," Donna said. "I keep trying to put myself in your shoes and seeing if I would believe what we're saying. To be honest, I don't think I would. It's too weird to be true."

"But if you put together some of the pieces yourself, keeping in mind what I've said, it does start to make a kind of sense. How about Larry Cole? You were there at the accident. Was his body so bad off it required a closed casket to keep from upsetting the family?"

Winfield shrugged as best as he could with his hands shackled behind his back.

"He was a mess, I already told you that," he said softly, trying to remember precisely what he had seen last Friday night, not colored by the details Dale had just given him. "I agree with you that Rodgers' insistence on a closed casket struck me as a bit unusual, but I wasn't about to go make an issue of it. His decision was his decision, and he did maintain that, in spite of what Larry's mother said, she had requested a closed casket."

"How *convenient,*" Dale said, mimicking the nasal drawl of the *Saturday Night Live* character "Church Lady."

"And you must have heard about Reggie Perry," Donna said. "From what his brother said in the bar, there was no reason for him to die like that. He'd been doing just fine until *pop!* He's dead."

"Things like that happen," Winfield said.

"Often enough for anyone to get suspicious?" Dale asked, arching his eyebrows.

"Possibly," Winfield said, scowling. "Look, "I suppose I can tell you this, now that, apparently, we're . . ." He snorted and spit over his shoulder onto the wall. "Christ, I'm starting to act like our host.

"I suppose I can tell you now that if there was one mistake made in all of this, it was that your friend Larry Cole got a little too close to this."

"What do you mean?" Dale asked, looking over at Donna and trying to read her reaction.

"He was right. And you're right, to a degree," Win-field said. "Lots of 'unusual,' shall say, things have been going for a long time around here, and I was conducting an investigation, trying to pin certain 'untimely deaths' on one or possibly two people who work in the hospital in Houlton."

"Like what happened yesterday to Reggie Perry?" Dale asked.

Winfield nodded his head. "Exactly."

"Do you want to mention any names?" Dale asked, feeling a sudden flush. Until now, he hadn't really considered how extensive something like this might be. If there's enough money involved it might be very big indeed.

"No," Winfield said. "I don't care to mention any names. I'd say, odds are we're going to have a bitch of a time getting out of this. I'm not really worried about compromising anyone. I can say that there is —should I say *was?*—an investigation in progress."

Dale chuckled aloud and shook his head. He glanced up at the cellar ceiling when he heard Hocker's heavy footsteps track from the living room into the kitchen overhead. Hocker said something to Tasha, but no one in the cellar could make out the words. Tasha shouted, "How the hell should *I* know who it is?"

"You know what's funny as hell?" Dale said, still shaking with laughter. "Now that I think about it, on the tape, Larry said something about his 'contact.' Were you his contact?"

Winfield nodded solemnly. "I had spoken with him off the record because I knew him from when he grew up here. Second, he worked for the state, and I wanted to sound him out on the possibility of getting the State Police involved in the investigation."

"What the hell would Larry have known about the State Police?" Dale said, shaking his head in wonder.

"I said I asked him off the record," Winfield replied. "I'd been working on my own and wanted to bring someone else in on it, but frankly I thought the whole thing—and I'm not talking *zombies* here, like you two; I'm just talking about some suspicious deaths locally—I thought the whole thing was strange enough to warrant my attention. I mentioned it to Larry one night, while we were drinking down at Kellerman's."

Sudden laughter burst out of Dale like a gunshot. His shoulders shook as he looked back and forth between Donna and Winfield.

"And all along," he sputtered, "I was thinking maybe you were in on it with Rodgers, working for him! Jesus, I guess that shows what kind of cop I would have made!"

Winfield tilted his head back and looked up at the cellar ceiling when they heard Hocker's hefty footsteps go across the floor again.

"And what do you think we can do about him?" he asked. "Because if I'm right, and Rodgers is responsible for several local murders, or you're right, and he's 'experimenting' with the corpses, if we don't get out of this goddamned coal bin, it isn't going to matter what we think."

"I've been trying to work these knots loose all night," Dale said, glancing at Donna. "This guy may be crazy, but he sure as shit knows how to tie your hands up nice and snug."

"I've been working on the girl all night, trying to scare her into helping me get loose. Thanks to her, I was almost sporting my left nut on my right shoulder." He briefly described his first encounter with Tasha in the church parking lot. "I think she's our best hope. It's obviously she doesn't really like this guy Hocker, but she feels some kind of security from him, too. I think if she realizes just how much trouble she's gotten herself into, she'll come around."

Donna sighed and leaned her head back against the cold stone wall. "You think she hasn't realized that already? God, I mean, what's it going to take for her to wake up?"

From upstairs, footsteps sounded in the kitchen again, running this time. The three prisoners heard Hocker call out, "You just make sure that back door is locked this time! I'll take care of this!"

"Could be one of my co-workers, looking for me because I didn't show up for my morning shift," Winfield said, his eyes brightening with hope that quickly faded when he remembered how easily Hocker had blind-sided him. It irritated him because it made him realize he was getting older and slower.

Dale was shaking his head, his eyes closed as he tried to slow down his thoughts. After what he had seen last night at the funeral home, his imagination had gone into overdrive, and he didn't like what he thought might be outside the house.

"I'll bet it's someone looking for us, all right," he said softly. "I'll bet you ten to one it's Rodgers, coming back with a little help."

# II

By the time dawn came, Hocker agreed with Tasha that it was time to head out of town. He had never really wanted to get involved here; things had balled up, and as much as he wanted to clear out, he just couldn't bring himself to do it. Maybe, he thought, it was because he hadn't had a chance to torch anything yet. He couldn't very well leave without leaving his mark on the town. Hell, those three dead guys buried back in the woods didn't count. Who was going to miss them?

Hocker hadn't slept well, because he didn't trust Tasha to guard the guests down in the coal bin. He figured she'd get cold feet and, when he was sound asleep, let them go. Then she'd betray him. Nah! It would be best to keep an eye on her and the hostages until they could slip out of here into Canada.

Sunlight slipped in through the living room window and, like a spear, lanced through a hole in the drawn window shade and hit him squarely in the eye. He jumped awake with a start and looked around, afraid that he had fallen asleep and, that while asleep, Tasha might have fucked him up.

But no, she was still sleeping, a quiet hump in her sleeping bag over by the fireplace. Hocker got out of his sleeping bag and hurriedly pulled on his jeans and socks. Damned, it was cold! But he didn't want to chance even the tiniest fire in the fireplace. Not after everything that had happened. Combining what he had taken from that old man, the cop, and the other guy tied up in the cellar, he had enough money to afford a motel room once they were in Canada. Hocker felt long overdue for a hot shower and a night's sleep on a real mattress.

Grumbling softly to himself, he hiked on his boots, buttoned his flannel shirt, and sauntered into the kitchen. None of the appliances worked, he knew, but he didn't want to bother with setting up the small camping stove, even though it was the only way he could get a cup of coffee. What he should do, he thought, was go in there and wake up Tasha; let her do the woman's work!

He decided against doing that, though, because he was enjoying the early morning quiet in the house. For a moment, he let himself wonder what it would have been like if he had grown up in this house instead of. . . .

"Fuck it," he whispered as he slammed open the lid of the cook stove and started working the valves to get the flame glowing. He cracked a wooden match with his thumbnail and lit the burner. The flame hissed loudly as it burned with a warm, blue glow, but it did nothing to cut the chill in the house. Hocker was still sputtering under his breath as he filled a small saucepan with water from his canteen and put it on the stove to boil.

"Morning," Tasha said sleepily. She was standing in the doorway, her eyes half-closed as she raked her fingers through her hair. Hocker, not wanting to let her know she had caught him by surprise, merely nodded her a greeting without turning around.

Before long, they were standing together in the frigid kitchen, sipping coffee from a steaming mug. The daylight outside was getting stronger, driving away the tangles of mist that clung to the hollows. The sloping hill was sharply lit by the slanting sunlight, and everything glowed with a gold light against the darkened sky to the west.

Hocker's eyes, though, as often as he tracked up the hill to the horizon, always kept coming back to the barn: the goddamned barn where I hid the goddamned cop's goddamned cruiser!

Something is going to have to burn in this town, he thought, feeling the hand holding his coffee mug tighten involuntarily. It was almost like a part of his brain began to *itch,* and he knew of only one way to scratch it. Burn! Burn something!

"What was that?" Tasha said, suddenly tensing.

Hocker tore his eyes away from his contemplation of the barn and looked at her. "I didn't say nothin'."

"No, that noise . . ."

"Just our guests knocking around. Probably lookin' for their breakfast." He chuckled and spit onto the floor.

He had been wondering most of the night what he should do about them. He couldn't leave them there in the cellar when he torched the barn! If the sparks drifted over and started the house on fire, they'd be trapped. He sure as hell didn't want to be a murderer!

Those guys in the woods don't count, Hocker thought. They attacked us, so they deserved what they got!

But he couldn't let them go, either, even if one of them wasn't a cop. They had seen him and could easily identify him. He had to make sure they didn't get free until he was safely across the border. Of course, that wasn't difficult, because the Canadian border was only a few miles from Dyer. He decided not to worry about it; he'd figure out what to do when the time came.

"No," Tasha said, her face creased with worry. "It sounded like a car pulled up outside."

Hocker put his half-empty cup down on the counter and hurried into the living room. Tasha followed two steps behind him, and they saw that she was right. There was a long, black limousine idling at the top of the driveway, squarely facing the house. The limo was missing one headlight, and the front and sides looked as though the car had tried to wrap itself around a tree. A man, dressed in a long, gray coat, and wearing a hat to shade his face from the morning sun, stood by the opened driver's door. One gloved hand rested on the top of the car door as he looked at the house, squinting into the morning sun; the other hand rested on the open door.

"Oh, shit," Tasha said. She slid one hand protectively up onto Hocker's shoulder. This guy sure didn't look like a cop, she thought, but who was he, and what did he want?

"Maybe we'll get lucky, and he'll just go away," Hocker said. He was clenching and unclenching his fists, and Tasha was thinking Hocker looked like he wanted this man to come up to the house, so he could add him to the collection downstairs.

"It looks like there's some other guys in the car with him," Tasha said, whispering close to Hocker's ear.

It was true. Behind the dark screen of the tinted windows, they could see silhouettes of a number of men. Hocker figured the limo could probably hold ten or more people comfortably.

"I'll bet this is the asshole who was out here last night, trying to ram down the front porch," Hocker said. The man was staring steadily at the house, and Hocker couldn't shake the odd feeling that this man could somehow see him and Tasha right through the wood.

Maybe, he thought, it's the way the sunlight makes his eye glow so strangely.

For several tense seconds, everyone stood stock-still: the man staring at the house, and Hocker and Tasha staring back. Finally, the man took one step away from the door and, cupping his hands to his mouth, shouted, "I know you're still in there, Mr. Harmon."

His voice was clear and strong, but it reverberated with an odd distortion in the early morning stillness. Tasha thought she heard the door window rattle from the force of his voice.

"Yup," Hocker said, nodding his head slowly. "It's those jerks down cellar he wants."

"Let's just send them out to him," Tasha said. "Maybe he's a cop or something and is after them. We might be able to get away from here while he deals with them."

"Shut the fuck up!" Hocker hissed between his teeth. "I'm thinking."

Tasha refrained from saying, "I haven't got that long." Instead, she took a deep breath and backed up toward the kitchen.

Hocker glanced at her and yelled, "You just make sure that back door is locked. I'll take care of this!"

Tasha did what she was told, then hurried back into the living room.

The man beside the limousine seemed to chuckle to himself and, shaking his head as though sadly concluding he had to scold a misbehaving child, he reached behind himself and opened the limo door. Two men, dressed in tattered work clothes, blinking fiercely in the glare of sunlight, stepped out onto the driveway. The man leaned close to them, then glanced back at the house.

"Mr. Harmon! Miss LaPierre! I think you must realize the futility of pretending you can't here me. I know you didn't leave the house last night. Now if you don't come out right now, things could get very unpleasant."

Hocker smacked his fist into his open hand. It made a wet sound. "Just come on," he whispered harshly. "Send your goons up here. I'll show 'em!" He eased Winfield's revolver from his belt and spun the chamber, making sure it was fully loaded.

"Come on, Hock!" Tasha said, backing away. "You can't just keep on killing people."

"I ain't gonna kill 'em 'less I have to," he said, smiling wickedly. "Why don't you make yourself useful and see if there's any more rope in the kitchen or somewhere?"

Tasha left him by the window, wondering how easily she could simply slip away out the back door. But she didn't; she went into the kitchen and rummaged through the closet until she was certain there was no rope in there. When she rejoined Hocker in the living room and looked out at the driveway, her heart nearly stopped. The man was pointing at the house, and the two shabby men, walking as though their limbs were stiff with age, started up the walkway to the house.

"You've had your chance," the man by the limo shouted. The smile on his face was broad, eerily lifeless and chilling as though he was going to enjoy what would happen next.

Hocker gripped the revolver tightly, raising it up in front of his face as he watched the men slowly approach the house. He, too, had noticed the peculiar way the men walked. He was thinking, since they were so damned stiff, they wouldn't be any problem to take out of the picture.

When the two men were halfway up the walkway, Hocker swung open the door and stepped onto the porch. He pointed the revolver at them. Tasha saw an expression of genuine surprise on the man's face when he saw someone he wasn't expecting. He opened his mouth to call out but then apparently thought better of it.

"If you fellas don't stop right there, I'm gonna fill you so full of lead you'll be able to use your dicks for a pencil!" Hocker shouted, his breath puffing a thin cloud of steam in the morning chill.

The men continued walking toward him as though they hadn't heard him. If they did hear him, they didn't care. Their eyes were fixed vacantly on the house door, and Hocker, standing there, waving a gun, didn't seem to bother them in the least.

These guys look like those old coots I wasted in the woods, Hocker thought. A cold dash of fear gripped his stomach, and he thought, for a flickering second, that these *were* two of the men he had killed! A line of sweat sprang out on his forehead as he listened to the *crunch-crunch* of the men's boots on the gravel walkway.

"I mean it!" Hocker shouted, brandishing the revolver.

Tasha was watching from inside the house, and she thought she heard a serious waver in Hocker's voice. She was thinking, if these guys got past Hocker, she could probably outrun them in the woods, at least.

"One more step!" Hocker yelled. His voice rebounded from the hill, sounding thin and pale.

The man next to the limo was watching with the sunlight catching a wicked gleam in his eye. He had taken a few short steps forward and now stood at the foot of the walkway with both hands in his coat pockets.

*"I fucking-A mean it!"* Hocker shouted, and now, before his voice had a chance to echo back, there was the loud snap of the gun . . . once—twice—three times.

The revolver kicked back solidly in Hocker's hand, sending a small measure of reassurance to his brain, but that reassurance quickly died when he saw the two men continue toward him without flinching.

"What the fuck?" Hocker said, turning the revolver over in his hand and looking at it. A thin wisp of smoke drifted from the muzzle and stung his nose. Was the damned gun loaded with blanks?

Tasha came forward and leaned on the open door, preparing to slam it shut as soon as the men reached the porch steps.

Hocker raised the revolver and pointed it at them again, this time sighting carefully along the bead at the head of the man on the right. He held his breath just as he'd been taught to shoot, and *carefully* squeezed the trigger. The gun kicked twice, and Hocker knew there was no way he could possibly have missed; the dirt slope behind the man kicked up twice as the bullets tore into the ground. But the man who had been his target paused for no more than a second, snapped his head to the side quickly twice, and then continued walking toward the porch.

Hocker knew there was only one bullet left before he would have to reload. He wanted to beat a retreat, but as he stood there, looking dumbly at the useless revolver in his hand, the porch steps creaked under the weight of the men as they started up them.

Frantically, Hocker fired one last time, point-blank at one of the men's faces.

*Yes!* his mind suddenly screamed when he saw the waxy skin and dull gleam in their eyes. These are the two guys we *killed* in the woods!

And then they lurched forward. Their bony hands made a surprisingly quick grab at him. Yellow fingernails snagged the side of his shirt as he dodged to one side. One of the men, the one who had taken most of his bullets, made a deep-bellied grunt, as though moving with any speed was an immense effort. Hocker saw that he hadn't been firing blanks; there were three dark holes in the man; two in his face and one in his neck just about his shirt collar. The holes were as clean as if he had shot the bullets through rotten wood. No blood, no ripped flesh, just three clean holes, dry and as black as the night. He could have easily put two fingers inside each hole.

*Impossible!* Hocker's mind shrieked as he lurched to one side just as the men grabbed at him. The revolver was empty, but a dim corner of his mind told him, shooting would be useless even if the gun had been loaded!

Both men, now, were moaning as they came at him, their arms stretched out as though to embrace Hocker. Hocker backed up, but accidentally tripped on a piece of the fallen porch. He fell, sprawling onto the porch floor. His arms and legs clawed wildly, trying to get him up and away, but then something grabbed his foot and held on tightly.

"Oh, Jesus! Oh, *shit!*" Hocker wailed as he turned and saw both men looming over him. Their jaws were crunching up and down, and their yellowed and cracked teeth, smeared with dirt, made harsh, grating sounds.

The hand holding his leg was as unrelenting as a bear trap. The fingernails pierced Hocker's thick denim pants and dug into his skin. All sensation in Hocker's foot was gone, and he was wondering if he could get up and run with a dead leg, if he could break the hold on him.

He looked frantically at the house and was stunned to see that Tasha had slammed the door shut. She was gone! He'd been deserted! Left alone with . . . *them!*

The two men leaned over Hocker, fixing him with their empty stares as they brought their open mouths closer and closer.

Hocker rolled onto his back and, bracing himself with both arms spread wide, placed his foot onto the chest of one of them. With a great effort, Hocker pushed back as hard as he could. The man's chest caved in to the pressure of Hocker's foot, as if the thin shell of flesh and ribs was about to break, before he stumbled backward, his arms waving wildly for balance. He backed into the railing, hit it above the backs of his knees, and cart-wheeled into the shrubbery.

Hocker quickly twisted around and planted his foot on the other man's chest. He could hear the heavy grunting of the first man as he scrambled to get back onto the porch. Fear and revulsion charged him as he cocked back his leg and kicked the other man several times viciously in the chest. Each time his foot landed, the man made a horrible grunt as air was forced out his lungs. It washed over Hocker in sickening, sour waves. Never in his life had Hocker smelled something so foul or rank coming from a human being. It reminded him of the time his grandmother had her septic system pumped. The heavy aroma of human waste had lingered in his nose for days, it had seemed, and the same smell now emanated from the open mouth of this man.

Each time Hocker kicked, the man sagged back. But a mindless determination drove him on, like a bone-dumb football player, intent on pushing and pushing until all resistance gave. Hocker couldn't shake the impression that the man wanted to take a bite out of him, wanted to *eat* him!

One wild kick caught the man a glancing blow on the side, and his tattered shirt suddenly split open, revealing the man's pale, thin chest. With the next kick, his boot heel hit the man in the ribs, just below his left nipple. The white skin, as sickly white as the belly of a dead frog, split open with a loud tearing sound. Again, just like when he had shot them, there was no blood! The man's chest pulled open as easily as the flannel of his age-rotted shirt. An oval gash more than a foot long opened like a wide, toothless grin. Hocker got a horrifyingly clear view of dark strands of muscles and blackened rib bones, sticking out like wheel spokes. "Jesus Christ!" Hocker wailed. His brain was still trying to reject the reality of what he was seeing. The man still gripped Hocker's other leg, and in a sudden, blinding panic, Hocker drove his foot at the leering face. His boot heel caught the lower edge of the man's chin, smashing his teeth together. The next time the man opened his mouth, a shower of teeth fell out, rattling like pellets onto Hocker's chest.

No matter what Hocker did to this man, he never showed any change of expression. His face was immobile, as inert as if he were having his fingernails clipped.

How can he not feel the pain? Hocker wondered.

But he didn't take too long to think about it now. He was filled with fear for his life and for his own sanity if he did not get away from this *thing!*

The man's toothless mouth, still gnawing mindlessly and dropping splinters of teeth, pressed closer to Hocker's face. The eyes seemed to drain the will from Hocker, and he knew he would be dead shortly if he didn't get this guy off him. From the side, he could see motion as the man who had fallen finally made it back onto the porch.

With one last effort, knowing this was it—he would either break free or die within a second or two —Hocker swung his hand with the revolver down as hard as he could on the back of the man's head. The impact sent a jolt of pain up his arm: he had no doubt he had cracked the man's skull. In his mind, he pictured the revolver butt smashing an old, clay vase. Again and again, he slammed the revolver into the man's head, and each blow did little more than force a shallow grunt from the man. Finally, though, as Hocker twisted beneath the man's weight, he broke the hold on his leg and rolled free.

Scrambling quickly to his feet, Hocker glanced at the second assailant, who was standing up with slow, stiff movements. With a quick turn, Hocker drove the toe of his boot into the fallen man's chest, satisfied by the sharp breaking sound he heard on impact. Then, turning quickly, he ran to the front door and hit it hard with his shoulder. The door didn't budge when he twisted the knob and leaned heavily against it. It was locked from the inside!

Hocker looked behind him as both men struggled to regain their feet. *They should both be dead!* his mind screamed, but the one who's teeth he had kicked out didn't even look stunned as he lurched from side to side, trying to catch his balance. The other one moved slowly and deliberately toward him, his hands stiffly flexing and unflexing.

"Tasha! You goddamned *bitch!* Why'd you lock the fucking door!" he shouted as he slammed his fist repeatedly on the door. "Goddamn Tasha! Where the fuck *are* you?"

*Can I break it down, or will it hold?* he wondered. *If I was safely inside, would the door stop them or would these bloodless things tear through the door as if it were paper?*

A hailstorm of fists pounded the door as Hocker shouted until his throat was raw. He heard footsteps behind him and knew he was dead unless he tried something else. Spinning on his heel, and counting on his speed to save him, he dashed down the length of the porch, hoping to Christ the kitchen door wasn't locked. These assholes may be tough, he thought, but I hope to Christ they're slow!

# III

Tasha surprised herself; she did exactly what she had told herself she would do. As soon as the first man's foot touched the first step, she swung the front door shut and ran into the kitchen. For only a second or two, she hesitated, her eyes darting back and forth between the front door and the back door.

She knew she could unlock the door and run like a son-of-a-bitch for the woods; once she was clear, she could find a phone and call home collect. Her father could easily arrange for someone to pick her up before the sun set that evening.

The man out there by the limo had called out for "Harmon," not the cop she had kicked in the balls. Maybe the "limo man" was a cop, too, and he and Win- field were both after this guy Harmon. And maybe she should trust this cop, when he tells her he'll help get her out of any trouble she might be in. He may not know about that old duffer Hocker knocked out cold, or the truck they had stolen, or the three men in the woods. ...

Oh, God, she thought as fear rippled her insides like an earthquake. I killed one of them, too! I'm in it just as deep as Hocker is!

From the front of the house, she heard the blast of gunshots and then sounds of scrambling as Hocker fought on the porch with the two men. A part of her told her she had to go out there and help him, she couldn't let them hurt Hocker who, in spite of his craziness and everything he had done, had taken care of her along the road. She couldn't very well leave him out there alone to face those men!

But what good would I be? she wondered, feeling a sharp stinging in her eyes as tears welled up and overflowed. What goddamned good am I to anyone? She was standing in the middle of the kitchen floor, rocking back and forth on the tips of her toes. Her eyes were fastened on the back door. "Escape," her mind whispered. *Freedom!*

But the sounds coming from the front of the house were too loud to ignore. Her hands tightening into fisted balls, Tasha took several steps back toward the front door, but then something caught her eye and brought her up to an abrupt stop. The cellar door was open a crack, and through the narrow opening, she could see a sliver of sunlight slashing across the floor.

In a flash, a single word filled Tasha's mind: *Help!*

There were two men down there and one of them was a cop! Any help was better than none at this point, she decided. She quickly went over to the door and raced down the stairs. The two men and the woman looked up at her with surprise in their eyes. They, too, had heard the gun shots, and the question of what was happening above them hung between them, unspoken.

"Which shoe has the key?" Tasha snapped, her voice jittery as she knelt down in front of Winfield.

"The left," he said, turning slightly so she could reach it easily.

Tasha hurriedly untied the lace and shook the shoe until a small, silver key fell out into her hand. Winfield twisted around so she could get at his hands cuffed behind his back.

"What's happening?" Winfield said, making a conscious effort to keep his voice steady; he could tell something had her all worked up, and if what agitated her would get them set free, he didn't want to jeopardize it.

"There's some men out there," Tasha said with a gasp. "Two of them are fighting with Hocker."

Dale and Winfield exchanged knowing glances, but it was Donna who said what all three of them immediately thought.

"Rodgers!"

"And company," Dale added.

Tasha's hands were shaking so badly, she couldn't get the key into the small hole. She huffed with frustration, barely noticing her blurred vision as tears filled her eyes. Finally, she got the key into the lock and gave it a twist. With a small clink, the cuffs fell to the dirt floor, and Winfield immediately jerked forward and began working to free his legs.

"Get them," he snapped when Tasha tried to help him.

"Do you know what that man wants?" Tasha asked as she worked on the ropes holding Dale's hands behind his back.

"Yeah," he said, grateful as he felt the bounds on his hands loosening. "He wants to make sure no one else finds out what we've found out about him."

The rope slackened enough so Dale could pull his hands free. As he worked to get his feet untied, Tasha moved over and started on Donna's ropes. By the time Dale had his feet free, Winfield had put his shoe back on and was standing up, shaking his hands and bouncing from one foot to the other to restore his circulation.

"This guy Hocker took my gun," Winfield said when Dale stood up.

Dale was about to reply, but the suddenly flow of blood to his cramped legs drained his head of blood, and a wave of dizziness seized him. Bright pinpoints of light squiggled across his field of vision, and darkness started to close in from the edges. He sagged back against the cellar wall, wishing frantically that the sensation would pass.

Wouldn't that be funny? he thought, to drop dead here of a heart attack, and wake up on one of Rodgers' marble slabs!

By the time Donna was free and trying her damnedest to get the feeling back in her arms and legs, the dizziness had passed from Dale. Taking a deep breath of the damp cellar air, he joined Winfield, who was over in the far side of the cellar, searching through a pile of rusted junk for anything that could function as a weapon.

Through the cellar floor, they heard the sudden clomping of footsteps as someone raced the length of the porch. This was followed by the steady "clomp-clomp" of heavy boots on the porch.

"This'll do," Winfield said, grabbing the splintery shaft of an old shovel. The blade was coated with brick-red rust, and it looked like it just might cut through butter, if the butter had been left in the sun on an August afternoon.

Dale could find nothing better than the rotted leg of an old saw horse, but with that in hand he quickly followed Winfield up the stairs to the kitchen. Donna and Tasha were close behind them.

Through the kitchen window, they saw someone flash by the window, and then Hocker was at the back door, his eyes rounded with fright as he banged his fist on the door window and shouted, "Unlock the goddamned door! Jesus Christ! They're after me!"

Winfield moved quickly to the door, flipped the lock, and swung the door inward. Just as he did, though, the man rounded the side of the house. One of them slammed like an express train into Hocker, pitching both of them onto the kitchen floor. In the wild scramble of fists and knees, Winfield couldn't tell, at first, who was who. All he could see was a blur of action.

Dale, though, knew exactly who—or *what*— had tackled Hocker, and he moved swiftly forward, raised his saw horse leg over his head, and brought it down swiftly onto the head of the attacker.

There was a loud crack, and Dale wasn't sure if what broke was the piece of wood in his hand or the attacker's skull. The blow seemed to get the man's attention, and when he rolled over and looked up at Dale, Donna, who was standing right behind him, let out a piercing scream.

"Mother of God!" Dale said, his voice sounding like a rasp on metal.

The man's eyes looked as though he should already be dead. There was a milky glaze over the pupils, and the eyeballs protruded from his skull as if his eyelids were gone! *He couldn't blink his eyes if he wanted to!* But the round, dead ivory balls that glared up at her weren't what made her scream. It was something worse.

"Jesus Christ!" Dale sputtered as he staggered backward, letting the board drop to the floor. "Jesus! It's *Larry!*"

Winfield, too, recognized Larry Cole; in spite of the hollow cheeks and pasty complexion, there was no doubt that this was Larry Cole the same man who, just last Friday night, he had pulled from the crumpled wreck of his car, *dead!* Winfield stood there, stunned by what he was seeing, as if this were a nightmare and if he could somehow push it away from his mind, it would go away.

A wide smile split Larry's face, but there wasn't the slightest flicker of recognition in his eyes as he scrambled to get onto his hands and knees. He moved slowly and deliberately as he shifted his weight forward, treating the fallen Hocker as nothing more than a rug he had tripped over. As Larry struggled to stand, his mouth dropped open, and with a sudden, reflexive muscle spasm, clamped shut again with a hard, chomping sound.

Winfield was frozen where he stood. Everything Dale and Donna had told him during their night of captivity came flooding back into his mind. Everything was a jumbled mess of thoughts, voices, and ideas; but one thing rang in his mind stronger and louder.

It's all true! his mind chattered, and he was afraid those words would suddenly spiral upward, higher and higher, louder and louder until they were an insane buzz.

*It's all true!*

*ITS ALL TRUE!*

Dale, however, didn't freeze. In Rodgers' Funeral Home, he had already confronted the idea that Larry could still be alive, which, in a manner of speaking, he was. Dale wrenched the shovel from Winfield's suddenly slack grasp and, cocking his arms back as though about to launch a harpoon, he drove the spade tip as hard as he could into the smiling face of his "dead" best friend.

There was a sickening crunch as the rusted blade caught Larry's throat just under the chin, severing the windpipe and biting downward into the spine. The rotten flesh tore open, with a hiss but no blood flowed. Larry's head sagged to one side, but the crazy glow remained in his eyes, and the wide smile remained on his face. His teeth kept clacking together hungrily, and all Dale could think was, *He wants to take a bite out of me!*

Larry managed to get up and, sitting back on his heels, slowly raise his hands. Whether it was to protect himself or make a grab for him, Dale didn't know; but he didn't bother to wait to find out. He pulled the shovel back, tensed his shoulder muscles, and then swung again, aiming for the same area of Larry's neck.

Dale was only vaguely aware of what was going on around him in the kitchen. He had a sense that Winfield was still standing there, numbly staring at the impossible thing that was happening. Someone was screaming. It was a high-pitched wail that cut Dale's nerves like a dentist's drill. Hocker was still trying to extricate himself from the weight of the man on top of him. He was fighting a panic he had never thought was possible for him to feel.

Dale's second swing was wide of the mark and merely glanced off Larry's shoulder. The swing carried Dale around, and for a flashing moment, he was afraid he would fall. His mind filled with the terrifying thought that, as soon as he hit the floor, Larry's mashing, grinding teeth would tear into him.

Larry made a low grunting sound as he darted forward, his hands like dirty claws, trying to snag Dale and bring him down. But Dale kept his balance and, turning to one side, brought the shovel down squarely on the back of Larry's neck. With a loud snap of breaking bone, Larry's head dropped forward and then fell off. It hit the kitchen floor with a dull thump and rolled with a crazy, lopsided spin toward the living room door. For several sickening seconds, the headless body remained sitting; then it sagged to the floor. Dale wanted to scream as he watched Larry's arms and legs twitch wildly, then lie still.

I'm going to pass out, Dale thought as darkness swirled around his mind like a black tide. In the distance, someone still screamed shrilly and long. Dale wanted to know who it was, to help if he could, but he couldn't because suddenly he found himself on the floor, kneeling on his hands and knees. His stomach felt like it was in the icy grip of some oversized hand that was squeezing out the remains of last night's supper. Not much was there, though, so Dale had to suffer several waves of painful dry heaves before it passed. He looked up just in time to see another dark bulk coming through the doorway.

Winfield finally snapped out of his shock. The second man lurched forward and, because Hocker was still on the floor, attacked the first person he saw. His hand flashed out and caught Hocker by the seat of the pants and started to pull him toward him. His mouth opened wide, exposing a mess of broken and cracked teeth. Before Hocker could twist out of the man's grasp, the attacker darted his head forward and chomped down hard on Hocker's shoulder.

Hocker let out a piercing wail as the broken teeth worked their way into his shoulder muscles. Then he distantly heard someone yell, "You have to cut its head off to stop it!"

Hocker was suddenly jolted downward several times as someone beat the man who was attacking him. After what seemed like hours, the grinding teeth released their hold, and Hocker felt the weight of his attacker lift off him. As he scrambled to safety, he felt the warm flow of his own blood running down his back inside his shirt.

When he turned around and saw what actually had happened, his mind wanted to block it out. The sight of two headless corpses, sprawled on the floor, instantly brought back the memory of the night in the woods when he and Tasha had killed those other three men. He was sure the man was one of the men he had killed in the woods that night, impossible as it seemed!

With both attackers dead on the kitchen floor, the small group of people hastily reorganized. Tasha and Donna were standing by the doorway to the living room; neither one of them could believe what they had just witnessed. Dale and Hocker were both standing, now, close to Winfield as all five of them looked numbly at the bodies on the floor. Winfield was holding the shovel tightly in his hand as his eyes darted from the bodies to the open kitchen door.

"Tenacious sons-a-bitches, aren't they?" Hocker said. He coughed up a wad of mucous and spat onto the floor. "I suppose you let 'em go," he said, turning to Tasha.

She looked down at the floor, then squarely at him. "If I hadn't, you'd be dead right now."

"And I wouldn't give a fiddly-fuck either way," Hocker said before spitting again.

Dale and Donna exchanged glances, then walked slowly toward each other and embraced. Each of them felt the other sag into the hug and were grateful that they could keep each other from collapsing.

"It isn't over yet," Winfield said gruffly. He bent down and rolled the second attacker onto his back. The gaping black hole in his chest ripped open a bit more with the motion, and a horrible, rotting odor rose from the wound. The exposed bone looked yellow and spongy.

"It's that prick up there with the fancy car, ain't it?" Hocker said, suddenly tensing. He suddenly realized that he was still clenching Winfield's service revolver in his hand, and he reached into his pocket for a handful of bullets.

As Hocker was reloading, Winfield came over to him and held his hand out. "I believe you have something of mine," he said, his voice low and firm.

Hocker gave him a flickering, angry stare as he shoved the last bullet into the chamber and clicked it shut with a flick of his wrist. The black hole of the muzzle slowly swung up and pointed at Winfield.

"If there are any more of these freaks around, you certainly don't expect me to go unarmed, do you?" he said.

The revolver pointed unwaveringly at Winfield, but he didn't back down. He was thinking, there are worse things than being killed by a punk like you, but that's not what Winfield said. Keeping his voice low, he simply said, "By the sounds I heard, I figure you already tried to shoot these guys. You know it isn't enough to stop them."

"It's like I said," Dale said, stepping forward to stand beside Winfield facing Hocker. "To stop these 'freaks,' you have to cut off their heads. That's the only thing that will stop them."

Hocker's eyes shifted back and forth and between the men. He knew — *Oh, Christ! Did he ever know!—they* were right. The man he had fought with on the porch had at least *four* bullets in him, fired at point-blank range. Those bullets had enough kicks to turn his brains into pudding hadn't been enough to stop him from barreling through the kitchen door and biting the shit out of him.

Hocker suddenly felt his knees buckle, and only now did he become fully aware of how badly he had been bitten. The blood was sticky and warm as it streamed down his back and soaked into the top of his pants.

"Give me the fucking gun," Winfield commanded, "and I swear to God, if we get out of this alive, I'll personally see that any and all charges against you, including assaulting a police officer for you and your lady friend, are dropped. And if you need a ride somewhere, I'll make sure you get where you want to go."

"Maybe I could have my cash and credit cards back, too," Dale said.

Hocker was finding it difficult to look directly at the police officer. The pain in his shoulder was building to a powerful crescendo. He could feel a steady pulsation, thumping from his biceps to the base of his neck. The flow of blood had abated, but it still felt as though a warm sheet was wrapped around half of his back. The early morning light in the kitchen should have been warming and comforting, but instead it looked hazy and dull.

"I think you'd better consider just how deeply in trouble we all are here," Dale said, looking at Hocker. "If we're going to get out of this, we're going to have to pull together. That man who sent those two to attack us is not going to let any of us out of here alive . . . not if he can help it."

"What the fuck does he want?" Hocker asked. He wanted to sound angry and tough, but the pain in his shoulder was spreading like fire in summer-dry woods.

"Are you ready for the truth?" Dale said, casting a glance at Winfield and wondering if, after what he had just seen, he had finally accepted the truth.

Hocker nodded. It hurt to hold his head up any more. He held the revolver out, handle-first. Winfield took it and slid it into his holster. Then he took the folded money and credit cards and handed them back to Dale, who slipped them into his pants pocket.

"Those men we just killed," Dale said, his voice catching for a moment. "They were already dead when they walked up onto the porch."

Hocker snorted, wanting to spit but finding his mouth had gone desert dry.

"They were already dead," Dale repeated. "And if we don't figure a way to get out of here, we're all going to end up just like them!"

# IV

Rodgers had watched with detached interest as two of his creations approached the farm house. He had earnestly wished he could have seen Harmon's face when he *finally* got to see the body of his dead friend . . . just before his buddy *killed* him! His interest turned to irritation and then to outright anger when he saw the man on the porch struggle with and escape from the two "men" he had sent to finish him off. Trembling with rage, he had watched as the man had run around behind the house to be followed by the two shambling figures.

Several anxious minutes later, the front door to the house opened, and two figures appeared on the porch. In the darkness beneath the collapsed porch roof, Rodgers at first mistook them for his two men, returning after dispatching everyone in the house.

Rodgers let out a loud gasp when he saw, instead, Dale Harmon and Jeff Winfield come to the edge of the porch and look at him.

"They're both dead," Harmon shouted. *"Really* dead this time."

Rodgers listened as Harmon's voice rebounded from the woods behind him. He had three more of his creations in the limo, but he had assumed that two of them would be more than enough to take care of everything. Obviously he had underestimated the situation. He vowed not to do that again.

"Did you enjoy seeing your friend again, Mr. Harmon?" Rodgers asked, his voice as sharp as a razor.

In reply, Dale flipped his middle finger high in the air.

"You could save us all a vast amount of unpleasantness if you just give yourselves up," Rodgers said.

Winfield was studying the man's position. With one hand on the limo roof and the other draped over the opened front door, he didn't present much of a target. In training, he had hit much smaller targets at greater distances, but this was one of those times when one shot and one alone was going to count. When he saw his opportunity, he wanted to be positive he would finish it with a single shot.

"Those two are nothing compared to what else I have at my beck and call. By this afternoon, I can have this house entirely surrounded by my creations. You won't be able to kill them all."

"We'll take out as many as we can," Dale shouted.

"And when it's over," Rodgers said, "I'll have you and your friends inside there to replenish the ranks."

He snapped his fingers, and the two back doors of the limo swung open. Squinting and turning their heads to avoid looking at the direct sunlight, three zombies slowly stretched to their full height. Rodgers glanced at them only briefly before turning back to Winfield and Harmon.

"These three should be able to finish the job," he said, his voice booming. "But I'm not about to take that chance."

With a quick motion of his arm, he gave each of the three a command. Dale and Winfield watched as one zombie walked forward, stopping at the foot of the walkway. The other two each walked out across the lawn, one to the left of the house and the other to the right. When they reached their positions and stopped, Dale and Winfield understood what Rodgers planned. From where the zombies stood, every side of the house was covered. They were trapped!

Winfield's hand, holding his revolver, was itching to rise, aim, and squeeze the trigger. Now was the time to shoot, before Rodgers could go back to his funeral home to get help. But the angle was bad, and Rodgers kept himself shielded by the open door.

Rodgers beamed with satisfaction when he saw that his creations did exactly what he had told them. He was disappointed to see how poorly the other two had fought, and he wasn't sure these three alone could to better. He only had four zombies left at the funeral home, but Higgins, owned several more; they could miss one afternoon of the harvest. Rodgers would ask to borrow Higgins' zombies, and Higgins would have to comply.

With a sudden intake of breath, Rodgers made a motion to get back into the car and get the assistance he needed to finish this messy job. But he caught himself and stood up, shielding his eyes against the morning sun as he called out to Dale.

"I understand, Mr. Harmon, that you've been rooming at Appleby's during your stay here in town. Is that correct?"

Dale wanted to reply, but his throat choked off as if Rodgers had his hands wrapped around his neck.

"Perhaps on my way into town, I'll stop by to give my regards to your daughter. What is her name—ah, I recall. She signed the guest book. Her name is Angela." Rodgers followed this with a laugh that sent waves of chills up Dale's spine.

"You won't get away with this!" Winfield yelled. He was boiling with frustration that he couldn't get a clear shot at Rodgers.

Rodgers tossed his head back, looking up at the blue vault of sky and laughing even louder, said, "But I *can*" He sputtered between gales of laughter. "It will be over for all of you before anyone suspects anything. But if you're worried about your daughter, Mr. Harmon, don't be. Not in the least. By tomorrow evening at the latest, you will in all likelihood see her again." His laughter pierced the sky, echoing from the surrounding hills. "The only problem will be you won't *recognize* each other!"

# V

Angie was relieved that the nurses had not strapped Lisa to her bed as they had said they might. After they cleaned her up and gave her a mild sedative, she had fallen asleep and was sleeping peacefully. For several hours, Angie and a nurse sat near the hospital bed watching her, helpless to do anything else.

As much as she wanted to stay awake and keep an eye on her friend, Angie was having trouble keeping her eyes open. Every few seconds, her head would start to nod, and then she would suddenly come to and sit upright with a startled gasp.

Lisa's grandmother had finally gone home sometime in the early morning. Angie had thought she was looking quite pasty and drawn; *Who wouldn't be?* she thought as she flirted with sleep. Even just the scare of Lisa falling off her bike and banging her head could have been too much for the woman's nerves— ending up in the hospital . . . and then finding her grand-daughter in the hospital walk-in, chomping on raw hamburger, was probably too much for *anyone's* nerves.

Angie's other concern was her father. He hadn't come rack to Mrs. Appleby's yet. She wanted to go back to the house with Mrs. Appleby, to see her dad. She wondered if he was back at the house yet. She knew he was with Donna, and she *knew* what men and women who feed each other might end up doing. But surely, she thought, not *my father!*

Mostly, though, Angie's concern was for Lisa. In the short time they had spent together, she had felt a bond of friendship growing between them that seemed much stronger than any of the friendships she had back home. She felt a genuine affection for Lisa, as if they had known each other for years before they met.

Several times in the pre-dawn stillness of the hospital, Lisa stirred in her bed. The crisp sheets crinkled like plastic under her as she tossed and turned. Often, she cried out in her sleep, and raising her hands to her mouth, she made loud munching sounds, smacking her lips and clacking her teeth as though she was eating. Angie, remembering the image of her friend, squatting on the floor as she chewed raw hamburger, her hospital johnny stained with meat juice, would awake with a start and lean over her friend, ready to either to calm her down or, if necessary, restrain her.

Each time Angie was torn out of her sleep by Lisa's thrashing, it seemed to her that Lisa was less agitated. The little bit of rest she was getting seemed to be restoring her to herself. And that was what had been bothering Angie all night: she hadn't known Lisa for very long, but ever since Stephen Wayne had been to the house to see Lisa, she had seemed very *different*.

Angie found herself wondering if, maybe this guy Wayne had done something to Lisa that had hurt her instead of help her. Maybe he had given her the wrong medicine, or maybe Lisa's injuries were more serious than he could determine. Thoughts like that mixed with other, scarier thoughts, giving Angie, in what little sleep she got, cold, stomach-dropping nightmares.

The worst nightmare was when Angie dreamed Lisa had her father, pinned to the floor in Mrs. Appleby's living room. Straddling her father, and keeping his shoulders pinned with her knees, Lisa was leaning over Angie's dad. Her face was down, close to his, and if it hadn't been for the loud munching sound, she might have thought Lisa was kissing her father. But they weren't kissing. As a matter of fact, Angie's dad wasn't even *moving,* except for a slight tremor in his legs. Lisa had her face down on top of her father's head, and Angie could vividly see thick rivers of blood spilling onto the floor, soaking into the carpet like spilled wine. Lisa had pried open the top of her father's skull and was chewing on what looked like a twisted bed sheet, stained pink and gray. Then Lisa raised her head and looked at her with a wide grin. The entire half of her face, from her nose down, was sheeted with blood and large chunks of gray stuff that looked like thick, gray worms . . . only Angie knew it wasn't *worms*.

About an hour or so after dawn, Lisa's eyelids fluttered open, and she smiled warmly when she finally focused on the face of her friend, leaning over her bed, smiling down at her.

"You're awake," Angie said softly. The relief she felt, that Lisa had stopped thrashing and moaning in her sleep, was compounded by the warmth of her smile. It wasn't anything close to the horrible smile she had seen on Lisa's face in her dream! Her eyes looked normal, too not distant and glassy, like they had after Stephen Wayne's visit, just sleep-heavy.

"How do you feel?" Angie said, keeping her voice low. The nurse who had been sitting with them had left the room while both of them had been asleep.

"I, uh," Lisa said, and then stopped and smacked her lips to moisten them. Her voice sounded thin, weak. She propped herself up on one elbow. Angie got the pitcher of water from the bedside stand and filled a plastic cup for her.

Lisa took the cup of water and drank it down greedily, her throat making loud gulping sounds. Angie almost laughed aloud at her friend's gusto, but when she remembered seeing her chomping the raw hamburger she just let one corner of her mouth twist up into a smile.

"Umm," Lisa said, handing her the empty cup and signaling that she wanted more. "That tastes so-o-o good."

"You had quite a night," Angie said as she refilled the cup and gave it to Lisa.

As if for the first time, Lisa noticed that she wasn't at home in her own bed, and she sat bolt upright in the bed, looking around with frantic eyes.

"Where am I? In the hospital?" she asked. She slapped one hand to her chest, clutching the lightweight cotton Johnny, not her flannel nightie at all!

Angie nodded her head and grunted softly. "Yeah. Do you remember that you fell off your bike?"

Lisa nodded, and the hand clutching her johnny slowly released and went up to her forehead. She gingerly touched the thick sterile pad taped over her head wound.

"Yeah," she said, squinting as she looked around for a moment. "I remember that. And I can kind of remember supper, but then it all gets sort of mixed up."

She suddenly cut herself off and looked at Angie with fear-stricken eyes. Her nostrils flared, and her teeth came together with a loud *click.*

She shivered and pulled the hospital sheet up around her neck. "I had some really scary dreams. I can remember I was in the police station, I think, and I was fighting with Officer Brooks! I was having this fight with Officer Brooks! Why would I dream about *him?* And I remember feeling really hungry in the dream— so hungry I wanted to— Again she cut herself off and shivered wildly.

"Look," Angie said, placing her hand reassuringly on her friend's shoulder. "You just lie on back and relax. I think that bump to your head kind of scrambled things up a bit. And I'll bet the medicine they gave you had something to do with those dreams you had."

A small part of her was crying out, wishing she could confide in Lisa about her own dreams, of Lisa bending over her father and eating his brains, but she knew she couldn't. After what Lisa had been through, what was just one stupid old nightmare, anyway?

"Is my gram here?" Lisa asked, her voice tight as she struggled to put aside the thoughts that kept intruding. "Does she know I'm here?"

Angie nodded, and for the first time in her life, she did something adults sometimes do. She would tell what her dad always called "little white lies," those lies you tell, not to deceive, but to protect someone from the painful truth.

"After supper," Angie said, "you were feeling really lousy, so your gram and I brought you here. She's home, safe and sound." Angie glanced at her wristwatch. "It's not even six o'clock yet, and she was up pretty late, so we can call her in an hour or so to let her know you're up and feeling just fine."

"I am," Lisa said, easing herself out from under the sheets. She wrinkled her nose as she looked around her hospital room, then nodded her head in acceptance of what had happened. "I hope I'll be able to go home today. But right now, I just want something to eat. I'm *wicked* hungry."

# PART FOUR

"O, might I see hell, and return again safe, how Happy were I then!" — Marlowe

# CHAPTER TEN
## "WAIT UNTIL DARK"

## I

"I don't think Rodgers will do anything until dark," Dale said. "He'll have the advantage because we can't see as well at night as they can."

All five of them were sitting cross-legged in a wide circle in the center of the living room floor. Tasha, after much protesting from Hocker, broke out their meager supply of canned food. Everyone shared it, but they all agreed it would be a good idea to eat sparingly, in case they were in the house for long. And how long they might be there was the topic under discussion.

"Look," Winfield said, casting a worried glance out the living room window. "We've got to keep in mind that we don't really know what we're dealing with here." About fifty feet from the house, he could see a figure, standing stock-still, arms hanging loosely at its side as it stared blankly at the house. It hadn't moved an inch in the nearly three hours since Rodgers had sent it there.

"We know what we're up against," Dale said. "I don't think after what happened in the kitchen this morning, there's any doubt."

"Fuckin-a," Hocker said as he gingerly reached a hand toward his wounded shoulder. Without water to clean the wound, they improvised with the ointment and gauze pads in the medical kit Hocker had stolen from Winfield's cruiser.

"We don't really know anything about them," Winfield said, nodding his head toward the window. "We may think we do, from whatever half-assed horror movies we've seen, but this is the real thing! We have no idea what we're up against!"

"We know we can kill them," Donna said.

"As many times as we need to," Dale joked.

Donna's mind filled with the image of those two headless corpses, bloodless stumps where the necks were, sprawled on her family's kitchen floor! Shivers danced up her spine. She was glad that, while she and Tasha tended Hocker's wound, Dale and Winfield had pushed the bodies and severed heads out the back door.

Dale shifted on the floor, trying to get comfortable. After spending most of the night tied up and leaning against the cellar wall, what he wanted to do most was get up and jog a few miles. With a couple of Rodgers' creatures close at his heels, that might not take so long. The thought that dug the deepest into his mind was concern for his daughter. Is Angie safe? he wondered. Would Rodgers really do something as cold-blooded and cruel as to attack a defenseless girl?

He hated to admit it to himself, but the answer was easily *yes!* Rodgers could probably do that, and worse!

Dale wanted to voice his concern about Angie—at least to Donna—but then, what could *she* do? Their immediate concern was to get out of this house—especially if Rodgers was on his way here with more of those *things*.

"I still think our best shot is for all of us to make a break for it all at once," Hocker said. He stood up quickly, went to the window and, leaning down, stared out at the guard who had been posted by the driveway. "There's only three of them and five of us. If we all go in separate directions, I figure at least two of us will get away."

"That's a great thought," Tasha said, shivering. "Why don't we have a little game of Russian roulette first?"

"No," Winfield said, shaking his head. "I don't like the odds. And who's to say Rodgers doesn't already have a whole swarm of those things hiding out there, just waiting for us to make a break for it?"

"Aww, shit," Hocker said. He spit onto the living room floor and, standing up, began pacing back and forth. "That's pussy! What do you want to do, have all of us huddle here in this fuckin' house until they break in and get us all?"

"No," Winfield said, shaking his head. "But I do want to make sure everyone of us gets out of here. Even you."

He remembered promising Hocker that he would try to get dropped any and all charges against him, but now he thought there'd be nothing better than slamming his ass in jail for a couple of nights. What irritated him most was the way he exerted his warped control over Tasha. He didn't like Hocker's abuse of power.

"I'm scared," Tasha said, glancing around the circle of faces, her lower lip trembling. "And I certainly don't want to be here tonight, after dark!"

Dale smiled at her and, reaching out, patted her on the knee. "Don't worry. We'll get out of here." He looked directly at Hocker. "We'll make sure we *all* get out together."

"I think the first thing we should do, then, is try to barricade the house," Winfield said. "Last night, when I left work, I told Ernie, at the desk, that I was heading out here to check the house." He cast an angry stare at Hocker, as if to say *"this is all your fault, asshole!"*

Hocker caught the stare and stopped his pacing for a moment, squaring off with Winfield. "And I think you're so full of shit, your eyes are brown," he said, his voice low and controlled. "I think it's bullshit to sit around here, waiting for him to come back with more help."

"We went to the station yesterday afternoon, looking for you," Dale said. "I don't know who I spoke with, but he said if you weren't home yet or down at Keller-man's, you were checking out some *place*. He didn't remember where."

"And you didn't tell him," Winfield said, raising an eyebrow.

"Remember that tape?" Dale said. "What we were going to talk to you about wasn't exactly something we wanted to broadcast."

Winfield scratched behind his ear. "That must've been Ernie. That 'bout figures for him."

"Wait a minute!" Dale said, snapping his fingers. "There's the cruiser in the barn. We can just drive on out of here if we can get to it. Why the hell didn't we think of that before?"

He got up quickly and ran into the kitchen with Winfield and Donna close behind, but they drew up suddenly when they saw one of Rodgers' creatures, standing directly in the path from the kitchen door to the barn.

"Damn!" Dale shouted, clenching his fists and slamming the counter top.

"It was a good idea," Winfield, "and maybe it still is, but from the damage you said Mr. Asshole did to it, I'd be surprised if it even worked."

"We can get it to work," Donna said, her face suddenly lighting up.

Dale and Winfield looked from the zombie by the barn back to her. "If you've got an idea, let's hear it," Dale said.

"Well, I'm not really sure if it's true or not, but down in the cellar near the coal bin is a doorway that leads into a tunnel. I never had the guts to go all the way down it because it's so small, but supposedly the tunnel leads all the way underground to the barn."

Dale and Winfield exchanged excited glances.

"This house is over two hundred years old," Donna said as they all started toward the cellar steps. "When we were kids, we always thought it was an escape tunnel, in case the house was attacked by Indians in colonial times."

"That tunnel's there, though? You know it for a fact?" Winfield asked. He snapped on the flashlight he had clipped to his belt and led them down the stairway into dark cellar.

"It was there when I was a kid, sure," Donna said, moving carefully down the steps. "I can't really say it goes anywhere, though, because I never followed it."

"It's worth a try," Dale said as they crossed the cellar floor. Donna took the flashlight from Winfield and directed it over to the corner of the cellar wall behind the coal bin. It was hard to spot, but set low to the ground was a small square of rough-cut boards flush inside the wall. Thick coal dust and cobwebs covered it, and the wood had turned sooty black with age. The bottom edge was punky with rot.

"It's on the right side of the house," Dale said, looking out the grimy cellar window at the small portion of the barn that was visible.

"Worth a try," Winfield said.

While Donna held the flashlight for him, Winfield ran his fingers along the rough edge of the door. He destroyed several spider webs, squashing the small egg cases that hung like tan berries.

"It's built right into the foundation," he said as he probed for a finger hold. "It's nailed right into the frame."

"We used to open it up and look inside," Donna said. "My sister used to threaten to put me in there and shut the door, so my father sealed it off."

"But if the tunnel's still open-" Dale said.

"We can get to my cruiser," Winfield finished for him.

"If it still runs," Donna reminded him.

"We won't know unless we try," Winfield said. "Here. Give me a hand."

Dale knelt down beside Winfield and tried to find an edge where he could work his fingers under the boards, but the door was set perfectly flush, and he couldn't find a hold.

Winfield, frustrated, sat back on his butt and raised his feet. With a loud grunt, he slammed both feet hard into the door. The wood, in spite of its age, was not rotten; it sprang back, sending a resounding shiver up Winfield's legs.

"Again," Dale said.

Winfield braced himself as best he could on the floor and kicked again, this time with just one foot. Using loud grunts with each kick, he hit the door five times in rapid succession, then leaned forward to check his progress.

"I think it gave a bit," Dale said, testing the edges of the wood. "It feels a little looser. Try again."

"You try it," Winfield said, huffing from the effort as he shifted aside to make room for Dale. "That's a killer on your feet."

Shaking his head, Dale took a position on the floor and, imitating Winfield's shouts, kicked the door as hard as he could. After three savage kicks, one of the boards in the door started to break inward, and it took just two more hits to knock it all the way in.

"All right," Winfield said as he reached past the splintered board and tried to pull the board next to it loose. He grunted with the effort and, pausing to catch his breath, said to Donna, "Christ, what did your father use, rail-road spikes?"

Donna shrugged as she concentrated on keeping the flashlight beam fixed directly on the doorway.

After another few minutes of effort, the rest of the door finally came away. The three of them knelt down and stared into the black square they had un-

covered. Donna shivered with her childhood memories of what she had imagined was waiting for her down in that tunnel.

"I don't think I can even fit down there," Winfield said, patting the bulge of
his stomach. "And I don't particularly relish the thought of getting stuck half-
way down there if it narrows any more."

"It does look pretty small," Dale said, looking over at Donna. She had shifted
a few feet away from the doorway and the memories her imagination had
started to rev up.

"You're not going to get *me* to go down there," she said, her voice trembling. "No way!" She shook her head quickly from side to side.

Winfield took the light from Donna and crawled forward, until half of him
was swallowed by the square doorway. "It looks like there's a turn up in there,"
he said, his voice muffled. He stayed with his head in the tunnel for a few seconds, then backed out, brushing away the dirt that had gotten on his face and
hands.

"Do you think we could enlist our good buddy Hocker to go down there?"
Winfield asked, looking at Dale.

Dale shrugged as he ran his hand over his forehead. "I don't know," he replied. "And even if he *did* go down there, I kind of wonder if he might not just
take off by himself and leave us to fend for ourselves."

"You honestly think he'd do something like that?" Winfield asked, his face
wrinkling with irony as he stroked his chin. His dirty hand left a black streak
beneath his eye.

"I can't imagine he'd do something like that," Donna said. "He couldn't be
that cruel."

"After getting clobbered over the head and spending a night trussed up like a
pig compliments of him, I don't think we can underestimate his lack of loyalty,"
Winfield said grimly. "For Hocker, it's himself, first, last, and always."

"I don't like the way he treats Tasha, either," Dale added. "The guy's obviously a nut case."

"So what are we going to do?" Donna asked.

"Donna, let me put it to you this way," Dale said. "If there were twenty of
Rodgers' zombies after you, do you think you'd find the courage to go down
there?"

Donna looked from him to the open doorway. Just the image of the small,
black square sent waves of fear rippling through her. She knew her fear of that
tunnel was irrational but the fear was also very real to her. The mere thought of
entering that tunnel made her stomach tighten up until it felt about the size of a
golf ball.

"I . . . don't know if I could," she stammered.

"Well I sure as shit won't fit," Winfield said, "and you say you won't go, so
here we are. I'd say our next best bet is to do like I said, reinforce the doors

and windows, and hope to hell we can hold off whatever Rodgers throws against us, at least until someone at the station remembers to check out here."

"I'm not holding my breath for that," Dale said. His unspoken thought was—*I have to get to Angie!*

While they were talking, Donna had gone over to what had been her father's workbench years ago. Most of the tools were gone, and the few that were there—a hack saw and a couple of screwdrivers —were rusted, but there was one thing she saw that she knew they could use. Years ago, her father had nailed two rows of jar lids to the ceiling rafters. After filling each jar with assorted nails, he screwed them back onto the cover. There were enough nails in the jars hanging down from the ceiling to build a whole house, by the looks of it.

Dale went over to Donna, who was pawing around behind the workbench, throwing aside old cans and age-stained cigar boxes. The noise she made was almost deafening in the close cellar as she rummaged through the junk.

"Seek and you shall find," she said as she straightened up, holding an old ball-peen hammer over her head. "We have the nails and we have the hammer!"

"We can take some of the bedroom doors and the shelving to cover the windows," Dale said. "So if we finally decide we can't trust Hocker to get the cruiser for us, we can at least hold out as long as we have to."

"That won't be very long, considering how little food there is for all of us," Donna said.

"We won't have to worry," Winfield said, standing up from his inspection of the open tunnel. "I've got a hunch Rodgers isn't going to let things drag along."

# II

As Rodgers drove back into town from the farmhouse, his anger grew and blossomed like an evil, black flower. He was positive that the people in the farmhouse had managed to kill the two creations he had sent after them, and that thought disturbed him. He knew his creations weren't invulnerable, but the fact that those people had "dispatched" them apparently so easily gave him pause.

He felt confident they wouldn't dare escape from the house, confronting the three he had left on guard, but still he felt a need to hurry back to the funeral home to get the two creations he still had there, then contact Sam Higgins and ask him to "loan" him as many creations as he could spare. He also should pay Mrs. Appleby—and her teen-aged boarder—a little visit, maybe in the company of Steven Wayne in his new *condition!*

Rodgers laughed as he considered just how firmly he had things under control. Oh, granted, a few ends had frayed a bit, especially now that that damned cop, Win-field, was involved; but Rodgers had his suspicions about him long before Harmon showed up, asking questions about Larry Cole.

Maybe, he thought, in the long run this is all for the better. He could take care of everything cleanly and completely now that the "frayed ends" were gathered together in the farmhouse. The only other person he needed was just waiting for a visit at Mrs. Appleby's. Wouldn't her father be so pleased to see his daughter again, Rodgers thought maliciously. *"Yes! ... so pleased!*

# III

Mrs. Appleby left the hospital as soon as Lisa had been found, cleaned up, and put back to bed. She prayed to God to make her forget the way Lisa had looked, squatting in the walk-in, stuffing clumps of raw hamburger into her mouth! Angie had insisted on staying at the hospital, but Mrs. Appleby had suffered enough. Her first thought was to get into bed and try her best to get some sleep before she fell apart entirely. During the drive home, she feared having nightmares of Lisa, eating raw meat.

The gray light of dawn had slowly brightened her bedroom window, but it wasn't until a beam of sunlight lanced through the curtains and hit her in the eyes that she stirred in her sleep. She pulled her pillow over her head and rolled away from the window, settling back into her thin, dream-disturbed sleep. The ding-dong of the door bell echoed distantly in her dreams, and it was only after the sound had been repeated several times that she woke up, got out of bed, and, tugging on her flannel robe, went downstairs to answer the door.

"Mr. Rodgers?" she said, forcing a sleepy smile, wishing she was still in bed. "What can I do for you?" Her first thought was that something had happened to Lisa during the night: Maybe she died! she thought, tensing; Rodgers was here to make "arrangements."

She looked past Rodgers and saw someone else standing on the steps, but he stood with his face turned to one side. She didn't know who it was at first. After a moment, though, she recognized the young man as the physician's assistant who had been to see Lisa last night, the one who had insisted he wasn't a doctor.

"I understand Mr. Harmon's daughter is staying here," Rodgers said. His voice was low and mellow, but there was an edge to it that immediately put Mrs. Appleby on guard.

"She and her father are renting a room, yes," she replied. She was leaning on the open door, and now she started to swing it shut, just a bit. She was telling herself not to worry, that there was nothing wrong, and Rodgers just had some business with Dale . . . but why would he ask for Angie?

"Is her father here?" Rodgers asked politely.

Mrs. Appleby couldn't stop staring at the man's left eye. The dilated pupil, ringed by a thin line of blue iris, seemed to swell and pulsate hypnotically.

"I—actually—I was out quite late last night," Mrs. Appleby said. She decided that telling a small lie right now wouldn't hurt anything. "Both he and his daughter are still asleep." She glanced over her shoulder at the clock in the entryway. "It is still quite early."

"I really must speak with Mr. Harmon's daughter," Rodgers said, his voice suddenly growing cold. "May I?"

Mrs. Appleby sensed trouble. And the way that Stephen Wayne looks! Good Lord, Mrs. Appleby thought, he looks like he hasn't bathed or slept in days! She eased the door shut a fraction more, leaning her weight onto the doorknob and mentally checking the position of the dead bolt lock.

"I'm sorry," she said, forcing her voice to stay calm even though she could hear a feathery pulse beat in her ears. "It's my policy not to disturb my guests when they are sleeping. Bad for business, you understand;"

She smiled to herself with the passing thought that Rodgers couldn't say the same: nothing was going to disturb *his* guests.

"Well," Rodgers drawled, "if you would be so kind as to check their room you'll see that Mr. Harmon did *not* come home last night. I have an urgent message for his daughter."

Maybe it was the man's strange eye, maybe it was the rather peculiar way Mr. Stephen Wayne lurked on the front steps, or maybe it was simply that she hadn't had enough rest after the tension of yesterday's events. Whatever it was, something tripped the alarm in her brain, and Mrs. Appleby was suddenly very resolved that under no circumstances would this man be allowed into her house.

"If there's been an accident of some kind — " she started to say, but Rodgers cut her off.

"Nothing of the sort," he said smoothly, the edge disappearing from his voice. He suddenly realized he didn't have a reasonable lie prepared to get past her defenses, so with a sudden lunge, he shouldered the door open, sending Mrs. Appleby reeling backward.

"In the name of God!" she sputtered as she bounced back hard against the grandfather clock. The impact made a loud gong sound as the heavy door swung open and banged against the wall, rattling the side light windows. Rodgers burst through the doorway, followed slowly by the young man who had attended Lisa.

"I don't have time for any games," Rodgers said, snarling as his eyes quickly scanned the rooms to the left and right. Then he tracked up the stairway.

"If you don't leave this *instant!*" Mrs. Appleby said, her voice nearly choking with rage. "I'll call the police."

In response, Rodgers turned back to Mr. Wayne and, with a quick nod of his head, pointed his forefinger at her and said simply, "Her! She's yours!"

A scream tried to build in Mrs. Appleby's chest and find its way out, but not even a faint hiss of air came from her lungs when she looked directly at Mr. Wayne. His face was drawn and pale, and there were heavy, black circles under his eyes. But when she looked at him squarely, she felt all of the gumption drain out of her. His eyes were glazed over, looking more like the blank stare of fake glass eyes than the eyes of a living person. The smile that spread across his face as he moved slowly toward her, his arms stiffly raised, was twisted, exposing his bottom teeth.

"You . . . you can't do this!" she shouted, raising her arms to protect herself. "You can't!" But her voice suddenly cut off when Mr. Wayne's hands grabbed her throat and steadily began to tighten. She tried to pull away, but the steely strength of the man's hands drove his fingertips into her throat. Colored star-bursts of light exploded across her vision, and then a swirling blackness began to spread inward, clouding over and blocking out the face that loomed closer to her.

From far away, as though he was in the next room, she heard Rodgers say, *"There you are Stephen . . . your first meal!"*

# IV

By early afternoon, they had the front door and all of the first story win-dows boarded over. They figured they might need the back kitchen door to get to the barn, so they left that unblocked but guarded by at least two of them at all times. Everyone's best guess was that Rodgers would send the zombies to the two doors. He wouldn't try a subtle approach.

Dale and Donna pawed through the junk down in the cellar, and after much searching, they had come up with an assortment of old tools that could be used as weapons. The best was an old axe. The handle was loose, but Dale secured it with a few strategically placed nails. Donna almost threw up when Dale pro-duced a rusty saw and described how they could use it to decapitate the crea-tures.

They found some lengths of two-by-fours and cut three of them to baseball bat length. Donna set to work, sanding and shaping one end of each into a smooth handgrip. She didn't like Dale's suggestion of driving some long nails through the other end to make a spiked club, but after she fashioned one, she decided it was a good idea.

"Maybe we can use this, too." Dale said. He had found several old gallon cans of paint on the bottom shelf of the workbench. He gave each one a shake, and found five that felt as though they still had something in them. Sitting down on the cellar floor, he pried off the lid of each. Three were almost full; two others were half full. The oil had separated to the top of the can, but by using a headless hammer handle, he broke the rubbery skim and mixed the paint.

"What good would that be?" Donna asked. She was busy shaving the ends of the two-by-fours. Her hair hung down in her face, and a slick of sweat glistened on her face and arms. She barely glanced up, but when she did, she couldn't help but gasp with surprise.

The light pink paint she recognized from the last time she and her mother had done over her bedroom. How old was I? she wondered. Maybe twelve or thirteen? Seeing that color, and all the memories it aroused, sent a wave of longing through her as she tried to connect the distant pleasure of her childhood with the terror of their present situation. She couldn't shake the disorienting feeling that this was someone else's life, not her own.

"Last minute desperation," Dale said, forcing a smile. "Throw a bucket of this into their faces, and even if they are already dead, they won't be able to see."

Donna shook her head and went back to work fashioning clubs, but her mind continued to replay fragments from her childhood.

Inside, the house was a shambles where they had torn apart cupboards and built-in bookcases, and hacked apart bedroom doors to nail into place. The house was also considerably darker in spite of the bright, late summer sunshine; only a few bars of light made it between the gaps they had left between the boards so they could see outside.

With only one hammer and the butts of Winfield's and Hocker's revolvers, the hammering had been frustrating and sloppy. When they were done, Dale and Winfield had their doubts that their barricade would hold up against even the least determined assault, but they still had the tunnel to the barn; at least he, Hocker, Tasha, and Donna, if she could get over her fear of the tunnel, could get away if worse came to worst.

"I still think he won't do anything until after dark," Dale said. They were all standing by the counter in the kitchen, passing around a cold can of Campbell's Minestrone soup, for lunch. Everyone was tired, and tempers were touchy after spending the morning preparing their defenses.

"I have a hunch these creatures can see better at night," Dale said. "When Larry was chasing us last night, he moved slowly, but it was very deliberately, as though he could see as clearly as if it was daylight."

"You said you thought this zombie drug Rodgers is experimenting with is made from potato plants, right?" Donna asked, looking at Winfield.

Winfield nodded. "Yeah, well, it seems pretty likely. You know, potato plants are in the same family as belladonna, deadly nightshade. I know back in the Renaissance, Italian women used a liquid form of Belladonna in their eyes, to make the pupils swell. It was considered a sign of great beauty."

Dale and Donna both looked at Winfield, barely able to suppress their laughter.

"And what," Donna asked, holding back a chuckle, "makes you such an expert on deadly nightshade?"

Winfield shrugged. "You live up here in potato country, you pick up plenty of interesting facts here and there. I think I learned that in a college literature class."

"His eye." Dale said, suddenly astounded. He brought his hand up to cover his mouth as his mind filled with the memory of Rodgers' left eye, the pupil swirling like a black pool.

"Huh?" Donna said.

"Rodgers' left eye." He looked from her to Winfield. "I didn't like it the moment I saw it; it bugged the crap out of me. Maybe he was using the drug on himself, too. Maybe he was experimenting on himself as well as the bodies of dead people."

"Right," Hocker said, snorting with laughter. "And the evil scientist, who's uncovered this dark secret of the universe, is being warped and twisted by this powerful *zombie* drug. It's turning him into a hideous creature! *Hah!* Bullshit!"

Winfield looked up at him, thinking if Hocker wanted a fantastic example of a hideous creature, all he would have to do is check out a mirror.

"Maybe," Dale said, his gaze drifting out of focus. He suddenly frowned as he looked at Hocker, who had the can of soup in hand and was freely swallowing great mouthfuls. "I've seen what they can do. So have you." He indicated Hocker's wounded shoulder. "I don't think this is just some bullshit fantasy I'm concocting here."

"Well for Christ's sake," Tasha said. She hadn't spoken much while they worked boarding up the windows, and her voice surprised all of them. "It doesn't really matter *what* these things are or what this guy Rodgers is doing with them. The point is, if we don't get out of here, we're all going to be dead soon!"

Dale wanted to say something to reassure her, but when he looked at her and thought how close in age she was to Angie, the numbing fear that Rodgers would try to hurt Angie to get at him gripped his bowels and wouldn't let go. He vowed to live long enough to kill Rodgers, with his bare hands if necessary, if he so much as looked at Angie!

"I still think this is bullshit," Hocker said. He spat over his shoulder, and everyone involuntarily watched the glob of spit splatter against the wall. "I say that fuck-face is bluffing us, and if we just run the hell out of here, we'll all get away."

"You first," Winfield said, glaring at him. "The back door's open."

"Fuck off," Hocker said, and he walked out into the living room, leaving the rest of them to finish the can of soup.

"I wish to hell we could get past that one out there," Winfield said, looking out the kitchen window at the man guarding the barn door. The slumped shape hadn't moved or flinched since it stopped there, and if he didn't know better, Winfield would have thought it was a mannequin or a scarecrow. He pounded his fist onto the countertop once in frustration, and then began pacing back and forth.

Dale was going to say something about the tunnel being a last resort, if they could trust Hocker not to take off without them, but before he could open his mouth, he noticed some movement outside. A dark figure, walked over to the man already standing by the barn door and took up a position beside him.

"Oh, shit," Dale said, pointing out the window. "Reinforcements just arrived."

As if in answer, Hocker shouted from the living room, "It's show-time, boys and girls! Your friend Rodgers just drove up!"

There was a wild flurry of activity as everyone moved into the positions they had decided upon. Winfield and Tasha stationed themselves by the kitchen door. Winfield held his revolver in one hand, and a nail-stubbed club in the other. Tasha gripped both hands tightly around the shovel handle. Dale considered their weakest point to be the kitchen door, so he had left all five cans of paint open on the counter. The smell added to the tension that was making Tasha's stomach churn.

Dale and Donna joined Hocker in the living room, where each of them took a post by one of the boarded up windows. Donna was holding one of her clubs, and Hocker held another one. His revolver was tucked into his waistband; he already knew, from painful experience how useless a gun was against these things.

As he leaned forward, squinting through a gap at the black limo parked in the driveway, Hocker tried not to think about the pain in his shoulder. He had put up a macho front when Tasha and Donna had cleaned and dressed the wound, but the truth was he felt as though he had been splashed with acid. The wound itself really hadn't been that bad. The zombie's smashed teeth had more shredded than actually gouged his skin; but the pain had continually gotten stronger, until it was now a steady throbbing. Every nerve, from the back of his neck to the base of his spine, was humming; and Hocker was positive it was spreading, as if the zombie's saliva was soaking through his skin like poison.

Dale and Donna were also peering out at where Rodgers had parked, and they watched, horrified, as several pale men dressed in heavy work clothes emerged from the limo and, under Rodgers' direction, positioned themselves around the house.

"If they come all at once, we don't stand a chance," Donna said softly. Her grip on the nail-studded club was so tight her fingers were going numb.

"How many do you think he had with him?" Dale asked.

"I counted at least twelve, maybe fifteen in all," Hocker said. He spat on the floor. Dale noticed Hocker was holding his wounded shoulder at an odd angle, but he didn't complain.

"Look, though," Hocker said with a grunt. "He's trying to get them to cooperate, but some of them are sort of drifting."

Sure enough, while Rodgers stood by the open limo door, shielding himself from any gunfire that might come from the house, he was indicating to each man where to go; but a few of the men seemed dazed as they wandered toward the house.

"If what you said was true about the drug," Donna said tightly, "maybe it takes away their will or something. They seem and act so mindless."

"That may be our only hope," Dale said. His hand tightened on the axe handle when one of the zombies lurched toward the house and stumbled up onto the porch.

The three of them waited tensely, and then there came a solid thump on the front door. Donna thought it was probably her imagination, but she was positive she had seen the door and the blockade buckle inward from the impact.

Dale shifted over to one side of the door and stood at ready, his knees slightly bent, the axe up over his head. As soon as a face or a hand came through the door, he was determined to lop it off with a single stroke. He didn't consider for very long whether or not the rusty axe head could really do that.

Then a harder blow shook the door. Hocker smiled, but Dale and Donna exchanged worried glances.

"It sounds like he could punch his way through the wall, never mind the door," Dale said.

Donna took another peek outside, and what she saw made her gasp. Three more of the zombies had approached the house. A twisted, snarling face loomed up in front of her, filling the crack where she was looking out. With a squeal, she fell backwards, covering her face with her arm when the glass exploded inward. She saw thin but strong-looking fingers reach in through the break and start clawing to remove the blocking wood.

"Hold tight!" Dale said. "If he starts getting through, whack him!"

The sound of breaking glass continued as the zombie pulled the window sash apart, clearing it out of his way, and then began hammering his fists on the wood nailed over the window. Donna watched with open-mouthed horror as the boards bounced with each hit. She focused on the nails, holding the wood to the inside window frame, and prayed earnestly for them not to slip out.

Hocker stayed where he was, watching Dale and Donna with a slight smile across his face. He kept glancing out through his slit to see if his window was also going to be the focus of an attack, but so far it wasn't.

Dale stood, frozen into position, as the zombie outside the door continued to rain heavy-fisted blows on the door. Everything, the door frame included, shook under the impact, and as much as he wanted to deny it, he was sure the barricade was gradually giving to the assault. His anger at Rodgers flared and grew stronger when he wondered if he had already been to Mrs. Appleby's and done something to Angie. He knew he had a responsibility to Angie to survive and find out if he had and take his revenge.

"It's not gonna hold," Donna said frantically.

"Be ready! Be ready!" Dale shouted, not taking his eyes from the door. As soon as he said that, the end of one of the blocking boards popped out and swung down. The hammering sound from outside grew louder and faster. Dale became convinced there were at least two of the creatures working to get the door down.

Finally, with a loud crack, one of the upper door panels broke inward in a shower of splinters. A big-knuckled fist shot in with it. Once inside, the fingers snapped open and reached blindly for something to snag onto. Dale tightened his stance and brought the axe down as hard as he could. The blade caught on the shattered wood, but enough of it hit the exposed wrist to do some damage. Dead and rotting muscles and tendons were torn open. The hand snapped back, flat against the inside of the door.

"Take that, you son-of-a-bitch," Dale snarled, curling his lips back and exposing his teeth in a savage grin. The fingers twitched, and the hoary fingernails made a weird tap-dancing sound on the wood. Dale pulled the axe back and swung it around quickly, before the creature could pull its hand out.

There was a loud snap as the hand severed at the wrist, and Dale watched, horrified, as it fell to the floor. For a second or two the fingers continued to twitch, but then they stopped, and the hand lay still, truly *dead*.

"Weird, huh?" Hocker said, standing there, watching. "No blood. No blood at all."

"Yeah," Dale said with a gasp, thinking he was going to throw up. "At least we won't make a mess on the floor."

Donna, meanwhile, was too busy watching her own window to pay attention to what was happening to Dale. Above the sound of shattering glass and breaking wood, she could hear the deep-gut grunting the creature made as he rammed his shoulder into the blockage. Every time he hit, the wood groaned. When it finally gave way, though, it wasn't slowly, as Donna had expected; the entire barricade suddenly shot inward, and right behind it was the bulky, dark shape of a man.

One piece of the flying wood caught Donna on the side of the jaw. The suddenness of the impact caught her by surprise, and she staggered back, dazed, as the coppery taste of blood filled her mouth.

It was more out of reflex than thought that Donna acted. She took a quick step forward and swung the club around with a low, whistling whoop. She hadn't even checked to see which side the nails were on, so only a corner of the wood connected with the man's head as he lunged through the open window. There was a satisfying sound that made her think of a baseball player swatting a home run, and the man collapsed with only half of his body inside the house.

Hocker let out a loud shout as he darted over beside Donna and brought his club down, time and again, on the back of the zombie's head. Each blow produced the sound of breaking bone as hair and skin peeled back, exposing the shattered skull. Splinters of bone stuck up through the dead skin, and Hocker caught a glimpse of the dark mess of exposed brain. The creature never flinched or stopped trying to propel itself into the house, though; arms and legs scrambled for purchase, and still the zombie struggled forward.

"Watch his hand!" Donna shouted, and Hocker had to take a quick leap backward to avoid getting tripped up. He knew how strong a hold these creatures could have, and there was no way he wanted to let this one get a hold on him.

"For Christ's sake! Don't just *stand* there!" Hocker shouted as he moved forward and continued to hammer on the man's head and shoulders, to no avail.

Donna wanted to help, but she couldn't bring herself to join in. All she could think was, not so long ago this man had been a living, breathing human being. It wasn't *his* fault he was what he was now. Even if he was just an empty shell, totally drained of true life, she couldn't bring herself to savage a human body. It was like corpse mutilation!

The zombie's fingers were clawing frantically at the floor. As Hocker pummeled its head, the nails of his club tore away large swatches of dead flesh. Then, one lucky swat severed the man's spine, and this, finally, had the desired effect. With a sudden growl, the zombie slumped to the floor face-first, his head hanging over his right shoulder at an impossible angle, looking up at the ceiling.

"That'll do it," Hocker shouted gleefully as he swung one last time at the twice-dead man. The head loosened some more but didn't quite come off; but Hocker could tell this one, at least, would give them no more trouble.

"See," Hocker shouted to Dale. "You just have to disconnect the brain from the body! Pull the plug on these bastards!"

"Great!" Dale replied. The handless arm had pulled back from the hole in the door, but the hammering on the door continued unabated. He glanced over at the corpse on the floor and the broken barricade. "Get that wood nailed back up if you can," he shouted, "before any more come."

Another face suddenly filled the hole in the door. When Dale swung the axe at it, the creature retreated. The axe head caught on the edge of the hole, and Dale almost lost his grip from the impact. As he was straightening up, regaining his balance, two more door panels broke inward, and soon the entire door and blocking wood were caving in.

# V

While Dale, Donna, and Hocker were defending the front of the house, Tasha and Winfield were busy at the kitchen door. Their problems were slightly less for two reasons: the door they were defending wasn't boarded over, so they had a clearer field of vision; and the two zombies who had been protecting the barn hadn't been joined by any others.

*Still, two of those creatures was problem enough, Winfield thought.*

Before the two zombies made their move toward the kitchen door, Winfield and Tasha had a few minutes to speak. Tasha maintained her quiet reserve, an attitude, Winfield had no doubt, she used with all authority figures, but she did, after a fashion, apologize for kicking him in the balls.

"Hey," Winfield said, "I've got to hand it to you. I've rousted drunks and dead-beats and vagrants for a good many years around here, and then it takes a teenage girl from Florida to scramble my eggs." He snorted with laughter and was pleased to see the slightest of smiles flit across Tasha's face.

"I've figured it out now, too," he said, keeping his eyes on the dark figures standing in front of the barn. "After you nailed me, I saw you run off into the woods, heading south when, actually, you wanted to be going north. You were trying to misdirect me, in case I caught my breath and gave chase, right?"

Tasha shrugged and looked down at the floor. "Yeah, it seemed like the thing to do."

"I think it was a pretty clever move, but I don't think your reason for doing it was very smart."

Tasha looked at him, her expression suddenly steely.

"I mean, if you were protecting *him!*" Winfield said, hiking his thumb toward the living room.

Tasha's gaze went in the direction he indicated, then she looked back at him and sighed deeply. She wanted to say something, but she didn't want to defend Hocker. She knew he was an asshole; he was just a little bit less of an asshole than most of the other men she had ever met.

What she didn't like was another thought that had reared up on her like a spooked horse: she was scared to death! And she knew they all were facing death here. Everything else Hocker had done—knocking that old man cold, stealing his truck and money, burning the truck—was like a joke compared to what was going on now! That man out there in the limo was using these *things* to try to kill them!

And even though she tried like hell not to react to this cop, calling her a "teenage girl," that was exactly what she was. She was a kid, and suddenly, actually without realizing it until it was too late, she had gotten in too damned deep. A phone call to her father wasn't going to patch this one up! Her parents' "emotional band-aids" weren't going to get her through this! What she was fighting was the feeling that all she wanted to do was just break down and fall apart. Let this big, tough cop and those other people in the house solve this problem for her. All she wanted to do was curl up in a corner somewhere, close her eyes, and cry until it was all over and she was safe ... or dead!

"You know, I meant what I said earlier about getting you off the hook," Winfield said, intruding on her thoughts.

Tasha looked at him, feeling equally attracted and wary. "And what makes you think I need your help?" she said. Even as the words were out of her mouth, she was angry at herself for acting so nasty, so stupid.

"Why?" Winfield said. "Because I've seen a lot of guys like Hocker in my time. They're what we cops call *Triple-P's*. That's short for 'piss-poor-protoplasm.'"

Tasha snickered and shook her head. "Aww. He ain't that bad," she said. "He may be a little fucked up, but who isn't?"

"Yeah, well, the offer stands," Winfield said. "If we get our butts out of here intact, I'll make sure you don't get in any deeper."

Oh, great, Tasha thought, just like dad: Mr. Fix-it!

They didn't have a chance to talk any more because just then both of the zombies by the barn started moving slowly forward, their blank gazes fixed on the kitchen door, arms extended.

Both creatures clambered up onto the porch at the same time, but the narrowness of the doorway forced one behind the other. The lead zombie thrust both hands straight through the glass, shattering it inward along with the snapped wood of the window grid. The creature's knees pounded against the door, making the whole frame rattle as it pushed forward.

Winfield watched, fascinated, for several seconds as the creature mindlessly tried to grab at them through the broken window. The door was just a momentary impediment, he knew, but he couldn't keep himself from staring at this *thing* that had been turned from a human being into a monstrous parody of life.

Tasha was cringing back, away from the door. One hand loosely held the shovel; the other was clamped across her mouth, muffling the screams that vibrated her throat. Winfield gave her a quick, reassuring nod, then raised his revolver and fired rapidly, point-blank, at the zombie's face.

The revolver kicked in his hand as it spat out lead, but the bullets had about as much effect on the creature as if they had shot through paper. Small, dark holes like black marbles appeared in the zombie's forehead, but his eyes never blinked; his face never flinched as he reached into the kitchen.

"Hocker told you that wouldn't do anything!" Tasha screamed, shifting backward toward the cellar door.

Winfield smiled grimly and, not taking his eyes off the creature, said, "I just had to see for myself." He slipped his revolver into its holster, gripped his makeshift club with both hands, and leaned into a vicious swing at the creature's head.

There was a satisfying whack upon impact, and the creature sagged to one side, but still there was no change of expression in its eyes. It unblinkingly groped forward ... to *kill!*

Tasha's screaming rose shrilly when the door, with the added weight of the second creature bearing down on it, suddenly caved in. Winfield was caught by surprise and was knocked backward against the counter. His club clattered to the floor. When he dove for it, his hands just missed it. A sudden, crushing weight dropped onto his back, forcing the air from his lungs in one big burst.

Tasha almost turned and ran, but she felt a sudden loyalty to this man. She brought the shovel around in a whistling swing, and she couldn't help but smile when the shovel blade caught the first zombie under the right ear and sliced cleanly through the putrid flesh.

Winfield never made a sound as he worked under the weight of the zombie to get his club. In less than a few seconds dirt-crusted teeth would be working their way into his living flesh. The panic that seized him was nearly blinding, and even though he couldn't breathe, he kept his focus clearly on the club; that was the only thing that was going to save his ass!

Glancing over her shoulder, Tasha saw the second zombie lurching through the door, its eyes fixed blankly on her. She swung the shovel again and caught this one squarely in the chest. The shovel *thumped* into the creature's chest, ripping it open to expose a xylophone of yellowed ribs. The creature was knocked back a few steps, but he regained his balance and started forward again just as Tasha swung again.

"Die! Goddamn you! *Die!*" Tasha wailed as she swished the shovel back and forth like a razor-sharp pendulum. Each swipe cut into the creature, exposing bone and blackened muscle, but it didn't stop coming at her!

"You son-of-a-bitch! *Die!*"

She spied the opened cans of paint on the counter top, with a few quick sidesteps, moved between the door and the scrambling mass of Winfield and his attacker. When one particularly firm hit had sent the zombie attacker reeling, she quickly turned and grabbed a can of paint and tossed it straight into the zombie's face.

The effect was exactly what she had wanted! The creature didn't hesitate as it continued to move forward, but now it was blind; she had the edge! With that to bolster her confidence, she braced the shovel close to her body, like a knight's lance, and jabbed it directly under the creature's jaw. Pink paint dribbled and splashed everywhere, a crazy parody of the blood this thing should have been shedding. The zombie's head snapped backward, and there was a stomach-wrenching snap as the rotted spine broke. The head dropped to the floor with a dull thump, and the body crumpled down after it, landing right in the puddle of paint.

Winfield, meanwhile, was struggling to keep the creature's open jaws away from him. He knew he couldn't keep this up for long. His lungs felt like they were on fire, and his arms ached as if he were trying to bench-press a Mack truck. With a frantic lunge, he finally managed to grab his club and bring it around. Using the heel of it, he pounded the zombie's face just as it was opening its mouth and leaning down to set its teeth into his neck. The only sound Winfield was conscious of was his own roaring intake of breath as the weight on him eased up enough to breathe.

The creature's long fingernails scraped across his scalp, spreading neon-bright pain along his nerves. The teeth, clicking and clacking, came closer to the top of his head.

All Winfield could think was, *This is it! I'm done for!* But then the creature suddenly lurched to the side and, looking up, Winfield saw Tasha, standing over him, smiling grimly. She had brought the shovel blade down hard onto the back of the creature's neck, and the blow had severed the spine, disconnecting the brain.

The zombie's head hung back over its left shoulder blade as it fell backward onto the floor. Winfield hurriedly kicked the dead body aside, stood up, and took a quick inventory of himself to make sure he wasn't wounded; he knew the adrenalin charge of fighting could numb the pain of a severe wound, and he didn't want to find himself collapsing suddenly from loss of blood. But the scalp wound was the total of his injuries, so he and Tasha set to work, cleaning up the damage.

"Where are we gonna put . . . *those?*" Tasha asked, wrinkling her nose as she pointed down at the two headless corpses.

Winfield glanced around the kitchen, then smiled when he saw the storage closet by the cellar door. "Stuff 'em in there, I suppose," he said. "I don't particularly relish the thought of dragging 'em outside. First, though, I want to get that door back up and nail as many boards over it as we can. There'll be more of them!"

Tasha shivered as she looked at the smashed down doorway. "Maybe we can put something across it, like those bars they used to block castle gates. I don't want to get trapped in here with all the doors locked."

Winfield looked at her, his gaze suddenly darkening. "If I tell you something, will you promise not to tell your friend Hocker about it?"

Tasha smirked and, shaking her head in agreement, said, "He's not my friend. We sorta ended up together on the road. You don't know how many times I wanted to dump him and take off on my own."

Winfield understood the dynamics of the situation. As crazy as Hocker was, Tasha felt secure with him, probably because he had never tried to put the make on her, and because he was nuts enough to do some fairly outrageous things. She probably thought that would translate into protection for her if worse came to worse.

But worse had come to worse, Winfield thought, and Hocker hadn't shown any signs of untapped nobility.

"But you didn't leave him," he said. "And you've got to admit, you're in pretty deep this time."

Tasha had to look away, and when she did, her stomach did a quick flop over. Spread on the floor in front of her were two dead men and these weren't the first she had helped kill. She was sure, now, that the three men who had attacked her and Hocker in the woods two nights ago had been creatures like these. She knew how lucky they were to have survived that attack. Pink paint, the color of Canada Mints, was splattered all over the walls and floor. The splintered door was wide open, an invitation to enter if there were any more of those *things* out there. And she *knew* there were more out there!

Tears welled up in her eyes, blurring her vision of the kitchen, so she kept her face turned away from Winfield. But when a deep sob shook her body, she knew she couldn't hide it any more, and with a shuddering groan, she fell into his arms and buried his face in the hefty warmth of his chest.

"It's okay," Winfield said softly as he stroked her hair. He was glad she had finally broken down. He knew that's what had to happen before she would find the courage to shake herself free of the control Hocker exercised over her. Winfield was keeping his eyes fixed on the opened doorway, positive that, as soon as he let his guard down, more of those creatures would come piling through the door and swarm all over them.

Tasha's shoulders shook as she cried into his shoulder. Her tears were hot, and her breath caught in her throat. Sniffing, Tasha looked up at him, her face streaked with tears. He found himself imagining that she was his daughter, and that made him think about the wife he had never had and the children he would never raise.

"Over by the coal bin where Hocker kept us tied up last night, there's a narrow tunnel way that leads out to the barn," Winfield said. Only with great effort could he keep his voice from breaking.

Tasha started to say something, but her voice chocked off.

"Dale and I have been thinking about it, and we think if things get really bad up here, the rest of you, including Hocker can easily fit through. Once you get to the barn, you can either high-tail it into the woods or, if my cruiser still runs, drive on out of here."

"What about you?" Tasha asked, sniffing loudly and running the back of her hand under her eyes.

Winfield chuckled. "A few too many sugar donuts at Kellerman's," he said slapping his paunch. His other hand was still resting lightly on Tasha's shoulder.

"And then what are you gonna do?" Tasha asked, her eyes suddenly darkening.

Winfield smiled and winked at her. "I'll be waiting for you by the back door," he said.

"There's just one problem I see," Tasha said with a deep sigh. "You've got to tell Hocker 'cause he's got the keys to your cruiser."

Winfield raised his hand to his forehead and gingerly probed his scalp wound. "Well, yeah, he does ... but I'd be a pretty big fool if I didn't have my ass covered, wouldn't I? Remember the hand cuff key in my shoe?"

Tasha nodded.

"On the cruiser, inside the rear wheel well on the passenger's side, if you reach way up inside there, you'll find a small metal box, stuck up there by a magnet. Inside is a set of keys to the cruiser. I haven't even told Dale this, yet, so I'm trusting you to keep my secret, just in case we get the keys back from Hocker."

"But why won't you tell him about your plans?" Tasha said. She couldn't deny that she felt quite a bit better, now that she had gained Winfield's confidence; but she still felt some shreds of loyalty to Hocker. He had, after all, stuck with her all the way from North Carolina to Maine!

"We'll tell him when we're ready to tell him," Winfield said. "He's not exactly number one on my list of favorite people, and there's no guarantee he won't take off by himself."

Tasha smiled and snickered. "He's not exactly tops on mine, either," she said.

"Well—uh, we have some work to get done here," he stammered, rubbing his hands together. Tasha was smiling, but he could see the fear, the jacked-deer nervousness, returning to her eyes. "Come on, give me a hand with this."

She helped him lift up a corner of the broken-down door, and together they wrestled the remains of the door back into place. They got the ball peen hammer from Dale and some nails, and while Tasha held crossing boards in place, Winfield started banging in the nails. By the time they had the door barricaded again and the two headless corpses crammed into the closet, the sun was high in the sky, hammering down with a last burst of summer heat. It was still hours until sunset, and everyone in the house knew they had to come up with some kind of plan, *soon!*

# VI

After the first wave of zombies at the doors things quieted down for a while in the yard. Through the slats of wood, Dale and Winfield kept watch over the limo parked in the driveway, but there was no sign of either Rodgers or his army of zombies.

The supply of food Tasha had bought in town was nearly exhausted, and so were the defenders. The lack of sleep the night before and the strain of watching and waiting in the darkened farm house were starting to wear on everyone's nerves, especially whenever Winfield and Hocker were in the same room. While one person watched in the living room and another guarded the kitchen door, the others tried to catch a few minutes of sleep, but it didn't do much good for anyone.

At three o'clock that afternoon, Dale, unable to sleep, came into the kitchen where Donna was on watch. Her face was drawn and pale from lack of sleep, but underneath it all, he could still see her beauty shining through. He tried, not very successfully, not to think what she would look like if she became one of Rodgers' creatures.

"You know, sometimes I just can't help but think this is still just some wild nightmare I'm having," Donna said. "It's like all the bad things I ever said about this town and this house have come back to destroy me. I keep wondering, too, if, when I wake up, will I even have returned to Dyer." She looked at Dale, and he didn't like the darkness he saw reflected in her eyes like storm clouds. "I keep wondering if, when I wake up, I'll even have met you yet."

"Don't be silly," Dale said softly. He touched her lightly on the cheek, and she kissed his fingertips when they brushed her mouth.

"But that's all life is, isn't it?" she said, her eyes darkening even more. "Just one big dream and then— *poof!*—it's over." She chuckled and shook her head. "I remember, even when I was a little girl that song, 'Row, Row, Row Your Boat,' used to scare the shit out of me sometimes."

Dale smiled widely. "Now I know the strain's getting to you."

"It was always that last line in the song," Donna said. "'Merrily, merrily, merrily; life is but a dream.' I remember, sometimes we'd be singing it in kindergarten or first grade, and I'd get this chill. I'd get so freaked, thinking, Oh my God! This *is* all just a dream! . . . Crazy, huh?"

Dale shrugged. "I don't think so," he said. "I never thought 'Row Your Boat' was particularly scary, but everybody has things that unnerve them."

"I wonder what it's like for *them,*" Donna said, her voice distant, as though she had barely registered what Dale had said.

"Who?" he asked.

"For those *things* Rodgers is sending after us," Donna said, looking at him with a cold, hard stare filled with unspoken fright.

*Life may be just a dream,* he thought, *but ours sure as shit is turning into a nightmare!*

"I wonder if they even know they're alive, or dead, or whatever!" Dale said. "Are they in some kind of zombie twilight zone, where they know they're *neither* alive nor dead?"

"I wonder if, Larry . . ." her voice cut off, but she forced herself to continue. "I wonder if he *recognized* you. If somewhere a tiny, little spark in the back of his mind registered that you had once been his best friend long ago, like in another life, or something."

"You know what I think?" Dale said, suddenly very firmly. "I think if you keep wondering things like that, you're going to screw up your mind. What we have to deal with is getting out of here! We don't have to figure anything out about these things! We just have to get away from them!" In his mind, he added—*And find Angie!*

"And how are we going to do that?" Donna snapped. "Are we just going to sit here and wait for him to send more? How many more do you think he has? He may have been doing this for years and have a whole Goddamn army of them. He'll wear us down. And even if he doesn't have many more, as soon as it's dark he'll finish us off. If we don't get out of here before sunset, we've had it!"

"Maybe not," Dale said. He paced across the kitchen floor, slapping the axe head repeatedly into the flat of his hand. "But I think-I can't help but think that it's run its course for Rodgers. Winfield is missing, and you didn't show up at your sister's, and I never returned to Mrs. Appleby's. By now, Angie's got to be wondering where I am. She'll call the State Police, the National Guard, and the FBI to find me!"

Donna looked at him and felt a deep ache of longing. She didn't want to remind him that Rodgers had threatened to visit Angie *first*. If Dale believed they had a realistic chance to get out of here, then so what? Let him be.

"I've been thinking, though," Donna said, "that maybe we should try to get out through the tunnel. I'll make myself go down there if I really *have* to."

"Go down *where?* Hocker said, entering the kitchen. His mouth spread into a thin, wicked smile as he walked over to them. *"What* tunnel are you talking about?"

# CHAPTER ELEVEN
## "A NARROW ESCAPE"

## I

The afternoon slowly slipped away. There was a gradual lessening of light in the house. Only a few bars of light made it through the gaps between the wooden slats. The living room faded grayer and grayer, until only a dim duskiness remained.

Winfield spent most of the day sitting in the living room, talking with Donna and Dale. He seemed to be particularly avoiding Hocker, although it seemed to Dale that as though he was waiting for an excuse to nail Hocker a good one. Hocker, for his part, realized how Winfield felt about him because he made a point of avoiding the cop, too.

Tasha talked with Donna because, she said, she was sick of being around Hocker. She seemed interested in Donna's childhood, growing up in this house, it was so different from the world she had known, growing up in Florida. When Tasha mentioned how foolish she had been to hook up with Hocker in the first place, Donna told her about her own foolish attachment to Bradley Phillips.

When they had gotten trapped in the house, Donna had only half a pack of cigarettes in her purse, and throughout the day she smoked them all. Now that she needed cigarettes, she told Dale jokingly that they'd better get out of there real soon. But the zombies milling around in the yard, waiting for the word to attack the house again, convinced them not to try anything rash.

At four o'clock, Winfield and Dale cornered Hocker in the kitchen and demanded the keys to the police cruiser.

"What makes you think I want to give them to you?" Hocker asked, his upper lip snarling back.

Trying to keep his voice as even as possible, Winfield said simply, "Because if you don't, I'll kick your ass so hard your sphincter is gonna pop out your mouth. That's why."

Hocker wasn't quite sure what a "sphincter" was, so to cover his ignorance, he laughed and spat onto the floor. He stood with his arms folded defiantly across his chest.

"Look, Hocker," Dale said, playing the pacifist, "we're all in this together. If we can get to the cruiser, we're home free. We'll be able to nail Rodgers before he gets anyone else."

"You'll also be able to nail my ass," Hocker said, staring harshly at Winfield. Again he spit, this time at the wall. The glob of spit slid slowly down to the baseboard.

"Listen, asshole," Winfield said, taking a threatening step toward Hocker. "That's my cruiser, state property, and if you don't cooperate, you can bet your last ass-hair I'm gonna hang you out to dry. I don't know what you've done on your way up here, but I've got you on enough counts so by the time yon get out of jail, your clothes will be long out of style."

Hocker pointed at Dale, his forefinger shaking, but whether from nervousness or anger, Dale wasn't sure. "I still want to know what he was talking about with his woman."

"Donna isn't my woman," Dale said, finding it difficult not to detest this guy. The thought of leaving Hocker behind as an appetizer for Rodgers' creatures arose in his mind as an attractive option.

"Whatever," Hocker said. "I want to know what she meant about this tunnel."

Dale and Winfield exchanged glances, then Winfield spoke. "You just hand over the keys to the cruiser, and we'll let you know." He fell silent when Tasha wandered into the living room and sat down beside him.

Now, Winfield thought, is the test. Will she tell Hocker about the spare key under the wheel well?

"We're *all* going to get out of here if any one of us does," Hocker said. "And I ain't giving you the keys until I know what the hell you guys've been planning."

Tasha opened her mouth, started to say something, but then shook her head and walked away.

"All right," Winfield whispered softly to himself. He then turned to Hocker and, holding out his hand, keeping his voice as friendly as he could, said, "Hand over those keys, and I'll forget all about the charges I could press against you."

"Yeah . . . sure," Hocker said, studying him in the gloom of the living room. He had fought hand-to-hand with two of those *things* out there. The last thing he wanted was to be left behind when everyone else made a break for it.

"What about other stuff I might have done, laws I might have broken?"

"Give me the keys and we'll talk about it," Winfield said, bringing his hand closer to Hocker. He fought the urge to grab his shirt, curl it into a tight-fisted ball, and shake the living shit out of him.

"You don't need to know shit about what I've done," Hocker said angrily. "Get me off the hook, and I'll . . ." He dropped his hand down. For a flickering instant, Winfield was sure he was going for the gun stuck into the top of his pants. Winfield's hand snapped down to his service revolver but then stopped when he saw Hocker's hand slide into his pocket. He slowly withdrew and held up the ring of keys, sparkling unnaturally bright in the dim room.

"Thanks, boy." Winfield said as he snatched the keys from Hocker's hand. He bounced them reassuringly in his hand a few times, then slipped them into his own pants pocket.

Hocker took one threatening step closer to Winfield, his face contorted with anger.

"Don't you ever call me *boy* again!" he said, his voice low and gravelly. "You understand?"

Winfield smiled, completely unfazed.

"Sure thing," he said, his smile widening. "No problem, boy."

# II

Half an hour later, Hocker was sleeping soundly. He had probably missed more sleep than anyone else, and after his confrontation with Winfield, he went upstairs, explaining he needed to get some rest away from their senseless chit-chat.

Leaving Tasha at the foot of the stairs to guard against Hocker or the creatures, Dale, Donna, and Winfield went into the kitchen to plan their next move. Donna was convinced Rodgers hadn't called things off. She believed he was waiting until dark, when darkness would handicap them enough so he could finish them off. Dale and Winfield agreed with her.

"What we need first of all is something for light," Dale said.

"Let's call up Northern Maine Power and ask them to hook us up," Donna said. Her attempted humor fell flat.

"If Ass-face here didn't dump them out when he trashed my car, I have a tank of gasoline and a package of roadside flares in the trunk of my cruiser," Winfield said. "We could wrap some cloth around a couple of two-by-fours and use them for torches."

"The problem there is getting the damned gas," Dale said. Glancing at Donna to gauge her reaction, he asked her, "Think you could hack it?"

"Hack what?" Donna asked.

"Going down the tunnel to the barn, to see if there's anything left in the cruiser we can use. I don't want to bring Hocker in on this yet. I don't trust him."

Donna shook her head. "I know I sound like a wimp, but I just don't think I could do it."

Taking a deep breath, Dale held his hand out to Winfield and said, "Let me have the keys. I'll give it a try, but I've got an idea. It might be kind of crazy."

Both Donna and Winfield gave him questioning looks.

"I think we've seen enough *crazy* to accept anything you might have in mind," Winfield said.

"I think we've got a chance here to do a little more than get away," Dale said. "Winfield won't fit in the tunnel, so we'll get him out another way. Maybe we can try to lure a lot of those creatures into the cellar after us. We could then touch off a fire using the gas from the cruiser and get rid of the whole lot of them at once."

"You're right," Winfield said. "That *is* crazy."

"Do you want to let those things keep living?" Donna asked, turning on him. "Maybe Dale's right."

"It's just an idea," Dale said, pressing the point. "But we can assume a couple of things. First of all, I think Donna's right. Rodgers has just pulled back and is waiting for the opportune time to send every thing he's got against us. And two, I think we can be pretty sure our defenses aren't going to hold out for long under a determined attack."

"If we get out of here with our skins, that should be enough," Winfield said. "To stop these things, all we've got to do is nail Rodgers' ass to the wall!" His upper lip glistened with sweat, and it was obvious to Dale that Winfield was thinking how it was easy enough for the rest of them—they had their escape route, he didn't.

"We're going to have to deal with Rodgers," Dale said. "If we've wiped out most of them, we'll be in a little bit better position."

Winfield winced when he unthinkingly scratched his scalp wound, then nodded in agreement. "I suppose we have to try it," he said. "So what's the first step?"

"The first step," a voice suddenly rang out, "is to let *me* set the fire."

There was a heavy tread of boots on the stairs as Hocker came downstairs, shouldered past Tasha, and came into the kitchen. Tasha followed behind him, but Dale asked her to go into the living room and keep an eye on the front of the house.

"Light sleeper, huh?" Winfield said, cocking an eye- brow at him.

Hocker ignored him and spoke to Dale. "God puts everyone on this earth with a talent, right? Well, the Good Lord saw fit to make me pretty fucking good at setting fires."

Winfield's eyebrows suddenly shot up. "So you *are* the guy they've got on the A.P.B.? The one who's been torching buildings all the way up the East Coast."

Hocker smiled with pride and nodded. "I might have had a little something to do with a few of them. Call it a hobby."

Winfield's fists clenched, and he took a threatening step toward Hocker. "It's a damned expensive hobby! It's assholes like you who start fires, but it's the local firemen who have to breathe the smoke and risk their lives putting them out."

Hocker shook his head, holding his ground against the cop. "I never torch a building that's being used, ever! I do empty warehouses or barns. *Never* houses!"

"The fires still have to be put out!" Winfield shouted. Nothing would please Winfield more than to wrap both hands around Hocker's neck and squeeze until it snapped.

"That ain't the point right now, pencil-dick," Hocker said with a snort. "If you want this house to go *whoosh,* I can set it up so it'll go up *good."*

Donna shifted uncomfortably. "Wait a minute—all of you," she said, her voice trembling. "This is my family's house, for God's sake! And you're talking about burning it down as if it meant nothing to anyone."

Dale turned to her and grasped her by the arms. "This isn't something we're taking lightly. But we have to destroy as many of these creatures as we can. We certainly don't want a whole army of them parading down Main Street, do we?"

"Of course not," Donna replied, shaking her head. "But this is where I grew up. This is my home."

"Lookee-here," Hocker said, rubbing his hands together vigorously. "You want this place to burn, I can do it. You . . ." He pointed at Dale. "Do what the man says, 'n go get that can of gasoline from the cruiser."

"Get the road flares too," Winfield added.

"Road flares," Hocker said appreciatively. "Nice touch. You bring 'em back here while we scramble up some nice flammable material and we'll have ourselves a regular weenie roast."

# III

Dale descended into the cellar with only a flashlight, no weapons because he needed one hand free to carry the gasoline tank. Anyway, if he met any of those zombies out in the open, any number of weapons weren't going to help him.

Winfield and Tasha were posted at the kitchen door, and Hocker stood guard in the living room, ready to signal if Rodgers or his creatures knew Dale was heading toward the barn. Except for Rodgers' limo, still parked in the driveway, the yard had been deserted for the past three hours.

Dale tensed as he knelt down in front of the black opening and aimed the flashlight beam along the dirt-lined floor.

"You know," he said, "I keep hoping you'll suddenly say something like 'Hey! Wait a minute! I'll do it for you!' "

He looked at Donna, his mouth set in a curious twist.

"I wish I could," she said, her voice low, "but if you only knew what I went through with this place when I was a kid, you'd understand. I'm terrified."

"For us to get away later, you're going to have to do it," Dale said.

Donna nodded. "Yeah . . . maybe. But it'll only be once. And with all the rest of us. I could never do it alone."

Dale smiled weakly, wondering if he was ready to do it alone. The fear that, somewhere down that tunnel, the walls would suddenly narrow and close in on him, kept whispering in the back of his mind. But it was either him or Hocker, and they all agreed that Hocker couldn't be trusted to do *anything* once he was out on his own. With Winfield's key ring in his pocket, a flashlight in hand, and one last kiss from Donna on his cheek, he got down onto his hands and knees and started to crawl.

The tunnel was narrower than it had looked, Dale soon found out. The tight, dark walls closed in around him like a huge throat threatening to swallow him. The beam of his flashlight cut a sharp V into the blackness which he followed, not even knowing when—or *if*—he would find his way out. His hands and knees were scraped raw on the tunnel floor, but the worst pain was in his back. It scraped repeatedly against the stone ceiling, and he could feel the bleeding on his back.

Can they smell fresh blood? Dale wondered with a tingling sense of fear as he forged ahead into the darkness. Will they sniff me out?

He kept talking with Donna as he moved down the tunnel, which slanted to the left slightly and seemed to be dropping a bit. His words echoed around him with an uncomfortable closeness, and soon, Donna's replies were nothing more than a garbled distortion of sound. His breath felt hot and close to him, like the breath of an animal waiting to pounce.

Dale followed the jiggling flashlight beam as he baby-crawled forward, wondering where this tunnel was leading. The floor was bone-dry, and every time he placed his hand down, a small puff of choking dust would rise like smoke. Sooty gray cobwebs shifted in the disturbance of his passing, and all along the tunnel there was evidence of rodent droppings.

Dale feared that somehow Rodgers knew about their plan; he had discovered the opening of the tunnel at the other end and had already sent one of his zombies down to intercept him. In the pressing darkness, Dale tried not to think what he would do if the face of one of those dead creatures suddenly loomed out of the darkness in front of him. The only reassuring thought was that, hopefully he would die of fright before those teeth tore him apart.

The further he went, the more Dale became convinced Donna was wrong: this tunnel didn't lead to the barn at all. His best guess was that he already had passed underneath the barn and was heading God knows where! He wanted to look behind him, to see if he could see the light of the cellar opening, however dim; but the tunnel snuggled him like a strait-jacket, and the few times he reflexively turned his head around, he banged his forehead on the stone wall.

This is *bullshit!* he thought, and he laughed. Was that his own laughter echoing in the darkness ahead of him, or was it . . . one of *them?*

The urge to turn around welled in him like a hot spring, ready to explode into the upper air. If the tunnel didn't lead up to the barn—and it should have done that by now! his brain screamed—but dead-ended instead, how in the name of Christ was he going to get out of there?

Would he have to crawl, slowly and painfully, backwards the whole way?

Donna's fear of entering the tunnel suddenly made sense. In the short time he had been down here in the pressing darkness, he felt his mind slipping its gears. If this went on for much longer when he ever made it back to the surface, he would be a blithering idiot for the rest of his life. He'd leave the last shreds of his sanity down here in. the cold, dark earth.

All the lights are on, but nobody's home, his mind sang in a high-pitched, singsong voice.

Was that him laughing again?

Or was it someone else?

Maybe *something* else?

The tunnel gradually curved around to the left, and as he crawled along it — faster, now, as his anxiety rose—he was sure, at least he *hoped,* the floor was pitching upward. If it was, could it mean he had misjudged? Maybe he would still come up inside the barn, as Donna had said he would.

He tried to force certain thoughts out of his mind.

—*that even if he did come up in the barn, he would find the place swarming with Rodgers' creatures . . .*

—*that he would find the trap door up into the barn, but it would be nailed shut, or Winfield's cruiser would be parked right over it—that he wouldn't be able to get out . . . he would have to return to the cellar, crawling backwards! . . .*

—*that he would emerge into the barn, a pale, aged, white-haired corpse-like creature, and Rodgers would be sitting on the fender of Winfield's cruiser, smiling as he said . . . "Welcome . . ."*

—*that he would get the gasoline and flares, and once he got back to the house, he would find ail of them —even Donna—dead!*

— *that the dust from the tunnel floor was caking his nose and throat shut—that moistened with his own mucous, the dust would become as hard as cement and seal his breath in his lungs as surely as his body would be sealed in the earth.*

The flashlight was slippery in his sweating hand as he forced himself to forge ahead. What choice is there, anyway? he thought. The chances were that none of them would make it safely out of here. What he was doing now was a fool's mission. Soon they would all be *dead* fools!

He pushed ahead, not sure at all how long he had been underground or how far he had come. The gradual rise of the floor continued and in that Dale found a sliver of hope. When he angled his flashlight toward the wall, his eyes caught a dull, glowing gray light up ahead.

*Daylight?*

His heart stopped for a moment, and, holding his breath, he snapped off the flashlight.

*Yes! There it was! Up ahead!*

Suddenly, all of his fears melted away. This was definitely a way out. The clear light of day was filtering down into the mouth of the tunnel's end. I'm going to make it!, Dale thought joyfully.

He realized the need for caution now. If any of Rodgers' creatures were in the barn, there was no sense alerting them to his presence. The dim glow of light up ahead was enough to hearten him as he crawled slowly forward until he came to a blocking door almost identical to the one they had removed in the cellar. Pressing his face close to one of the several thin openings between the planks of wood, he looked up and saw to his amazement the arching roof of a barn.

"Hot-damn!" he whispered, slapping his fist onto the tunnel floor. He craned his neck, trying to see around inside the barn, but his field of vision was severely restricted. There might be zombies up there. He was just going to have to chance it.

As best he could in the tight confines of the tunnel, Dale wiped the sweat from his face with his shirtsleeve. Then, bracing his feet on one side of the tunnel and his back on the other, he leaned his shoulder against the wooden doorway and pushed up. He pushed until his pulse pounded in his ear and sweat dripped down his face. Soft grunts came from deep in his belly; but the doorway didn't yield an inch. He pushed until pin-pricks of light popped in the darkness, until his breath built up inside his chest like a fire, waiting to burst into the open air. He pushed, but the door wouldn't budge!

He fell back against the tunnel wall breathless from the exertion, his muscles trembling. All he could think about was how much trouble they had tearing down the door on the cellar end of the tunnel, and he cursed himself for being a fool and not bringing the ball-peen hammer to help him tear this one down! It was so damned stupid, to come this far and then not be able to make it!

"I want to speak with Mr. Harmon!" a voice suddenly called out from the front yard.

Hocker, who had left his post watching the driveway, darted to the window and looked outside. The sudden, bright sunlight stung his eyes, but he saw Rodgers, standing beside his limo, shielding his body with the open car door.

"Can you hear me in there?" Rodgers shouted, cupping his hands to his mouth. "I said I want to speak with Harmon!"

Hocker glanced over his shoulder as Winfield came into the living room and took a look for himself out another window. In his hand, Winfield held the axe Dale had been using.

"I know you're still there!" Rodgers shouted. "I've had the entire building surrounded all along. There's no way you could have escaped. I insist on speaking with Mr. Harmon."

"He don't wanna talk to you!" Hocker yelled, pressing his mouth close to one of the openings. He stuck his gun out through a crack and fired off one shot. The bullet went wild, and Rodgers didn't even flinch.

"You're wasting my time," Rodgers said. "I wish to make you a sort of offer."

"An offer I can't refuse, no doubt," Winfield said, smiling grimly. He was taking his time, studying the man. On the outside, he looked completely composed and in control; but Winfield thought he detected signs of strain in the tightness of his voice and the way he stood. Things had started to unravel, quite seriously. Rodgers was going to have to do some very creative covering up if his experiments weren't going to be "found out" by the authorities.

"You can take your fucking deals and stuff 'em where the sun don't shine!" Hocker shouted. He was feeling agitated, not so much from the strain of being trapped in the farmhouse as from the anticipation of torching the place off. It had been a long time since he had seen those gorgeous tongues of orange flame licking skyward.

"May I speak with Mr. Harmon?" Rodgers called out. "You can tell him I have his daughter with me."

"He's bullshitting us," Hocker said, glancing at Win-field with a deep frown.

"No shit," Winfield said. He was no fool at reading people, and he knew right away that Rodgers had played it all wrong. He had thrown his trump card before he should have. A fool could see he had no idea where Angie was, and he was using this simply to draw Dale out into the open.

"Harmon isn't talking with you," Winfield said. "He's asleep. Your friends kept us awake all night. Anything you've got to say. you can say to me."

"Who the hell are *you?*" Rodgers yelled. His face looked pinched with frustration at not getting what he wanted.

Winfield let out a loud burst of laughter. "Rodgers, this is your old buddy from town, Jeff Winfield. I didn't think you knew I was here."

"Winfield . . ." Rodgers said, his voice soft but still carrying across the yard.

"Uh-huh. And I'd bet right about now, you're starting to think things may be a little worse than you thought," Winfield said, seeing the advantage and taking it. He raised the axe and slapped the rusty head into the flat of his hand.

"Who else is in there with you?" Rodgers asked.

"Just some friends we picked up along the way," Winfield answered. "I think I'd like to keep you guessing."

"No matter!" Rodgers suddenly yelled, stiffening his back. "I half-suspected you were on to me back when our good friend Larry Cole was asking so many embarrassing questions around town. Poor Larry. I suppose he's *really* dead now."

"For good," Winfield replied.

Rodgers paused for a moment, turned and looked over at the abandoned barn, then he continued, "Do you want to hear my deal?"

"Talk all you want. I'm not going anywhere," Winfield shouted.

"I want all of you in there to give yourselves up!" Rodgers said. "You can make it easy, or you can make it hard, but one thing is certain: all of you are dead as it is. If you give yourselves up now, I'll promise you one thing."

"Yeah, and what's that?" Winfield asked in the brief pause that followed.

"That after you're dead," Rodgers said, and a wicked smile flashed across his face. "I promise I'll let you *stay* dead!"

"The son-of-a-bitch!" Hocker sputtered. Flecks of saliva shot from his mouth and dribbled down his chin. He wiped them away with the back of his hand.

"Rodgers, the jig may be up for us, but it's also up for *you*," Winfield said. "I'm overdue for my shift and you can bet they'll be out looking for me once they check at my house and find I'm not there. Ernie'll be wondering where I am, and he'll get Chief Bates involved. And then there's the rest of us here. This isn't going to be as easy as running one man off the road late at night on Casey's Curve. You're going to have a bit of a problem covering *this* one up."

"Difficult ... not impossible," Rodgers replied.

"Fuck you!" Hocker shouted. He banged his fist in frustration against the wooden blockade, wishing just for a second he could get a clear shot at the bastard!

Winfield shot Hocker an angry look and said sharply, "For Christ's sake, don't give him the satisfaction!"

"Have it your way, then," Rodgers yelled. "By tomorrow morning, all of you are going to be like *them!*"

Rodgers pointed off to his right behind him, an expression of smug satisfaction on his face. As if on cue, a dozen or more zombies came into sight over the crest of the hill. The figures were, at first, nothing more than dark dots on the landscape, as they moved inexorably closer to the farm house.

"You had your chance," Rodgers said, and then he backed away from the limo and disappeared out of sight around the side of the house.

Neither Winfield nor Hocker saw where he had gone. What they had to do now, they both realized, was to hold off this horde long enough for Dale to do what he had to do in the barn. The zombies fanned out and surrounded the house. Once they were in position, they stopped and just stood there, waiting for the command to attack.

"Jesus H.," Hocker said, whistling under his breath as he watched the mass of men waiting silently in the front yard. "There's his reinforcements! There's at least twenty more of 'em that I can see."

"Yeah, and where the hell's the cavalry?" Winfield said softly, wondering how Dale was making out in the barn. "When do *they* come charging over the hill?"

# V

Dale, if he was the cavalry Winfield was hoping for, was still behind the solidly nailed trap door at the tunnel's mouth. After a while, pushing as hard but as quietly as he could at the door with his shoulder, he had decided Screw it! What the hell? If I attract any zombies, maybe they'll break the door for me!

It took an amazing feat of contortion, but finally he got onto his back so his feet were pushing up on the door. He could feel the veins pop out on his neck and his muscles strain as he forced his legs upward against the unyielding wood. Tight, tingling pain shot up his thighs to his hips, but even with this added leverage, the door wouldn't give.

Dale drew his legs back and, grunting as he counted each blow, kicked upward.

"One . . . two . . . *three* . . ."

The door did not even shake with his kicks, but he gritted his teeth and hit it with as much strength as he could gather in such a confined space.

". . . four . . . five . . . *six* . . ."

The bottoms of his feet tingled with each kick. His back slammed against the ground with each rebound, knocking the breath from him.

". . . seven . . . eight . . . *Yes!*"

On the ninth kick, he felt the door budge. The sound of the rusty nails yielding set his teeth on edge as badly as fingernails being raked down a chalkboard; but he didn't care! It was loosening! He was going to make it!

He was only vaguely conscious of the long tube of the tunnel behind him. In his efforts to loosen the boards covering the exit, he had entirely forgotten about it. But now, he heard something shifting in the darkness behind him. He froze and listened. Lying on his back with his feet up in the air, he felt both ridiculous and extremely vulnerable.

*They're coming after me!* he thought. Somehow, the creatures under Rodgers' control had already taken the house by storm, and one now was coming through the tunnel.

He wished he had checked his watch when he had left Donna in the cellar and started along the tunnel. For all Dale knew, it had been an hour or more that he had been crawling along in the dark. Plenty could have happened since he had left her!                .

No matter how lightly he tried to breathe, the sound of air rushing in and out of his nose blocked out everything else; but as he strained to listen, he was sure there was a faint scratching sound coming from behind him. As it grew louder, his breathing got louder, too, keeping the sound barely audible.

The dust from his efforts swirled in the close quarters of the tunnel, choking him; and as he waited tensely, he imagined that at any second a horribly dead-looking face would suddenly spring into the glow of his flashlight, and with one, short cry end his life.

If there was one of those things in the tunnel with him, Dale's only hope was to get that damned door open! With a sudden yell, he kicked up with an adrenalin-charged kick. The wood suddenly exploded as easily as if it were balsa-wood. Dale imagined he was already dead and was now bursting out of his coffin, newly reanimated.

It took some effort to shift around so he could climb out of the tunnel. The guttural sounds he made masked the sound of something else, but then: *yes!* He definitely heard a scrambling sound in the tunnel, getting closer!

Fear tightened around his throat like cold hands as he shifted to get one arm up over the splintered doorway. He wanted to scream, but his throat was so caked with dust, all that came from it was a dry rasp. His head broke out into the fresh air and light. He felt like a swimmer, piercing the surface after going down for the third time!

In an instant, he saw the police cruiser, smashed and dented, over by the barn door. He saw the spanning rafters of the barn, dusty gray with hay chaff and cobwebs, and bats hanging up there in the darkest corners. He saw the window, looking out toward the house, and he wondered if Donna was there in the kitchen, waiting frantically for some sign that he had succeeded. He instantly registered all of these things, and the sense of freedom that surged through him drove him to push himself upward with one muscle-tearing effort.

He struggled to get his other arm into the open and, bracing himself, kicked wildly to gain a purchase. His mind suddenly went cold, and his eyes felt like they were going to pop out of his head, literally, when, just as he felt himself rising clear out of the wrecked doorway, a hand grabbed his ankle in a steely grip and started to pull him down.

# VI

As soon as Dale had disappeared down the tunnel and was out of ear-shot, Donna lit her next to last cigarette and went upstairs to rejoin Winfield and the other defenders. She had to keep blinking her eyes to keep from crying; she couldn't shake the feeling that she would never see Dale alive again ... at least not alive as she knew it!

Winfield was near the kitchen door, keeping an eye on the side of the barn. Hocker was in the living room with Tasha, watching and waiting for Rodgers' creatures to make their move. Everyone in the farmhouse was armed and waiting, but Winfield still felt certain Rodgers wouldn't try anything until after dark.

Donna inhaled the smoke and let it out in a thin, whistling stream as she looked out the kitchen window. She saw that the sun was already slipping down toward the hill. Night was closing in on them like a trap.

"He'll be all right, you know," Winfield said, placing a strong, reassuring hand on her shoulder.

Her hand tightened into fists as her gaze drifted toward the barn, to the small rectangle of window, reflecting the sky. All she could do was wait and hope to see Dale's face, looking back at her once he made it to the barn.

"I ... I know," she said, fighting the voice inside her that told her she was lying. In one regard, life wasn't a dream. In her dreams, she sometimes felt a sense of control, like a movie director, who could make certain things happen. Well, if she was the director of *this* movie, she would cue Dale to come to the barn window and look at her, smiling broadly.

"I think we've got to start preparing for the next attack as soon as it's dark," Winfield said.

Donna looked at him, searching his face for strength she knew she was going to have to find within herself. She flicked the cigarette ash into the sink, then, wrinkling her nose, ground it out and dropped the butt down the drain. "Do you think this will work?" she asked, her voice shaking.

Winfield smiled and nodded. "Course it will," he said. "Come on, let's get organized."

The plan was relatively simple. The door leading into the cellar opened inward. It wasn't one of those modern, hollow-core doors; it was a hefty paneled oak door, with a glass door knob and strong hinges. Winfield and Hocker constructed two cross beams that could quickly be lowered from inside the cellar* to hold the door shut. Winfield had no illusions; he knew that, with a determined effort, the door could eventually be broken down, but not before everyone had plenty of time to crawl along the tunnel and get out.

The only flaw with the plan was that *he* wasn't going to go down the tunnel; he wasn't even going to be in the cellar. He figured, when the last attack came, both front and kitchen doors would be smashed in. If Tasha and Donna were already in the cellar, Hocker could wait until the zombies saw and pursued him before going down into the cellar, shutting the door behind him. Winfield's part of the plan was to hid somewhere in the house. As soon as the zombies followed Hocker down into the cellar, Winfield would go out the kitchen door and join everyone in the barn. By then, if they timed everything right, Hocker could touch off the fire and they would destroy the creatures trapped inside the cellar.

It was a simple and rather elegant plan with a minimum of risk, Winfield thought. The worst risk was his, and he was willing to take it. Now all they had to do was make it work.

"I want to put up something on the outside of the cellar door, too. Something strong enough to keep them down there so they can't get out once the fire starts," Winfield said to Hocker once the inside barriers were prepared.

"I'll see if there's any more wood down in the junk pile," Hocker said as he ran down the cellar stairs.

Donna stood there by the kitchen sink, looking out at the barn. It had been almost half an hour since Dale left, and she was thinking he had had plenty of time, he should have reached the barn by now.

But what if the tunnel is blocked or it caved in on him?, she wondered, fighting back a ground-swell of panic. And what if, once we're down there, we can't get out?

As she stared out at the barn window, her vision suddenly blurred. Hot tears carved tracks down her cheeks, and her breath hitched in her throat.

Behind her, she heard Winfield say, "Tasha, why don't you go down the cellar and help Hocker get some more wood?" Then she heard Tasha's footsteps going down the stairs and Winfield's coming over toward her.

"It's taking too long," she said, her voice catching. "We've got less than half an hour until dark."

"He's gonna be all right," Winfield said. "We're all going to be all right. You just wait and see."

"I can't believe all of this is happening," she said. She had one hand clenched into a fist, covering her mouth and distorting her words. Her knuckles were bloodless knobs. Her body shook as though she had a fever.

A sudden splintering of wood drew their attention, and they both looked over their shoulder to get a fix on the direction.

"That you, Hocker?" Winfield called out. He gripped the axe firmly as he started toward the living room. He glanced back at Donna and, with a nod of his head, indicated that he wanted her over by the cellar door, just in case. Thinking that facing Rodgers' creatures was preferable to entering the tunnel, she ignored what he said, picked up one of the nail-studded clubs, and followed closely behind him into the living room.

Diffused gray light cast an eerie gloom into the living room. Through the wooden slats covering the windows, they saw dark silhouettes shift by, cutting the light. A weird silence laced with tension filled the room as Winfield tiptoed to one of the windows, resting his axe on his shoulder like the baseball bat of a Home Run King.

"Jesus Christ, Jeff," Donna whispered when she saw more figures move silently past the window.

Everything was nailed back the way they had originally had it, but much of the wood was splintered from the last attack. Winfield knew their defenses wouldn't hold as well as they did last time and they hadn't done too well last time!

"I think we're gonna be in some deep shit if Dale doesn't get back here soon with that gasoline," Winfield hissed, never taking his eyes away from the windows.

"Should we try to hold them off here?" Donna asked. The backs of her knees felt like rubber.

"Christ if I know," Winfield said. "Maybe we should just make a break for it to the barn. A couple of us will get away at least."

More shapes shifted by the window, their passing made real only by the faint creaking of the porch floorboards.

Winfield shifted closer to her and bent close to her ear. "Why don't you go see what the Christ is taking Hocker so damned long!"

Donna almost said something about preferring to stay here with him and fighting, if necessary, but she turned to leave. Just then, though, the sound of breaking wood, as loud as a string of firecrackers, filled the room. When Donna looked back toward Winfield, her mind went suddenly numb, trying to register what she was seeing.

Both windows and the front door almost instantly collapsed inward, and through all three openings, a tangle of arms and legs poured into the house. The sudden burst of light in the darkened room hurt her eyes, and she was momentarily disoriented until she heard Winfield shout to her.

*"Get the hell out of here!"*

Before she could react, a wave of dead human beings crashed into the living room and crested over Winfield. The last thing Donna saw and registered in her shock-numbed brain was Winfield, wildly swinging his axe back and forth, as he crumpled beneath the weight of those creatures.

Donna didn't know exactly what to do, and more out of reflex than thought, she ran to the cellar door and slammed it shut behind her. Her breath was raw in her throat as she stood at the top of the stairs, trying to think clearly. She had seen several zombies lurch past the mass that had buried Winfield and, arms reaching out, come after her no more than six steps behind. With a frantic grunt, she rammed first one, then the other blocking bar into place just as the weight of several dead bodies slammed into the door.

"Jesus Christ!" she wailed, looking down the cellar steps at Tasha, who was looking up at her with a pale, blank expression. "Where the Christ is Hocker?"

Outside, the cellar door took a steady hammering as the creatures smashed against it, furiously pounding to get at her. She had seen the dead glow in their eyes as they registered her—*a living thing*— and came at her. In the instant she saw them, she had recognized one or two of them. They were people she had known around town, back when they were *alive!*

Donna pressed herself against the door, even though she knew her added weight would do little to stop the onslaught. The cross-bars sagged inward from the pressure, and already the ends were digging divots into the plaster wall, slowly losing their brace.

"Where's Hocker? Did Dale come back?" Donna screamed. Her throat was vibrating so hard, she thought for sure it was being shredded. "Tasha! Answer me! Don't just stand there! Where the Christ is *Hocker?"*

She glanced over her shoulder, down the steps at Tasha, who was standing there motionlessly, shrugging and shaking her head.

"I don't know where he is," Tasha said. "He wasn't here when I got here. Are you sure he even came down here?"

# VII

Dale thought for sure he was going to shit his pants when he felt the hand grab his ankle. With a scream bubbling in the back of his throat, he tried to kick free but only succeeded in slamming his knee against the tunnel mouth. Pain shot up to his hips, and blind panic filled his mind like lightning.

"No . . . *No!* . . ." he wailed as he kicked to release the hold on his leg. His arms trembled as they strained to boost him upward, and miraculously he did get himself up enough so his hips were clear.

His left hand still gripped the flashlight tightly, and counting on a sudden blast of light to startle the creature that held him, he swung the beam downward.

In a flickering instant, he saw a dirt-smeared face glaring up at him with a wide smile, and then, in a sudden rush, he recognized who it was. "Jesus Christ, Hocker!"

"Jesus Christ, *yourself,* man," Hocker said, laughing deeply. "Your sure are jumpy."

Relief flooded Dale so fast it almost took away all of his strength. With a sudden outrush of breath, he settled back down into the tunnel opening, wishing to God the rapid hammering of his pulse in his ears would slow. His arms felt like frayed elastic.

"What the fuck do you think you're doing?" Dale asked once he had regained a bit of his composure. Sweat dripped from his forehead and ran from his armpits down his side, making him shiver.

"Go on," Hocker said, chuckling. "Get your ass out of here so I can get out."

Dale wiped his arm across his forehead, he hoisted himself up into the barn and rolled over onto his back. For several seconds, he lay there, staring up at the barn roof. Hocker quickly scrambled up after him and, standing up, stretched his arms over his head.

"Sure is cramped down there, ain't it?" Hocker said, looking down at Dale with a wide smile.

"I can't *believe* you," Dale said with a snarl as he slowly stood up and stretched his legs and arms. "Why the hell'd you follow me?"

"I didn't want to miss any of the fun," Hocker said as he moved over toward the cruiser. "'N I figured, this was my gig, so I ought to help you with the gasoline."

"You came down that tunnel without a flashlight?" Dale asked, raising his eyebrows in astonishment.

Hocker shrugged as he leaned into the open cruiser trunk and grabbed the five gallon can of gasoline.

"No problem," he said casually. "I figured it would be pretty straight and you'd be up ahead. Hey, you know, I don't think they've been in here since I parked the cruiser here last night. It doesn't look like anything's been disturbed."

Dale whistled through his teeth as he gave Winfield's cruiser a quick once-over. The lights were smashed out; the fenders and sides were dented; and the radio and huge chunks of the interior had been blown away by the shotgun blast.

"You did a damned fine job of it," Dale said, shaking his head with disgust. "Think it'll still work?"

"I don't think the trunk light, being on all night, would be enough to drain the battery." He brightened and looked at Dale. "You got the key? Give it a crank."

Dale glanced at the window toward the house, fearful that at any moment a dead man's face would fill the window. He knew Donna was waiting for him to signal her, but he wasn't so sure he wanted to do anything to draw attention to the barn.

"Let's just get the flares and gas and get the hell back there," Dale said gruffly. "If we trap enough of those creatures in the cellar when you torch it, we'll probably be able to make it back to town through the woods if the car doesn't start."

"Fine by me," Hocker said. There was a sing-song tone in his voice that irritated Dale as well as warned him to keep a close eye on this guy. Dale took the package of road flares from the trunk, then slammed the trunk lid shut. Hocker carried the can of gasoline to the tunnel entrance. What neither of them saw, as they lowered themselves down into the opening, was the pair of eyes watching them from the crack between the two large, sliding front doors. One of the eyes had a wide, dilated pupil, fringed with a cold, blue iris.

# VIII

"We're in deep trouble!" Donna said when first Hocker and Dale emerged from the tunnel into the cellar. Their faces were smudged with dirt and streaked with sweat.

"What's going on?" Dale asked, glancing around the cellar. The steady pounding sound coming from up the top of the stairs immediately drew his attention. "Where's Winfield?"

Donna cast her glance down at the floor and sadly shook her head. Her lower lip was trembling when she looked at Dale and said simply, "I think . . . they got him."

"What? What do you mean?" The flood of anger and frustration that swept through him was almost too much to handle. All he could think was, I shouldn't have gone! I should have stayed here!

"We were waiting in the kitchen, for some sign that you had made it, and those creatures broke into the living room. He tried to fight them off, but there were just too many. I . . ." Her voice choked off, and tears flowed down her face. "I turned and ran down here just as they piled all over him."

"Holy Mother of God," Dale said, shaking his head as he tried to absorb this new loss. He felt that same numb rush he had felt when Nichols had called him Saturday morning to tell him Larry Cole had died . . . that same cold hand on his neck that he had felt when the call had come eight years ago, informing him that Natalie had been hit by an on-coming truck.

"You're . . . you're sure he . . . didn't make it?" he stammered, looking up at the door where the pounding continued, unabated.

Donna nodded, wiping at her eyes with the heel of her hand.

"Well, fuck it!" Hocker said. "We've got some fun ahead of us!"

He held up the can of gasoline and sloshed it back and forth. There was a wicked gleam in his eyes. Tasha recognized it as the same look from the night he had torched the old man's truck and sent it off the cliff into the river.

Dale turned toward him, his jaw chattering with sputtering rage. He clenched his fists and, for the first time, fully understood how much Winfield had hated this man. The least he could do, he thought, in memory of Jeff Winfield, was throttle the shit out of this jerk; but he stopped himself: there might be time to throttle him later! First, they had to get everyone including Donna down that tunnel and out of the house!

The harsh sound of tearing cloth drew his attention, and he looked over to see Tasha, kneeling over her opened backpack by the coal bin, shredding one of her shirts. Hocker smiled and said, "Well, at least someone knows how to have a good time! If you two feel like helping, I could use a *lot* of flammable material—cloth, those wood shavings over there . . . anything to help the fire get along."

He walked up the stairs to the closed door, still vibrating with the heavy hammering from the other side, and started to splash gasoline around the doorframe and on the stairs.

Dale and Donna stood in the middle of the cellar, watching while they both tried to register the loss of Winfield in their numbed brains. Neither one of them had noticed that Tasha's shoulder shook with wrenching sobs as she worked. She was thinking how she wasn't going to need any of her clothes anymore; she was either getting out of here and going home, or she was going to be *dead!*

"If we can get enough gasoline, maybe use those road flares to get it real hot, to make sure the stairs go up good, we should have 'em," Hocker said as he backed slowly down the steps, splashing gas as he went.

Dale suddenly had an idea. He went over to the space beneath the cellar stairs and trained his flashlight upward. The three stringers were made of well-seasoned wood, free of any rot. Clumps of black cobwebs hung in the corners, drifting lazily with the stirring of the air as Dale poked around. In a few spots, funnel-shaped stains of Hocker's gasoline seeped through between the steps and dripped down.

"Hey! Hocker! Come here," Dale called, once he was sure by the sound that Hocker had finished dousing the stairs.

With the gas can hanging at his side, sloshing with a hollow, near-empty sound, Hocker came around under the stairs. Dale directed his flashlight beam upward, toward the source of the heavy pounding.

"Think we could use the saw and maybe help this sucker collapse once they start coming down?"

Hocker snorted a loud laugh, and a fleck of mucous shot from his nose. He wiped his hand across his face and nodded. "Those fuckers are probably so *stupid,* they'll keep coming even if the steps are gone. Christ, Harmon," he said, slapping Dale on the shoulder, knocking him off balance. "There might be some hope for you yet!"

The comment made Dale miss Winfield all the more, but as waves of grief swept through him, he forced himself to smile and said, "Let's get a move on. That barrier up there isn't going to hold them all day."

"You do the cutting," Hocker said, "I want to check out where I can pop a few lighted flares, where they might get the floor boards upstairs burning."

Dale got the rusty saw and, propping the light upward, set to work. The sounds of his efforts were almost completely drowned out by the noise Rodgers' creatures were making in the kitchen upstairs. As the rusty teeth chewed into the first stringer, dry sawdust, almost as dry as the dust in that tunnel, sifted down into his face. It fell down his neck and inside his shirt collar, mixed with his sweat, and started to itch fiercely. It wasn't long before his neck and shoulders were screaming with pain.

Donna came over and held the light for him as he worked. She didn't say a word while he was hacking away at the underside of the stairs, but when he stopped, gasping from the effort, her glance caught him, and he knew she had something on her mind.

"Don't hold back on me," he whispered. "What's bugging you?"

He craned his head around the stairs to see what Hocker was up to. He was over by the workbench, pawing through the accumulated junk. Every time he found a can of paint or turpentine he'd shake it to see if there was anything left. The expression on his face reminded Dale of a kid on Christmas morning. He was having the time of his life. And maybe the threat of death added spice to it all, Dale thought.

Donna's eyes flickered briefly. "It's Tasha. She's really freaking out."

Dale nodded, sighing deeply as he regarded his work. So far, he wasn't even a quarter of the way through the first stringer. The old wood had dried until it was as hard as steel.

"She's really freaked that . . . *they* got Jeff."

Dale nodded again. "I still can't quite accept it, either," he said.

"I don't know," Donna said, shrugging helplessly. "She keep saying there's no reason for us to make it out of here, that she can't think of many reasons to live anymore."

"Look, we've got things to do if we're going to get out of here," Dale said, suddenly charged with anger. "I mean, think about what I've got to deal with! For all I know, Rodgers has already been over to Mrs. Appleby's and got Angie. You don't think I'm a little anxious to get out of here? Tasha's been through a lot for a kid her age. And I can imagine she feels pretty alienated, but I'm not going to let her bullshit slow me down! Tell her to get it together and come along for the ride! I really don't have time to be her goddamned shrink!"

With that, he turned back to his sawing, attacking the wood with renewed fury. The saw dust flew everywhere, sprinkling the dirt floor like snow.

"Well, Mr. Sensitive," Donna said, but she didn't leave; she continued to hold the light for him while he worked in spite of the awkward silence that had fallen between them.

"I have no fucking idea how much to cut these," Dale said, sounding totally frustrated after a short-lived round of furious cutting. His face and hair were covered with sawdust, making him look like he had a case of terminal dandruff.

"I don't know," Donna said, laughing at how funny he looked. "As long as no one's going up there, I'd say go almost all the way."

She couldn't account for her sudden giddiness. Maybe, like Tasha, she was finally buckling under the strain . . . only she was going to end up *laughing* hysterically in the corner of the coal bin while Tasha *cried*.

Either way, she thought, we're both going to end up in the rubber room, writing letters home with Crayolas.

"Aww, screw it! That's enough for that one," Dale said, snorting as he brushed the sawdust from his face. He rotated his shoulder, trying to get the circulation back into it, then set to work on the middle stringer.

When the second stringer was almost cut through, both of them jumped when the stairs suddenly snapped and sagged. Wood popped, sounding like a gunshot.

"I think you're through with that one," Donna said, smiling and still fighting the urge to burst out laughing.

Dale scowled at her, lowered his arm, and, after giving it a quick shake, started on the last stringer. He had finally gotten his second wind with it and went to work slowly and steadily.

"Christ, man, are you about ready?" Hocker said as he came around under the stairs. "I've got everything else all set to go." He glanced up the edge of the stairwell and saw plaster powdering where the cross bars were digging into the walls. "I don't think they're getting any more patient."

"I—just—have—a—bit—more," Dale grunted, each word timed with the stroke of the saw.

Hocker bounced up and down on his toes, a book of matches clenched in his hand. "Well," he said, snorting and spitting onto the floor, "it doesn't have to be a fuckin' masterpiece, you know."

"You do what you do, and leave me the Christ alone, all right?" Dale shouted. He turned and faced Hocker, the saw held up like a sword.

"Hey, hey . . . just checking, man," Hocker said, holding his hands out and backing away.

Dale was exhausted from the effort, so after a few more passes, he dropped the saw to the floor. "Screw it ... if it works, it works," he muttered. He used his left hand to massage his right shoulder, but he knew that tonight his back and shoulder would feel like he had been wrestling a bear.

"Come on, man," Hocker said. He was standing at the foot of the stairs, anxiously looking up. Bending forward and trying to take deep breaths, Dale came over and looked up, too.

the door was sagging inward as the combined weight of Rodgers' creatures pressed against it. The steps were stained dark where Hocker had doused them with gasoline.

"Okay," Dale said, turning to Donna and Tasha, "why don't the two of you start down the tunnel?"

Donna looked at him, her eyes widening to perfect circles. Her mouth opened to say something, to protest, but the firmness in Dale's voice told her, clearly, that it was now or never!

"Tasha? Will you go first?" Dale asked. She looked at him, and he saw for the first time how bad she looked. Her eyes were dark and rimmed with red, and the paleness of her face only made her eyes look worse. She looked like she had become a victim of anorexia in the span of a few hours, and Dale suddenly regretted his callous treatment of Donna's concerns for her.

Tasha silently nodded, looking back toward the coal bin where her sleeping bag and backpack were stacked. She made a move to pick them up, then obviously thought better of it.

"Come on!" Hocker shouted, waving his arms in frustration. Dale thought he was just getting over-anxious to touch off the fire, but then the cellar door suddenly gave inward with a loud crack, and one of the blocking wood bars came tumbling down the stairs.

"Look, Donna," Dale said, approaching her and gripping her firmly by both arms. "We don't have time to dick around here. You've got to do it! *Now!*"

"I —know," she stammered. Then she turned and, directing her flashlight beam into the opening, walked over to the tunnel, got down on her hands and knees, and crawled inside. Tasha was no more than a pace or two behind her. Dale darted over as the two women were swallowed by the thick blackness.

*Oh, he remembered that darkness all right!*

"See you on the other side," he called after them, then he turned and faced Hocker.

Hocker was standing at the workbench. With a quick glance over his shoulder at Dale, he lit one of the road flares and dropped it into the collected junk. Dale shielded his eyes from the sudden brightness as the red flames hissed and caught. In an instant, tongues of flame were licking upward toward the ceiling.

"Damn . . . he's good!" Dale said to himself, watching, fascinated, as Hocker dashed over to where he had propped another flare. He lit it and, casting a worried glance up at the sagging door, stuck it up into the crossbeams. There was a tiny "whoosh," and flames started flickering to life.

The cellar door was groaning inward, and Dale could dimly see faces, peering down at him through the crack in the door. Thin but strong-looking hands scrambled to gain a grip inside the door and pull it off its hinges.

Hocker touched off a third flare and planted it up under one of the floor joists. Glancing at Dale, he spat and said, "Hell, man, you might's well get your ass moving down the tunnel. I'm 'bout done here."

Dale hesitated, but a final glance at the door convinced him to move. The second wooden bar gave way, and the door exploded inward. There was a dark, seething tangle of arms and legs as the zombies all tried to get through the doorway at once.

"Move your ass, man!" Hocker shouted. He touched off another flare and stood there, about six feet from the foot of the stairs, smiling as he watched the creatures pour through the doorway. The last thing Dale saw before ducking his head into the tunnel was the harsh lines of Hocker's sweat-streaked face, glowing madly in the red glow of the flare. His teeth were bared in a wide, crazy smile, and just before he tossed the flare into the gasoline, he dropped his head back and laughed like a madman.

Dale didn't directly see the flames once the flare touched the spilled gasoline, but being only a few feet into the tunnel, he saw the sudden orange glow and felt a *blast* of intense heat slam him from behind.

At least the second time down the tunnel wasn't as bad as the first: he knew there was safety at the other end. What scared Dale was what he'd find there. The heat from Hocker's blaze cannoned down the tube with him, sucking air in as if the tunnel were a huge straw. Swirling dust made it difficult to breathe, but by keeping his head lowered, he made good progress.

All the time, though, he couldn't help but wonder how Hocker was going to get out of the house. It was out of the question that Hocker would have done something so noble as to sacrifice himself so the rest of them could escape. He certainly seemed to know what he was doing; he probably wouldn't have miscalculated.

Much sooner than he expected, he saw the dull gray light of the opening appear up ahead; and as he got closer, he heard Donna frantically calling his name. Although his lungs felt as though they had been char-broiled, and his arms and legs were knotting with cramps, he re-doubled his efforts. In another few seconds, he was out of the tunnel mouth and standing in the middle of the barn floor, hugging Donna so desperately he thought he would never be able to unclamp his arms from around her back.

"Where's Hocker?" Tasha said, her voice frayed with panic.

"He ought to be along right behind me," Dale said, sputtering.

Tasha was looking down into the tunnel mouth. She couldn't see the glow of the flames. The air sucking into the tunnel made a low, warbling whistle, and then suddenly thick black billows of smoke erupted outward.

"How's he gonna make it through that?" Tasha wailed. She didn't want even to think about losing the one person she felt had looked out for her through all of this.

Dale ran to the barn window and, crouching, slowly stood until he could see the kitchen door over the window sill. The sun had dropped below the horizon, and the sky was stained deep indigo, blending into black. The cold pin-point light of two stars winked over the house, but there was no sign that Hocker's fire had caught.

The sudden slamming of a car door made Dale and Donna jump. Turning, they saw Tasha, sitting in the cruiser on the passenger's side. She rolled down the window and waved frantically to them.

"Come on ... He ain't gonna make it," she said, glancing over at the tunnel opening. The smoke boiling out of it was thicker, now, and it started to fill the barn.

The kitchen window suddenly sprang to life with a dull orange flicker. Dale imagined he could hear the roaring of the flames as they licked up the stairway and into the house.

Donna, who was standing beside him, burst into tears as she watched the fire gain strength, feeding into the kitchen and spreading from the flares propped under the floor joists. Her mind was filled with hundreds of colliding memories, swirling and mixing like paint until there was nothing but a muddy blur.

The glow in the kitchen window intensified. Dale was about to go to the cruiser when a sound came to him, vibrating the window with a low but gradually rising tremor. At first it sounded like the huge timbers of the house, groaning as they burned and sagged beneath the weight of the house. But after a moment, Dale realized that the sound was sustaining and building, until with a sinking sensation of horror and the thought, *I've become a murderer!,* he realized it was the sound of ten or twenty throats, crying out in pain and anger as the flamed consumed them.

*Dead flesh!* he reminded himself, seeing his own horror reflected in Donna's terror-stricken expression. "They were already dead! Remember that!" he commanded himself, but nothing could erase those horrible, groaning wails.

"Hocker ain't comin'!" Tasha yelled from the cruiser, banging her fist on the dashboard. *"Come on!"*

Dale turned away from the window first and, digging into his pocket, started for the cruiser. For a freezing instant, his fingers couldn't find the key, and he thought they wouldn't make it! But then he found Winfield's key ring and slipped the key into the ignition as Donna opened the back door and hopped inside.

"Come on, now, baby," he said, coaxing the car as he turned the key and the starter made a low grinding sound. He stared up at the ceiling, focusing all of his mental energy onto the cruiser's battery. The trunk had been left open all night —would that be enough of a drain on the battery to kill it? he wondered.

"Come on now! Sears *Die-Hard,* show your stuff!"

The ignition cranked but didn't catch. Dale stepped down hard on the gas pedal and kept the key turned.

"Come on you royal mother-/fucker" he snarled. His fingers were wrapped so tightly around the steering wheel, he was positive he'd need surgery to get them off.

After more than a full minute, the engine caught and roared into life.

"All right!" Tasha shouted, clapping her hands.

Dale adjusted the mirror and, putting his right arm over the back of the seat, turned around to back out of the barn. His foot was on the brake, and the brake lights cast a weird glow onto the inside of the barn door. He was just going to pop the shift into reverse when a blackened face popped up over the back of the car.

"Ahh! Jesus!" he screamed. His foot slipped off the brake and onto the gas, sending the engine roaring. There was a loud *thump* on the side of the car, and both Donna and Tasha screamed when a face loomed up by the side door.

"Unlock the fucking door!" Hocker shouted.

Even though it was his voice, his face was unrecognizable beneath its mask of soot and dirt. For an instant, Dale thought that maybe Rodgers had already gotten him and turned him into a zombie, but he saw the wide-eyed smile beneath the soot.

"Get your ass in here," Dale shouted, reaching over the seat and unlocking the door. "We're going to have to take down the door with us."

Hocker dove into the back seat and slammed the door shut behind him as Dale hit reverse and stepped on the gas. The cruiser shot backwards, spitting a shower of dirt up against the chassis as the tires spun out.

"Buckle up," Dale said just before the cruiser smashed through the barn door. Slats of wood and metal flew everywhere, but he could see the dark shapes of several people moving toward them across the lawn.

The car heaved heavily to the right as Dale turned, raced the engine for a split second while he snapped on the headlights, and then popped the shift into drive and stepped down hard on the gas. Twice there was a heavy thump sound, and everyone in the car knew exactly what it was; Dale had driven over two of Rodgers' creatures. But the impact didn't slow the cruiser, and in an instant, it had shot past Rodgers' parked limo and swung out onto Mayall Road.

Dale glanced at the rearview mirror, and the other three looked back over their shoulders at the flames gathering strength and raging like angry tongues out of the house windows. Thick smoke spiraled into the night sky and was lost.

Donna had both of her hands covering her mouth and was sobbing as she saw her family home destroyed. Tasha, white-faced and trembling, watched silently. Dale was too numb to say or think anything. But Hocker was suddenly brayed with laughter and slapped his open palms on his legs.

"Oh, God, Jesus! You should have *seen* it!" he said, cackling with laughter. He was shaking with excitement, doubled up with pleasure. His only real regret was that they had to leave the scene so soon; he enjoyed sticking around as long as possible to watch the effects of his handiwork.

"I threw that flare into the gas just as they started coming down the stairs. And boy, oh boy, were you right about wanting to collapse the stairs. Under their weight, they came tumbling down like nobody's business. When they hit the flames, *Christ!* You should have heard 'em wail!"

"I'm . . . I'm glad you enjoyed it so much," Dale said, even though his throat felt like it was no more than pencil thick.

Hocker started to speak but before he did, he rolled down the window and spit out into the night as the cruiser headed back toward town. He cleared his throat, but he next words were simple; he said, "Oh-ooh."

"What?" Dale asked, glancing again in the rearview mirror. What he saw reflected there was answer enough. A single yellow headlight like a sinister, evil eye was speeding toward them out of the darkness.

# CHAPTER TWELVE
## "Endings and Partings"

# I

There was darkness all around her . . . darkness ringed with flameless heat
that came in long, steady pulses. There should be some kind of light, she
thought . . . how can there be such heat without light?

—*Is the house on fire?* . . .

—*Am I on fire?* . . .

She knew who she was, at least; and that was a start, but she wasn't even
sure if she still had her body. It didn't feel like she did. All she felt was a curious, floating sensation, as if she were drifting in a hot darkness, like the
womb.

-*"Am I dead?"*

Did I speak those words aloud, or were they words without sound, like
the heat without light? she wondered.

Her thoughts swam in her mind like fish in a midnight ocean. There was
no up or down, no left or right, no center . . . there were hints and sensations
of who she was ... or at least who she had been, but she couldn't drag herself
onto the shore, as it were; she couldn't even conceive of the shore. Now that
she thought about it, she wasn't even positive she was *breathing!*

-*"Am I dead?"*

The words came to her again with a sharp-edged brilliance: Yes! Brilliance!
Here, sounds have light!

*"...Am.. ."*

Yes! That is my voice. The single word glowed with a deep violet just on the
edge of perception; it came out of the darkness and quickly fell back into it, a
memory tracer spinning crazily, like a sky rocket spiraling into the dark ocean.

Brighter, stronger purple light this time. It blossomed from the darkness like a flower, exploding outward from the center. What center? she thought; How can no up or down, no left or right have a center? *". . . dead. . . ?"*

This *word quickly throbbed into life, changing for* a fraction of a second into a deep blue ... the blue of the evening sky in winter once the sun has dropped. Memory stirred like a sleeping beast.

And that third word brought something more than light; it brought a sense of heaviness of her drifting, floating, and then suddenly being pierced by tiny hooks that sank into her flesh and started drawing her downward.

*—There can't be a downward in a darkness with no center!*

*—"Do I still have my body?"*

"No, you're not dead," said a voice close to her ear. The voice was not her own.

"Do I still have my body?" she said. Each word began as pulses of light, rapidly shifting from purple to blue, through the spectrum to green then yellow and orange and, finally, to red, until the last word was no color at all; it was all *sound!*

"You're in the hospital, Mrs. Appleby," the voice said gently. "You were brought here early this morning by Police Chief Bates, from Dyer. Do you recognize the name?"

She thought for a moment. Her thoughts, as her words once had once been, were colored lights, not voices in her mind. They twisted and tangled like swirls of oil in a puddle, shimmering and bright like insect eyes. They could be *seen* only if she took the time to notice them. "Yes," she said. "Sure I know who you mean." "Mrs. Appleby," another voice said, this one male. "I'm glad to see you're awake."

She moved her eyelids allowing only the thinnest sliver *of yellow light to strike her eyes. It felt like* a splash of acid, making her eyes water. But the relief she felt, that her eyes *could* water, made her want to shout with joy. "Don't try to sit up or even open your eyes," said the woman. There was a gentle downward push on her shoulder.

"You've got a fractured skull. It's quite a serious fracture," the man's voice said. "I'm afraid you'll be here for a while."

"And Lisa . . . ?" Mrs. Appleby said. Again, she wanted to sit up in the bed. She knew now she was in a hospital bed. "Is Lisa all right?"

"Your grand-daughter is doing just fine," the woman's voice said. "Her friend has been sitting up with her all night, and she's feeling just fine."

"Funny," Mrs. Appleby said, letting herself sink back into the coolness of the pillow. "Isn't it funny how, within a day, we both ended up in the hospital with head injuries."

"There was nothing funny about how I found you this morning," the man's voice said. "What can you tell me about what happened once you got home last night and early this morning?"

For an instant, she wondered as the timeless, directionless darkness started sweeping back over her.

"They called me at the office as soon as they told me you were coming around," the man said. "Do you recognize my voice? This is Police Chief Bates."

"I don't remember much," she said. Trying to push her memory back only intensified the darkness, and she didn't want to go back there!

"I have a quite serious problem on my hands, Mrs. Appleby," Bates said. "Due to the incident with your grand-daughter, I have one policeman out of commission with a serious arm wound. Another man failed to report for duty this morning, leaving me short-handed. Now Officer Brooks has informed me that yesterday a man and a woman came to the station looking for Officer Winfield. It turns out this man has been rooming at your house and is the father of the girl who is staying with your granddaughter. After I was notified of the incident at the police station, I decided I had to ask you a few questions. When I arrived at your house, early this morning, I found you unconscious on the floor in your entryway."

"What day is it?" Mrs. Appleby asked. She made no motion to sit up, but her eyes opened a bit more, and she could just barely distinguish him: a hazy blur, leaning over her, big as a mountain.

"It's Tuesday evening," Bates said. "You were brought here early this morn-ing. It was right after you left here from visiting your grand-daughter."

"You said Lisa is fine," Mrs. Appleby said. "Were you telling the truth?"

"She's doing just fine," Bates replied, shifting his gaze to the nurse by the bed. "What I need to know is, who came to your door, either late last night or early this morning?"

"I . . ." she said, and that was all she could say. Her eyes slid shut, and the darkness started to return and embrace her in its warmth. She tried to ignore it was happening, but when she had spoken the word *I,* she had seen it in her mind as a burst of violet light.

"You might be pushing her too hard," the nurse said softly. Mrs. Appleby could feel someone tucking the sheet up under her chin.

"No," Mrs. Appleby said. It took great effort not to cry out when the word pulsed a blue light in her mind. "I remember." Blue light exploded like lightning at the word "I." A flash of green like a handful of emeralds tossed into the air accompanied the word "remember."

"Who was it?" Bates said. He knew he was pushing, but he had to find out what the hell was going on. Her boarder, this Mr. Dale Harmon, shows up at the station, looking for Jeff, and then first thing next morning, Jeff Winfield is missing, no sign of him or his cruiser anywhere! In all his years of service, Jeff had never been late or missed a shift without notifying the station.

"His eye," she said, feeling a sudden chill when the word *eye* glowed a pale blue exactly the color of the eye! "I remember his eye."

*"Whose* eye?" Bates said. "I want you to tell me. Whose?"

"And the *pupil,"* Mrs. Appleby said, suddenly clenched with a bottomless terror. That black pupil, like the heated darkness swelling to embrace her, wanted to embrace her . . . to *smother* her!

There was a sudden high-pitched beep. For the sheerest instant, Mrs. Appleby thought the sound originated in her head, that perhaps a blood vessel had suddenly burst from the effort of speaking, and she was dying. But as the sound got louder, she managed to get a direction on it. Then, as suddenly as it had started, it stopped.

"Excuse me a moment," Bates said, switching off his pager. "I have a call. Can I get an outside line on this phone?"

"Just dial nine and then the number if it's local," the nurse said.

Mrs. Appleby let herself settle back into the pillow, grateful for its coolness, an escape from that hot blackness, while Bates hurriedly dialed. He cupped his hand up close to his mouth and mumbled into the receiver for a few seconds, then hung up.

"It never rains but it pours," he said as he turned back to Mrs. Appleby. "That was a call from the station. You remember I said that yesterday a man and a *woman* were asking for Officer Winfield? The man was your boarder, and the woman was Donna LaPierre. Well, it seems as though the old LaPierre homestead is going up in flames even as we speak."

"Rodgers!" Mrs. Appleby suddenly said in a barking shout. Pure reflex made her snap open her eyes and try to sit upright in the bed, but she just didn't have the strength. She groaned with pain and closing her eyes again, collapsed back onto the bed.

"What?" Bates said. He was already at the door, ready to leave.

"This morning," Mrs. Appleby said softly. "The man who came to my house this morning . . . was Franklin Rodgers. And he had . . . Stephen Wayne with him."

"Thank you very much," Bates said. Within a few minutes, he pulled out of the hospital parking lot and, blue lights flashing and siren wailing, sped down Route 2-A toward Dyer.

# II

"We're fucked," Tasha said as she leaned over the back seat, staring like Donna and Hocker at the pursuing car. There was no doubt who was chasing them; the only question was, could Winfield's cruiser, smashed and dented as it was, keep the distance? Dale was thankful that Hocker had only smashed one of the headlights, otherwise he'd be driving stone blind. The slide windows were nothing more than a mass of spider-webbed cracks. Chilly wind whistled through them.

"Can't you call for help on the radio?" Donna asked from the back seat.

In answer, Dale held up the shattered plastic of the microphone. His eyes flickered between the road ahead and the rapidly approaching headlight behind them. The cruiser held the road with a firm grip, and Dale found something else to be thankful for: Hocker hadn't slashed the tires.

"We've got some simple chores," Dale said grimly as the cruiser shot down Mayall Road toward town.

"I say we stop and kill the bastard," Hocker said. He raised his revolver up in front of his face and cocked back the hammer. In the glow of the dashboard lights, Dale saw Hocker's crazed expression. The wind ruffled his hair wildly, and Hocker's face, leaning toward him out of the darkness, sent a ripple of chills through him.

"We can either stop in town at the police station, or we can try to out-race him."

As soon as he stopped speaking, Dale felt a cold touch on the back of his neck. He looked in the rear-view mirror, and saw Hocker leaning close to him. The cold touch on his neck was the muzzle of Hocker's gun.

"You ain't stoppin' at no fuckin' cop station," Hocker hissed close to his ear. "So I guess the decision's just been made. You're gonna have to outrun the bastard."

"Hocker! For Christ's sake! What the hell are you doing?" Tasha said.

"I ain't going to no goddamned cop station, that's all," Hocker said, glaring at her.

Donna cringed back in the seat, wondering if she would even dare to try to stop this crazy man before he did something *really* crazy. Then again, she wondered which one of them wasn't going to end up in the funny farm after what they had been through in the last twenty-four hours.

Up ahead, Dale saw the stop sign at the intersection of Mayall Road and Main Street. With just the slightest bit of pressure on the brake pedal, he looked to the left, prayed that it was clear, and, tires squealing like an animal in pain, swung onto Main Street. The yellow headlight behind him shifted around the curve just seconds after him.

"Maybe we'll get lucky and someone will see us and call the cops," Donna said. Her voice was tense, and she couldn't take her eyes off the gun brushing against Dale's neck.

What, if we hit a bump and the gun accidentally goes off? she wondered, feeling sweat break out on her forehead.

"We'll just get us a good stretch of road and dust this bastard," Hocker said, his voice low and leering. "Won't we?" The revolver's muzzle pressed harder against his neck. "These cop cars can out-do anyone!"

"Whatever you say," Dale said, setting his jaw firmly as he sped toward town. When he shot past Mrs. Appleby's house, he couldn't help but look up to see if anything had happened up there. He saw that no lights were on and felt a wave of chills much worse than those he got from the gun at this head. If Angie's not all right, Dale thought, let Hocker pull the trigger now!

In a flash they raced down Main Street. The few people they passed on the street barely had time to look up and register what they were seeing: a smashed-to-pieces police cruiser being pursued by a sleek, black limousine. In seconds, they were out of town, heading south on Route 2-A. Before Dale could even think to respond, the police station and all help was behind him. If he was going to get all of their asses out of this, he was going to have to do it alone!

"You know were you're heading, don't you?" Donna said, her voice a faint whisper from the back seat. Dale barely heard above the whistling sound of the wind.

"Shut the fuck up, will you?" Hocker snapped, turning to her with an angry leer.

Dale nodded, fixing his eyes unblinkingly on the road as it unraveled in front of his single headlight. Behind him, the light of Rodgers' car kept pace with him, but he hadn't gotten any closer.

"Come on, man," Hocker said. "You can get some more out of this baby. Goose it!"

"I'm doing over seventy as it is," Dale said, forcing his voice to stay level. "And there's a hair-pin turn not too far ahead. I'd rather not lose it there."

"If you don't dust this bastard behind us, we're all gonna lose it. We'll *all* end up fuckin' zombies!"

"That's gotta be worse than going to jail," Tasha said. "Come on, Hock, put the gun away." She put her hand out in an attempt to take the gun from Hocker, but he jerked away from her.

"I ain't going to no jail, and I ain't going to end up one of those things," Hocker said. "I can see the gas gauge. We've got better than three-quarters of a tank. We can go all night if we have to."

"And where will we go?" Dale asked. "Even if we manage to lose Rodgers, he's still going to be alive back in Dyer. He'll still be doing what he's been doing. And my daughter's still there."

"You think / give a sweet shit?" Hocker said, jabbing the gun harder into Dale's neck. "You lose this guy and drop me off, you can do whatever you want. Call out the National Fucking Guard to nail his ass, for all I care! Right now, you just drive!"

"We're getting close," Donna said. She realized that she was the only local, and so was the only one who knew exactly where the curve was. Dale had only been out here once, when they had checked out the site of Larry's accident. She had to tell him exactly when Casey's Curve was coming up.

"I think we might be losing him," Dale said after glancing in the rearview mirror. It certainly looked as though the limo had fallen back a bit.

"Naw," Hocker said. "He's just playin' with our ass."

The cruiser sped through the night, swinging solidly around each twist in the tree-lined road. When they went over one bump, though, something underneath the cruiser snapped. The rear bumper dropped down started scraping on the road with a loud, grating noise. Donna looked behind them and saw sparks trailing out from underneath the cruiser.

"Oh, shit!" Dale said when the pursuing headlight suddenly shot forward. For a flickering instant, he had the sensation of standing still as the limo bore down at them. The single headlight became a swimming pool of yellow, filling the rearview mirror.

"Punch it!" Hocker said, close to Dale's ear.

"You're coming up on the curve," Donna said, her voice laced with tension. "You've got to slow down for it!"

"You ain't slowin' down," Hocker commanded. "You'll take it!"

"For Christ's sake," Dale said but then they shot over the rise just before the curve. It felt as though all four tires left the road as the cruiser rose, then dropped with a belly-floating bump. The metal dragging behind them hit the road with a loud impact that shook the car. Donna prayed the sparks wouldn't make the gas tank explode.

In the glare of his single headlight, Dale saw the solid wall of rock suddenly right in front of them. It seemed to leap forward out of the darkness, solid and tall . . . *instant death!* He jerked hard on the steering wheel, conscious only of the piercing screech of the tires and his instant conviction that, within a fraction of a second, he would be joining his friend, Larry Cole.

"Hold on!" he shouted as the cruiser skidded around the curve, leaving a thick skim of rubber on the asphalt. Time suddenly dilated, and everything seemed to happen in slow motion as the cruiser swung to the left, its tail-end trying to take the lead. Everyone in the car was thrown to the side, but Dale gritted his teeth and held the steering wheel firmly in line. Metal cried out in the dark night as the left rear fender of the cruiser glanced off the sheer rock wall.

Dale quickly straightened out the steering wheel and the front tires held onto the road. We just nicked it! he thought triumphantly.

The road straightened out up ahead, and with a bit more pressure on the accelerator, the cruiser shot forward, leaving Casey's Curve behind them. Dale let his breath out in a roar just as he chanced to look in the rearview mirror. The glow of Rodgers' headlight was suddenly gone, leaving only thick, impenetrable blackness. But as suddenly as the glow of the headlight switched to darkness, the darkness suddenly blossomed into an orange blast.

"Oh my God!" Dale muttered as his nearly numb brain registered what he had seen. A gentle curve in the road suddenly blotted out the orange glow. By the time Dale could tell anyone else to look behind them, there was nothing to see except the night-stained road.

"Well, all right," Hocker said, the second person to register that Rodgers' headlight no longer followed them. "You did it. Either he gave up on the turn or . . ."

"He didn't make it," Dale said as he gently applied the brakes.

"Hey, motherfucker! You don't stop yet!" Hocker shouted, poking the gun painfully into Dale's neck.

"Take it easy, will you?" Dale said as he pulled over to the side of the road and, putting the shift into park, draped himself over the steering wheel. He was bathed with sweat, and he wondered when he would be able to take a breath without shuddering. He could barely uncurl his hands from the steering wheel.

"What makes you so goddamned sure?" Hocker snapped, glancing back along the empty road.

"I saw flames," Dale said, still leaning over the steering wheel.

"Come on, Hock," Tasha said gently. She put her hand on the gun and tried to take it away.

Hocker resisted and glared at her. "Back off, you *bitch!*" he shouted. "Now, I want you to get moving that-a-way." He pointed straight ahead down the road. "You get me a good hundred miles away from here and then you can come back and do whatever you want."

His voice suddenly cut off and was followed by a loud, pained shout. With a sudden flash and explosion, the gun went off close to Dale's ear. The bullet tore a hole through the cruiser's door and skimmed off the road with a high-pitched whine.

"Jesus!" Tasha screamed.

Dale tried to say something, but his throat had closed shut. He twisted around in the seat, saw the gun and had sense enough to make a grab for it before the next bullet went through him. He jerked it out of Hocker's hand, feeling almost no resistance.

Hocker was sputtering with fury and groaning in pain at the same time. Once he had the revolver, Dale sat up and looked into the back seat. Donna had hit Hocker, either on the neck or shoulder; he was doubled over, his face almost on the car floor, covering the side of his head with his hand.

"What'd you do?" Dale said. He found it necessary to shout to hear himself above the ringing sound that filled his ear.

"I didn't hit him that hard," Donna said. She was sitting back, away from Hocker, who was using just about every swear word any of them had ever heard.

"My fuckin' goddamned shoulder, you fuckin' bitch!" he wailed, stamping both feet on the car floor. "Aww, Jesus! You hit me right where that fucking zombie clawed me! Aww! Jesus H. Christ on a cross!"

"That'll teach you," Dale said, still speaking unnaturally loud as he opened the car door and stepped out. He looked back up the dark road and could just barely distinguish a flickering orange glow above the tree line. "Come on. Get out," he said as he swung open the passenger's door. "Let me take a look."

Hocker eased himself out of the cruiser and stood on the side of the road, still doubled up with pain.

"Here," Donna said, handing him a flashlight through the open door. She had taken it with her from the house and seemed to realize now that she had been clutching it in her hand all during the chase.

Dale clicked it on and, peeling up Hocker's shirt, directed the beam onto his shoulder. What he saw made him gasp in shock. There were four gouges, running from the base of his neck down over his shoulder blade and around to his side. Each gouge was about a half-inch thick. Some of the blood had dried to a powdery rust color, but the wounds had opened up from Donna's punch. Fresh blood mixing with yellowy pus ran in thick streaks down Hocker's back.

"That doesn't look good," Dale said.

"No shit," Hocker sputtered, still doubled over.

"I think we should get you to the hospital," Dale said.

In the back of his mind was the thought that, if Hocker resisted in any way, he'd use the revolver. What he was going to do was, Hocker be damned, was go back to town and find Angie.

"I don't need no fuckin' hospital," Hocker snarled. He straightened up and pulled his shirt down. The fabric scraped against the freshly opened wound and made him wince. He cried out in pain.

"You will if you don't get your ass into that cruiser and shut up," Dale said. "And if you don't behave yourself, I'll see if Jeff left a pair of handcuffs around." It was now his turn to direct the revolver at Hocker, and he enjoyed turning the tables, except that his concern for Angie made the pleasure short-lived.

Hocker stammered, but he was in such obvious pain that Dale wasn't surprised when he meekly obliged. He grunted as he dropped onto the backseat and pulled the door shut.

Dale got in behind the steering wheel and handed the gun to Tasha. "Make sure he stays quiet," he said.

Tasha started to protest but then fell silent and sat with one elbow over the back of the seat, the revolver clenched in her fist.

Dale put the cruiser into gear and backed around, heading back toward town. The orange glow he had seen over the treetops was now faded. He had a moment of doubt, that Rodgers had somehow set a trap for them on the curve. Maybe, Dale thought, his shoulders shaking with chills, he's waiting for us back there and will nail us as soon as we turn the corner.

*"Keep your eyes open,"* he said, looking nervously out his window. The breeze coming in was chilling, especially on his sweat-drenched neck. He knew, later tonight, he was going to be seriously stiff.

"He ain't back there," Hocker offered from the back seat. He kept glaring at Tasha, unable to believe she could turn on him like this. When he could catch her attention, he would flash her his "winning" smile, but she maintained an icy distance. Once they got out of this, and were back on the road Hocker thought, she was going to pay for this!

Driving slowly through the thick night, the road seemed much longer heading back to Casey's Curve. Dale was expecting, at any moment, to see a single beam of light suddenly snap on and come careening toward them out of the dark. He figured, if they were lucky, they would have about half a second to register it before the impact killed them.

But as he rounded one turn near Casey's, the glow he thought he had seen suddenly became very real. The surrounding trees were underlit with wickedly glowing flames that brought out, in harsh relief, the silhouette of the smashed and twisted limousine. The spray-painted wall of rock looked like the inside of some huge fireplace.

"Oh, my God," Donna said, sitting forward and staring at the wreck. "Oh, my *God!*"

Tasha was silent; Hocker let out a slow whistle. All Dale could feel was immense relief as he slowed and then stopped the cruiser a safe distance from the hammering heat of the flames. He tried to see into the crumpled wreck, to determine how many bodies there were.

The *limo had to have been moving at least seventy* miles an hour when it hit the rock; it looked as though the impact had shortened it by half its length. Broken glass glittered like diamonds in the flickering light, and thick, oily clouds twisted up into the sky. Bent chrome littered the road. The smell of burning rubber was sickening.

Burning rubber, Dale thought, his stomach doing a quick flip, or worse . . . *Burning flesh!*

"Do you want to get out and make sure that's Rodgers?" Hocker asked, pointing at the human figure sprawled on the front hood of the burning car.

Rodgers had been propelled through the windshield and lay with his legs still in the car and his torso twisted around so he was facing up, staring blankly at the sky. His clothes were blazing, and it looked as though the heat was peeling away the skin from his face. Dale tried not to imagine that, even in death, Rodgers was *grinning at* him. This man had somehow conquered death; Dale was prepared to see this burning corpse suddenly lurch up into a sitting position and look at them, a maniacal laugh tearing from its charred throat as he slowly came forward after them.

"You wanna get out and check?" Hocker repeated. "Make sure that's him."

Dale snorted and shook his head. "Sure. Why not? You want me to leave the car running when I do?"

Hocker clicked his tongue and sat back heavily in the seat. "Shit, man, I can't pull one over on *you*."

Dale chuckled. "I'm not as stupid as I look."

"How *could* you be?" Hocker muttered.

They sat there a while longer and watched as the flames roared skyward. Hocker, especially, enjoyed the sight. He was thinking this had been a goldmine: *two* fires in one night! If it wasn't for the pain in his shoulder, he'd really have enjoyed tonight.

"Satisfied?" Dale asked, turning to look after Hocker.

Hocker's face was rippling in the light of the flames. He was smiling, and his eyes were almost perfect circles, trying to take it all in. "Never," he said softly.

"Well, I am," Dale said. He put the cruiser into gear and took off for town. His only thought was that he had to find Angie right away. Nothing else mattered.

"Where to first?" Donna asked as the few lights of town came into view. She felt drained. What she wanted was to go to sleep, but she also was terrified at the thought of what dreams might come, and earnestly wished she could first get about a thousand miles away from Dyer.

"Gotta go to Mrs. A's," Dale said grimly.

As he drove past the police station, he wondered if anyone would notice the battered cruiser. He had begun trying to frame his story in the mind, but he knew that, as soon as he and the rest of them started relating what they had been through, the authorities would be getting the nets ready to throw on them. He knew that as soon as he had found Angie and made sure she was all right, they would have to decide how much of what they had seen even *they could accept.*

When Dale saw Mrs. Appleby's house up ahead on the right, his stomach did a cold flip. Sitting on the hill, well back from the road, what had once looked like a cozy, happy Victorian house suddenly took on the scary aspect of a haunted house. All of the windows were dark, reflecting the night back like polished marble. The glow from the streetlight washed the front of the house with a powdery glaze.

"It doesn't look like anyone's at home," Dale said, his voice tight in his chest.

Donna let out a sigh, shifting her gaze rapidly back and forth between Dale and the house. "Maybe they've gone out for the evening," she offered.

Dale rapidly shook his head and gritted his teeth as he turned the cruiser into the driveway. "I've been missing for a whole day," he said. "They've got to be wondering what's happened to me. If Angie's . . ." But he let the rest of the thought remain unspoken as he pulled to a stop in the driveway.

"The car's still in the garage," Hocker said.

"I don't know if I can go in there." Dale said after stepping out of the car and looking up at the silent and empty house. He dropped the cruiser's keys into his pocket and waited for Donna to get out and join him.

The night air was chilly, and he put an arm over Donna's shoulders as they started up toward the house. They were a few steps from the cruiser when they heard a loud thump that made them stop in their tracks. They turned, expecting to see Tasha or Hocker getting out of the car to go up to the house with them, but neither had left the car. Dale was just opening his mouth to ask them what that noise had been when the sound came again another loud thump.

"I think it was at the back of the car," Donna said, taking a tentative step forward.

"Maybe the bumper finally fell off," Dale said. What they had heard was muffled, as though coming from inside the cruiser.

Dale and Donna went to the rear of the cruiser and stopped, looking down at the closed trunk lid. Suddenly, a question hit Dale that he had not allowed into his conscious mind until now.

"The trunk lid . . ." he said, thinking back to when he and Hocker had first climbed through the tunnel to the barn. They had gotten the gas and flares from the trunk easily because the trunk had been left open from the night before, when Hocker had rummaged through it.

"The trunk!! I don't remember closing it. Hey, Hocker?"

"Yeah?" Hocker said. He had been waiting tensely the cruiser, counting the time until Dale and Donna were in the house so he could make good his escape. With or without Tasha, he had a hefty bank roll in his pocket, and he intended to strike out on his own.

"In the barn," Dale said. "Did you close the car trunk?"

Hocker turned and looked at him, wrinkling up his nose. "What the fuck? I don't remember. I thought you did."

Dale was staring down at the trunk lid as if his eyes were lasers and could cut clear through the metal. He was searching his memory, trying to replay exactly what had happened. As best he could remember, Hocker had started into the tunnel first. So, if *Hocker* hadn't shut the trunk, and unless he himself had done it so automatically he had forgotten about it . . . *who* had shut the trunk?

Both he and Donna jumped, and Donna make a tight little noise in her throat when the thump came again from inside the trunk.

"You going to take a look?" Donna asked. She didn't know whether to pull closer or to back off and let Dale handle this.

Dale was fishing in his pants pocket for the keys. The only thought in his mind was the question: *Who closed the trunk?* His fingers closed onto the key ring, and he drew it out slowly. It made a faint jingling sound that startled Donna.

With a sudden exhalation of his breath, Dale looked at her and smiled. "For crying out loud," he said. "We're just getting ourselves worked up about nothing." He slid the key into the trunk lock and gave it a twist. The trunk popped and swung upward.

"Holy Mother of God," Dale said, taking an involuntary step backward.

Donna let out a strangled cry that instantly brought both Hocker and Tasha scrambling out of the car. They both got to the back of the car just as Dale was backpedaling away from the opened trunk.

"Jesus H.," Hocker said with a whistling breath.

On the floor of the trunk, lying in a fetal position with his legs curled up, his arms clasped around them, was Jeff Winfield. One side of his face had been sheered away, exposing the milky-white bone of his skull. The dim light gave his face a cold, pale cast; his eyes were closed, and even at a safe distance, Dale knew there was no warm breath stirring.

"Well," Dale said, "that answers one of the questions I still had," he said, sadly regarding the corpse of the man who, in a short time, he had come to consider a good friend. Donna stared silently.

Hocker let the faintest of smiles cross his face. He was thinking it served the cop right! With Winfield out of the way, and the roll of bills in his pocket, he was starting to feel free and clear all the way. He glanced down at the road and at the woods behind the house, wondering which way would be easiest and fastest to get away. Certainly, none of these people were going to bother chasing after him. The only thing that held him back was the pain in his shoulder. He would have been fine if Tasha hadn't hit him and reopened the wound. Now it was throbbing worse than it had when he first got it!

"What are you going to do with him?" Donna asked tightly. "You can't just leave him there."

Dale glanced at Hocker and then nodded toward Win-field's body. "Come on. Help me get him up to the house at least. We're going to have a lot of explaining to do."

Hocker spit onto the ground, then stepped forward and reached into the trunk along with Dale. "This is it, though," he said as he wedged his hands up under Win-field's shoulders. "I'll help you lug his sorry ass up to the house, but then I'm splitting."

"Hocker," Tasha said, almost a whine. "You've got to stick around until we explain what happened."

"I'm sure you guys can handle it without me," Hocker said. He snorted and spit again, aiming carefully over his shoulder.

Dale winced as he took hold of Winfield's cold, stiff legs. He was surprised how thin the man's ankles were, for such a hefty man. He was bending down, bracing himself for the lift when a scream suddenly ripped the night, shattering his nerves.

In a second of blinding panic, Dale let go of his grip and straightened up. His head slammed into the opened trunk lid, sending a jolt of pain along his nerves to complement the fear.

As soon as Hocker shifted Winfield's body upward, he saw a subtle motion on the dead man's face. Hocker had a fraction of a second to wonder if it had been a trick of light, but then the dead man's eyes snapped open and, before he could react, Winfield's hand shot out and grabbed him by the throat.

Both Donna and Tasha screamed, scrambling to get away from the cruiser as Winfield lurched upward, swung his arm around, and clamped it solidly down onto Hocker's wounded shoulder. The scream that ripped from Hocker's throat was a blend of perfect pain and horror as the dead man opened his mouth and started to pull him down.

"No! No!" Hocker wailed as he stared down at the gaping mouth. Wide teeth gleamed like knife blades in the night as they chomped up and down, coming closer to Hocker's face. He could smell the man's sickly sour breath, reeking with decay.

In the first instant of surprise, Dale reeled backward, tripping on his own foot and almost falling. He regained his balance and dove forward, not exactly sure what he could do. From experience, he knew these things of Rodgers' were much stronger than they had been in life, and Dale was sure Winfield was no lightweight when he had been alive.

*Rodgers' last shot,* Dale thought as he tried not to imagine the full strength and fury animating this corpse.

Hocker's feet were scuffing the driveway; his screams were muffled inside the trunk as the thing that had been Winfield pulled him closer and closer. He felt the steely fingers of one hand dig like hooks into his torn flesh; the other hand clutched the side of his neck, just missing the windpipe, as it yanked him down.

"Do . . . *something!"* Hocker managed to cry out. There was an intense hammering in his ears, and his vision spun wildly.

Suddenly, out of the night, there came a huge explosion that filled his mind with thunder and lightning. Thick fumes of spent gunpowder entered his lungs, choking him; but even in his thunderstruck confusion, he sensed a slackening of the hold on his throat and shoulder. With a moaning shout, he leaned back with what little strength he had left and fell backward. He was unconscious when he hit the pavement.

Dale was almost as surprised as Hocker was by the sudden report of the gun. He thought for an instant that he himself had been shot. He believed his body just needed another second or two to register the lead that had ripped through it, then he would drop to the ground, a lifeless heap. After another second, though, his mind registered what had happened: Tasha had fired point-blank into Winfield's face.

The zombie hadn't been hurt. He *couldn't* be hurt. Maybe the shock of the gunshot startled him for an instant; maybe because he had just recently been transformed into one of Rodgers' zombies, he still had a living reflex and remembered that bullets could hurt him. Regardless, in the instant the thing that had been Winfield cringed back and released his hold on Hocker, Dale acted. His hand clamped down on the tire jack, then he raised it over his head and brought it down as hard as he could onto Winfield's upturned face.

The first impact sent a bone-deep shudder through Dale's arms, but Dale knew one hit wouldn't be enough. He knew he had to disconnect the brain from the body, so body and brain could die alone.

Dale was surprised by the power he felt zinging through him as he repeatedly raised the jack up and brought it down on Winfield's head again and again. Each hit made a sickening thumping sound. The creature that had been Winfield scrambled to protect itself, as a low, pained moan issued from its throat. Dale had to tell himself, over and over, that the man he had known as Winfield was already dead: he was putting an unnatural and ungodly thing to rest.

In spite of Winfield's superior strength, Dale had the advantage. Unable to stand or even to avoid the successive hits, Winfield thrashed on the trunk floor as Dale hacked away at him. Finally, with a fortunately placed shot, the metal edge of the jack split the creature's spine. All strength went out of the creature's limbs, and with one feeble grunt, the zombie collapsed back into the trunk, truly dead.

Dale dropped the jack, oddly bloodless, to the ground. When it hit, it rang like a bell. Until now, killing these things hadn't been easy, but it certainly was necessary, even when he had had to *disconnect* Larry Cole's brain from his zombie body. But having to do this to Winfield left Dale feeling weak and hollow himself, as if *he*, now, was nothing more than a re-animated corpse. All feeling and emotion had been twisted so horribly out of shape, he wondered if he could ever feel truly human again. His stomach suddenly revolted, and before he knew what was happening, he was on his knees beside the cruiser, vomiting. He dimly suspected that once he found Angie, he would be all right, but right now, all he could think was: You can only take so much death before you start feeling dead yourself!

# III

As it turned out, there had been no one in Mrs. Appleby's house, and no message left behind to let him know where anyone was. Dale and Donna loaded the unconscious Hocker into the cruiser and, with Winfield's body still in the trunk, drove back to the police station. There they had found Chief Bates, and after showing him the body and giving only the briefest of explanations, enough so Bates could dispatch an ambulance and a fire truck to the accident site, they drove to the hospital in Houlton where Bates assured Dale he would find his daughter safe and sound. Still, before they left the station, Dale called the hospital just to hear Angie's voice to confirm it.

Tasha rode in the ambulance with Hocker, whose torn shoulder, seen in the harsh glare of the ambulance, looked more like raw hamburger than human flesh. Dale and Donna accompanied Bates in his cruiser, thankful for small things, such as car windows that rolled up to shut out the cold night air and two headlights, clearly *illuminating* the road ahead.

On the way to the hospital, Dale and Donna tried to fill Bates in on what had happened. He listened to their story in disbelief, interrupting them several times to question them on certain points that didn't make sense and probably never would. Several times, Dale had to tell him not to worry, none of it made sense in the way he was trying to understand it; he was going to have to see the basement of Rodgers' Funeral Home in order to begin to accept what had been going on. Dale wished he still had the tape from Larry's dictating machine, but it had been destroyed in the fire at Donna's homestead.

When Dale and Donna burst into Lisa's room, Angie shot up out of the chair where she had been dozing. Lisa, who had been contentedly watching TV, looked up and smiled as Angie and her father embraced and wouldn't let go.

"Good God, Almighty, I thought I'd *never* see you again," Dale said as tears streamed down his face. He held her back at arm's length, looked at her, then hugged her tightly to him again, patting his hands on her shoulders as if in disbelief.

"You don't look so hot, Dad," Angie said. "Why didn't you call and tell me where you were? God, I was *wicked* worried!"

Dale glanced at Donna and gave her a feeble smile. "Well, you see, we were kind of in a place where we couldn't get to a phone. I'll tell you all about it . . . later," he said. In the back of his mind, though, he was already wondering exactly how much he would tell her. He certainly couldn't tell her he had had to kill Larry . . . *a second time!*

"Have a seat, Mr. Harmon," Lisa said, her voice bright and chipper from *the bed.* "I've got some ginger ale here you can have. Haven't even touched it. I'm still waiting for the nurse to bring me that hamburger I asked her for."

Dale smiled. Lisa looked thinner than he remembered. He took the clear plastic cup from her. Dale considered for a moment, then took it and handed it to Donna, who eagerly gulped down half of it before handing it back to him.

"So," Angie said, eyeing him with a slight smirk and a suspicious gleam in her eye. "You two haven't been ..."

She waved one hand back and forth in front of her face as if she had just burned it on a hot stove.

"No ... no, nothing of the sort," Dale said after taking a sip of ginger ale. The carbonation exploded on the back of his throat like a string of firecrackers. "I only got part of the story from Chief Bates. What's Lisa in here for?"

Angie and Lisa exchanged glances. At last, Angie cast her eyes downward and said, "I guess it was my fault, kind of."

"It was *not*," Lisa said, shifting forward on the bed. A magazine slid off the side and fell to the floor. "It was my own stupid fault. I fell off my bicycle and banged my head on the sidewalk."

"But you wouldn't have if I hadn't surprised you from behind," Angie protested.

Lisa waved her to silence. "I would *too* have!"

In the course of the next fifteen minutes, the girls filled Dale and Donna in on what had happened. They explained Lisa's biting of Officer Brook's arm as simply an hysterical reaction, brought about by her head injury. What they left out, by mutual and silent agreement, was any mention of Lisa's hamburger "snack" in the hospital refrigerator.

When it was Dale's turn to tell Angie and Lisa about his last twenty-four hours, he also conveniently left certain details out of the picture. Some, he knew, he would eventually tell her; others, she would never hear from him. When he was finished, he and Donna left to see how Mrs. Appleby was faring.

He gasped when he saw her. If he had thought Lisa looked worse than he remembered, there was no doubt Mrs. Appleby had been through a lot. He and Donna both smiled cheerful greetings at her as they entered the room and sat down at her bedside, but both of them were instantly worried about her.

"Chief Bates told me what had happened out at your place," Dale said. Police Chief Bates had told him Mrs. Appleby said Franklin Rodgers had done this to her.

Mrs. Appleby's eyes fluttered and shifted to the side to look up at him, but she didn't—or couldn't—turn her head. Her mumbled greeting was just barely louder than the bubbling glucose solution in her I.V. bottle.

As soon as Dale heard that Rodgers had been to Mrs. Appleby's house, his suspicions were confirmed: Rodgers had been looking for Angie and, not finding her, had made Mrs. Appleby suffer for his bad luck. He was chilled by the thought that, had she died, she wouldn't have even been allowed the luxury of finally resting. It gave him another reason to be happy about Rodgers' death.

"I'm . . . feeling . . . better," Mrs. Appleby said, her voice a strangled caw. With each word, her eyelids flickered, and her pupils jerked back and forth. If Dale hadn't also seen the flickering smile on her face, he would have been very concerned; but he knew what a determined woman she was, and he suspected she'd be on the mend soon enough.

"I don't want to tire you out," Dale said softly, "but I did want you to know that, if you'd like, we could have Lisa stay with us until you're up and about."

Mrs. Appleby smiled. Her lips opened with a papery smack. "If it's . . . no . . . problem."

"It's no problem at all," Dale said. His eyes were beginning to sting, and he knew it wasn't from lack of sleep. "I feel like I owe you a lot." His unvoiced thought was that she had almost died, essentially protecting Angie; he owed her more than his life!

Donna was standing by the door. The accumulated strain of the past few nights was beginning to tell on her; she felt she was going to collapse if she didn't sit down soon.

"You saw . . . his . . . eye," Mrs. Appleby said. Her voice dropped to no more than a low moan. "Didn't . . . you . . . His . . . *eye!*"

The mere mention of Rodgers' eye sent chills racing through Dale, but he knew he couldn't let her see his true reaction; he couldn't allow any chinks in the armor.

"His . . . *eye!*" Mrs. Appleby, her voice winding upward, bordering on a scream that she didn't have the strength to produce.

Dale nodded and gave her hand a reassuring squeeze. "Yes," he said. "I saw it. And I saw a lot of other things I'd just as soon not remember. Right now, you have to worry about getting better."

He patted the back of her hand and stepped back from the bed. It saddened him to realize how small and frail she looked in the hospital bed; it was difficult to see her as anything but the robust, life-filled woman in her house on Main Street.

"Let's let her rest now," Donna said softly.

"Don't worry about Lisa," Dale said. "We'll get her discharged, and she can come to Thomaston with us. He glanced over his shoulder at Donna, standing in the doorway. "I'm pretty sure we'll be coming up to Dyer on weekends quite a bit this fall." He almost laughed aloud at the understatement.

"Thank . . . you," Mrs. Appleby said. Her eyelids fluttered and sank down, staying shut this time. As Dale and Donna walked out into the corridor, they were unaware that the old woman had drifted off to a warm, dark, "centerless" place where her words glowed with purple and blue light. She knew she would find her way back eventually, but for now, at least, she wanted just to stay there a little while longer.

# IV

While Dale and Donna were visiting Mrs. Appleby, Tasha was down the corridor, visiting with Hocker. He had remained unconscious through most of the drive to the hospital, and by the time he realized what was happening, he didn't have the strength to resist. They admitted him, stuck his arms full of needles, and wheeled him into this room before he could say, "Boo!"

The pain in his shoulder convinced him to stay right where he was rather than try to leave. After the nurse and doctor washed and dressed the wound, he was content, for now, to float along with the roller-coaster ride of pain killers they had given him.

But that had been a couple of hours ago. Now, once his mind cleared, he was royally pissed! Because Tasha was the only one there at the time, he lashed out at her as soon as she walked into the room.

"Why the Christ'd you let them bring me here?" he shouted. His face was nearly purple, and saliva flew from his mouth. "You know what they're gonna do? Huh? They've got me now!"

"Hock," Tasha said as tears filled her eyes. She was angry at herself for feeling anything about this man; this was her chance to head home and be done with him! But no matter how much she wanted to, she just couldn't leave until she knew he was going to be all right.

"Jesus Christ, Tasha! They've got me! They're going to check me out now. Hell, that friggin' cop probably already has my face and name out on the wire. They're gonna find out that I escaped from that mental hospital down south. They're gonna find out about the truck we stole, that old man and those three guys in the woods."

As soon as he reminded her of the woods, Tasha's face went cold. The back of her head suddenly started to tingle. In the frenzy of fighting their way out of the farmhouse, she had forgotten all about the three men who had attacked them in the woods. If they hadn't been some of Rodgers' zombies, if they had been real, living men, then both Hocker and she were . . . Her mind formed word and denied it simultaneously:

*Murderers!*

The creatures they had killed in the farmhouse were one thing. It hadn't been like killing real people. Bates had assured her that the authorities wouldn't press charges against any of them for that. Then again, it was going to take Bates and the authorities a big leap into the irrational to believe that there actually had been zombies out there.

But there still was those three men in the woods! They had killed them!

"They're gonna connect me to thirty or more fires from here to Georgia," Hocker said. "They're gonna put my ass away forever!"

"What?" Tasha said, almost a bark.

Hocker looked at her, his eyes skimmed with pain like thin ice now that his first jolt of pain killers was wearing off. One corner of his mouth twitched into a smile.

"Yeah," he said, shaking his head and staring out the hospital window at the solid brick wall of the adjacent building. "I, uhh, might have set a few warehouses on fire . . . you know, while we were traveling north."

Tasha opened her mouth, but no words came out as she sank back in her chair. She remembered the look of pure ecstasy on his face the night he had torched the stolen truck and sent it off the cliff. She remembered the joy that had filled him when he had looked back at the old farmhouse as it went up in flames. She remembered the way he had craned his neck to watch the flaming wreck of Rogers' limo as long as he could. And suddenly it all made sense. Now she understood why, when they were hitchhiking north, Hocker had taken all those detours; he was setting fires as they went!

"Look," Hocker said. "What I want you to do is help me get out of here."

She shook her head and, standing up, started backing toward the door. "Uh-uh," she said. "No way. I've already done too many things I regret. I'm not going to do anything like that."

I'm not under arrest or anything!" Hocker yelled. He punched his mattress, but the sudden shock sent a wave of pain through his shoulder, and he cried out.

"Not yet, you aren't," Tasha said as she eased open the door. "But if what you say is true, you *will* be, and I'm not sticking around. I don't wanna have *nothing* to do with you!"

"Oh, yeah?" Hocker said, his upper lip curling back in a snarl. The pain helped him make it look mean. "Well, you may not want to, but you already do! You actually think I'm gonna let you desert me like this? You think I won't tell them you were with me every step of the way?"

As Tasha started back out the door, every word he spoke hit her ears with needle-sharp pain.

This is very serious she was thinking as she squirmed inside herself. It might have started as a lark, a joyride, running away from home and heading north, but it had gotten very serious very fast; if she didn't get out now, she was never going to escape.

"You won't," she said, keeping her voice as low and steady as she could. "They're going to spend all their time trying to figure out what happened out at the farmhouse. They won't bother to check on your background."

Hocker snorted with laughter. He coughed up a wad of mucous and spit onto the floor. Shaking his head from side to side, he closed his eyes and rubbed his brow.

"I thought there might have been hope for you," he said, "but there ain't." Looking up, he nailed her with the harshest look he could muster. "You're *always* gonna be an ignorant bitch, so fucking ignorant you don't even know how fucking ignorant you are."

Tears welled up in Tasha's eyes, blurring her vision.

"No," she said, clawing at her cheeks to wipe away the tears. "I think you are. I ran away from home, thinking I could find something I was missing at home. But what I learned, and maybe knowing you had a little something to do with it, is, I won't find it anywhere unless I find it inside myself."

Hocker roared with laughter so hard it shook the bed. The motion sent a shock wave of pain up his shoulder to his neck, but he ignored it.

"That is so much bullshit!" he gasped as his laughter built even higher. "Such . . . total *bullshit!*"

"Maybe to you," she said, so softly she wasn't sure and didn't care if he heard. "But not to me. I'm gonna go home to Port Charlotte."

She went out the door and let it swing shut softly behind her. All the way down the corridor, she could hear him back in his room, wailing with laughter.

Maybe he'll learn someday, she thought. She pressed the button for the elevator, and when it arrived, its door opening with an hydraulic hiss, she glanced down the corridor at Hocker's closed door. His laughter echoed like a madman's in the corridor.

As she stepped into the elevator and pressed the button for the lobby, she thought, then again ... he probably won't.

# V

"This is sort of how it all began, isn't it?" Dale said, smiling as he put his arm around Donna's shoulder. "Only last time, as I recall, we were sitting in my car." He tried not to think about the flattened wreck he had left in the farmhouse driveway.

They were parked in front of Donna's sister's house, directly under the streetlight on purpose. Donna had driven them back in her car from the police station where they had spent most of the day, answering the same questions over and over, filling in more details then seemed necessary. Dale, Donna, Angie, and Tasha grabbed a quick supper at Kellerman's. It was take-out because they didn't want to sit and eat with everyone in the restaurant staring at them, asking questions with their eyes. Word had traveled fast about the accident out on Casey's Curve and what had happened out at the LaPierre place.

The facts, at least, were simple.

Franklin Rodgers was dead in the car wreck at Casey's Curve, along with four other bodies, only one of which had been identified—that of Stephen Wayne, a physician's assistant who lived and worked in Houlton.

The LaPierre farmhouse had burned flat to the ground, and twenty-eight charred corpses had been found in the remains, mostly in the cellar. The smashed barn door, the remains of Dale's car in the driveway, and the shattered pieces from Winfield's cruiser, strewn around inside the barn, helped confirm the basic outline of their story, but the authorities who interviewed Dale, Donna, and Tasha, were skeptical when given the full explanation.

Jeff Winfield's battered cruiser was returned to the Dyer Police, and his decapitated body was taken to a funeral home in Haynesville. Dale saw the irony but no humor in the fact that he was resting— *finally*—in a closed casket.

The State Police sealed off Rodgers' Funeral Home, and as Bates seemed so fond of saying, "the boys from the lab" were going through the place. Yes, Bates had also said, "with a fine-toothed comb." The people who interviewed Dale and Donna remained tight-lipped about what they found, but Dale learned that they had also brought Sam Higgins in for what Bates called "routine questioning." Dale got the usual police reaction whenever he mentioned the body he had seen on the marble slab in Rodgers' laboratory: flat, expressionless faces with not a hint of emotion.

Probably, he thought, like typical bureaucrats, they'll cover this one up . . . *real deep!*

"It's been a hell of a few days," Donna said. She let her breath out slowly, and the breeze, angling upward, ruffled her hair.

"I always like to show my dates a good time," Dale said, forcing a laugh. "You know, really impress them."

When Donna looked at him, he could tell she was trying to soften her eyes, but they still looked haunted and scared as though she expected to see one more of Rodgers' creatures lurch out of the darkness at them.

"Do you think," she said, licking her lips to keep them moist, "they're all dead for real now?"

Dale shrugged and tightened his hand on her shoulder. He didn't want to think about any of it any more, but he knew he would.

"I'd say the chances are fifty-fifty," he said, after letting his gaze drift out the window, up and down the street. "The cops didn't say anything about finding any others at the funeral home."

"As if they'd tell us what they found," Donna snapped.

"True, but you've got to figure, Rodgers probably threw everything he had against us. And I think, if there are any left, they'll probably die off for good when they can't get more of the drug or whatever Rodgers was using to keep them going."

"Seems like kind of a frail hope," Donna said. Her eyes continually shifted to look around the car. She was remembering the man in the cemetery, trying not to wonder if *he* had been one of those things. Maybe he had been up there, digging up corpses and eating them! she thought with a shiver.

"Overall, I'd say we both can thank frail hope," Dale said with a snicker. "If you had ever asked me what our odds were for getting out of the farmhouse, I think I might have mentioned something like 'frail hope.' "

Donna suddenly turned and looked squarely at him. Her lower lip was trembling, and she seemed on the verge of breaking down entirely. He admired her courage and stamina, but he wouldn't have blamed her if she *lost control of herself right* now.

"What kind of 'frail hope' do *we* have for the future?" she asked.

Dale leaned his head back, rubbed his neck, and sighed. "Well, that's as much your choice as mine, I'd say. Lisa will be staying with Angie and me until Mrs. Appleby's out of the hospital. I just can't believe how much that girl eats. Did you see the size of that hamburger the nurse got for her? And she ate it all just about in one bite."

"She needs to regain her strength," Donna said.

"Anyway, like I told you, I'm sure I could get you a job in Augusta if you want it. What are you looking for?"

Donna shook her head, covering her mouth with her hand. Dale had the impression it was so she wouldn't scream.

"I'd like to think," she said, her voice muffled by her hand, "that sometime in the future I'm not going to jump at every shadow I see after sunset. I'd like to think I won't wake up half a dozen times, like I did last night, screaming and covered with sweat."

"I'd like to think that, if you do, I'll be there in bed beside you to calm you down," Dale said softly. His hand rose and began to stroke the side of her face.

Donna's hand dropped, but her mouth remained in a hard line. "I know you would," she said huskily, "and I think I would, too."

"*Think?*"

She nodded. "Yes. I need time to think. I told you why I came back to Dyer in the first place—to think my life through a bit. The last year, not to mention the past few days, was absolute hell!"

"Look," Dale said, trying to draw her close enough to kiss; she resisted for a moment, then gave in. The kiss lasted a long time, and the longer it went one, the softer and more yielding Donna's lips became.

# VI

Lisa was released from the hospital early the next morning; Angie, Dale, and Donna went in to pick her up. As they left the hospital room she and Angie were chattering excitedly about her coming to stay with them.

Angie was thinking it could have been a really fun holiday if Lisa didn't have her grandmother to worry about. But she *did*, and when she saw Mrs. Appleby for the first time since she left Lisa at the hospital yesterday morning, Angie couldn't help but feel a twinge of guilt that she had caused all of this, too.

Mrs. Appleby smiled when the three of them entered her room. She spent a bad night, but now, in the clear light of morning, she found that the nightmares were receding. She knew her sleep had been filled with images of Rodgers' strange eye and expressionless face as he reached for her again and again in night, trying to choke the life from her. Once she had her strength back, maybe this afternoon, she knew she would have to tell Chief Bates more of what she remembered. Her memory was coming back to her now, and as much as she didn't like it, she knew she would have to tell him everything.

While those three were with Mrs. Appleby, Tasha decided to pay one last visit to Hocker. She couldn't quite admit to herself that she cared even a little bit how he was doing; she simply told herself that, since she hadn't gotten to go straight home yesterday, because the cops had so many questions for her, she'd check up on how his shoulder was healing.

As she walked down the corridor, she was swept by a sudden feeling that something had gone wrong. It wasn't anything that was going on in the hospital. The two nurses at the nurses' station nodded a cheerful greeting to her. The corridor was quiet and calm. But there was a foreboding sense of something going wrong, the way she believed she could *smell* a thunderstorm before it hit.

Her hands were shaking when she raised them up to the door of Hocker's room and gave it a push. The door swung silently inward and hit the rubber tipped bar that stopped it from banging the wall. The curtains were drawn, and the room was cast in an heavy yellow glow. Tasha cringed, remembering the dim light that had filtered through the barriers into the farmhouse living room.

"Hock ...?" she called out, sticking her head into the overheated room. On the nightstand was the vase of flowers all of them had sent. The heater was running full tilt, rattling as the fans spun. Below the whirring of the fan, though, was another sound, a soft *thump-thump*.

Hocker's bed was disheveled, the sheets draped onto the floor. It looked to Tasha as though one side of the sheet had been torn.

"Hey! Hocker!" she called out, a bit louder.

As she walked over toward the bed, she saw that the bathroom door was closed. Stepping up to it, she pressed her ear against the warm wood and listened. She jumped when she heard the thump sound again. It came from the bathroom.

"Hock?" she said as she raised her hand and rapped gently on the door.

There was no response from the other side, and the feeling that something was wrong grew much stronger.

"Hey! Come on," she said, her voice warbling with tension. "Don't play any games with me, all right?"

Again, she knocked on the bathroom door, this time hard enough to hurt her knuckles and to knock the door open. When she saw Hocker, his head was cocked to one side as he dangled from the curtain rod in the shower, a twisted length of sheet tied around his neck. Tasha let out a scream that echoed through the entire wing. Several people on staff thought, at first, that it was someone having a particularly tough time in the delivery room.

For several seconds Tasha stood there, frozen, as she stared at Hocker's twisted, broken neck. His eyes were opened and rolled back, showing only the bloodshot whites. His tongue protruded through his teeth, almost bitten completely through. A thin streak of blood ran from one corner of his mouth. The crotch of his hospital johnny was drenched with urine, and tiny drops had fallen from the cuff and puddled on the floor. As his body swung slowly around, his toe flipped the edge of the lead-weighted shower curtain; it hit the tub edge with a dull *thump*.

Within seconds, two nurses rushed into the room. One of them left immediately to notify the head nurse who, Tasha assumed, would call the police. The other one, unsure what to do, took Tasha by the arm and led her over to a chair. She gently shut the bathroom door behind them.

After the initial shock, Tasha was too stunned to react with any emotion. The nurse was kind enough; she kept trying to help by talking to Tasha, to comfort her. But Tasha wanted nothing more than to be left alone.

Now, maybe, it's really over, her mind kept repeating.

When the nurse asked her if she would like something to drink, Tasha asked her for a cup of coffee just to get her out of the room. Once she was alone, Tasha leaned back into the chair, closed her eyes, and tried as best she could to blank her mind. She didn't want to feel anything, so she filled her mind with thoughts of all the stupid, idiotic things Hocker had ever done. She remembered all the things he had done to scare and intimidate her, to keep her under his control, even up until yesterday when he threatened to turn her in to the cops if they started checking up on what he had done.

"Not any more, you bastard," she whispered.

She opened her eyes, surprised at how much they were stinging. It was then that she noticed a piece of yellow, lined paper, torn from a notebook folded in half on the bed stand. Her mind went numb when she registered her name, scrawled along the top in heavy pencil strokes. The "S" in Tasha was backwards.

Tasha was reaching for the paper when the nurse returned with her coffee. She snatched the paper up quickly, crumpling it as she jammed it into her jeans pocket.

"Oh . . . thanks," she said, taking the coffee from the nurse but then not bothering to sip it.

"If you'd like to come down to the staff room, you can. You might not want to be here when the police arrive," the nurse said softly.

Tasha nodded and stood. She quickly brushed her hand on her leg to flatten out the paper in her pocket, then followed the nurse out of Hocker's room. She paused for a moment at the closed bathroom door and, touching the wood lightly, said, "See yah, Hock."

Much later that evening, back at Mrs. Appleby's house, after being questioned again by the police, Tasha found the courage to read the letter. With trembling hands, she unfolded the crumpled piece of paper, flattening it on her leg. The words were scrawled in a mixture of cursive and printing, but with a bit of effort she made out what it said.

*Dear Tasha,*

*By the time you reed this I'll be dead. This is no idal threat, it's reel. You were wrong and I was rite. I just finnished talking to Bates. He says he did check into me and found out a lot of stuff. Not everything tho. He says I'm gonna have to go back to the hospittel in Georgia, that that's where I'll be safest—for me and everyone else. But I can't do it. If I gotta be in a hospittel it's just like being in jail so I'm gonna kill myself. I just wanted to say GoodBye and that I was rite and you were wrong. But because I'm not gonna tell them about you being with me all along I'm gonna ask you a favor. I don't know how your gonna do it but you have to make sure once I'm dead I stay dead. Okay? I think when it comes right down to it, your the only person I'm gonna miss but so what? huh?*

*Your friend, sort of, Roy Moulton "Hocker"*

# ABOUT THE AUTHOR

**RICK HAUTALA** has had more than thirty books published under his own name and the pseudonym A. J. Mathews, including the million copy, international best-seller *Nightstone*, and *Bedbugs, Little Brothers, Cold Whisper, Four Octobers, The White Room, Looking Glass, Follow*, and *Unbroken*. More than sixty of his short stories have appeared in a variety of national and international anthologies and magazines. His screenplay *Chills* was recently optioned by Chesapeake Films. Born and raised in Rockport, Mass., he is a graduate of the University of Maine in Orono with a M.A. in English Literature. He lives in southern Maine with author Holly Newstein and Keira the Wonder Dog. Visit him at www.rickhautala.com.

# ALSO AVAILABLE FROM BREAKNECK BOOKS

**By Jeremy Robinson**
*"...a rollicking Arctic adventure that explores the origins of the human species."* -- James Rollins, bestselling author of Black Order and The Judas Strain

www.breakneckbooks.com/rtp.html

**By James Somers**
*"...a nice read of battle, honor, and spirituality... that left me wanting more."* -- Fantasybook spot.com

www.breakneckbooks.com/soone.html

**By Sean Young**
*"...captures the imagination and transports you to another time, another way of life and makes it real."* -- Jeremy Robinson, author of Raising the Past and The Didymus Contingency

www.breakneckbooks.com/sands.html

**B**REAKNECK BOOKS
PUBLISHING COMPANY

# ALSO AVAILABLE FROM
# BREAKNECK BOOKS

**By Eric Fogle**
"This will definitely be one of my top ten reads of the year and I would recommend that this book makes everyone's 'To Read' list..." – Fantasybookspot.com.

www.breakneckbooks.com/fog.html

**By Craig Alexander**
"...an action packed race against time and terrorists. Absolutely riveting." – Jeremy Robinson, bestselling author of Raising the Past. And Antarktos Rising

www.breakneckbooks.com/nineveh.html

**By Michael G. Cornelius**
"A dark and dangerous book with suspense and surprises aplenty...a remarkable novel."- -A.J. Mattews, author of Follow and Unbroken

www.breakneckbooks.com/ascension.html

**B**REAKNECK BOOKS
PUBLISHING COMPANY

## ALSO AVAILABLE FROM
## BREAKNECK BOOKS

**By Jeremy Robinson**
*"[A] unique and bold thriller. It is a fast-paced page-turner like no other. Not to be missed!"* – James Rollins, bestselling author of Black Order and The Judas Strain

http://www.breakneckbooks.com/didymus.html

**THE DIDYMUS CONTINGENCY**

**By Jules Verne**
This Special Edition of the original high speed thriller features discussion questions, a design challenge and the complete and unabrideged text.

www.breakneckbooks.com/mow.html

**By Edgar Rice Burroughs**
This Special Edition features all three Caspak novels (*The People that Time Forgot* and *Out of Time's Abyss*) in one book, the way it was originally intended to be read.

www.breakneckbooks.com/land.html

**THE LAND THAT TIME FORGOT**

BREAKNECK BOOKS
PUBLISHING COMPANY

# ALSO AVAILABLE FROM
# BREAKNECK BOOKS

**By Kristina Schram**
*"An amazing adventure to a unique and mysterious subterrainean world."* — Jeremy Robinson, bestselling author of Raising the Past and Antarktos Rising

www.breakneckbooks.com/anaedor.html

**By David S. Michaels with Daniel Brenton**
*"This is not just among the best first novels I've read in years, it's among the best novels, period. Red Moon is a masterpiece."* -- Paul Levinson, President Science Fiction Writers of America and author of The Silk

www.breakneckbooks.com/redmoon.html

**By Paul Byers**
*"A high flying thrill ride exploring the Nazi's last ditch effort."* -- Jeremy Robinson, bestselling author of Raising the Past and Antarktos Rising

www.breakneckbooks.com/catalyst.html

BREAKNECK BOOKS
PUBLISHING COMPANY

Printed in the United States
113154LV00001B/151/A